12/18

osbkm

D1530822

THE SOLACE OF WATER

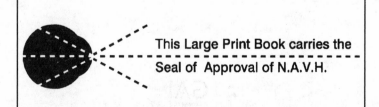

This Large Print Book carries the
Seal of Approval of N.A.V.H.

THE SOLACE OF WATER

ELIZABETH BYLER YOUNTS

THORNDIKE PRESS
A part of Gale, a Cengage Company

Farmington Hills, Mich • San Francisco • New York • Waterville, Maine
Meriden, Conn • Mason, Ohio • Chicago

Copyright © 2018 by Elizabeth Byler Younts.
Scriptures are taken from the King James Version. Public domain.
Thorndike Press, a part of Gale, a Cengage Company.

ALL RIGHTS RESERVED
This novel is a work of fiction. Names, characters, places, and incidents are either products of the author's imagination or are used fictitiously. All characters are fictional, and any similarity to actual people living or dead is purely coincidental.
Thorndike Press® Large Print Christian Fiction.
The text of this Large Print edition is unabridged.
Other aspects of the book may vary from the original edition.
Set in 16 pt. Plantin.

LIBRARY OF CONGRESS CIP DATA ON FILE.
CATALOGUING IN PUBLICATION FOR THIS BOOK
IS AVAILABLE FROM THE LIBRARY OF CONGRESS

ISBN-13: 978-1-4328-5666-3 (hardcover)

Published in 2018 by arrangement with Thomas Nelson, Inc., a division of HarperCollins Christian Publishing, Inc.

Printed in the United States of America
1 2 3 4 5 6 7 22 21 20 19 18

For Pam and Alicia

■ ■ ■ ■

Mid-April 1956

■ ■ ■ ■

DELILAH

My skin was the same color as the soil. I pushed my hands into the ground and it had hardened some since my visit a week earlier. My hands barely left a dent when I lifted them. I put them back and pressed harder. Tiny bright-green blades of grass were growing and the dirt didn't look so newly turned over no more. Made me mad. Grass growing over my boy's grave. Should have known it would happen quick in an Alabama spring without no shade overhead. Still wasn't ready to see the ground looking so settled in just a month.

But in that month's time there had been a whole lot of rain to tamp down the old dirt. Even though the gravediggers didn't sow grass over the colored folks' graves, these seeds found this soil anyhow. But I still didn't like that. No, sir, I didn't. With life coming up from what was dead and buried. It was unnatural. That's what it was.

"Come on, Deedee." My husband's voice softened around me like a down pillow. He put his hand on my shoulder, and he would've had to bend over real far because he was tall and I was on my knees. "Brother Jake is waiting for us."

I leaned forward away from his touch. My tears dripped and the wetness slipped between my fingers and watered the new grass I hated.

"Just a minute, Malachi." He didn't mean to rush me, but part of me just wanted to tell him to let me be, to take hisself to Brother Jake's Ford and wait on me 'til I was done. Might never be done though.

I rubbed my hand against the rough concrete gravestone. But it wasn't just concrete. We didn't have enough money for a whole bag, so we had to add in sand from the river. The sand made it weaker though. But it didn't look different from all the other colored folks' stones in the graveyard. Most didn't stick up out of the ground like the white folks' stones. They just lay flat. Flat and dead. I traced his name with my finger. I thought I'd do the lettering just like that — with my own finger — 'til Brother Joshua offered to do it up nice with his tools. He done a good job.

What I didn't like was that someone had

added a shell from the Alabama River to the corner. Just about all the gravestones at this cemetery had them embedded somewhere. But I didn't want that for my boy. No way. I didn't need to explain why, but that river shell got no business on his marker. I knew who snuck the shell to Brother Joshua and there wasn't no way I was going to leave it be.

I pulled out a hammer from my handbag. I'd taken it from the box of tools Malachi had packed a week ago. With one quick swing I set a crack in the corner of the gravestone.

"Delilah Evans, why you do that? Gimme that." Malachi grabbed the hammer from my hand. When he got mad he lost a little of his polished-up preacher voice. "Look what you done."

"You know why." My gaze was still on the gravestone.

I didn't like that the corner was chipped off, but it was better than having that shell there. I tucked the shell in my pocket and it felt heavier than was right.

With my pinky I brushed off bits of concrete from the gravestone onto the grass. I took a few minutes and just stared at what I'd done. But getting that Alabama River shell off was like a little bit of right in all

11

the wrong.

With my handbag still open I took out my coin purse, my white church gloves, my hankie, and my sunglasses. I handed my stuff to Malachi without turning around. He fumbled a little but he took them. Now my handbag was empty.

When I dug my fingers into the dirt, the grit got under my nails. Beneath the surface the dirt was a little damp, but that don't stop me. After I put the first handful in my purse, Malachi grabbed my shoulder real firm this time.

"Delilah." He almost never used my given name, and now this was the second time in a few minutes. 'Course he was worried about me, but I wasn't going to stop. "What you doing, baby?"

"I need some of his dirt. Dirt don't die. Dirt don't die." I set my purse down and used two hands. I got some urgency down in my gut that I hadn't felt since the day I heard my little boy was in trouble. "I'm taking little Carver's dirt with us. Pennsylvania got to know my boy."

When my handbag was full, I sat back and let my breathing calm down. I got dirt all over my black dress, but I don't care none. And Malachi's sigh got all sorts of heft to it and I felt it all down my backside.

12

After a few more moments in the new morning sun, he started talking again in that calm way he do. "Sister Lois say she'll come by to take a picture of the headstone and send it to us. Her grown boy got a nice new camera."

I nodded and sniffed again. I closed my handbag and when it clicked shut, I got half a mind to throw it across the ole misty graveyard. It just felt too finished.

"Time to go." Malachi offered his hand.

I let him help me up. My strength all gone.

I looked at my husband and his big, brown, glassy eyes got a sadness in them that I wonder will never leave. 'Course he was hurting too, but two weeks after our baby boy died he preached from the pulpit. It was about forgiveness and he sang along with the choir in proclamation of the Lord's goodness. I couldn't do that. Some fingers of my gloves stuck out of his pocket, like they was grabbing at something. I looked back at Carver's grave. Nothing felt right.

Malachi took my dirty hand in his and we walked away. Brother Jake sat with his hands on the wheel. He tried to smile at me but didn't get far. I glanced in the back seat before I slid in. My kids filled it up. Malachi Jr., Mallie, sat by the door and just looked out. I could almost hear his brave voice tell

13

me again that ten-year-olds were too old to cry. I almost slapped him smart when he said it. Got no business keeping dry eyes when his brother died. Little Harriet sat next to him. She gave me a smile because that girl always tried to give away happiness.

Next to the other door was my oldest girl, a new young woman really, Sparrow. I raised my eyebrow when I looked at her, dug that shell out of my pocket, and held it out for her.

"You keep it, girl. Don't you lose it." I wanted to add *too* but held back the reminder.

She took that concrete-crusted shell from me and curled it in her hand and turned back toward the window. Her gaze traveled to the distant stone with the cracked corner.

I let my gaze trail down to little George sitting on Sparrow's lap. He had this lost look on his four-year-old face.

It was his other half that was buried in the deep down.

EMMA

Secret hive, whispering wind — no — *breeze.*
Swaying branches, dancing trees. I repeated
the words over and over in my mind. I
didn't want to forget them. My fingers
thrummed against my knee, itching for the
pencil and paper I had at home. What would
come next? What would it be like to have
the freedom of trees?

"Life is a vapor. It's just a breath." Mervin
Mast, the preacher, released a puff of air as
an example. He was a new preacher who
had just moved into our small Sinking
Creek, Pennsylvania, settlement. It wasn't
in the mountains with the miners or in the
valley where it was lush and green, but just
in between. Mervin's beard was neat and a
rich auburn, declaring that he was younger
than the preachers with long *schtrubleh*
beards — the messy beards had always
bothered me. Mervin came from Lancaster
and his *frau,* Lena, fancied her *kapp.* She

15

was round and plump and pretty. The very opposite of me.

"But the world doesn't live like that. Their lives move like the blowing wind. They go wherever it leads. They travel fast like the many streams and creeks that come down from the mountain and just let the current lead their way without thought."

I turned away from the sea of white and black coverings of my fellow Amish *schwesters* to the nearby window. Several bees buzzed around the hanging potted plant. I imagined the murmur of their collective wings. Like the hum of these same fellow sisters who surrounded me, who talked with quiet voices behind their hands.

Preachers on occasion referred to Amish communities as beehives or colonies of ants — living in groups and always working at their ordained responsibilities. And just like bees always had their golden honey ready for harvest before the summer faded to autumn, we always had to be ready too. For whatever was to come.

The cry of the most recently born baby in our church caught my attention away from the window. It was like looking backward into a past life I'd lived. I'd been about the age of this girl — the new mom — when I'd had Johnny. The bliss and wonder of

16

new motherhood had captivated every part of me. I'd suddenly realized why my mother glowed every time she introduced me to our family's new baby. It made sense that my *alt mammie,* even at the risk of her health, would travel to see the fresh little face. Through my old grandma I learned to see this new life stretch before us and it brought so much hope.

That's what it was. Hope.

And even as I thought this, my hands rested in my lap, so close to where my son had grown. He was across the room somewhere now — tall, lanky, and as handsome as his *dat* had been at sixteen. I looked at my hands. They were so empty.

"Emma." The whisper came from near me and a warm hand tapped my knee.

My daydreaming — my past-dreaming — had taken me through the rest of the service. It was time to kneel and pray. Then we would file out. We would eat. We would talk. I would hold many babies and I would hand them all back to their mothers.

A few hours later I was in the buggy with my husband, John, trying to forget my reminiscing and remember my lines that I'd thought up during service instead. I mouthed the words a few ways before I recalled the exact lines. The *clip-clop* of the

17

horses offered me a rhythm. I whispered them. *Secret hive, whispering breeze. Swaying branches, dancing trees.*

"Vas wah sehl?" John asked what I said, with his eyes trained on the road through the open windshield — now that April had turned nice.

"Nix." I told him *nothing* because he didn't appreciate what he called my fancy lines and ideas and warned me against vanity.

"Larry and Berthy are coming on Tuesday. For a week or so."

"In two days your brother and sister-in-law and their seven children are visiting from Ohio and you are just telling me now?"

Since Berthy couldn't read or write, Larry usually wrote to John. I remembered seeing the letter weeks ago but had forgotten to ask John about it. This had happened enough times I should not be surprised. The last time was before Thanksgiving and his parents and two unmarried *bruders* came to visit for a week. My oil and flour ran dry and my faith was dashed clean away.

"Ich hap fageseh." He was a plainspoken man and would not provide more explanation.

"How can you forget? We don't have close to enough food to feed nine more people." Of course, I knew why he'd forgotten. He

18

knew also. But it wasn't something we talked about.

"*Nah,* Emma, you're making something bigger out of this than it is. Most of the women around here are feeding more than nine for every meal. You got it easy with just me and Johnny. Stop being spoiled. You just need to make our food stretch. We make more money than Larry does, and Berthy still finds a way to feed all nine of them. Why don't you ask her to show you how?" He never looked at me when he spoke. He remained elbows to knees with the reins loose in his hands.

The mild weather was suddenly too hot for me because I knew he was right. I only had one son and husband to feed and care for. Berthy worked small miracles to feed her brood. But feeding twelve instead of three without time to prepare made my stomach drop. I wasn't good at working without a plan.

"We got all those empty rooms — shouldn't complain about filling them up. You cry because they're empty and get ornery when they're filled."

"John —" My response was disrupted by a buggy racing by, throwing gravel toward our horse, Brian.

Johnny.

John let out a hoot and holler and our son offered a wild response. Johnny had just turned sixteen and John had paid for half his buggy to help the boy out. I wished I'd had a say in the matter. Johnny was an irresponsible rabble-rouser and should've had to save the entire amount for the buggy himself. He would be prepared for baptism this fall, which could calm some of the ambitions of the young people. Maybe it would settle him down.

"Sehlah buh muß schlake." I was half teasing.

John laughed and the heartiness of it softened me a little. We didn't often laugh together. "I'd like to see you try and spank that boy — you're too hard on him."

While racing buggies was normal behavior for our youth, I worried about Johnny's irresponsible ways.

The chickens and geese scattered as we pulled into our drive. If we turned to the left it would take us to the back of our white farmhouse and the walkout basement, but we went off to the right to park in the red barn.

"Last week I found him watching television." Though a typical rebellion, it still concerned me. Johnny was far too comfortable with the English neighbor's son, Arnold. "I was taking some herbs to Lisa — she hasn't been well for weeks — and Johnny was sitting with Arnold in the living room watching something on the television. He didn't care that I saw him because he knows you won't do anything about it."

"Emma, I remember the two of us raising a little Cain when we were running around."

I hadn't seen the twinkle in his eyes for so long my heart flopped. I played along and jabbed him in the ribs. He smirked. He had raised Cain; I had not. I'd done little more than hem my dress a little higher and write poetry that I was told was prideful. His twinkle didn't remain and his stern jaw returned, set like stone.

I reverted just as fast, returning to my concerns about our son. "I know all about *rumspringa*, but because you're the *aumah deanah*, people expect certain behavior from the head deacon's family."

His chest tightened and his movements were stern and snappy when securing the reins. "Listen, you don't have to remind me of what I am." He threw the words over his shoulder as he stepped out of the buggy.

I hopped out and walked around to his side as he unhitched the horse. I got close to him, but his hands didn't stop moving and he didn't turn toward me. He didn't

21

want to have this conversation. I didn't either, but Johnny —

I moved my hand to cover his so he would look at me but then laced my hands together instead. "He knows he can get away with anything, John, because —"

"Because what?" He turned toward me.

I couldn't remember the last time he'd looked into my face so fully. His brown eyes squinted at me. I took in his appearance. His dark hair still without a single gray strand — unlike mine that mixed evenly with my dark blonde, making me seem older than my thirty-seven years. He'd been so handsome when we first married almost twenty years earlier, and remnants remained, but in the last few years his cheeks had become unnaturally red against the edge of his beard. The strong features in his face had hardened and I knew why. His tall body had become softer, but it wasn't because of age — he wasn't even forty yet.

His jaw tightened and his Adam's apple bobbed. "Because what?" His voice was thin and his face twitched when he repeated his words.

I could smell the peppermint leaves he chewed for his breath and as a comfort. He always had some handy, even if pressed between the pages of his Bible. His question hung unanswered. Because the answer would bring pain to us both. I avoided all pain. And I loved my husband and I didn't want him in pain. I wanted to be what brought him solace even when he was lost in sin. It was what drove me.

But as I walked away the answer still plagued me. Johnny knew he could get away with anything because the *aumah deanah,* his own father, was a drunk and no one but me was the wiser.

DELILAH

We drove so long I thought I would always feel the hum of the Ford on my backside and feel the green vinyl embedded there too. And driving so long put all these thoughts in my mind — like how I ain't never been so far north. Malachi had. He got his growing up in the north, in Sinking Creek, Pennsylvania, where we were going. In these fourteen years married, *middle of nowhere* was about all I heard when he talked about Sinking Creek. He always said they weren't miners who had their own way of living up in the mountains to the west, but they weren't in the valley neither, where everything was pretty and green. Sinking Creek had a bunch of creeks and streams that came from the mountains and fed the valley. But the water was just passing through; it didn't stay.

The sun was just about falling asleep when we drove into town. It wasn't sweltering hot like Alabama neither. The four near the doors had their arms hanging out the windows. Mallie was cupping the breeze in his hand real carefree like. I wanted to do that also, but I was stuck in the middle of the front seat.

We drove in and Malachi started tripping us down memory lane. He got as fidgety as my boy Carver does — did. I just about gave him a pinch under his arm to make him sit still, but instead I hugged my dirt-filled purse closer.

He started pointing out this place and that place and he was smiling. I couldn't help but feel a little betrayed by how he was acting. Where were his cares? They just gone like the Pennsylvania wind moving past us, I guessed. All I could think about was how far away I was from home. Montgomery was home. The South. My people were there and I wanted to be there. Carver was there.

Sinking Creek, though, was a place to start over. None of Malachi's family was there no more. His parents had moved to Montgomery when Malachi took on our church, but they was both gone now and his brothers and sisters was all over — Montgomery, Atlanta, and even New York City. We never gave moving away from Montgomery a thought until he got a letter from an old friend who heard about our loss. She told him to come back home and take up the church. It was all Malachi could think about from then on.

Mallie looked at everything we passed with such hungry eyes and asked about everything he could. He thought the motel just on the edge of town was fancy and the streets were so clean and how all the stacked-up wood at the lumberyard looked like a playground to him.

Main Street was just like Malachi described. Small storefronts and diners with them cloth awnings hanging over most of them. I heard him explain everything but tried to take it in for myself too. I took a special notice of the women milling around and a handful of them looked so different from home. All the white ladies back home wore them nice wide skirts that fluffed so far I wondered how they could sit. But these ladies looked like poor folk from before the war even. Drab brown dresses that hung on their bones. Their hair wasn't done up but just hung down their backs or in a small twisted bun at the nape of their necks. Everything was neat but just not like the modern women I was used to. It was almost like we went back in time. Malachi said those was the mountain folks who came

26

down for supplies.

Of course there were those that looked like the kind of lady who hired up us colored women to clean for them. I did see those ladies too. They walked past the plain women almost like they'd walk past me.

There were some friendly looking folks — talking on the sidewalks. When we drove past a few buggies — that's what Malachi said they was called — the kids just about wet themselves with excitement. They were unusual enough to me too. I looked hard at the black carriages. The people looked like they was wearing a costume.

I saw a grocery, a butcher's, and even a barber with the spinning red-and-white pole in the front. I'd only ever heard of those poles. There was a beauty parlor next door called Pretty'd Up. Then Miller's Diner and Stolzfuss Restaurant and The Beiler Bakery. Malachi said the Amish had the corner on all the restaurants in town.

A few people waved at us until they got a closer look, then their hands would still and retreat down to their sides. I knew why. They kept staring though. This was the same for both the white and the colored folks who were out.

"Everybody knows everybody in town," Malachi said, and while those might've been

some nice words to put together, I wasn't
sure that knowing everybody was a good
thing. "They'll warm to us once they know
I'm a local."

My eyebrow went up and my mouth said,
"Mm-hmm," quietly. I knew they saw what
color we were and the white folks didn't
want more of us and the colored folks probably wondered who we were and didn't
want no trouble. Maybe we were too different from the colored community up here.
Didn't even know as I cared about all that.
Didn't know as I cared so much about making friends. Even with all my decades of
friends in Montgomery, when I lost Carver
I didn't fit in with nobody. Just myself.

"Notice anything different here, Dee?"

What did Malachi want me to say? There
was a whole lot of different. Where did he
want me to start? Mallie said he wondered
if they played the same yard games for
recess and all Harriet was worried about
was eating dinner. That girl's mind didn't
stray far from food.

"Look around, kids. No signs." The man
fairly jumped out of his brown skin like he
been keeping this as a gift to us. Even
though we knew it was different from the
South, that things weren't segregated the
same way. But I don't know that the kids

understood that meant no signs that said Whites Only or Colored Only.

He got a whole chorus of talk from Mallie and Harriet about walking through the same door as the white folks, using the same bathrooms, and eating at any table in a restaurant — that last one was Harriet, of course, and she said it like we ever go to restaurants.

Malachi told us how the men that run most of the shops were the ones he came up with. They were boys together. And I think he must be fibbing. All the shopkeepers I saw were white but for a few, and colored boys and white boys didn't *come up* together.

"What you mean *come up with?*" I asked. "You make it sound like you went to school together."

He shook his head. "No. It was better than that." His eyes twinkled. "We played together."

I didn't pay it no mind because it don't make much sense to me. My childhood in the South was just too different to understand that.

I could tell right away when the white neighborhood ended and the colored one started. No signs were needed, not even for a blind-as-a-bat granny. As we left town the rows of pretty houses where the white folks lived went for a few blocks on either side of us. The lawns were nice and most of the houses looked the same. In the distance you could see the farmhouses and their big barns poking up out of the fields. The few who were out in their yards didn't wave when we passed but just looked at us like we was something to be looked at.

Then we drove on a little bridge that crossed over one of the many creeks around here, that's when the colored part of town started. The houses were smaller, shotgun style, with small yards. I thought that maybe it would be different because we was up north now. But it wasn't.

We drove through Malachi's old neighborhood. He said lots was the same — just older. But he didn't stop to talk to nobody. We all just wanted to get to the new house.

Then we drove just out of town to where our house and the church sat. All I could think about was how I didn't trust none of this. Didn't trust that these northern white folks was any different from the ones I knew in the South. That the colored folks up here ain't coming out greeting us neither. And all this talk about no signs for whites and coloreds — it don't sit well with me and I just laid another row of bricks along my wall.

EMMA

Just half a spoonful of my dried herb in cold water each week — that was all it took. It seemed so simple to say it like that, but there was nothing simple about secrets.

I tapped the jar on the dresser so the herbal powder settled. I replaced the lid and buried the jar in a drawer and covered it with my clothes. Over the next few months I would do what I'd done for over a decade. I'd gather more wild turnip — or Jack-in-the-Pulpit root — to dry, grind, and offer me the miracle I needed.

The drawer caught and when I pushed harder the dresser hit the wall. A flap of wings sounded through the screen window to my right. I left the drawer ajar and investigated. In the eaves near my bedroom window was a small bird's nest. Beyond the nest on the porch roof was a brown-and-gray bird. It hopped around before flying off, leaving me alone again. It flew over the smooth-as-glass pond and into the woods.

As I walked downstairs John came in from outside. He sat with a loud huff and grabbed his Bible. He needed to prepare for an evening visit with a neighboring couple. It was church business. This made him more restless than normal. I wanted to help him because he was doing important work. Handling it sober, however, was the problem. And unless we had Communion he did his best not to drink on Sundays.

An hour before the meeting I handed him a steaming cup of coffee. When he looked up from his first sip, I pretended not to notice. I had put in it several hearty swallows of wine. For many years I had kept a small dark-amber bottle in the back of my cabinet once I'd caught on to his need for help when we had company. It was how we kept his secret. *Our* secret.

It was John's oldest brew and overly fermented. Just enough of it to help calm him. Every time I did this I was guilty for helping him sin and keep a secret, helping him not be the man I'd married. I was helping him continuously hurt our family in order to hide the truth. But even knowing this was wrong, I couldn't see him in pain without fixing it.

A short time later I watched him leave and

was glad that it was not my place to attend these meetings with him. Sins against the church were private though still well known in the community — this couple had had a double-tiered wedding cake. Only single-tiered cakes were allowed. They'd followed this up with being found with a radio. I could not have sat across from this couple to tell them that they were in sin because of a cake and radio when I knew what we kept behind our closed doors.

How John was able to do this, I could not understand. How many other head deacons, who had the responsibility to manage the Communion wine, had had John's dependency?

We had both been surprised when the lot had fallen upon John to be the *aumah dea-nah* when he was not yet thirty. This person was in charge of addressing the discipline issues that arose throughout the community — and to brew and store the church wine. He didn't answer to anyone regarding the wine. He'd also found other ways to get more alcohol than his own brew. I could smell the difference now.

We had each once given a confession in front of the church — him for having left the church for several months after his baptism but before we were married, and myself after dressing Johnny entirely in white. Though I hadn't meant my confession — knowing nothing purer than a baby.

But being in such an honorable role helped keep the deacon's family in good order, to be humbler than necessary and to exceed even the *Ordnung* standards. We were taught that the *Ordnung* was for our protection — to keep us safe. But my efforts to keep our secrets hidden were to keep us safe — like the bird in my window with her head curled under the protection of her wing. She had only herself to depend upon.

DELILAH

The white siding got crack lines like an old lady's face. It had age spots around the porch and windows and that floor sagged like the skin on a granny's arms. But it was our new home. A white family had lived in it for years and I wondered, since now it was all used up, if that made it okay for us to use. If I said that out loud Malachi would tell me I needed to stop speaking like that.

Truthfully I was thankful. The house was about a quarter mile outside of town and out here there was more green grass and trees than the entire colored neighborhood back home. When Malachi just cracked open the car door, Mallie pushed it wide and all the children tumbled out of the old Ford like they never seen the sun and they started running. Even little George laughed. Malachi climbed out next. I took an extra few moments before I stepped out.

When I got out I saw where the garden

used to grow. Could I revive it when I ain't never had a garden? Couldn't even keep houseplants alive. The back of our new yard was lined with woods instead of a bunch of other houses. My babies never did have no land like this where they could run and play. They were cooped up in my old granddad's place before. We had the upstairs and my older sister, Deborah, had the downstairs — we shared the kitchen. That upstairs boiled me up like a crawdad, but right now a good breeze came up from the valley like it was rolling up here just for me. Not sure if it wanted to cool me down or blow me away. Didn't know where I'd go if it did. Didn't know if I cared.

Before I saw my children I heard them. When I saw them running in circles, I tried not to be slighted by their happiness. My eyes stung like they was trying to find that joy they needed. My arm clutched my handbag of dirt close and I leaned on the open car door in front of me. It hurt. It hurt so bad.

My poor boy Carver ain't never going to know this new place. I ain't never going to hear his giggle fly up to those cotton-candy clouds. He ain't never going to know life without the signs.

"Deedee? You all right?" Malachi set his

hand on my shoulder.

Sometimes I just wanted to smack that man. He was a good husband, but it was a dumb man to ask if I was all right. 'Course not. I gave him the stink eye and then sighed when he raised his eyebrows at me. I knew what he meant. He didn't mean no harm. He just wanted me to be back to my old self.

"Don't know how this is gonna give us a fresh start. It just don't seem right," I said.

A heavy sigh fell out of his mouth and stacked onto my shoulders.

"Let's go on inside. I think the house will do nicely." Malachi was always so positive about everything. He never did like to talk about all that was wrong about his life.

"Think it might fall over if I walk in?" I meant this twofold. I had gained lots of weight after the twins were born and never did lose it. Then when my baby died every church lady in Montgomery brought over biscuits, beans with pork fat, and pound cake. We liked to fill our bellies when our hearts were empty with grief. But more than that, I had this burden on my shoulders that I couldn't put down. I would carry it with me to the grave. It got heavier every day.

Malachi tilted his head at me, chastising me with a smile.

"Come on." He winked at me and I gave him a smile in return even though I thought it would break my face in two. "Where did those children run off to?"

"What?" I looked around and I didn't hear them. My heart started jumping and I pushed past Malachi to find my babies. "George? Mallie? Harriet?"

I yelled their names a few times while I ran my heavy legs 'round the side of the yard.

"Mama." Sparrow's voice sounded as light as birdsong. I used to like that sound. "We're right here. We found some peas over there." She held up a handful of pea pods. A little early, but when they're wild they get to do what they want.

The two youngest ones came running with pea pods in their mouths and smiling while they chewed. Harriet and George were like a salve to each other. They was four years apart in age, but they clung to each other still.

"Where's Mallie?"

Harriet looked behind her. "He was with us."

Did she lose another of my sons? I wanted to pinch that *don't care* expression off her face. But then it shifted and her gaze went to the ground, like she knew what I was thinking about her.

"Mallie?" I yelled but kept my eyes on Sparrow when she walked away. "Answer me, son."

He didn't say nothing but instead came skulking around the corner, chewing on the long stem of a green onion. He walked right by me without a word. If it ain't that we just buried a son, I would've smacked the back of his head. But he was hurting. Little man said he wanted to be all "growed up" and be like his daddy, but he was a child.

It was time for me to gather my babies 'round like they chicks in my henhouse and cluck around them like I used to.

Like when Carver was still with us.

I took a deep breath and tried to act like the mother hen I was before all this hurt.

"Mallie, don't you walk by me without a 'yes, ma'am.' " I stepped in stride with him and he recognized my old ornery voice and looked over. The whites of his eyes caught mine and I gave him my special smile. He knew it and that it meant "I love you even when you think you too big for them britches."

"Harriet, you and your sister go pick your room." I waved toward the house and smiles crossed over their faces.

Sparrow pulled at her sister and they

bounded up the three creaky porch steps. It was a wonder they didn't stomp through the wood slats.

Mallie looked at me with that darn hope in his eyes. He wanted to know if it was his turn.

"Go on, boy. You and George go see what the girls left you with."

The boys took off running.

"Y'all, look," Harriet called from an upstairs window. "I like this one. I can see the church."

I turned to see the church house. Our new church. I knew it was there all along, but a new flock was as hard to accept as a new house. I hadn't been ready to settle my eyes on it more than a passing glance. I took in the view. The sun was setting just on the other side of the church. It looked pretty.

Pink. Purple. Orange.

God was painting His love across the sky, but I didn't deserve to see it. All I could think was that the sun had already set for the last time on Carver's life. I'd give up all the sunsets for the rest of my life if I could just have Carver for one more hour . . . the hour before I sent him to his death.

EMMA

The grass was so long that I saw every blade turn and twist instead of it looking like a soft green blanket. Even though I was frustrated that Johnny hadn't mowed the lawn, I still felt a line of poetry move in the breeze and I pulled out my pencil and notebook from my bedside table. I jotted down a few words. I had to be quick before they flew away — and because I had dumplings in the oven and a house full of company. I crossed through a few words and replaced them.

The blades of grass twist and turn.

I didn't know what came next until I saw a storm rolling in from the western woods behind our house. A gust of wind washed the trees. I extended my arm and smiled as the heaviness of the wind cupped in my palm.

"Emma, *vas bish en du?*" John bounded

into the bedroom asking me what I was do-ing.

I pulled my hand inside like I'd been burned. I closed my notebook and stuffed it away. "I just had to put something away." This was true until the open window had wooed me.

"Bish du en schravah?" He shook his head as he asked if I was writing. "That's non-sense. Your time would be better spent see-ing to what's burning in the oven."

I didn't say anything to my husband, but I hated being scolded like a child even though he was right — I was not a good hostess. I was embarrassed and stayed silent. As I passed him he grabbed my arm, and though my instinct was to pull my arm away, I didn't want to make things worse. He was too sober.

"Don't give them a reason to gossip." His voice was low.

The brew on his breath lingered just over the chicken and noodles since he'd been drinking just before his brother's family's arrival. It was how he would get through the evening. He'd slip into the basement again after everyone was asleep. This was always an issue when we had overnight visi-tors. We didn't want anyone to know about the things that happened behind our closed doors. And even we didn't talk about them openly with each other, like an unspoken agreement.

"If you don't want gossip, you might want to chew on some peppermint leaves," I said through clenched teeth and pulled my arm from his grip. My anger toward him in this moment frightened me.

"Emma. You know I need your help." He whispered, "I — I can't — can't do it." His lips pinched together and his eyes were steeped with a familiar desperation.

I lifted my chin but didn't respond. I would help him. I always did. I didn't want us to lose our lives with my husband losing his reputation. But I couldn't agree to it like this — it was too humiliating.

The air downstairs smelled more of sweat from the added bodies than of the scent of my overcooked dumplings. When I got to the bottom of the stairs, I ignored the curious sidelong glances from those who sat in the living room. How long had I been upstairs? My fourteen-year-old niece, Rebecca, pulled the dumplings from the oven when I entered the kitchen.

Berthy sat at the table and rested her hands around her swollen abdomen that held her eighth child. I was accustomed to the ache I felt inside at the sight, but for just a moment I stared.

I smiled at Rebecca. "*Dangeh*. Maybe I should get you to make the dessert tomorrow."

A shy smile crept over the girl's face. "They're only a little dark," Rebecca said with the gentleness of a lamb. "With some ice cream it'll . . ."

Her words faded when John strutted into the kitchen. Though he appeared eager for dessert, I knew why he stayed close to me. Was he worried that in my nervousness I'd surface his secret? I would never let that happen though. I was too afraid of the consequences our whole family would face.

We made eye contact and after a few moments his face softened slightly. I knew he didn't want to hurt me, but protecting himself was more important than anything else. He watched me for a few more moments, then returned to the living room. I cleared my throat to disguise the shudder that ran through me.

Rebecca asked me what was wrong. "*Vas ist letz,* Aunt Emma?"

"*Vas?*"

"You winced."

"*Hap ich?*" Had I?

For dessert I put on the table the shallow bowls we'd just washed, dried, and stacked.

What was one more round on rarely used dishes? I sent Johnny and my nephews for the ice cream I'd made earlier that day when my laundry was on the line. From the living room my husband cleared his throat and I turned to watch him fidget worse than a child. He needed another drink.

"Larry, coffee?" I asked my brother-in-law, who was engrossed in talking about how their bishop was allowing *Englisher* farm equipment. He looked over and nodded with a thumbs-up but kept talking.

I took two mugs and filled one all the way and one halfway. With Berthy and several of her children behind me, I whisked from the back of the cupboard the unmarked wine bottle and filled up the second mug.

"I'll take them." Rebecca stood right behind me and started for the mugs.

I panicked and handed her a mug. "This one is your *dat*'s."

"They're both black?" Rebecca was confused.

"John takes his sweet." The lies I told to hide our truth were starting to suffocate me.

My niece smiled and picked up the other mug with an "okay" on her lips.

And as I fumbled to put away the amber bottle she seemed not to notice, I held my breath. I had no way to stop her and

46

breathed a prayer — as if God would hear such a prayer.

I turned as both Larry and John thanked Rebecca. My gaze met John's as he lifted the mug to his lips, and before I knew which mug he'd gotten, Larry sprayed his first swallow of coffee all over the living room.

"What's this?" he yelled and started laughing. "Emma, you got me good. I know John put you up to this because he knows how much I like my coffee."

Rebecca started laughing and pointed at me like I'd played a good joke. Everyone else joined in, thinking I had accomplished quite a prank.

"Gotcha, Larry," John said and laughed with his brother. I played along and made a few jokes while I cleaned up the coffee spray and let Rebecca fill another cup for her *dat.*

I couldn't look at John. In all the years this had never happened before and it made my every nerve twist and turn like my writing about the blades of grass in a burning wind. Later that night I thought John was going to hit me. He never had, but maybe he would start. Surely my stupid mistake would bring it. But he ignored me like I didn't exist.

I began to wish I didn't.

DELILAH

A man as dark as pitch stood at my door the second morning. It was our mover.

"G'morning, ma'am. Clyde Green." His voice was so deep it touched my toes and maybe dug through the floor. It reminded me of my daddy's voice, like he chewing on every word before he spit it out. "Would've been here sooner, but the truck broke down."

I waved him in. "Coffee, Mr. Green?"

I turned back to my kitchen and had to take it in again because it didn't feel quite right yet. The sink was ahead under the window. I'd hide the water pipe with a curtain this week. The stove was to the left. A small fridge was against the same wall. The cabinet against the opposite wall was painted the same cream wall color. It looked like it was built right in, but it wasn't. My table would sit between the kitchen and the front door. Bigger kitchen than Montgomery, but it wasn't home.

"Thank you, ma'am." He ducked through the doorframe when he stepped inside and his shoulders filled up the space.

"You better call me Deedee, Mr. Green." I handed him some instant coffee.

"Thank you kindly, Ms. Deedee."

"I'll go get Malachi. He over at the church."

I left the man standing in the kitchen. When I walked out the breeze caught the skirt of my dress and I pushed down the pleats. It was my darkest shirtwaist dress, an olive color. Didn't seem right to grieve in the springtime when the outdoors was coming back to life. But the dress was thin enough to grieve in the Montgomery heat and dark enough to be respectful. But this place was different. It was warm, not hot, and the trees and grass was always moving around.

My Harriet was dancing with her doll in the morning sun. Mallie and Sparrow was picking through the garden ruins for more wild vegetables. And my little George was chasing butterflies with a fistful of wildflowers.

When I caught Sparrow's eyes I pointed at the church. She yelled, "Okay," and returned to weeding through the wild onions and beans. Even from a distance I saw she wasn't a little girl no more. She looked like a young woman with curves that come from chicken-fried chicken and beans and an extra serving of growing-up stuff happening under that skin of hers.

She reminded me of myself when I was fourteen. My mama wrapped my bosoms under my church dress because she said the boys wouldn't look at my face or hear my words no more. Made me sweat like the choir director. Mama finally gave up on her notion and just sewed me up some new dresses.

But this wasn't as easy as that. I didn't know what to do with Sparrow — not just because she was growing up but because of Carver. I just kept her at arm's length and knew it was wrong. Everything changed when we lost Carver.

The moment after Sparrow was born Grannie Harriet put her in my arms and she looked like a little brown bird. She made the littlest sounds from her puckered lips and her eyes opened to look right at me. She was so small, a little early, and God just said to my heart, *My eye be on her.* He named her Sparrow. Grannie Harriet thought I was nuts so I made sure to name my next daughter after her.

When I walked into the church, the door creaked and a mouse scurried across the floor. My gaze roamed over the old building. I hadn't even come inside yet. Just kept my distance. It wasn't nothing fancy. Just four walls and a roof. Six rows of old wooden pews on a wide plank floor — an aisle down the middle. There ain't no choir loft, no altar, no pulpit to preach behind neither. But there was a cross. It was way up high — the highest point inside. It all felt so heavy on my soul my knees let go of my weight and I grabbed hold of the pew in front of me. The commotion echoed in the dusty air.

Malachi stood from the front. His face wet. He pulled out a hankie from his pocket and wiped it down his face. I'd seen him cry plenty — preaching at the pulpit, at funerals, and when our boy died. But those times we were together as a man and wife or as a church family with all of us sniffing on tears. But these tears was different — lonely — and for nobody but hisself. Did this happen often without me knowing?

"Deedee?"

I wanted to ask him what's he crying for but I don't. Carver. Leaving Montgomery. Maybe 'cause I wasn't the woman he married so many years ago.

"Clyde Green here with all our stuff." I threw a thumb over my shoulder toward the house. "Anyone coming by to help unload?"

"Baby, I don't know. Sister Marlene said they needed a preacher but nobody is here."

At the mention of Marlene my back stiffened. She was Malachi's longtime old girlfriend and the one who brought us to Sinking Creek. His burdened-filled voice tramped on down the aisle toward me, but I stood stiff so it didn't touch me.

"I tried to talk to them yesterday but nobody answered their doors."

"Is that why you crying?" I just 'bout lost my breath. We had a boy in the ground and he was crying about this?

"I just want our family —" He stopped for a long swallow, then he looked at me real serious. "This should be a new beginning for us. I thought they would welcome us and make you feel —"

"Make me what? Feel better?" I raised my eyebrows and let out a breathy laugh. "You think a group of strangers from this Podunk place are gonna make me feel better just like that?" I snapped my fingers.

In the distance I heard Sparrow's voice and then the door flew open. Mallie rushed in, his eyes so big all I seen was white.

"What's the matter, boy?" I said it like he

52

was exaggerating real good because I didn't want to believe that something could be wrong. There was too many things wrong already.

"George is gone," he said between deep breaths.

"What you mean, George is gone?" His face formed in my mind, both him and Carver. They were identical. But George had that special way about him. He didn't breathe right away when he was born, almost didn't breathe at all, and it made him — special. Carver had always looked after him. But Carver gone now.

"Mama, come," Mallie yelled.

Then Sparrow's voice came at me so loud it made me think of church bells calling for everyone to come. I ran.

Emma

I studied my reflection in my pond. My face was too thin to be pretty. It hadn't always been that way. When I was young my *mammie* told me I was her prettiest granddaughter so I wouldn't have to try quite so hard with my baking to catch a husband. She knew I wasn't as good in the kitchen as most Amish girls. I told her I'd rather write pretty lines about nature than bake. Later my *mem* told me that I wouldn't need to finish the eighth grade, that working at home was more important than school. I never went back to school a day after that, but I already had the love for words in my heart and I never stopped writing my lines. It didn't matter if anyone else thought they were pretty. I liked them.

Looking glass lake.

I imagined my new words floating in the water next to my face — I would write them down later. My love for words about nature was in part due to all the time I spent in it. From the beauty and peace of it to the harvesting of wild herbs. The need for the herbs drove me now.

The clinking of metal a short distance away made me stand and stare back at my house. Berthy's younger children cheered. Someone had gotten a ringer, playing horseshoe. Berthy had pulled a chair outside. She sat near her children with a bowl of snap peas held between her knees.

Since we were all eager for wild mushrooms in our dinner tonight, it was my job to gather them. I picked up my basket with tools. There weren't many other things I would rather be doing than redeeming the good from the earth.

I glanced to the tethered boat that floated next to the small dock, then pushed past the long grass toward the woods. The young trees greeted me with their low swaying branches and my hand brushed against the thin bark of several before I got to the sassafras trees. It was a little late for digging up roots for tea, but I had been so consumed with my sugar maples earlier in the spring, I had forgotten. I used my trowel to find a root, severed it, then pulled it up. After cutting it with my knife to fit in my basket, I moved on.

My sugar maples waved at me as I continued farther in to find nettles and yarrow with my eyes out for mushrooms. After a few minutes the road noise and the squeal of my nieces and nephews playing had disappeared. The cry of hungry baby birds and the long whistle of the cardinal tickled my ears instead, along with the rustle of wildlife against the dead leaves and twigs that had lain under the snow.

In this part of the woods nettles grew everywhere. I put on my gloves and held the stalks to cut about five inches down. I cut, wrapped, and pinned them in cheesecloth — I'd been blistered by the nettles because of carelessness and I wouldn't do that again.

The deeper I walked the heavier the humidity became and sweat dripped from my jaw and onto my evergreen dress. Rain whispered against the high trees, but I stayed dry until I spotted mushrooms in a small, lush clearing. I rushed to cut them no matter the rain. With my basket full of mushrooms, I walked a short way to see about my wild turnips — Jack in the Pulpit.

My most-needed wild herbs were scant and not at all the hearty plants from previous seasons. We'd had a difficult spring with a freeze after everything had started to bud.

I'd check on them again soon. There wasn't much time left to harvest the root.

What would I do if my harvest was too light to last me for a year?

Just around the other side of that patch, I squatted down at a small grassy mound where my too-early baby had been tucked in so many years ago. I brushed away the wilted black-eyed Susans atop her place. This was not the first time I'd found the flowers here. Johnny didn't know about his long-ago sister and I couldn't imagine John doing this — he'd never shown any tenderness over our loss. As I let my mind linger on that time long ago and on how it had changed everything, I heard a distant scream.

It sounded like a child but too far away for it to be one of Berthy's children. I stood and looked around. It could've been an animal. When it came again I stepped through the brush and back onto the path. Then the screaming became continuous.

I ran toward the screaming. Twigs broke and leaves rustled beneath my feet. An overgrown thistle bush snagged my dress. My heart was pounding inside my ears. I didn't stop running until a small Negro boy came into view.

I dropped my basket. Herbs and mushrooms scattered everywhere. The boy was waving his arms around. Bees. His eyes found mine and he ran toward me.

A dozen or more bees swarmed him when I closed the gap between us and pulled him into the front of my skirt, covering him with my apron as much as possible. I swatted at the bees. After a sting of my own and more swatting, the remaining bees flew away.

The boy wailed and both of us shook with frenzy. I held him close for another moment before I nudged him back to kneel in front of him.

I inspected the boy and guessed him to be about four. His arms were covered in bee stings. I counted at least a dozen and they were swelling fast. What if his throat swelled shut? I had to do something quickly.

He grabbed and slapped at the welts. His wailing grew louder and his tears washed down his round, plump cheeks. I looked around and spotted what I needed.

"Stay right here," I said, first in Pennsylvania Dutch out of habit, then in English. I sidestepped the path and found plantain weed. I tore off several leaves, and after curling them I bit into them to release the healing juices. I spread the weeping leaves onto the little boy's stings and continued to use the poultice until his wailing reduced to sniffling. I'd used the herb many times over the years and was thankful it grew so plentifully in the wild.

"Feeling better?"

He gazed up at me with the biggest brown eyes I'd ever seen and nodded. Then he looked around as if just realizing he was lost in the woods and with a stranger.

"Mama." He was quiet at first but got louder and louder and began crying again.

When I tried to take his hand to lead him down the trail, he fought me. So I picked him up. He didn't fight but instead wrapped his arms and legs around me. I started walking in the direction he had come from. My arms and legs ached after a short time — he was a hearty child. How much longer would I walk? Where had he come from?

I knew the land well since the woods had been a womb for me to grow in when my own had rejected my daughter. It had betrayed me. I knew the houses that lined our woods in the direction the boy had walked from, so I continued toward them, but I didn't know any Negro families who lived in any of them.

The little boy kept calling for his mama through his crying. It had been so long since Johnny was small enough to fit into my arms or would let me comfort him for any reason.

"What's your name?"

He started crying louder so I began to sing. When all the songs that came to mind were in Pennsylvania Dutch, I decided on "Amazing Grace" in English. I soon wore out with the extra exertion and took a break.

"I'm sorry. I'm sorry." I had to put him down before I dropped him. My arms shook.

He wailed louder and I tried to comfort him. Nothing helped. He was still swollen, but it didn't seem to affect his breathing, thankfully. I picked him up again but didn't sing this time. I just walked with a singular focus. To find where he belonged.

After a few minutes I heard voices nearby. I couldn't see who was yelling or what they were saying, but my instincts pricked me to call out.

"Over here," I called out, ragged. "He's over here."

I kept moving toward the sound of the voices, then I saw a woman in an olive-colored dress with wild eyes running at me. Her brown skin glistened with sweat. Her short black hair curled around her chin. She had the same big brown eyes the little boy had. She had to be his mother.

"George, George," she yelled over and over as she stretched her arms toward us.

When she reached us she didn't grab him from me but pulled us both into her arms. The way she held us — all three together — I could almost feel what she felt. The fear of losing her little son. I didn't know how, but I knew she understood loss.

SPARROW

When I saw the lady's watery eyes, it was like I was looking back at myself. It wasn't that she looked like me — she was white — but she got this *something* in her eyes that I got since Carver been killed. It made me get fidgety and I started to rub the puffy scar on my finger. I got it on the day we buried Carver when I smashed my small mirror against the porcelain sink. I couldn't stand to see myself in it. Didn't like the way it felt now neither so I looked away. That's when I saw the rest of her.

Her clothes was plain — even plainer than Sister Imogen who still dressed in old-fashioned clothes. I didn't know what to think about the bonnet this white lady wore. I ain't never seen nobody like her. She reminded me of them Pilgrims from those broken-down schoolbooks the white school gave my colored school.

The white woman's chin sat just above

Mama's shoulder and our gazes met again. She breathed heavy behind Mama's corn bread–fed body and her face and lips was whiter than fresh butter-cream. I was embarrassed that Mama just threw her arms around a white woman. A *white* woman. But the woman didn't flinch none. It was a sight.

Maybe it was 'cause she gonna faint and she need somebody to hold on to. That's what I seen grown ladies do when they got a shock. Mama did that when she learned about Carver. I didn't. After I done told Mama about what happened to Carver, I vomited all my insides in the dirt alley by my house.

I ain't never told nobody about that. I got rid of the milk, hash browns, and corn bread I'd eaten for breakfast. But it was all colored up with the black licorice Mira and I stole earlier from her brother. I left it all there in that muddy alley right next to my heart that I'd thrown up first. Now I was emptier than that godforsaken church across from our new old house.

Mama's shriek echoed in my hollow insides. Daddy peeled Mama's arms from around the white lady. Then the woman stood on her own; she didn't faint. No one did — yet. Mama knelt with George and checked him all over. Her hands touched his face. His hands. She checked his legs.

She done all those things with Carver too, when he was found, but no matter how much she checked him, it didn't bring him back.

"What happened, George? Why'd you walk off, son?" she said.

I recognized the voice well. Part relief, part fear, and part stuffed-away anger so she don't whip the boy for walking off — or me because I wasn't watching good enough. Again. But it was George and that boy ain't never been right in his mind. Ain't his fault he didn't understand the mess he caused.

While she said that a few times, the white lady said something about bees and chewing on a weed. I couldn't follow nothing she said because of all the racket Mama was making. But then the white woman took a few steps back. She lost even more color in her face. Didn't know how. Her hands shook and her eyes darted back and forth between Mama and George, then came back 'round to me.

"I have to go," she said with a voice filled with breath and air.

"Mama, the lady. She leavin'."

I didn't think Mama heard me so I started repeating myself when she stood and smacked my face so hard my jaw cracked.

"Don't you never, girl, let your eyes leave *my son* again. You hear me?" Her voice weren't sweet and tender like when she talked to George. It sounded like half a devil coming out of her.

Mama's finger was in my face and I wanted to slap it away. But it was my fault. All my fault. First Carver. Now George. But at least George ain't dead. I saw from a distance that the woman saw the slap and turned away and left faster.

George started yelling, "Mama," even louder and Mama turned back to him like she got nothing more to say to me. Like she got nothing to hear neither. Not that I'd say a word right now — but I got lots inside. I pushed all my words away, far from the front of my head, and looked down the forest path. The lady just 'bout out of sight.

I didn't wait to ask or get permission or tell nobody. I just left. Mama didn't hear the crunch of grass and branches under my feet or when my foot splashed in a puddle that made me want to dry heave the nothing in my belly.

Dirty water on my feet. Water that don't cleanse — there ain't no water that worked like the Bible talk about.

The path ahead was clear enough but not well worn, but the woods scared me. I ain't never seen so many trees. When I got to the first bend in the path, I looked back once and nobody noticed that I ain't with them. So I kept going. I got to know about this woman. She rescued George. Maybe saved his life. I couldn't let her walk away. She done what I couldn't.

She saved my brother and I killed one.

My hand went to my pocket where I kept Carver's shell. I folded my hand around it and held it while I walked. We always pressed shells into gravestones to make them pretty, but Mama said she wouldn't have that for Carver. I knew why, but I done it anyhow. I dropped it back in my pocket.

Why did God choose to save George but not Carver?

It started raining again. The tops of the trees blowed around like ghosts in a graveyard. The sky cried some big drops and made splash marks on my skin. I ran faster.

Not too far down the path I saw a basket on its side. It got some stuff scattered around it — mushrooms and weeds — and a cloth inside. On a hunch I grabbed it — it got to be that woman's. I'd lost sight of her by now, so I just walked along the main trail that had a creek to the right. It was louder than a snaky little creek seemed like it should be.

Just when I thought I'd gone too far, the path turned to the left and into a clearing. The rain had stopped but the breeze was still warm and wet and there was a smell I knew. Just ahead was a big ole watering hole, a pond, wrapped partway around with tall grass, but there was a dock and a small sandy shore. A little metal boat was floating around.

I smelled my haunts. I smelled that old Alabama River. I smelled something dead.

Seemed like flat land didn't last long in these parts and a yard rolled up and down on the other side of the pond that led to a nice two-story farmhouse. Nicer than mine. The white siding wasn't chipped. The porch floor was dark green and so was the door. The porch was big with rocking chairs that looked like a bunch of tree branches bent around each other. And there was a porch swing. Made me think of the porch swings in Montgomery. But they was all that would fit on the porches — one porch swing. We could swing on ours and have a talk with somebody across the road on their swing. Everybody was close.

A woman with a baby in her belly peeled taters on a porch that curved around the front of the house too. Some little kids giggled as they raced up and down the wet porch steps. Another few ran out of the house and started playing horseshoe. They were dressed in the same strange way — like them Pilgrims from our falling-apart schoolbooks.

I was there a whole minute at least before the lady from the woods rushed out of the house. The screen door slapped behind her and she jumped. My white lady's face was shining with sweat when she snapped the wrinkles from her apron. She fumbled tying it around her tiny waist.

The lady with the taters said something to her, but I just caught mumblings. My white lady, that's how I saw her now, used a hankie from her waistband to wipe her face up.

As I watched them talk I remembered the basket in my hand. Maybe I just blended in with the grass and woods — maybe that's why nobody saw me yet. Maybe I should just set the basket down and leave. Before I made a decision a little boy pointed at me. Then both women looked over. It was too late for me to pretend I hadn't seen them.

Before I knew what I was doing I started walking toward them. "This yours? I thought I'd —"

My white lady was real surprised.

The other white lady just stared at me

with her mouth wide open with a tater in her hand, dripping with water. Mama scolded me if I hung my mouth open, catching flies. Fresh rainwater dripped from the eaves and the sound drilled into my ears. I wanted to snuff away the dripping. The wicker basket started digging into my skin and I loosened my grip. All of these things pressed against my insides.

I walked a few steps closer before the woman started coming toward me. A little girl, maybe five years old, ran up to me. She looked up at my face and squinted. Her head tilted. She was sweet looking. Big brown eyes like mine, only her skin be the right color. White as cream.

She spoke some words I didn't understand. And when I didn't respond she looked back at the women. The lady from the woods was close now and the other hadn't moved none. The little girl talked again and the lady on the porch said something to her. Couldn't understand nothing.

The girl looked at me again, then ran off.

"Thank you." She had a strange accent. Her face and her hair were just 'bout the same color but weren't the bright, pretty Hollywood blonde white ladies wore. She reached her hand toward me and I handed her the basket. In our nerves we dropped the basket and the cloth with the weeds inside fell out onto the lawn. I squatted to pick them up and the woman grabbed my hands.

"Don't," she said quickly, kneeling down. "They're nettles. They'll sting you."

Why did this white lady care if they stung me? Why was she touching me at all? I stared at the contrast of her milky hand against my darkness. I ain't never been touched by a white person before. When I spread my fingers to show her that I wouldn't touch them weeds — whatever she called them — she let go of my wrists. My gaze went to the woman's hands as we both stood. They was calloused more than Mama's, more like Grannie's. Why would this woman want to gather stinging weeds?

"Emma, Emma." The little girl from before ran back to us. The rest of what she said I didn't understand, but what she done was not lost to me. Her face, arms, and legs was covered with pond muck. She was trying to be my color.

Emma inhaled loudly. She grabbed the little girl by the arm and spanked her in the direction of the house. The other woman came running and took up the girl real mean like and started her toward the water pump. That water come out so fast and cold and the girl started wailing and carrying on. The child didn't know she done wrong. I'd have felt bad for her if I still had my heart.

Even without a heart I knew I had to leave right away. I had to run home. Back to Alabama if I could — but that meant back to Carver's grave. When I turned to leave Emma grabbed my arm, touching me again — on purpose.

"Don't go. What's your name?"

I saw that same *something* in her eyes from before.

"Lemme go." I exhaled the words. They weren't loud but I meant them.

When Emma released my arm I lost my balance and fell. My skirt ran up my legs. I pushed it down and got up as fast as I could and got out of there. I ran fast back into them woods and when I was far enough in, I stopped and turned. Emma hadn't followed me. She hadn't.

I caught my breath for a moment. When I turned back around I slammed into someone's chest. I stumbled and grabbed two fistfuls of shirt. Two hands caught around my forearms and kept us both steady.

I looked up and into the eyes of a boy. Maybe a little older than me. Same blue eyes as the woman — Emma, the little girl had called her. White. But he got this dark, wavy hair laying all over his forehead that was different from the greased-up hair white boys wore.

"Whoa, there." A smile played over his lips and I smelled cigarettes on his breath.

"Where'd she come from?" another boy asked.

I tried to pull away. He looked into my eyes, really looked, before he let me go. That's when I saw there were four boys altogether. Three of them were dressed real funny with suspenders, plain shirts, and farmer hats. The other white boy was like any other boy 'cept his ears was too big for his dang head.

"Hey, Johnny." The boy with big ears cackled. "That your new girlfriend?"

"Shut up, stupid," Johnny yelled over his shoulder.

The other two boys were silent, but their eyes looked so close they just 'bout hurt my skin. I looked back at the one in front of me. Johnny.

"What's your name?" he asked.

I stepped back and looked over my shoulder. I couldn't go back that way. I turned to face Johnny. "Lemme pass." I lifted my chin and promised myself I wouldn't say *please*.

When I moved around him off the path, he blocked my way. I had to bite down on my jaw to keep it from quivering.

"I just want to know your name. I'm Johnny."

I took in a long breath when I heard him introduce hisself. Our eyes locked together for a short spell. I pulled my brows together.

"What you want with that girl — she's black as mud," the boy with the ears said. Then he called me that word that always made me flinch.

Ain't like I never heard that word, but it don't feel nice anytime.

"Knock it off, Arnold," Johnny yelled.

"You been rolling around in a black bog, girl?"

He called me that nasty word a couple more times, like it was made just for him to say.

"Lemme pass," I repeated with control, just like my mama do when she got madder than mad. I wasn't gonna let Arnold see I didn't like that word and moved my eyes far away from him. Ain't got nothin' for that boy.

I pushed as hard as I could and he moved easily, like I didn't have to try so hard. Then I ran. The whole way, though, I got that feeling of Johnny's hands on me burning through my sleeves onto my arms.

I'd finally felt something.

DELILAH

Sparrow was ghost white when she ran through the front door. The screen door slapped shut and plucked my nerves like a wire. I spun 'round from a kitchen box of pots and pans and my hands found my hips quicker than my words could spit out of my mouth. "Where you been, girl?"

She was faster, though, 'cause my words only met up with her backside as she pounded up them stairs. She didn't even so much as pause at my question.

I craned my neck and hollered, "Sparrow, you get on down here. Now."

When after a few moments I didn't hear her respond, I slammed down a pot onto the kitchen table. It didn't get dinged up moving here, but I just done it. I heard footsteps traveling down the steps, but I know they ain't Sparrow's. They too soft and patient to be that harebrained girl.

It was Malachi. He'd put George down

for a nap after all the mess from earlier, then helped Mallie unpack their room. We didn't have much so it didn't take much.

"Leave Birdie be, Dee." Malachi used Sparrow's pet name. I ain't used it since Carver.

"Don't you call her that," I snapped.

"Why?"

"She don't deserve it, Malachi. You forget what she puttin' us through?"

He told me he didn't forget, but I didn't believe him. He got all soft when he said that she was still his *Birdie*. Well, he could keep his *Birdie* for himself. What I wanted to say was maybe if he'd been paying more attention to her before Carver, he might'a known that she was kissing on boys and making a ruination of her life and Carver died because of it.

I didn't know how he still got any softness left for her. Mine was all buried and bones. It made me think of when I was a child and digging and playing and finding a small rock with marks on it — like the imprint of a lizard. A fossil. That lizard had been a living, breathing being, but it was long gone by the time I found it. But that old, faded outline was proof that it had once been there. My fingers found the dent I'd just made on the wooden table and I rubbed it.

Was this proof that I was here? But I didn't want to be.

"She done walked on by me. Where she been all this time? She should be helping —" I gripped the handle of the pot so hard I felt the pale on my knuckles. The next mark I'd make would be on that girl's backside, not on my table.

"Dee, give the girl a break. She just needs some time." Malachi flattened some of the empty boxes with his feet.

"Time? What you talking about *she* need time?" I broke my words up so he knew I was serious and about to let him have it. "She done —"

"Is that the Reverend Malachi Evans?" A wrinkled-up voice came through the screen door and interrupted my spat-out words.

Malachi turned and started for the door. He took big steps, and even though his back was to me, I knew he wore his wide preacher smile.

"Grannie Winnie," he said with his arms flying up like a praise Jesus.

He opened the door to an ancient, miniature woman dressed in her funeral best. The old lady walked in and Malachi offered his hand. The woman took it with both of hers with her cane dangling on her arm. She pulled him down for a hug and a kiss on the cheek.

When she released him she kept his hand and looked up into his face. Her skin was almost gray compared to my husband's rich brown. "You done growed up. I can't believe you remember me." She patted his hand.

"How could I ever forget you, Grannie Winnie?"

"Oh, you a good boy." She pulled him down. "Here's another kiss."

I remembered him telling me about her. I pulled some numbers up in my head and I figured up that Grannie had to be close to a hundred.

She got my husband close and put her hand on his head and shoulders and back and muttered words that sounded like she was praying a blessing. Malachi was accustomed to this, but I found it a bit foolish — like them ladies think they something special to bless my husband. She released him after several moments.

"I know'd what you're thinking, young man." She tapped his hand again and motioned to the nearby chair. Malachi helped her sit and pulled up another to sit with her. "Your grandmama was somewhere 'round a year older than me. That makes me ninety-nine years young — one hundred real soon."

Then she threw her head back and laughed out loud. She act like she got freedom by the tail with a laugh like that. Where'd she capture that? But if she was born in the North, she had been born free. Though I knew she'd still seen a lot but different from all the old southern biddies.

How was it that she came visiting but nobody else had? And someone as old as her couldn't have walked all the way here from town. If she knew, shouldn't others know? Shouldn't the church body have come to welcome us?

"I can't say as I was sad when I heard that Ruthie passed. She in glory and I still stuck here in this in-between place." She looked over at me and twinkled when she burst into laughter. I tried to bubble over with her, but I knew it came out forced. It was like she knew it too. "Well, ain't you pretty and plump."

She looked back to my husband. "I like a plump girl. Make her look like she cared for. I was always bony myself. Never had much food."

She called me a girl. An almost warmth for the woman came into the corner of my stomach. Malachi knew better than to say a word about my being plump, but it wasn't the first time I heard it from an old lady.

"That's my bride, Delilah." Malachi looked at me like he done fell in love with me all over again, but I was still thinking about being called plump.

"What was your mama thinking calling you after a harlot like Delilah in the Bible?" the old woman asked.

"My daddy named me. He wanted a boy called Samson but then I came — he said Delilah was my rightful name." I fed her the story I'd repeated so many times. Too many times.

"People call you that?"

"I go by Deedee."

Before she had the chance to disapprove of my nickname, Malachi changed the conversation and I went back to unpacking.

"What you doing here all alone?" Malachi asked.

"I was the one who told Marlene to write you and ask you to come home, but she didn't tell me it was gonna happen so fast. We ain't had a good preacher here for a good long time. Sometimes the men take their turns, but more often we just fellowship on the Lord's Day with a meal and singing."

"Church building was looking pretty rough and dirty. Don't look like anybody has been in there for a long time." Malachi shook his head.

I listened to Grannie Winnie, interested, while I unpacked. I wanted to hear this. It bugged me that we arrived in Malachi's hometown without so much as a casserole brought over. Nobody came to see us. In Montgomery ain't no new family settled into a new house without everyone chipping in.

"You're right about that. I ain't happy about it neither." Grannie Winnie nodded.

"Where is everyone?" Malachi used his sincere voice. "Nobody even came to say hello."

"Listen, son." She waved her hand at him. "People are nervous and a little upset over old stuff."

"What? But I'm from here."

"But you left." She put a finger up like a mother would to a child. "You remember how those last few years went? All you talked about was getting away from this place — even though you was engaged to my Marlene. Then one day you was just gone — just like that — and in a few years everybody else in your family was gone too."

My ears just about turned to horns when she said that he'd been engaged to Marlene. I eyed him and I knew he felt it, and when he looked over I raised my eyebrow so high it just 'bout lifted off my forehead.

"It wasn't just like that, Grannie. I'd applied to all sorts of colleges; everybody knew that. Marlene knew it. Besides, that was a long time ago and I know she's married and has kids now. She isn't still mad over old stuff like that when we were little more than children ourselves. And I wasn't the only one to leave either."

"No, you weren't. But everybody wants you to know that you need to earn their trust back. They don't want that old Malachi back who always thought he was better'n everybody else." This time Grannie's eyebrow rose.

Malachi sighed through his nose and his shoulders slumped like a little kid who just took a scolding.

"Marlene's husband, Titus — and the other men 'round here — aren't too sure about you, Reverend. When you made something of yourself in Montgomery with your big church, we got wind about how you was fixin' up your neighborhood and helpin' with that bus boycott." Grannie clicked her tongue. "All good things — but it made people 'round here feel like you just too good for ole Sinking Creek folks."

Malachi nodded and I wanted to throw something at him. He don't need to feel bad

81

about doing good in Montgomery.

"Listen, I know people build high walls around here toward outsiders. Mama and Daddy were the same way. But I will earn their trust back." He was straight-backed again.

There he go again, not staying down too long. He done the same over Carver. Just bucked up so fast it made me mad.

"How'd you get here, Grannie? You didn't walk all the way over here."

"Marlene." She winked. "Don't worry, Reverend, things will get better. Just will take some patience — and a couple of doses of prayer."

"You don't have to call me Reverend, you know." Malachi took Grannie's hand.

" 'Course I do. Listen here, sonny." She slapped him playfully, then got serious. "I got this distant cousin in Montgomery and she wrote me 'bout your burden." My arms grew weak and I set down the pan I was holding. "I was so sorry to hear about your boy. Ain't natural to bury your child. Just ain't natural."

She looked over at me and her old eyes looked more tired than they had a minute ago. "Deedee, I know it don't feel like you ever gonna get through this grief, but you just got to see every break of day like God's gift to you. I know it hard."

She knew that, did she? My face was too numb to make the expression I was feeling. People always said that and it just made me want to box their ears. I bit the inside of my mouth so hard I just about tasted my bitter blood. It wasn't because I couldn't think of nothing to say. It was because I got too much to say — I got inside of me so many words and feelings that if I let them start coming out now, I couldn't promise they'd ever run out.

"Oh, bless your heart, child." The old lady looked right at me like she done heard my thoughts. She stood with help from Malachi's shoulder. With her cane she walked to me.

I stepped back. I didn't want her touching me. I didn't want nobody touching me. But when she get up close to me, I got nowhere to go and she grabbed my hands with a grip that startled me. "I know you's hurting, but it'll get better, Deedee."

When she patted my hand my anger bloomed. I felt Malachi looking at me and thought that he probably said some prayer to keep me from opening my big mouth to my elder. Mine and Grannie Winnie's eyes stayed fixed for a spell until I saw some of my sadness reflected in her eyes. I couldn't tell no more if I was looking at her or a reflection of myself.

"Can I get you something to drink, Mrs. Rivers?" I added emphasis to her name. "I just got water."

"Sometimes water is all there is, honey." She let go of my hands but not my eyes. "Call me Grannie Winnie. Everyone does."

I wasn't everybody, I thought when another knock came to the door. Grannie Winnie turned away and yelled, "Come on in," like it was her house.

The spring pulled on the screen door and almost a dozen ladies poured into my house. Most of them was carrying a dish with a pot holder over their hands. One lady got one of those Betty Crocker cake boxes — did Betty Crocker's show come in on the television all the way out here in the middle of nowhere? My sister Deborah and I debated about Betty Crocker's four-minute cake. She didn't like it, but I didn't bake a cake any other way no more. It made me miss Deborah.

"Everybody, this is your new reverend's wife, Delilah Evans — please call her Deedee so's we don't think on that harlot woman every time we says her name. Deedee, this is everybody — or some of them, anyhow."

She sure didn't mince no words, did she? "Hi, y'all," was all that came out.

So they had shown up after all. The ladies lined up and shook my hand and told me their names. I don't remember any of them in a minute but for Marlene. She got skin half as dark as mine, straight soft-looking hair to her shoulders, and a voice that even when she just talking sounded like she was singing. She was tall and had big bosoms with a small waist.

I sucked in my own waist when she stood in front of me with her hand out toward me. This was the woman my husband walked away from? Now look at what he got instead.

She handed me a stack of newspaper clippings. I raised an eyebrow and looked at her. Then she said in a nice cool, even voice that they were coupons for groceries at Coleman's Grocery. That was a nice thing to do, but I feel like she got some nerve assuming we would depend on coupons.

As soon as the line was through, Grannie Winnie was back in charge using her cane to direct everyone. She told them all what to do. And I just watched and didn't know where I fit into all of it. They brought in a bunch of cleaning sprays and rags and cleaned all my new corners full of old dust

I hadn't gotten to yet. I'd done the same for other folks back home but never thought I was ever going to be the kind of person who needed the extra help. They washed my baseboards, and when I looked around and saw the flats of their feet as they kneeled, cleaning and chatting with each other, I was humbled. But felt so alone.

But what I didn't like was that the husbands of these women were still staying away. They weren't so sure about Malachi yet.

Over the next two hours I just couldn't find nothing to say to all these ladies. There was some sense of home when you got help, but everything was still so different that it don't feel like my life or like I'm here in the middle of it. I just kept running my finger over the dent I'd made in the table to remind my own self that I was here.

EMMA

The rain whispered its burden to me before it stopped. *Dampen this old dirt. Fall on these buried seeds and be used.* If it fell on me, would I grow? Could I break open like a seed in the hopes that something new would spring forth? What goodness water held, but it still had to break the seed before it said *grow.*

How many seeds had I sown in my lifetime, and how many had just remained as seeds and died without growing? Did they resist the water? Did they fight the submission to it? Or were they already dead when I folded them into the damp soil? Water could do a lot, but I didn't think it could bring anything back from death. Sometimes too much water caused a seed or a young plant to die. They'd done their part and cracked open, grown, and submitted — and died when the water ceased to be good to them.

Was that me? When the rainy season came, had I just let too much of myself drown in my pain?

For two days it had rained, but this morning a faint glow came from the sun. It was past the tops of the trees — on the other side of the woods. It made me think of him. The boy. The mother. The daughter. I couldn't get them out of my mind, and even in the sliver of quiet that I knew these days — only at sunrise — I found visions of their faces. Sometimes they shone in the tin bucket before the pumped cold water washed them away. I saw them reflected in the pond behind the house. I saw them on the other side of my rain-stained windows.

Johnny came from around the porch and he was startled when he saw me. I hadn't known he was awake yet. I hadn't seen him when I gathered the eggs from our chicken house, though, and assumed he was still asleep. Because he had cousins visiting, he wasn't going to work with John and had even shirked some of his chores. It embarrassed me.

"Where were you?" My voice thinned the damp air around me. I looked to see if his cousins were with him. They weren't.

"Roy's. His cows got out." Johnny responded in English to my Pennsylvania

Dutch. A habit he had developed since he spent too much time with Arnold. He didn't look at me as he walked past. He pulled off his wet and muddy boots in even heavier silence before he went inside without another word.

The next few hours passed like walking through the haze of the fog lifting from the wet ground. The rain moved away. The birds proclaimed the wonders of the spring day. A rainbow rested itself amid the blue sky. My personal drought had settled in, however. Everyone had rushed outside once the breakfast dishes were done and gone about various chores while the younger children played in the yard and chased after my poor chickens.

Even though it wasn't Monday — laundry day — I washed a load of bedclothes and towels we were using at a speed I'd never known, since several of Berthy's children still wet the bed. As I was pinning up the last of the laundry, I heard tires roll over the still-damp gravel driveway. I left my place at the wash line and walked around the house.

A shiny green automobile idled in the drive. I squinted from the sun's glare. My sister-in-law strode up without hesitation and opened the passenger door. Before I had time to consider this, my father-in-law, Aaron Mullet, heaved himself out of the vehicle. My mother-in-law, Polly, was next, followed by a girl of around nineteen and then one of John's younger brothers, Paul.

I was too shocked to smile and walk toward them, so instead I watched as my sister-in-law shook everyone's hands, except she hugged our mother-in-law. Did she know they were coming?

John's parents had moved to another Pennsylvania settlement out east several years ago to be close to their other grand-children. They didn't visit often, but when they did it often came unannounced.

"Meh sint doh," Polly's voice called toward me as she caught my gaze.

Yes. She was right. They were here. The small crowd walked toward me and my thoughts rushed around. Four more people to feed. How long would they stay? Why didn't they tell me? Where would they sleep?

John walked out of the barn and our eyes met for a long moment before he turned away and greeted his parents. It was clear John was as surprised as I was and his shoulders sagged.

He would retreat even further into himself with more visitors. Even though it was because of his sin, I found myself hurting for him.

I knew I should move forward, but I used their momentary distraction with the others to take in a long, deep, wooded-air breath.

"Emma." Aaron thrust his large hand out to me. "John always says his *frau* loves surprises, don't you?" he called over his shoulder as John walked our way.

"That's right, Emma, isn't it?" John said so convincingly I nearly believed him as he caught my gaze again.

For a moment I saw the memories of past surprises play over his mind and through his eyes. Sometimes they lingered in my mind until either the blush of passion arose or the burden of our distance wiped them away. This time my father-in-law's laugh pulled us both back to the present.

I watched as John and Aaron walked away to the barn. Aaron believed his arrival was a surprise, but I knew better. John's forgetfulness was getting worse the more he drank. His gentleness toward me was diminishing like dampness whisked away in a May breeze. And anytime he *was* gentle, I was filled with my own regrets and in my guilt I pushed him away.

"Emma?" Polly walked closer. "Is that really you? You're all bones. You're going to blow away with the wind."

"Sis miehck," I answered her. We shared an awkward handshake. In an instant the feeling of that mother in the woods pulling her son and myself into her arms came back to me. I hadn't realized until that moment how hungry I was for something different from my veneer-covered life. How hungry I was for touch — John and I were so far from each other, and our intimate moments were not what they used to be, and seldom.

Later that day the bowls of potatoes were scraped clean and the talk at the table had begun picking up after a quiet midday meal. I bristled at the chatter because I knew John didn't like conversational meals. He preferred to eat quickly and silently.

Johnny and his cousins had been excused already. John sent them to continue helping our neighbor Roy with his fence after the storm the night before. I was glad the three of them were gone. Their jokes and laughter added to the noise that thinned John's nerves. This was what happened when he couldn't drink.

As the voices continued to pick up, I caught his eye and laid a gentle hand on the knee of the child to my left. Without explanation he looked at John and in a moment his hands were in his lap. Berthy and Rebecca made sure the other children were quiet. It didn't surprise me that Polly was the last to recognize John's desire for silence in order to begin the after-supper prayer.

Berthy's arm moved toward Polly next to her and a moment later the older woman's mouth stilled. John looked around at everyone before bowing his head. We followed him.

I didn't always try to pray. Sometimes I relied on the pace of the many words I always had in my mind, reciting some lines I'd written or wanted to. A few lines in and the prayer would be done. But today I wanted to pray but couldn't find words.

A moment later a soft knock came on the door. I'd never judged a knock before, but this knock almost seemed to be repentant — like it wished itself away. I jerked my head up and landed my gaze on my husband, whose eyes had sharpened. Everyone was looking at us for several long moments.

A second knock sounded. I pushed my chair back. I didn't rush, afraid my own nerves would begin to show through my veil of calm.

"I guess today is the day for surprise visitors." I smiled and feigned joy since it had been clear when my in-laws arrived that I was unprepared for more company. I hated to say that Polly and I weren't close, but it was more the difference between a field mouse and a barn cat.

I eased the door open and had to stifle my eagerness when I saw who stood there.

"Hello, ma'am." It was the boy's mother. She peered around my shoulder and then her gaze rushed back to my face. "I'm sorry to interrupt your meal." Her voice reminded me of a low breeze gliding over long grass.

"It's all right." When her brown eyes met mine, I took a moment to size her up. She was shorter than me and was wearing the same dark-green dress from the other day. Her stylish chin-cropped hair and her fancy hat gave her a very opposite appearance from mine. I felt even more common than I was accustomed to. The shine of her skin tone made the curves and turns of her face even more beautiful.

She and her daughter, who stood a ways off, had the same jawline and eye shape. But the young girl's eyes seemed filled with confusion or embarrassment, while her mother's carried something else. I didn't know what.

Neither of us spoke for several beats and then we both started and stopped.

"She's the same color as the girl who —" I heard Lissy speaking and imagined Berthy clapping a hand over the little girl's mouth.

Even though she'd spoken in our dialect, Lissy had used the English word *color,* making her words easy to interpret. My face grew warm.

"I brought you this." The woman lifted a pan along with her chin. "For what you done for my George."

"Emma," John barked. *"Ich bin en wadah."*

I turned around and looked at my husband. Didn't he know that I understood they were waiting for me? With a quick word for them to go on without me, I stepped outside with the woman and closed the door behind me.

"I'm sorry to disturb you, ma'am. I just wanted to give you this and you can go back to your family." Small beads of sweat dotted the woman's hairline. It wasn't hot, but she had just walked through the humid woods. I knew the walk so well and I imagined her following my lonely path. The idea that it was now a shared path quickened something deep inside of me.

"Is your daughter okay?" I nodded toward the young girl who was throwing stones into the pond.

"Is she what?"

"Is she okay? I'm afraid she was a bit — startled — when she came by with my basket. I never had the chance to ask her name or introduce myself or even say thank you before she ran off."

"Don't you mind her. She's addle-minded." The woman cleared her throat. "Let me give this to you and I'll be on my way. Me and my young'uns have taken up enough of your time."

The woman was rushed, but I was content. I didn't want her to go. I wanted to know who she was. Where had they moved from? Was George okay? I took the dish she handed me. It was heavy and still warm. I put my nose to the cloth that lay over it, and even though I was full, the scent made me hungry again.

"I'll say thank you again, ma'am." She turned to leave.

"Please, don't go." I set the dish down on the porch swing and met the woman as she took the first porch step. She looked sideways at me like she didn't understand what I'd said. I half thought that maybe, in my haste, I'd spoken Pennsylvania Dutch instead of English. "I'm Emma. Emma Mullet." I held my hand out to her.

She looked at it and furrowed her brow. She didn't take it and her refusal reminded me of the nettles I had gathered. Was I nettles to her?

"How is George?" I pulled my hand back.

"He fine. Just fine." Though she seemed exasperated, her voice was smooth, even, and nice to listen to.

"Good." I paused. "And the rest of your family? Are you at the old church house?"

"Old church house?" She dipped her chin.

"That's what we call it around here. The house has been empty for a few years. I was just guessing that maybe that's where you're living."

"Mm-hmm, that's the one." She took the rest of the steps down from the porch. I could see she was determined not to speak with me — but I wanted to speak with her. "Well, thank you again — for finding my George. I'll be saying good afternoon now and good-bye, ma'am."

"Please, call me Emma." I followed her down the stairs and walked in step with her.

"I think I'll stick with ma'am." She just looked straight ahead when she spoke and widened her stride to move more quickly.

Her coolness toward me made me stop in my tracks.

"Let's go, Sparrow," she said to her daughter.

Sparrow.

If my daughter had lived, I'd have wanted to name her something like that. Wild and unfettered. The opposite of me. The opposite of my life. I stood there and considered the girl's name and the woman who still remained nameless and watched them walk away.

SPARROW

I saw that boy, Johnny, when Mama pulled
me back through the woods when she was
done dropping off the food to that white
lady. Daddy had called them Amish. I didn't
know much about them 'cept they dressed
funny and didn't have electricity or cars. We
did see a few in town when we drove
through.

But in them woods, there was a little
thread of gray smoke that caught my eye.
Then I saw him. He was with them same
boys as before.

Mama didn't notice the cigarette smoke.
Her eyes done gone darker than usual. She
kept her eyes straight ahead and walked like
she trying to stomp holes in the ground.
She didn't turn her face when I almost stop
walking because that boy and me caught
eyes. He sat up straighter, and even though
trees and bushes were between us, I felt like
I could smell the cigarettes on his breath.

"Girl." Mama's voice snapped me back. "What you doing? Come on."

"Sorry, Mama." I didn't dare look back at Johnny, but my back burned and I know'd he was looking at me.

A crash like broken glass sounded. Then a loud laugh I imagined came from Arnold.

"What's that? Who's there?" Mama craned her neck.

"I didn't hear nothin'." I lied so hard it knocked me around inside.

I could tell when she saw them boys. She stopped like a statue and grabbed my wrist. The one boy, Arnold, stood and my chin lifted just a little because I remembered what he'd called me the other time. Still, though, my heart started thudding when he made like he was coming toward us.

My gaze darted around looking for Johnny's face, and when he stood I knew he wouldn't let Arnold do nothing. I didn't know why I trusted Johnny. But there ain't no question why I want to say curse words when I put eyes on Arnold.

"It's that dirty girl again."

Then he called me that word again and laughed like a devil.

My throat tightened. I never told Mama about the boys — or anything else about that day. My fear of Mama and when she would find out I didn't tell her was nothing like my fear of white people like Arnold. They could do just about whatever they wanted against us as long as they saw us as trash. I tried not to let that word break me, but it did a little. I know'd what I was. Ain't nobody else got to tell it to me.

When he spat that word out toward Mama he laughed even harder. The breeze picked up through the woods and threw his laughter around and I wondered if the wind was on his side or mine.

What I did know was that Johnny didn't laugh.

"Come on." Mama pulled me hard and her walk was almost a run — but she was a little too proud for that. Her breathing was heavy, like she working hard. She did this until she was sure them white boys weren't following us. She didn't talk to me while we was in the woods and didn't look at me neither. But as soon as we stepped out of the woods and the long grass was under my thin, flat shoes, Mama turned to face me.

"How do you know them white boys?"

I hesitated for a minute and my toes started wiggling inside my shoes like they wanted to run away with me.

"When I took —" I stopped. She made me nervous. I couldn't think. She stared so hard at me that the hate in her eyes soaked me through like rain.

"When you what? Come on, girl, spit it out."

"When I took the basket back to that lady, they was there." Why did I sound so guilty? I ain't done a darn thing wrong.

"You talk to them?"

I replayed it all in my head — 'bout how it went with them boys — but when I didn't answer fast enough, she grabbed my chin and gave me a shake.

"You stay away from them boys. You stay away from all boys. Ain't no good can come from you getting attention from boys. You mind me like I'm God. You hear me?"

She pinched my skin in her grip, and as much as I wanted to answer her, I didn't just then. She scared me worse than any other time.

"Don't you ignore me."

"I understand, Mama." My words squeezed out of my gripped mouth and chin.

Mama's fingernails scratched my skin when she let go, then she turned and walked away. As I watched her leave, I imagined living with her for the rest of my life. It was my fate. It was my sentence.

Later at supper I got to thinking 'bout

how there was so much the same now as before that it didn't seem right.

The table was the same. The dishes and silverware was the same. Mama's food was the same. The way we sat at the table was the same. The empty chair was the same. Daddy said that we should leave some place for the Master. But that empty chair wasn't for God. It was for a different master we'd brought from Montgomery.

I picked at my food and watched the screen door twitter in the light breeze. The scent of grass was too sweet for the likes of me. It weren't nothing like the muggy river air in Montgomery where I imagined all our real selves still living. That's where my old mama lived — the one who used to love me. The me before I killed my brother and damned my soul away from the good place.

My mind wandered 'til we was doing dishes. Mama was washing, Harriet was rinsing, and I was drying — just like in Montgomery.

"Harriet, you go watch television with your brothers." Too much salt seasoned Mama's words and I could taste trouble coming.

"Really?" Harriet raised an eyebrow. Mama flicked her head toward the TV and Harriet done run off quick like.

All I heard for the next few minutes was the sloshing of the water. Was Mama bothered with that like I was? The insects started to stir outside and covered up some of the water noise. The sun wasn't set yet, but I could see it heading that way and throwing some of that orange across the dim sky.

"What you know about that Amish boy and the red-haired one?" Mama's voice spoiled the sweet scent of the grass that came through the window.

"Why do you think I know something?" My question fell out of my mouth before I could pull it back. I know'd it would irritate her and she'd think I was doing it on purpose.

"Just answer me." She kept washing.

"I don't know nothin', Mama."

"But he looked at you like he knew you. That other boy said he saw you before. Girl, we been here for less than a week and you already getting yourself into trouble."

"I told you the truth before. I met them when I was coming home from the Amish lady's house. Just that once." I cleared my throat, wanting to give myself a moment to choose my words wisely. "The one boy who looked — normal — said some nasty stuff. The Amish one — Johnny — didn't. He was nice to me."

"Nice? What does that mean?" Mama's voice was as tight as a pulled rubber band.

"Just that, Mama. He didn't like what the other boy, Arnold, was calling me."

"Johnny. Arnold." Mama laughed — but it weren't the nice kind; it was the mean kind. "There you go again — you know them boys' names already."

I didn't say nothing to defend myself. It wouldn't matter.

"You see them, you turn and walk — no — you run the other way. I don't want you to think about them or remember them. That also goes for that Amish woman."

"Her name is Emma." I spoke just above a whisper.

"What was that?"

I didn't answer her right away but let a few moments pass. "Nothin'."

DELILAH

I saw a white lighthouse once a whole bunch a years ago. It wasn't a real one at an ocean or nothing. But it stood tall next to nothing more than a small pond — one that somebody dug up and made for themselves.

I'd been only fourteen but I still remember it all, even the heat that burned through the top of the car we traveled in from Montgomery. Sweat dripped off all of us — my parents, sisters, and brothers — like grease from fried-up bacon. But those were the days when bacon only showed up in my dreams and not on my plate. Those days was thin and half starved. We had driven to Georgia to go to Great-Granny Scott's ninety-fifth birthday party, and I ain't sure we didn't do it more for the food than we did for Great-Granny. Since Daddy lost his job, money, food, and smiles were scarce. But when that lighthouse came into view, thoughts about my empty stomach went away.

Since I was sure I would never get no-where where a lighthouse really mattered, I took it into my memory to make it a part of me. I stared at that thing until we was just next to it and I craned my neck so far I almost fell. A boy was at the top of the lighthouse and I remember feeling jealous. I wanted to go up there, but Daddy said not to be no bother.

But Great-Granny gave me permission to go to the top and said that I wasn't bother-ing nobody. When I climbed the stairs that went up in circles, the boy was still up there. I wished he wasn't so's I could have the whole top to myself.

He was reading from a book that didn't look like nothing I saw in school. His suit was smart. Was he sweating through that darn thing? Because I was pretty sure God was sweating through His robes just watch-ing us. I didn't recognize him so he wasn't no cousin.

The spring door screeched and the boy turned toward me. He seemed annoyed and looked me up and down when I stepped out. I was dressed more simply than most of the folks at the party and I felt the shame of it.

"You shouldn't be up here. This isn't a place for children." His manners were poor but his voice was so smooth and his words sounded like he was full of schooling. Why was he up here anyhow? Why was he wearing clothes a body couldn't even work in? Reading in the middle of the day? Did he think he was better'n everybody else? He wasn't no common colored boy wearing a smart suit. Even though all of this annoyed me, it also made me a little jealous of his ways.

"Great-Granny said I could," I snapped and lifted my chin at him. "And I ain't a child. I fourteen — almost fifteen. Why you up here anyhow?"

He started talking all big and calling Granny by her given name — Mrs. Cassandra Scott. That made me as mad as when my mama pinched the soft part of my arm. Everybody called Great-Granny "Granny" or "Great-Granny." He too good to do that with his obvious northern ways. I didn't like him. No, sir. Not one bit. He was so full of hisself, it was a wonder he could breathe normal air that everybody else was also using up.

"How you get an invite to Great-Granny's party?" I didn't think he belonged here.

"Reverend Carl Scott brought me. He

wanted to talk to me."

"That's my uncle. Why?"

"I'm just about done with college and he wants me to work at his church when I graduate — I aim to be a preacher in two more years but —"

"That's *my* church." I raised my chin. "Wait a minute, you going to college?" I stepped closer to him. I hadn't met many colored folks who were going to college.

He nodded like he knew he impressed me, but I didn't care about that no more. He was going to *college.* "Wow."

His chest puffed and he put his hand out to me. "My name is Malachi Evans — what's yours?"

I raised my chin up real high when I took his hand. "Miss Delilah Mae Scott."

"Dee?" Malachi's voice cut through my lighthouse memory, reminding me that there ain't no lighthouses in this old Pennsylvania land. "It's barely dawn."

I hadn't slept much last night. I moved around like a snake in a sack. I didn't want to be pent up in bed and left before the sun was up. It was like my body didn't know what tired was, or maybe it didn't know what awake was. I just went through all the motions I needed to do every day.

He sat with me on an old pew on the front

porch — he was too close. I wanted to be alone. He was disturbing me now like I disturbed him when we first met in that lighthouse. "Just needed to get up is all."

"There ain't that sizzle to the sun waking up here, is there? Not like it was in Montgomery."

"Mm-hmm."

"George's fussin' woke me up." He stretched his arms above his head for a moment before letting them flop back onto his lap.

"George?" I started to get up from the pew and my coffee mug tumbled out of my hands. The handle broke off on the old porch slats.

"Doggone it." The words were whispered but like a loud one that scraped against your throat.

Malachi bent down before I could and handed me the handle piece inside the mug. "He's fine. I checked on him." He patted my hand before resting his on top of it. I supposed he wanted me to hold his hand, but I didn't want to. After a few moments he put his hand back into his lap.

"What were you thinking about?" I was glad to hear he hadn't turned on his preacher voice. That was when his questions were just to get someone to talk out their own problems and then he'd go and slap a verse on top of it like a bandage.

Don't get me wrong — I loved the Bible — but it couldn't be used like that. But right now, in this quiet country morning, he was just Malachi, my husband. This was the only reason I started talking.

"You remember that lighthouse back when we thought we was so big?" I said and I felt the smile somewhere inside my words.

" 'Course I do. That was the day we met."

"You mean that was the day you called me a child and you was acting too big for your britches." I couldn't keep a smirk from my face, but I wiped it off in a moment. Even my grief wouldn't erase that memory. "You was so puffed up."

Malachi let out a loud laugh and poked my arm. "I wasn't the only one *puffed up*, you haughty peacock — Miss Delilah Mae Scott."

He laughed again at my old self and then grazed my face with his knuckle. "You were so pretty that day, but you were so young."

"I watched for you every summer at church. All us girls had our sights set." I let my memory go back and skipped over the stuff that hurt. I figured it was okay to do, just for a minute.

"I had my sights too." He nudged me with

111

his shoulder.

I had always wanted to marry a preacher. A smart man. One who wanted a whole bunch of kids. My parents loved him more than they loved me. I was extra hopeful when he told me that twins ran in his family. I'd prayed for twins since I was eleven, so I figured he had to be the one.

Twins. I'd had my twins. But I didn't no more.

A mourning dove landed on the chipped-up porch rail. It cooed but didn't seem to notice us. Then it turned all the way around and it was almost like it looked at me before it flew away. I was jealous of the way it could just fly off and not care about the worries that made a soul heavy and thick.

"You know, baby, there are lighthouses everywhere. In the sunrises every morning. The church bells." He paused and I fought rolling my eyes at the sermon I heard behind his words. "But, Dee, I don't think you're looking for a lighthouse right now. I think you're looking for an anchor so you don't go anywhere — so you don't go too far away from *him.*"

"Don't you go and try to figure me out." I stood and Malachi took my hand.

"Baby, don't go. Let's talk. We never talk

anymore. Ever since Car —"

"Don't say his name." I pulled my hand from his.

"Dee, come on now."

"Don't wanna talk." I said it like I meant it but I was lying again. I wanted to tell him just what I thought. "You always said you'd be my lighthouse. You said when I feel like I'm —"

I stopped. My mouth just wouldn't form more of my thinking into words.

"Say it, Dee. When you feel like you're *drowning.*"

"Don't you say that." I stuck my finger in his face.

"When you were drowning because your mama got sick — we got through it together. When you felt like you were drowning when the Robinson girl got attacked by those white boys and you were convinced Sparrow was next — I was right there with you. But now, with this — our baby boy — you're pushing me away. You think I'm okay? Don't you see I'm drowning alongside you? And Sparrow —"

"Don't you go saying all that. You stop it. Don't you talk about him like this is just one more burden to deal with."

"You can't even say his name. Say it. Carver. *Carver.* He was our perfect, precious

113

boy but he's gone." Tears rolled down his face and it made my own eyes burn. "He ain't coming back. He gone."

"You fixin' to make me hurt worse?" I could tell he had crossed into his other self because he wasn't using all his proper words no more.

"Nothing going to bring him back or hurt him. Not your sadness. It wouldn't even hurt him if you moved forward — if you'd let yourself. He won't hurt if you forgive Birdie — and forgive yourself. But instead you blaming me for not being your light-house. Like I ain't in those same waters with you trying to find my way."

We were quiet for a minute and then a car drove up. It wasn't nobody I recognized.

"Grannie Winnie's grandson-in-law, Titus, is taking me into town to find a car. I'll get to the grocery store too." He looked at me like he wanted me to say something, but I just didn't want to. I wanted to tell him to get potatoes, milk, butter, eggs, and bread mostly, and if there was any way to get his hands on some chicken, I'd be grateful.

But I didn't even want to tell him that. I just wanted him to suffer and not get what he needed from me. That was how I lived now. Not getting nothing I needed.

When Malachi came back a few hours

later, he was driving an old red beat-up truck. *A truck.* I pursed my lips in disgust. But he come bouncing out like he was excited to get that old clunker. He grabbed two paper bags out of the back. Mallie caught sight of him and opened the door for him.

"Daddy, is that our truck? Did you get that today? Can you teach me to drive it?" Mallie never did know nothing better than trucks and nobody better than his daddy.

Malachi laughed out loud.

"You got that right, son." He set the bags down on the kitchen counter. I wanted to riffle through them but didn't want to act too excited. "I think on these old country roads I could teach you pretty well."

"No, you ain't," I piped up. "He just a child."

He didn't know it, but I saw him elbow Mallie in the ribs and wink at him. I let it go.

"Why don't you go get the last bag out of the back," Malachi said, then looked at me. "Sorry about this morning, Dee. I didn't mean to come at you like that."

I believed him, but instead of saying anything, I looked at the bags and raised an eyebrow. "Can I get that food put away now?" But I forced out a small smile to

115

make him see that I still loved him. And I did. But all them good feelings were just covered up under all the bad ones.

He smiled back but then got this expression that I knew meant he was thinking on stuff. "The grocery store is okay. Pretty different from Montgomery."

"Different? How?"

"We can talk about it later. But Mr. Coleman, the grocer, is nice."

"*Mr.* Coleman? I thought you said his name was Carl and that you played together when you was boys."

"Same fellow, but he's Mr. Coleman to me now."

Of course he was.

EMMA

When I walked into my bedroom, John was sitting just outside the moonlight that cascaded onto the bed. The last I'd seen him he'd gone into the cellar, giving our company some false reason that I alone knew didn't make sense. My husband was a liar — but so was I.

I didn't know how or when he'd slipped back upstairs and then into our bedroom. He lounged with his back against the oak headboard, one leg on the bed and one leg off. Boots still on and the quilt — our wedding quilt — had bits of dried mud scattered nearby. His hat was hanging over the footboard corner and his hair was dark and pasted on his forehead where the sweat had accumulated.

He didn't hide his bottle when I walked in, and the mix of alcohol and his natural scent wrapped around me. Though he'd made drinking this *Communion wine* his evening habit for over a decade, it was still rare that I saw him with a bottle. But I always saw the drink. In his eyes, in his breath, and in his touch.

"*Blahp doh,* Emma." He told me to stay with more sobriety than should be possible.

"*Ich muss* —" I started to say *I must* before my throat closed up around my words and intentions. I tried again, stating his mother needed some help with something — anything — but didn't finish my untruth. "*Deh mem muss helve mit* —"

"*Neh.*" His *no* was simple but firm. I never believed that the Bible meant for a wife to submit to a man who pretended to be someone he wasn't, who chose control over love. But yet I chose to submit. I stood there with the doorknob in my hand — it grew warm and sweaty — but I didn't have the power to let go.

After he took a long drink from the green wine bottle, he got up from the bed with his usual slow movements. The kerosene lamp's small flame was so unfettered within its glass globe, and I fixed on it instead of considering what was going to happen. The bottle was over half empty.

"*Kumm.*" *Come.* He used his head to wave me over to him.

The tears in my eyes burned and then

blurred the setting in front of me. I didn't want to go over there. I knew what he was going to do and what he wanted from me, which I didn't want to do this way. Without my even blinking, a hot tear betrayed my supposed bravery and trailed down to my chin. I felt it drip onto my dress.

"Why like this?" I whispered.

"Because I need you, Emma." He set the bottle down. His hands went around me and he moaned as he leaned into my middle.

"Please, John. I don't want to — not this way."

"Come on." He pulled me over. "You know this way helps us. You know what to do."

Hot tears coursed their heat down my face. But I would submit to him because I couldn't say no to him. I'd never been able to. I would do anything, tell any lie, and hide his sin from everyone — all for him. But he didn't know what I did for myself.

That was my own secret and maybe it was my revenge on him.

"Go on." His voice wasn't his typical monotone but had a lift to it and was warm around the edges.

"I don't want to, John."

When his hand moved from its relaxed place on the bed to his lap, I knew not to test his patience.

"Please." His husky voice was nearly a whisper.

I reached out and wrapped my sweaty palm around the green glass bottle on the nightstand, and I emptied it. The warm liquid was strong as it traveled through my body, past my heart, and drenched my soul with such deceit I could not confess. But this was how we could be close.

The next morning I woke to the sound of a car door slamming and the sounds of voices yelling good-bye. I lifted my heavy eyelids and saw that my window was open. The light that spilled through stung my eyes. Why did my head ache? Why did my body feel so heavy?

A few long moments passed and I looked down at myself, not recognizing my condition. Naked. On top of the bed crossways. My hair loose. My covering smashed between the footboard and the mattress. Then I remembered.

He had made me drink. It was how he needed me when we were together as husband and wife.

My headache worsened as I stumbled out of bed. I couldn't pick up my dress on the floor or the straight pins scattered here and there. I didn't even try to piece together what happened after I'd drunk. I hated this frailty that I woke to but wore like a covering.

I should have refused to drink with him. Our intimacy was so rare and I didn't know when this had begun to be part of the ritual. Was it to lower the walls our guilt had built between us? But it wasn't the right way and I hated it.

I watched the drivers pull out with a car and a van loaded with our home-going visitors. Johnny walked toward Arnold's, and though John should've told him no, he didn't. John went to the barn where he would tend to the horse, a chore acceptable on the Sabbath.

I looked at the drawer where I kept my papers and pencils and my herbs. I wouldn't need to take the herbs today — tomorrow morning. Every Monday morning.

I fixed myself the hottest bath I could stand, though my body ached as I sat with my knees folded against my chest in the small tub. I didn't get out until the water had cooled.

It was our in-between Sunday, so we didn't have a church service. The house was empty again — and I was certain to be chastised in a forthcoming letter from my mother-in-law that I wasn't present to send them off. The now-empty bedrooms seemed to sigh in thankfulness. Or was that me? Scripture kept me from starting the washing of all the sheets and towels on the Sabbath, but it wasn't just that.

When I walked into the midmorning air, it was thick with invitation. A long walk through the friendly woods was within what was allowed on the Sabbath. I hadn't been in the woods since the day I'd found George and the very trees called to me. Sometimes it was in the way the wind wrapped around them and their leaves waved hello. This morning it was in the birdsong with its trill reminding me that there was something beautiful still to be cherished.

I repeated the word *trill*. I would have to use it in one of my written lines soon. I touched my pen and paper that I'd tucked in the waist of my dress.

I walked past the barn and saw John before he saw me. I had so many memories of Sunday walks from our early married days. A flutter of my eyelashes was all it took for him to drop everything and stroll with me. Every now and again these memories would cross my mind and I would try to feel them again to remind myself of what we once had.

Back in those now lost times, we would

hide out in the woods for hours. When our marriage was new, when everything was fresh and laced with love. We lived far enough from neighbors that we could slip away without judgment of the unpredictability of young romance.

One day we found a piece of earth that fit our bodies just perfectly. We conceived a child on one of those jaunts. But my body gave the child back to the earth when just half grown. The baby was a girl and I never forgot her. It was as if she'd never existed because her birth was her death. The precious unknown one never had a name until the season moved from summer to the wild colors of autumn, and that became her name, *Autumn.* She would've been thirteen this year.

Then I began to rename her as often as I liked. One spring day when I saw the first fawn of the year, I named her that — *Fawn.* And every time I saw the mixture of green and brown from a long view of the woods, I thought *Hazel* should be her name. It was always changing. But when I learned the Negro girl's name — Sparrow — I knew that my daughter would have that name now and maybe forever. A bird so uncelebrated by man but not forgotten by God.

"Emma." John spoke my name loudly,

pulling me from my spun memory web.

"*Ja?*"

"I was telling you that Simon Miller may stop in before lunch." His face looked stern over the top of the almanac he was reading. He looked down. "Just for company."

Simon Miller was a young man whose wife had passed recently. He came over for John's company some days. He'd been married only a short time and they had had no children, and now he was alone again.

"Should I stay?" I tried to speak normally, but my tongue felt fat and dry in my mouth. "Make sure you have coffee and pie?"

"No," he said too quickly, then paused so long that I started walking away. "There's some lemonade and the cookies that *Mem* made. That'll do."

With nothing more to say, I walked away with the thick, humid air slipping around my hands and pulling me to quicken my pace. It walked me toward the woods, past the pond, along the path that deepened my freedoms.

I breathed in the rain-washed woods. The growth had shrouded portions of my path and brushed against my dress. The nameless mother and Sparrow had walked this path. It was no longer lonely.

I hadn't walked far but my eyes knew what

I needed to find. The wild turnip, even after all the rain, looked to be faring poorly. The green and almost purple plant brought me freedom. The plants were so small, however, that the roots would not yield much when cooked and dried. In another week I would have to take what I could and hope. I allowed my eyes a quick glance at the eternal bed of my daughter. I would not stop today. The sorrow didn't seem right for the Sabbath.

When I continued walking, my foot rolled over something slick and I was on the ground.

I groaned, then noticed that I'd tripped over one of John's Communion bottles. It shouldn't have been out here. They were stored in the darkest corner of our basement. The bottle was green glass, which was the oldest brew.

I picked it up and looked around. I found a snaky, worn path heading off of the main trail. I followed it, holding the wine bottle. I entered a small clearing. It was man-made — or, as I suspected, *boy* made. Son made. Several sawed logs were rolled together like seats. Newly hewn branches were piled over the makeshift seats as if to hide them. I pulled them off — what more was Johnny hiding?

There was an old hankie wet on the ground with the initials *JM* in the corner. In my handwriting. Old, empty, weather-beaten packs of cigarettes and butts littered the ground under the branches. My heart hammered and my hand trembled as I tucked the empty bottle under my arm. Johnny was taking his *rumspringa* more seriously than anything else in his life, but seeing the proof broke too many pieces of me. It was time for John to get involved before real damage was done.

Rumspringa did not allow for worldly rebellion — experimenting with alcohol, smoking, and immorality. It was, at its simplest, a time for dating and finding a girl who could grow to become a good wife. But there were always a few youth who took this "running around" as a time to do as they pleased, regardless of right and wrong. The purpose was for small freedoms, but sometimes church leaders turned a blind eye to the foolishness of the young people, which only fueled their folly.

The new Lancaster preacher and his *fratzy frau* had spoken of wanting to hold the youth to a higher standard. They had seen the sinfulness within the booming communities of Lancaster and did not want that for our youth. The *Englisher* lifestyle was far more accessible in Lancaster. This was why I had never approved of Johnny getting so close with the neighbor boy, Arnold.

Under one of the logs, magazine pages stuck out. I rocked the log back and pulled. The moment I saw the cover I gasped and dropped it. I looked down at it and the shock of it filled me. Though the cover was tattered and faded, the picture was clear enough. I picked it up with the tips of my fingers — which still made me feel dirty. The woman on the cover was young and berry lipped and wore her wheat-colored waves no longer than her earlobes.

Her shoulders were bare. Completely bare. Her breasts were more uncovered than not and the magazine cut off just below them. How could this woman be willing to bare so much of herself? And who would even agree to take such an image with a camera and then more people agreeing to print it for many others to buy and see? Not to mention those who sold it in their stores. How could so many people agree to do the same wrong thing? It didn't take much to think about how Johnny had gotten this.

I glanced around before flipping through the pages. I had never seen anything like this, and as upset as I was about Johnny having the magazine, I was curious. What I found inside made me ashamed of myself. Articles about lifestyles I didn't approve of — drinking, smoking, and sex. Inappropriate advertisements. Photos of women who may as well have been nude. Before I knew it I was ripping it apart. Pieces of the pages fell around me like leaves.

Imagining my son looking at that magazine and suspecting that it was not the first made my stomach swirl. Had he exposed his cousins to it? If Larry or Berthy found out, I would never be forgiven.

Who was this boy I'd raised? He was a boy following after his parents with secrets just like John. Just like me.

SPARROW

There was a time years ago when I loved sitting in church and listening to Daddy preach. I remember many hot, muggy Sundays sitting on Grandma Evans's soft lap and looking up and feeling proud that it was *my* daddy who was preaching. I imagined what a shame it would be if he wasn't so handsome — everyone would have to look at some homely, sad-looking face for a good hour. But Daddy was the best-looking man at church. Maybe in all of Montgomery. And he could lead the choir just as good as Brother Jeremiah, who was the actual director.

But one day that changed. One day I noticed that the church ladies doted over Daddy something awful. He was so handsome I was sure every lady wished Mama was dead and buried just so they could snag him up. And Mama let them fawn all over him without no word. Not one. Even though

I was young when I noticed this, it stuck with me and I asked Mama about it. She just told me to leave it be — happy church women made a happy church — that's what she said.

But when George was born and everybody could see that boy wasn't gonna be *normal,* instead of all the doting it was pity. Pity expressions and pity talk too. I heard it with my own ears. Ladies saying stuff like, "Might be easier if there was only Carver," or "Don't think that comes from the reverend's side. I heard Sister Deedee had a cousin who was simpleminded too." Then the ladies would exchange a knowing look like they got it all figured up.

I wanted to yell at them that it wasn't true. Mama had no simple cousin and George was that way 'cause of how he wasn't breathing when he was born. What they mean by simpleminded anyway? That boy was as kind as a body could be. He was happy and tender. If that's what simpleminded was, then that's better than those old biddies could ever be.

Just like Mama knew what I was thinking, she always gave me that gaze that told me I got to keep my mouth shut and pay them folks no mind. Why didn't she fight back? Why didn't she tell them that we loved

George as much as we loved Carver? But she never said nothing.

But when Carver died the talk got worse. It went from people saying, "Well, at least they still got one of them twins," to "I thought an accident like that would happen to the simple one." Then they'd shake their heads like it was out of sympathy instead of judgment. But I know'd better.

Then I'd look at Mama and wait for that gaze telling me to stay quiet. But it never came. She just had those dead eyes — though I knew she heard every word. But I yelled my piece. I did. I told them church ladies they got it all wrong. That George wasn't just the leftovers — he was funny and tender and loving and didn't have a mean bone in hisself.

Then my too-handsome daddy dragged me away and made me feel ashamed — even more than I already did. But Mama just stared. She never paid those ladies no mind. She never paid me no mind no more. She didn't pay no mind to nothing no more.

Now that we moved to this Pennsylvania country, that time felt far away, like a different world. Daddy didn't look so handsome to me like he used to. Mama still stared off into nothing. But when I looked around at the people in the rickety church pews, ain't none of them talking about how burdened the reverend's family was with the simple-minded little son and how it was a curse that Carver was the one who died.

How long would that last?

We had a few extra families at church today besides us and Grannie Winnie. Daddy asked them all to introduce themselves to us. Titus and Marlene Carter had Kenny, Jake, Belinda, and Tootsie. Joshua and Tammy Randall had Calvin, Joy, and a baby on the way. Then a man named Lincoln Tripp with his daughter, Lois. She was about my age. Her mama died a long time ago. Then an old wrinkled-up man named Otis.

"G'morning." A hand was in front of me when everybody got up to shake hands. I looked up. It was that boy Calvin with his hand out at me. He was 'bout my age.

"Morning." I stood and limply shook his hand.

He was all-right looking even though his eyes were small and his smile was too big.

"I'm Calvin," he said and fixed up his three-piece suit that was a little tight.

"Hmm," was all I said. Of course I already knew his name. I wasn't trying to be rude but know'd Mama would say I was flirting with him if I spoke.

The quiet but constant buzz of voices stirred in my ears while I waited for him to leave.

"You're Sparrow, right?"

"Mm-hmm." He reminded me of the boy who'd kissed me behind Minny Lawrence's shed on my thirteenth birthday. It was a terrible kiss.

"Like the bird, right?"

I nodded a few times. "Yeah."

"I like that." Then he smiled and showed all his teeth. They was as straight as that path that Mama wanted me on.

It was hours later when the preaching was through and the potluck all ate up. Now there was the scrape of silverware against the plates to push off the little bits of okra and macaroni. These people knew how to eat as well as our church in Montgomery. Just a smaller crowd. Daddy drew a big crowd in Montgomery. The choir was larger than all the folks sitting in the creaky pews at the new church.

"Lois, did you know that I have an aunt in Montgomery?" One of two girls my age stacked a few plates next to the sink. She hadn't introduced herself to me, neither had the other girl, but they had been looking at me through the corners of their eyes.

The tall one with the mouth was Belinda

133

and she always dragged the shorter one, Lois, around. I didn't like neither of them. But I was a little jealous of how long Belinda's hair was. Mine wasn't even to my shoulders. No matter, though, they both thought they was better than everybody else. And Belinda crinkled up her nose like them white women do when we walk by.

I grabbed another plate and kept washing in the lukewarm water. As long as Mama didn't notice, I didn't care that it wasn't as hot as it should be. The three of us girls watched out the window for a few moments. I wasn't sure where the other two were looking, but my eyes went right to my daddy, and, of course, there was a woman talking to him.

"My aunt didn't go to her daddy's church but she knows of him."

Belinda's mean, snotty tone dirtied her words. I decided to say nothing. Maybe the girl would stop running her mouth. And if I had an argument with some girl at our new church, Mama would skin me. Yes, she would. Skin me.

"What did your aunt say about her daddy?" the short one said with her squeaky voice, then giggled a little. In the reflection of the window I saw Belinda elbow Lois.

"Oh, she just said that her daddy is too

soft at the pulpit — that he isn't tough enough on sin."

I dropped the plate and it clinked hard against the few others in the gray water. I pushed my hands back into it so they wouldn't see me shaking.

"Said if he was tougher on sin maybe *some* things wouldn't have been so grim by and by." Belinda's voice sounded sweet, but it was full of venom. "My aunt said that the boy died because of the reverend being too soft on sin — it was God's punishment."

She hung those words out like laundry on a line. They just waved and flapped in the wind, and I wanted to grab hold of them and crumple them and burn them up. Then it was like I could see little Carver standing by them woods in the back of the yard. Was it really him? He was wearing that sweet smile of his and his big eyes looked right at me. George never looked in our eyes.

I blinked and looked again and he was gone. My hands started shaking so bad the water was splashing. I couldn't make them stop. They convulsed like Tate Robert did back home when he was having one of his fits.

"What's wrong with her?" Lois's tone started out disgusted, but by the time she spoke the last word, I could tell she was as frightened as me. "Belinda, make her stop."

"What do you want me to do about it? She's the one who's losing her blessed mind."

"Go fetch her mama," Lois told Belinda, who wasn't used to taking orders.

"She's just faking. I'm sure of it. Girls like her always want attention. That's all this is."

They may have kept talking but I stopped hearing them. My mind dwelled on my baby brother. Did he hurt when he died? What was he thinking in his final moments? Did he hate me?

Then I stuck my face in that dirty sink water. I pushed it as far down as I could. I hadn't taken much of a breath before, but I guessed I would see how long I could hold it or what would happen if I couldn't. Someone was trying to pull me but they wasn't strong enough. I kept my face buried and gripped the side of the sink with all my might. When my hands had stopped convulsing, I wasn't sure.

I could feel the greasiness of the water and the bits of food floating around. But I wasn't gonna stop. Maybe I would find Carver somewhere in this murky water. Only the tips of my ears were above water and I could hear muffled voices. They sounded far away.

I started screaming in that sink, under that water. I yelled all sorts of bad, ugly words, but mostly I yelled for Carver. Like I had done that day. Had he heard me then? Did he hear me now? Would God let him? Or had Carver already forgotten all about us he left behind? I didn't have any air and my chest ached.

It was like a force I couldn't control when I lifted my head on up out of the water and gasped for air. Between my deep breaths, the yelling didn't stop. I heard some commotion in the kitchen but mostly I heard my own wailing. Why couldn't I just fall and twist down the drain and go away forever? I don't know how long it was 'til someone pulled me away from the sink. It was Mama. I knew her grip. Her thumbnails dug into my skin.

The shaking came back without warning, and I couldn't control it or the noise that come out of my mouth. Water was everywhere. Water dripped down my neck and into my dress. Water went between my bosoms and all the way down me until I could feel that dirty sink water around my belly.

Even with Mama's tight hold on my arms, I couldn't stop shaking. My ears stopped working and I squeezed my eyes shut. I

137

didn't want to see nobody. Didn't want to see what their faces said about me. There came a smack across my cheek and my eyes opened. I continued to wail and yell for Carver.

Mama's mouth was moving and her brow was all wrinkled up, but I blocked out her words. Even in the madness of the moment I saw Mama in a different way, like I was looking through that dirty dishwater. I saw how old she was getting and that her skin was slack around her jaw. When had that happened?

The other church ladies were looking on like we was something to be watched. One of them, the old granny, pushed everybody toward the door. When that boy came in, they pushed him back out like cats on a mouse. The screen door shut, but I didn't hear the loud slap when it closed. I turned back to Mama who was still yelling something at me. She dumped me on a chair. But I couldn't hear nothing.

Every sound I made scraped against my throat now. Everything moved slowly, and when Daddy's face came into view, I got slapped back to Mama's view and her face was even angrier. Everything was foggy and filmy looking. My hearing came back, but everything now was in a whisper about what was wrong with me and that I was too old to have fits.

"Don't, Dee." Daddy pulled Mama away. He left her standing a little piece away, then came and folded his arms around me.

His mouth was by my ear and he whispered, "He gives power to the faint. Breathe, Birdie. He gives strength to the weary. You're okay now."

He picked me up like I was just a small thing and walked past Mama and went into the living room. Then he put me on the couch and nudged me to lay down. Daddy got down, level with me. I breathed heavy and I was still all wet. But his face calmed me.

I looked over his shoulder and saw a few of the ladies had returned and were looking on, but when they saw my eyes they turned and left the house again. They didn't think I saw them shake their heads, but I did. Mama stood there like she was afraid to come closer.

Daddy laid his hand on my shoulder and I looked back at him. I think he prayed 'cause his eyes was shut. Then he patted me and smiled. "You rest now. Okay?"

Then he just kept staring at me. Probably wouldn't leave me be 'til I closed my eyes. My eyes were so heavy and I let them fall.

After a minute the weight of Daddy's hand lifted from my shoulder and I heard him walk away. My body felt so mushy — like bread dough. Had his hand left an imprint on me? I pretended to fall asleep but I listened instead.

"Why'd you hit her?" Daddy asked.

"I was fixing to knock her out of her fit. What came over that girl?" Mama was breathing heavy like a bull with a ring in his nose. "She done stuffed her face into the sink full of water like she trying to —"

"Drown herself," Daddy finished.

"What she thinking embarrassing us like that?" Mama almost spoke right over Daddy's words.

"You might be embarrassed, Dee. But more than that you're mad. You're so mad that she's grieving and you don't think she deserves to." Daddy's voice got higher — he was agitated.

When his voice fell on my ears again, I knew he was watching me. "That scream."

"It was just like — that day." Mama's words weighed on me heavy like.

The recollection of my screaming and wailing and cursing came into my ears. I wanted to disappear.

"The girl's grieving hard, Dee. We need to be more patient with her." Daddy's full-of-burden voice swallowed up a little of my own burden for just a moment, and then it all came back because it was all my fault.

"You think your new flock of people gonna be patient with her?"

"They know what we've been through. They know why we're here."

"Should have left her with Aunt Doris."

What she mean by that? It was hard to lay still in my false sleep. I forced even breaths because I wanted to know more.

"What do you mean, leave her with Aunt Doris?"

Mama didn't say nothing.

"Deedee?" Daddy prodded.

"Aunt Doris told me that maybe she should keep Sparrow with her. Maybe give the rest of us a fresh start and she could —"

"What? And you didn't think to tell me what you was planning for my daughter?"

"Don't get in a fit over it now, Malachi. I told her no, didn't I?"

"But you wish you had said yes?" He was angry.

Mama snorted. "Shouldn't we both?"

"Dee, you need to forgive her. She's our daughter — our Birdie."

The silence got heavier with a whisper that

came across the room.

"I can't."

DELILAH

I should have known better than to think Sparrow was asleep. But as soon as I said I couldn't forgive that girl, I saw the smallest of flinches in her face. My soul told me I should explain, ask her to forgive my unforgiving heart. But instead I let my words stay in the air like a wall between me and my firstborn. She had been my little birdie-baby that cooed in my arms and I had let my words clip her wings. I'd just taken away her chance to fly and I knew it like I knew that daybreak came every morning whether I wanted it or not.

I didn't even give it a thought, leaving her there all night. Should have at least checked during the night. So when I woke and she was gone, my first thought was that she'd run away. But her shoes sat where they were left. She must have stumbled up the narrow stairs and lay in her own bed.

The kitchen looked so normal when I

walked in. Not like the place where my eldest had dunked her head in a sink full of gray water. Where she screamed and cursed with all the church ladies watching.

I don't know when Malachi left the house. He said he was going to the church for a bit to clean up and pray and read before he made his visits around town.

I poured myself a mug full of coffee and even though it was lukewarm I wished I could just sit with it quietly. Instead I heard footsteps upstairs. In minutes Mallie, George, and Harriet all came tumbling down the steps as loud as elephants. Harriet was the first to squeeze my middle. George was already chasing around his big brother with the kind of energy I wasn't sure I ever had.

After breakfast I spent over an hour cleaning up even though I had just cleaned on Saturday. But old houses liked to sneak the dust back in and I wanted to make sure I was ready for anybody who might stop by. Ain't nobody gonna see my dirt. It was just a moment after I threw a pail of dirty water out the back door when Harriet bounced in with Marlene Carter.

She looked at least as elegant as she had the first time I met her, maybe more. Her daughter was with her, also tall and perfect, and they were both dressed like they were about to meet the mayor or something. I pulled off my apron and hung it on a hook on the wall as I said hello.

"I hope it's all right that my Belinda and I stop by." Her voice was so northern, even more than my husband's. It sounded different to my ears. Her clothing fit her smoothly and she didn't have my lumpiness. She had a friendly smile, but I'd seen a lot of those same smiles in my time. Was she coming to gawk at the family with the crazy girl?

Probably should rouse her to be polite since Belinda was her age. But that girl looked like she smelled something bad. She didn't have one bit of friendly, even the fake kind, in her expression.

"Of course it's all right that you stop by. We ain't got much 'round here, but I was just fixing to make some sweet tea. Y'all just have a seat." I gestured toward the kitchen table.

Marlene looked at her daughter and nodded. Belinda's sigh sounded more like a grumble. She plopped her butt down on a chair and started riffling through the Montgomery Ward magazine on the table.

"Tea would be wonderful." Marlene offered a drippy-sweet smile.

"Harriet, go on upstairs and get your

sister." Then I turned to my company. "That girl could sleep the day away if I let her."

As if Sparrow hadn't embarrassed me enough already, now she was at it again. I suppose I had to give her a chance to try and show these two that she wasn't so crazy. She could act normal if she tried.

"Is she" — Marlene cleared her throat — "feeling better?"

I opened my mouth to say something about how she was just fine when Harriet come down and I don't get nothing out.

"She ain't up there, Mama. Can I go back outside to play with Tootsie?" Harriet was jumping up and down.

"What you mean, she ain't up there?" I tried to keep my voice even and calm. I turned to Marlene. "Excuse me, I'll be right back."

I rushed up the stairs expecting to prove Harriet wrong. Of course Sparrow had to be in her bed. Because my heart was thudding so dang hard and I hated running up the stairs, I was winded when I got to the top. I turned the corner and saw right away that Sparrow wasn't in her bedroom.

My whole body sagged. She'd heard my ugly words the night before. She had reason to run. But where would she go? It wasn't like she could've gotten on a bus or something to get back to Montgomery. The nearest bus station was in another town. She didn't have no money anyhow. Would she start walking?

I couldn't tell Marlene Carter that my girl ran off, and even if I could go find her, I'd have to cart Mallie, Harriet, and George with me. Malachi was off somewhere probably eating his fill of pie, cold chicken, and grace, and here I was — in this mess with Sparrow again. I started sweating and my underarms stung. I took slow steps down the stairs, thinking.

"Well now, sorry 'bout that, ladies." I put on my own fake smile — I knew it well. "Sparrow's not well, so she won't be coming down."

"Oh, we're sorry to hear that." I could tell that Marlene didn't believe me.

EMMA

When the sound of boots against wet grass brushed against my ears, I was surprised to find Johnny. He ran out of the woods like he was being chased. My mind went to the things I'd found at the small clearing. Had he seen that someone found it? His eyes smoldered and his face was tense. He was wearing his tall rubber boots as usual and they parted the long, uncut grass. His gaze was narrow and focused, and he didn't seem to notice me at the open kitchen window. I left the sink and pushed through the screen door and walked onto the porch.

He didn't see me until I spoke his name.

"Johnny?"

He didn't hop onto the porch like usual. His eyes were frantic in finding mine.

"Vas ist letz?" What was wrong was the simplest way to ask, though I could be asking why he was in the woods so early in the morning. Was he looking at that dirty

magazine? Did he want to become a drunk like his father?

"Sehl maedle." He lifted his straw hat before running his hand through his damp, dark hair. His shirt was unbuttoned and his chest gleamed with sweat.

"That girl? What girl?"

"Sehl dungel maedle?"

"Sparrow?" What other *dark* girl could he be talking about?

"She's in the woods. I found her. I think she's sleeping but — you just need to come."

I jumped down into the dew-covered grass and we were off toward the woods. My mind filled and spilled over like the eaves on my house. Why would Sparrow be asleep in the woods? Nothing I could imagine sounded reasonable except that she had gotten lost — but the woods were not so dense for a girl her age.

"She seemed so scared the other day. I felt bad for her."

I couldn't remember the last time Johnny had talked to me about anything more than the necessities of life. Yes, he was done with his chores. No, he didn't want a third helping. Yes, he would be going to the Singing. No, I shouldn't wait up for him.

As I considered these thoughts, I realized he'd lied to me. "You met her."

"Ja."

"Alone? What happened? Was she upset?"

He sighed loudly. "Arnold said — some things — things he shouldn't have said."

He didn't need to explain further. While I had not been around Negro people much, I knew what many white people called them. It was part of a world I didn't understand and tried to stay away from. But already, with just the little I knew of Sparrow, it pained me that anyone would treat her unkindly because of the color of her skin.

Over the next five minutes Johnny told me to hurry every few steps. "Over here." He grabbed my arm, making me run faster. "She's on the ground."

When I saw her it was almost as if she'd grown there right out of the earth. Like she was part of it. She looked so comfortable I hated to disturb her.

"She's breathing, right?"

Johnny's overflow of worry didn't make sense to me. I'd never seen him concerned like this. I put my finger to my lips, then mouthed *yes*.

I turned back to her and watched the shallow shift in the rhythm of her breathing. Her dress was a pretty green. The fabric was finer and thinner than my own. Hers had a collar, buttons, and short, pleated sleeves. Billows of frizzy brown hair surrounded her face. Her bare feet were dirty and scratched.

At first sight, because of the way she was nestled like a baby, she appeared to be sleeping peacefully. But with a closer look, I could see from the tightness in her brow to the curl in her toes that she was anything but peaceful. Her arms were wrapped around herself, her bottom lip was clamped between her teeth, and the space between her eyes was so wrinkled up it looked like it might just stay that way.

I touched her sleeve. She stirred a little and I pulled away. I was quiet for a while and just watched her.

"Mem." Johnny's voice broke in, reminding me that he was still standing behind me. "What should we do?"

My *kindisch* son. My immature boy who shirked many of his responsibilities wanted to be part of this? Wanted to help this girl? It made me nervous. I wasn't sure why. I found nothing wrong with befriending a Negro family, so what was I afraid of with regard to Johnny? It wasn't against the church to be friends with non-Amish people — *Englishers*. But his friendship with Arnold was destructive. This was not the same, was it?

151

Was I afraid Johnny was as drawn to Sparrow as I was?

"Go back to your chores, Johnny."

"*Neh,* I want to —" His whisper was louder than mine and Sparrow flinched but didn't wake.

I turned back to my son. His lips were pursed and he shifted from foot to foot a few times. Then he bobbed his head toward Sparrow — as if encouraging me to wake her. I took a deep breath and then agreed.

"Sparrow," I said just above a whisper. "Sparrow. It's Emma, your neighbor."

After repeating her name a few times, I placed my hand on her arm. When she woke her eyes opened wide as if in shock, and she gasped like she was fighting for her last ounce of breath.

Sparrow

Her words spilled over my ears like water. Then the water covered my face and filled my nose and I couldn't breathe. I heard my name but the sound of it smothered me. My mouth felt pinched together, like my lips been sewed up. Then I saw Carver's face but it was all blurry, like through water. I called for him but he didn't get no closer.

I had to get away.

I opened my eyes and gasped for breath.

The Amish woman, Emma, was in front of me and behind her was that boy — her son. Johnny. They both got those worry lines across their foreheads. Where was I? I was in the woods between our houses. All the stuff from the day before rolled over me like a big wave. But my mind didn't linger on that too long, because I got these faces looking at me.

My heart slammed over and over in my chest and my hand pressed against my bosom. The front of my dress was open. The boy looked away and I looked down at myself.

"Let me help." The lady smiled and buttoned my dress. Then patted my hand. That white woman done touched me. I nodded a thank-you and repositioned my legs as stiff as cold taffy. I winced.

"Are you hurt?" the woman asked and it made Johnny turn back around. Our eyes met and I got warm all over.

"I fine." My voice sounded small in the open air. I had to show the lady that I was just fine so I started to stand. The nice woman grabbed my elbows right away, then Johnny did the same. I never had nobody try to help me so much as these two. And they white.

The woman looked at me like I was hers but in a nice way — not the other way. Her hand was on me like it was okay and I didn't know where to put that in my mind.

And the boy. The heat of his hand went all the way through the skin of my arm and down to my bones. All the attention made me nervous.

"Look like you got a knack for finding lost people," I said before I heard how stupid it was.

"Johnny found you. He came to get me.

Why are you out here? Did you get lost? How long were you here?"

I didn't know which question to answer. I could almost hear Mama telling me that I should always give a respectful answer when an elder asks me a question, especially if the elder was white — 'cause we don't want no trouble. But I still don't know what to say. I couldn't tell her I had a fit and that Mama wished she left me back with my old, grumpy, spinster aunt. And that I just wanted to get away.

"Don't y'all worry 'bout me. I'll just walk back and let y'all get on with your morning." I smiled as much as I could even though I didn't want to go home.

"Let me walk you home." Emma started helping me to the path — touching me again. Someone needed to tell this lady that it ain't proper.

I looked at my arm where her hand was. "You shouldn't do that, ma'am." I gently pulled my arm from her. I looked down at my feet, ashamed at how dirty they was. I kept my face down. "I dirty and I wouldn't want you to get dirty 'cause of me, ma'am."

"But I'm . . . Please, call me Emma."

"Can't do that, ma'am. Mama would turn me inside out." I paused. Was that disrespectful? So I tried to explain myself. "I don't even call Sister Sandra Thompson by her first name and I knew her since I's a baby — she was my neighbor."

"What do you call her?"

"Mrs. Thompson or Sister Thompson, of course — ma'am." I wanted to dig myself a hole and crawl into it.

"If you called me Mrs. Mullet, about six other women along with myself would turn to answer. It's just our way." Her voice danced along the trees and sounded like music to me. "We see children and adults equally — and since many of us share last names, we all use first names."

"Everyone?"

She smiled and nodded.

I took in what she said, but besides my face maybe screwing up some, I don't know what to say but I know I got no business using her name. I'd be in even more trouble than I already was. Didn't need that.

"I better go. Mama will be —" I didn't finish my thought, didn't know how. Then I saw Johnny's eyes on me and turned around fast to start down the path. My feet would suffer because of this.

"I'd like to see you home." Emma caught up. Even just thinking of her as Emma seemed wrong to me and somehow Mama would find that out.

I wouldn't be able to stop the woman —
unless I was rude to her. I didn't know what
was worse — Mama knowing a white
woman was going to trouble for me or me
being rude to her so she wouldn't. If I was
being truthful, I wanted her with me. She
had this warm milk sort of way about her.
A body just couldn't walk away from somebody like that. You just want to drink it in
'cause you don't know if you ever gonna
meet anyone like that again.

"I'll come too."

Johnny's words made my insides burn.

We both stopped and turned around.

"No, Johnny." Then the woman spoke in
her other language. He said something back
to her before he looked over at me for a
second, then sighed.

I didn't have to understand her words to
know the conversation they were having.
Johnny wasn't supposed to be here at all —
he came 'cause of me.

My face felt all burned up when he set his
gaze back on me when his mama was watching. He seemed like he was about to say
something but instead he gave me a long
look. I didn't take another breath until he
walked away.

The woman went ahead of me on the narrow path. I followed her. I was glad that I

could just see her back and not her face when she started talking again.

"Who's Carver?" she asked.

I didn't respond, wasn't sure how to.

"You said 'Carver' when you were waking up."

"My little brother," I said after a time. Maybe I wanted her to know.

"I thought his name was George." The woman didn't turn around when she spoke.

I walked a few steps. "Carver was George's twin." I don't know why I was talking. This woman was a stranger. She white. Too many reasons for me to keep my mouth shut. My mama was gonna kill me dead. Maybe that was okay.

"Was?"

"Yeah. He gone."

There was a long bit of silence after I said that.

"What happened?"

I never did hesitate before I answered her with more truth than I'd ever spoke in my life.

"I killed him."

DELILAH

I couldn't see into the woods with the green leaves shielding my view. The panic I felt when George was missing came back. That, of course, took me right back to when I heard that Carver was lost to me for good. All because of Sparrow. Why that girl got to be so irresponsible and just about useless? I raised her better than that.

I got rid of my company after saying Sparrow wasn't feeling well. Nobody want to be around a sick house. And I decided it wasn't much of a lie. I hadn't said nothing about that darn girl being upstairs, in the woods, or on the moon. Just let them figure what they wanted to. Belinda looked glad to leave. Didn't think she got much for Sparrow.

Before I could make a decision about what to do, the front door creaked open and there she stood. Sparrow still got on her Sunday dress. It hung on her a little crooked like and her hair was mussed. Her shoulders were a little slumped. But she didn't hesitate to look me right in the eyes.

"Lord have mercy, girl, where you been?" My tone ain't nice or dignified like I tried to do when I got company. I got half a mind to pull that girl by the ear all the way upstairs and give her a spanking like a little child.

I looked her up and down again. She crossed her toes like she was trying to hide her dirty feet. I was just about to complain that she was standing on my clean floor when behind her came that Amish woman.

"Her name is Emma, Mama. And she's nice."

"Her name is *ma'am* to you." I dished it to her with my mad face. Then I tried to take a breath to calm myself, but I felt like an angry steer with my nostrils flaring. Why did she bring that woman into our home? "Now, ma'am, I am not trying to be disrespectful, but I'd like to know what you're doing with my daughter."

"She was asleep in the woods. I wanted to help." Her voice was so much softer than mine and I could tell she was a meek-spirited woman. She was probably thinking I'm just about the worst mama around.

She was wearing a light-brown dress and

her hairline was tidy, and she wore that bonnet, of course. This white woman found Sparrow only days after she found George. And she don't know nothing about Carver and don't know that Sparrow had her head in the clouds as bad as the bird she got her name from.

I gave myself an extra few moments. I had to remember that even though she was an Amish woman and might not be just like other white people, I still didn't want no trouble. I didn't want nobody spreading stories that I didn't know my place and that my children were wild and trespassing on white folks' land.

I shouldn't have walked through it when I took her the food. What was I thinking? I guess I didn't want to walk all the way around by the road and Malachi had the truck. I got all these thoughts still running through my mind when I spoke.

"I say thank you, ma'am. I don't know what came over my daughter to run off." I peeked out the sides of my eyes at Sparrow, who was still standing too close to that woman. What a lie I told and I was ready to tell another. "But I sure am grateful that we have neighbors who watch out for us. We won't bother y'all again. We know we shouldn't be on y'all's land."

161

"I'm sorry I'm intruding. Please, call me Emma." She went on before I had a chance to tell her no. "She, both of you — your whole family — are welcome in our woods and our home anytime."

If I'd said those same words, it might have sounded like it just came out of a viper's mouth. Poison and all. But when she spoke, it was like she meant her words. I done lost two of my children in the woods in a few days and she wasn't judging me?

"Well, bless your heart, ma'am." I almost tripped over my words because I got some sharp words I wanted to spit out at Sparrow. "Sparrow, tell her thank you."

"Thank you." It was almost a whisper and her buttery smile bugged me.

The woman looked at Sparrow like she knew her. Like she loved her. Like she was her kin. Like she want her for her own daughter.

She could have her.

Emma smiled at me but let it linger over Sparrow, then patted her arm. That darn girl didn't even flinch but fairly glowed. Emma turned around to leave, but just before she slipped through the door she looked back at me. "What's your name?"

Her blue eyes looked at me so nicely I couldn't be rude. "Delilah Evans." I didn't

162

say Deedee because I didn't want no familiarity between us.

She bobbed her head nervously. "All right then. It's nice to meet you, Delilah." She looked at Sparrow and then back at me. "And I'm sorry to hear about the son you lost." Her eyes diverted for a moment and they almost got bluer when they found mine again, and I saw that they got some grief in them. "I'm just so sorry."

Her words brushed against me like the silk scarf my mama once gave me — all pretty and soft. But after Emma closed the door behind her, the silk-scarf words done wrapped around my neck and pulled so tight I couldn't breathe.

Couldn't I have nothing to myself? The church got my husband. The Lord and Sparrow stole my baby from me. And now my grief was all spread out everywhere. But it was mine and I don't want to share with nobody. Not this woman. Not with my daughter. Not with nobody.

EMMA

As I walked back through the woods, the air around me was still. The branches hung silently. But Sparrow's words still echoed in the silence.

"I killed him."

Those had been her words. I had paused when she spoke them. Just for a moment. Struck by her confession. Then I had to push myself onward.

"I didn't mean to," she added.

Of course it had to have been an accident. Of course it had been a terrible mistake. Of course no matter my concern it was not my business.

Learning about the death of Carver made that day in the woods, when I found George, make sense. The ache in Delilah holding on to George and me when he was found. I wanted to tell Delilah how sorry I was to hear about her son. I didn't know her exact pain since my lost baby lost her spirit before she was born. Even my heartache had been worse than I thought possible. It changed everything, but still I didn't think it could compare to the hurt of losing a little boy after having years with him. Giving him a real name. Looking in his eyes. Knowing he was breathing one moment and then the next he wasn't.

I wanted to tell Delilah that while I hadn't experienced that kind of loss, I wanted to be her friend. Only two people knew about my lost baby — John and my sister, Judith. Judith lived in Ohio and John had become almost as lost to me as the baby. I'd grieved alone. John helped his own grief with the power of wine.

I began retreating farther and deeper into the woods in my mourning. This turned me toward herbs and what they could do — and how they could help me never to go through the pain of losing a child again.

When the path got closer to home, my heart beat faster. What if Johnny said something to John about the girl and that I had walked her back? I would have to talk to Johnny today and tell him that we needed to keep anything that happened with the new neighbors between us.

It wasn't that I'd ever heard John say anything particularly against Negroes, but I didn't want any of his input because I knew he would err on the side of keeping to ourselves. I didn't want to do that. I wanted to know my new neighbors — Delilah and Sparrow.

John had become distracted more than normal and didn't notice me unless it served his basic needs. I did the laundry, cooked, cleaned, and got our home back into order after our company. I watched John carefully. I needed to talk to Johnny and even prayed John would drink more than normal to make it easier for me to talk with my son about Sparrow. Praying for John to indulge in sin was my own personal hell. But I didn't know where else to allow my mind and heart to retreat to.

It was Friday before Johnny spoke to me of Sparrow.

"Have you seen her again?" he asked me as I washed dishes. He leaned over my shoulder and handed me a bowl from the table. John was in the living room with his Bible open.

I shook my head no. But I wanted to say more. This might be the one chance for a long time to have a conversation and maybe even start a new relationship with my son.

"We can't let *Dat* learn anything about her. He wasn't happy when her *mem* —" I paused. I didn't want to say anything that would raise questions.

A heaviness weighed between us and I took the bowl from him, letting him free. But he turned back to the table and picked up the pitcher of water and returned to me. He wanted to have this conversation. He wanted to speak to me.

"I won't say anything about Sparrow," he said. I saw he wanted to say more but he didn't. His gaze hung on to mine for a moment, then something shifted. "I need to go do chores," he mumbled and left.

SPARROW

"Go wash up, girl," Mama told me when the Emma lady left. I liked the way her name felt saying it. Not many adults wanted me to use their first name like that.

I didn't say nothing back to Mama when I turned on my heels to go upstairs to get clothes for my bath. Didn't have nothing to say to her and nothing she wanted to hear anyway.

"Don't you ever tell a stranger about our grief. Not our joys neither," she said when I was at the bottom of the stairs.

"What joys? Ain't none."

The silence was thin. I was sure she could hear me thinking. But then I realized I didn't just think those words, I'd said them. I hadn't meant to.

"What you say?" She stepped real close. But I wasn't nervous like other times. I imagined how happy she would be without me.

168

"I know you wish you could've left me with Aunt Doris." I about smiled when I spoke because it made me feel glad to be brave and just say stuff to her.

Mama's face went pale and any words she was gonna say got all stuffed back in her throat. I hoped she'd choke on them.

"Now, Sparrow." She used my name. That didn't happen much. She tried to open her mouth to say more but I cut her off.

"It don't matter. I wish you would've left me. Would've been nice to be so far away." I left out *from you.*

She don't say nothing when I walk away upstairs, like maybe I got her good this time. I never got the last word with Mama. Nobody did. But today I just did and I'm proud of myself because she needed to know that I heard what she said to Daddy. She was the reason I ran off and she couldn't push me around no more.

When I come back down she got the water going in the bathtub. She was standing in front of it. I still thought about how she had to swallow down them words and I wondered if they tasted as bitter as the words I said. I hoped they had.

When she turned she looked at me with her face like something cut out of stone. I felt myself tuck in my chin and pull back a little. She got that fire in her eyes that never went well.

"You think you is all big and brave for talking to me how you just done. But you ain't. You still that selfish little girl who was thinking about kissing on a boy instead of watching her baby brothers. I hope that's the last kiss you ever get, girl. Ain't nobody want to take on a selfish girl like you, who can't think of nobody but herself. That's just who you are and that's who you'll always be."

She walked past me and let her shoulder bump mine on the way. I wasn't feeling brave or smart no more. I wasn't feeling like I got my mama neither. She was right.

I stripped off my clothes and stepped into the lukewarm water and wished it was hot enough to scald away all my shame. But I figured it ain't gonna go nowhere for a long time. Maybe never.

The water wasn't very deep and it didn't take long for me to feel cold. Mama must've done it on purpose so I would finish fast. I bent my knees to get farther under the water, and when my ears went under I could hear him. Carver. His little laugh and his chatterbox way of talking that was so different from George. We had to remind him to take a breath sometimes.

My heart stopped a little when I thought of those words — *take a breath.* It all hurt so bad. His voice sounded so real to my ears when I closed my eyes and I just about saw him. I pushed my head down a little more. Just my nose and mouth were above the water.

All my sad memories weighed me down and my nose went under the water now.

My chest was tight but I stayed underwater.

Even though my lungs burned, I fought to stay under. I imagined a clock ticking and could see the second hand go around the clock face. One more second.

I didn't know how long I was under the water, but my body forced me to sit up and I gasped. Not my mind. If it had been up to my mind, I would've let myself breathe in this water and all of this would be over. Then I'd be close to him.

I pictured my own grave. Probably would be back in them woods hiding and not a cemetery to be visited. Mama wouldn't take no dirt of mine with her. There wouldn't be no marker for me. Soon enough there would be track marks all over the ground above me. Daddy would come. Maybe Emma and Johnny because they were so nice. But not Mama. Nope. She wouldn't care. She would be glad to forget me. I knew this.

At that thought I lowered my face into the water again. This time I tapped out the seconds with my hand against the porcelain. How long could I stay under? How long could I bury myself with water like Carver was buried in the dirt?

DELILAH

It didn't matter that the black clouds were white now. It had rained earlier and the puddles on the road were deep and muddy. The three little ones were under strict orders to keep far away from the muddy water. It was our first time walking into Sinking Creek and I didn't want my children looking like they weren't taken care of. Those wild children just run ahead and make wide swoops around the puddles with their arms out like airplanes. I walked with my purse gripped tight — I got Carver with me — trying not to breathe too heavy from walking fast and from my nerves about visiting town. Sparrow lingered behind me.

I'd already had to answer all sorts of questions from the little ones — were we walking because there was a bus boycott up here too? Told them that this town didn't have any buses. We hadn't ridden a bus in months, but the kids asked about it every time their daddy drove somebody some-where. But we didn't have much more than some breakfast cereal and it was time I got myself to a grocery store.

I heard a motor behind me and turned to see a pickup tearing down that gravel road like they were late for their own funeral. Somebody else's funeral was about to happen if we weren't careful.

"Mallie, y'all get off the road and stand in the ditch — far in," I yelled. "Pickup's com-ing."

I made toward the ditch myself and stood facing the road so I knew I was clear to let them pass. Sparrow did the same. The whole time my heart raced. Too many ac-cidents happened to walkers like us. The pickup didn't slow down none, and when it got closer it swerved toward Sparrow, and puddle water and gravel sprayed her. She was a mess.

The driver laughed when he passed. He looked like the young man with some awful carrot-colored hair from the woods. He yelled some awful words at us that I done heard enough already.

"Mama, let me go home," Sparrow whined as she wiped a hand down her face that dripped dirty water.

Her shirt was now more brown than blue.

Her too-tight trousers were dark at least, but her white stockings were almost the color of her legs. I heaved a sigh. Why? Not just why some folks got to act like that, but why now? We needed to make a nice impression in town, and now my girl looked like she was half pig and had rolled around in the mud. But I couldn't trust her if I let her go home alone.

"You're coming with us." I turned around and started walking. I waved at the little ones ahead of me that they could keep going. They listened right away.

"Mama, I can't go to the grocery store like this."

I didn't even turn around. She was going to listen to me like daughters were supposed to do. That was that.

When we got to the crossroads outside of town, the road became paved. We passed a few houses and businesses and then I stopped for a moment and looked at the road behind us. I couldn't even see the church steeple no more. I hated feeling like such a stranger.

We moved onto the sidewalk and took in the town. Saw the shopkeepers talking and sweeping. Now that we stood at the main street I took in the view. The municipal building seemed larger than needed for such a small town. Beyond the main street I saw a pretty white church and farther was the lumber mill and yard Malachi had pointed out. But everything was so small compared to Montgomery, like a different world.

I saw a shiny pink sign that said Soda Shoppe and The Filling Station next to it. Music was coming from that way and that was at least familiar. Everywhere got the same music that was new and popular, I supposed. There was a funny-named beauty shop, Pretty'd Up, and a barber like before. Several men in white aprons stood outside talking. The competing diners and a few other businesses, I couldn't make out much about them. A buggy came clopping on down the street and I thought my kids — all but Sparrow — were going to jump right out of their own skin. They got all tickled by the Amish carriages.

As we walked down toward the grocery store, we passed another barber. Why a small town like this got to have two barbers was a wonder. But when I got closer I saw that this one was run by a Negro man. A newspaper office and a doctor and dentist clinic was opposite us. Did they see colored folks? If they didn't it made me think on how the colored barber might be the pulling-teeth kind.

It was a strange thing, walking around a town without all the signs up telling me where we could and couldn't go — where we could stand or where we could ride. I'd seen those signs my whole life but not today. I got this measure of pride about how my children could come up in a place that don't tell them no with those dang black-and-white signs.

"Look, Mama, it's a candy machine," Harriet yelled in her cheerful way. Just like a happy, innocent puppy she started toward it, and I had just enough time to grab her braid to pull her back. "Ouch."

I took in every part of the grocer's entrance. I didn't see no sign at the door. No sign at the vending machine neither. I wished I could spare a dime so's we could feel what it was like to use something that was usually meant for somebody else. Somebody different from me.

"Mama," Harriet said and I let go of her braid.

She didn't say nothing. Her braided ponytail just stuck straight out and no one moved to fix it.

Once we got inside Coleman's Grocery, I saw that the supermarket was small. Several white women and their young children were inside. They all turned to look, then turned

177

away. The clerk at the counter looked at us a little longer. He didn't say hello before he turned back to his paperwork. If that was the nice owner Malachi told me about, I questioned his study of a person.

I looked around and saw a dozen or so shiny grocery buggies.

"Get a buggy for me," I told Harriet and I tried not to let my voice get shaky but it was.

"Ma'am," the clerk said with a small glance at me. His hand pointed. "Those carts are yours. Your produce is in the back."

"What?" I asked stupidly. But he don't got to answer. I knew what he meant and when he opened his mouth I said, "Thank you, sir," before he could say anything. And I smiled at him real nice. I didn't want no trouble. I directed the children toward the back.

Harriet ran ahead and picked out one of the five buggies waiting for us. She pushed it over to me with a twinkle in her eye as she pretended to be a haughty grown-up lady pushing that thing around the market. She got it to me while I was still in the *white* section that ain't marked. If it weren't that I was nervous to be there, I'd have thought Harriet was cute and funny. But my blood pressure was too high for that and I didn't know who was nice around town and who wasn't. My senses wasn't up for any horsing around.

"Mama, it's so clean," Mallie pointed out.

"Mm-hmm." I handed George's hand over to Mallie. "Hold tight now, boy."

He "yes, ma'am'd" me and little George winced a little at his grip. He loosened it up and I didn't have to say nothing.

I put the market bag next to my Carver purse in the front of the buggy. The front bar was cold in my sweaty, warm hands. It was an old buggy with the front plastic handle worn off and when I pushed it the front right wheel jiggled. I don't want to make something of it so I didn't replace it.

I missed my market back home. 'Course we got most of our vegetables from Ms. Maddie who had a big garden outside of the city. Every week she sold us city folk all sorts of good produce. But I still had to shop at the store for other stuff. But I knew the clerks and I knew how I would be treated. Of course, a white person would be served first, but we still got pretty good service anyhow.

But now I didn't know what to expect.

"Mama, can we get some?" Harriet picked up an apple. Her voice was loud and it carried around the produce displays. One of

179

the white ladies looked over at us with her little daughter sitting in the buggy seat.

"I didn't see —" she started.

"Harriet," I loud-whisper-scolded. "Just come over here. Our stuff's in the back."

Then I put a finger over my lips reminding her to speak low. I waved her to keep following. I didn't want to draw attention. We didn't need nothing to draw attention to us in this new town.

"Mama, I want one," the little white girl from the buggy yelled. "I want an apple."

"Not today," her mother said. The little girl started crying and carrying on and begging for an apple. "Patty, I said no."

I just got us all to the back and pretended not to notice the girl's fit. Out of the corner of my eye I could see a few other white women and the young moms exchanging knowing expressions.

"She never acts like this. I don't know what has come over her," the woman said, breathless, like you get when you get tired of the fussing.

"It's because that colored girl asked her mother for an apple — one of ours. And she's not supposed to touch the produce, but because she did, now your little girl wants it." The woman said everything over the sounds of the crying and didn't hesitate to check me over with her eyes a few times.

I pretended not to notice and looked at my list again, and I got to thinking about what I was led to believe about the North. We went from *no signs* in town to realizing that these northerners were just pretending to include us. This was not the freedom that the north acted like they could give to Negro families. No signs was one thing, but we weren't equal.

The woman was still prattling along. I just ignored her. It was better that way. I hoisted a bag of potatoes into my buggy and I was glad to see they looked good, then moved over to the tomatoes. Ripe and red. It made me wonder why we was separated. Didn't seem to mean we got the cast-off produce. Maybe this grocer was a nice man as Malachi had said. Then why separate us?

Before I got the chance to consider that for more than a minute, I heard Harriet's voice. I whipped my face around and wondered if I was dreaming. Or having a nightmare. What was she doing? It was like my feet was stuck in concrete blocks and my mouth was full of sand. I couldn't even yell her back over but just watched it happen.

"Well, bless your heart, Patty. Here's an apple for you and a penny. You can buy it all by yourself." Harriet's precious face smiled up at the girl sitting in the buggy. She even called her by the name she heard her mama use. The little girl got happy and took the apple and the penny from Harriet.

"Y'all stay right here," I tell the others and get a move on over there.

"Patty, don't touch that." The mother snatched the apple out of Patty's hand, who looked as hurt as if her dog just died. Her face went through several slow-moving contortions before a sound came of her unhappiness. But her mama kept at it. "And give me that penny."

The mother ain't getting very far though. Patty kept the penny tight in her fist and stuck out her tongue at her mother between her screaming. That's when I got there.

"Harriet, you know better than that." I took Harriet by the arm and pulled her behind me. Then I turned to the woman. She was even younger than I thought, almost just a girl herself, but she was a whole lot taller than me. Her skin was like porcelain and her hair shiny and she was wearing the prettiest yellow dress. "I'm so sorry, ma'am. She didn't mean no harm though. We won't bother y'all again. Have a nice day."

The young mother wasn't sure what to say. Her light eyes were big and round and she stammered a bit, but nothing real came out of her mouth.

"Sorry?" The older woman guffawed. "This is the reason coloreds should have their own stores."

"Harriet, go put the apple back." Of course she don't have the apple, my stupid mind forgot this, so my girl put her hand out to the young woman to give back the apple. Then I couldn't do nothing but wait for a moment.

The woman held the apple between two fingers and dropped it into Harriet's outstretched hand. She wiped her hand on her skirt after that. She hadn't even touched Harriet's hand though. My girl obeyed right away and took that apple back.

"She can't put it back," the older woman said. "Now the whole basket of them are ruined." She scoffed and rolled her eyes.

"Mama, those apples is for everybody, ain't they?" Harriet's southern drawl was so strong it was like she had a banjo tangled up in her mouth. "I don't see no sign that says they just for the white folks."

"Harriet," I whispered and scolded and tried to shush her all at the same time. And it all made me so sad even when I pinched her arm to stop talking because my girl was right. There wasn't no sign, but we just were supposed to know our place no matter there be a sign or not.

She started crying and I knew I pinched too hard in my nervousness. She leaned over to Mallie and he put an arm around her like a good boy and I just wanted to hide. What sort of mama was I anyhow?

The younger woman still looked panicked and glanced between myself and the older white woman.

"Is there a problem?" A brisk-sounding voice came from around the corner. A man in a grocer-white jacket with a broad smile now stood among us. His face was clean shaven and rosy. He looked friendly.

"That colored girl picked up an apple — one of ours — and tried to give it to Marcy's little girl," the older woman explained, her wild hands pointing at Harriet, then the apples, then Patty.

The man looked confused and made the same route with his gaze.

"Then she put it back in the pile of apples. Now we don't know which one she touched."

"So no one is hurt? Or bleeding?" the man asked. "Linda, I don't see the problem."

"Now, Carl," Linda responded. "I know you are a sympathizer to" — she looked at me — "coloreds. But don't think that

184

people won't stop shopping here if they think all their produce is being touched up. They got their own section. This was all handled in the town meeting and you know how we voted."

"Little girl, don't cry, please." Mr. Coleman squatted down and looked at Harriet. "Your produce is in the back and the white folks' is up here."

"But there ain't no signs like back home," Harriet said and I just wanted to be buried alive.

The grocer stood up and raised his own eyebrow like I never seen no white man do in all my born days and looked right at that Linda woman.

"We don't have signs because we are civilized and progressive in the North. Isn't that what you said in that same town hall meeting, Linda?" His sarcasm splashed across his smile.

I couldn't believe what I was hearing. Was he giving it to this lady? Had we just walked into some strange new world? If it wasn't that I was still breathing in and out, I would've thought we was sent to the moon. But just when I thought we got all the strange stuff out of the way, I saw Malachi roll a cart from the back toward the canned goods.

What was he doing? I kept watching him while he stocked cans. He didn't notice me. The children hadn't seen him yet neither — which made me thankful because I knew they'd make a fuss. I heard Linda walk off in a huff and Mr. Coleman smooth things over with the young mother, who walked away, but not before he had given the little girl an apple — not the same one Harriet touched, mind you. But my eyes stayed on my husband. He was wearing a white apron and a white hat that reminded me of a sailor.

The man stood next to me and noticed the direction of my gaze.

"You wouldn't happen to be Mrs. Evans, would you? And these must be your children."

"Yes, sir, I'm Mrs. Evans." I found my voice. I looked from Malachi to the grocer. I took a moment to gather myself. "I don't know what came over my daughter with picking up the apple. Things are different here, so she just got herself a little confused."

I was about to tell him that she was not the only one confused and ask why my husband was wearing an apron and pushing a cart around the store when Mr. Coleman held his hand out for me to shake. I shook it.

"Hi, I'm Carl Coleman. This is my store." His cheerfulness surprised a smile out of me, but I was nervous so it don't stay long. He shook my hand so hard that he jiggled my whole arm before he let me go. He looked over at my children. "Little girl who picked the apple, what's your name?"

Harriet didn't hesitate. She stepped forward and looked right at Mr. Coleman. "Harriet, sir." Her eyes looked puffy but she wasn't crying no more.

Mr. Coleman walked up to Harriet. My girl was doing her best not to be afraid. "Why'd you pick up the apple?"

"Because that little white girl wanted one so bad but her mama told her no. I just wanted to make her happy. She was pretty. And I gave her a penny to pay for it too."

"I see. Do you like apples?"

"Sure do. You know somebody who don't?"

The man laughed. "Well, since I am noticing that I don't have any in the back right now, why don't you and your brothers and sister each go get one. And get one for your mother too."

A smile spread over Harriet's face and I wished she'd have looked at me so I could give her the *don't you move* eyes.

"Mr. Coleman, please, you don't have to

do that."

He waved a hand at me as Harriet beamed, picking out an apple for each. I just watched and didn't know what to do. I knew better than to tell a white man no, but I didn't feel right about taking anything I didn't pay for.

"Now don't you worry about those ladies that were here. Linda Drake is my cousin and she likes to make a fuss about everything — she got folks in town riled up about *this stuff,* and I had to divide up the produce in order to stay in business." He shook his head. "But the other one, Marcy, won't cause any problems. She comes from a good family. Just doesn't know to speak up yet." He was still smiling. "I do my best to keep the Negro section stocked up, and I hope you find what you're looking for."

"I'm sure I will, sir."

"And look, there's my best new employee." Mr. Coleman pointed at Malachi coming with his cart.

I caught his eye this time and Malachi knew right away that he had some explaining to do. We didn't have much money, but he never said nothing about working for the grocer. I thought when he left in the mornings he was going to visit with church folks. I guessed he was okay that I believed something that wasn't true.

"Daddy," the little kids said and showed him their apples. He winked at them and then looked at me. He just smiled and looked like Harriet's innocence.

"Malachi, you didn't tell me your lovely wife and children were coming to see us today." Mr. Coleman clapped Malachi's arm.

While Malachi made introductions, Sparrow's attention wandered. I followed her gaze and saw a slow-walking boy going past the large windows in front of the store. He stopped and locked eyes with Sparrow. They didn't notice that I saw them.

But it was just a few moments and he started walking away. It was that Amish boy we saw in the woods, but I didn't know his name.

"Deedee." Malachi's voice cut through my thoughts. "Mr. Coleman wants to know how you like the house."

My husband had this big chiseled-out smile on his face. The one that told me I needed to be at my best.

"The house?" I questioned.

"Mr. Coleman is our landlord."

I eyed Malachi but didn't say a word. Didn't have to 'cause he knew what I was thinking. Why had he not told me before? I turned to Mr. Coleman with a smile.

"I know that the siding needs a good painting and the porch sags. It wasn't more than a week ago that Marlene Carter came and asked me about it, telling me that the new reverend was looking for a place to live. When she told me who it was, why, I was glad to rent it out to you. Houses are meant to be lived in, right? Not sit empty."

Of course, Marlene Carter. That woman. She had some nerve and so did my husband, for that matter. Keeping me in the dark like that.

"How do you know Marlene Carter, Mr. Coleman?" I asked.

"Everyone in Sinking Creek knows everybody else, ma'am. And her son Kenny does some lawn work for me and fixes stuff up around my place. He can fix anything and he's a nice boy."

"Well, I'm mighty grateful to you, sir." I smiled, purposing to end the conversation. "We are right comfortable in the house."

We each made our good-bye formalities to Mr. Coleman and then we were alone. As alone as we could be in a grocery store.

"Why didn't you tell me you was working here?" I said through my teeth. "Or about the house?"

Malachi looked at the three little ones who

were listening to us. He smiled. "Didn't seem like something to worry you over, darling. You have had your mind on — other stuff." I could tell he meant it, but I could also tell it wasn't the whole answer. Then his face changed and he looked around the produce department. "Where's Sparrow?"

And just like that, Sparrow had flown away again.

SPARROW

My shirt was still wet from the puddle water, but when I saw Johnny make a motion for me to come out of the store, I just went. Didn't matter I looked like filth. Mama and Daddy were too busy to notice me anyhow.

By the time I got to the door, he was gone. I walked a few steps in the direction he had been going and I was disappointed when I didn't see him.

"Psssst, Sparrow." A loud whisper came from the nearby alley. He was leaning against the alley's brick wall.

I looked back across the street where I'd seen some white men notice me when I walked out on the sidewalk. One bald man, who was reading a newspaper, peered up over it and I stood still until he raised it so I couldn't see his eyes no more. I turned around and took a step off the sidewalk into the alley.

As soon as I did I felt a light breeze flowing through the narrow path and the sun wasn't blaring bright neither. I wrapped my arms around myself, even though I wasn't cold, before I looked up at Johnny.

He had a nice smile. For half a second another smile flashed in my memory. The boy I was with that day Carver died. The one I was paying attention to instead of Carver. I shook my head to toss that vision away and blinked it gone.

For a long moment we just stared at each other without no words. Why would he want to stand in a dirty alleyway with dirty me? In Montgomery they always smelled like pee because colored bathrooms were hard to find. But then, this was Sinking Creek and the alley wasn't so bad. It didn't smell like pee. But I had mud on my clothes.

"I got splashed by a truck — puddle water." I glanced down at my clothes. I was feeling self-conscious.

"I think you're pretty," he said like I some white girl. I wanted to be pretty for him, but when he got his eyes on me like that, I started to remember that my shirt was a little tight and there was a gap between the buttons. My bosoms were too big for it.

"What are you doing?" Johnny got bluer eyes than I remembered and he was handsome the way he leaned up against the wall.

I nodded over to the store. "Groceries." My voice was small and thin and didn't sound right. I cleared my throat. "What you doing?"

"Just had to run an errand for my boss at the lumberyard. But I have to go to a wedding now." He shifted his lean body but kept his gaze on me.

I didn't think I ever talked to a white boy before. Well, not like this. Mama didn't like me talking to any boys ever, even before. This would make her furious.

"Why ain't you in school? It's still May."

"We just go to the eighth grade," he told me. "So I'm done."

"We?"

"Amish."

"Oh."

"Why aren't you?"

I shrugged. "We supposed to start next week, but I don't want to go no more."

Did he think I was a stupid Negro because I didn't want to go to school no more? He just didn't know that it didn't matter if I got any schooling because I ain't nobody special. Mama said I had to live at home with her and Daddy for the rest of my life, so there was nothing more I needed to learn to do that. For the rest of my life I would just do housework and sit around and think about what I done. That's all I got left now.

But still, he smiled at me. Why he do that? What did his smile mean? It was so different from the boy who had me behind the bushes when Carver died. When I thought on Carver, Mama's face came to my mind.

"I gotta go." I could almost feel a smack against my cheek from Mama. I took a step backward.

Johnny stood up tall and his face seemed as bright as a sliver of moon in a dark sky. "Can we meet sometime?"

"What?" I was confused. "You a white boy."

He flipped his hands back and forth a few times. "I know. Does it bother you?"

His smile made my heart turn in a few twists. "When?"

"Sunday. Daybreak."

"Where?" I asked.

"In the woods. There's a clearing by the creek."

I bit my lower lip and said, "Okay." I turned the corner and my face was in the broad chest of a real big man. Before I could step back, I could smell him. My stomach didn't like it.

"What are you doing?" His voice was like a roll of thunder and scared me.

"Sparrow?" Daddy's voice came from behind the man.

The big man turned around toward Daddy and I was lost behind his back. I took a moment and looked back down the alley. Johnny was gone. How had he disappeared so quickly?

"This your girl?" the booming voice asked.

I stepped from around the giant man and found Daddy's eyes. His forehead scowled and I lowered my gaze to the ground. I was in trouble — again.

"Can't let her wander around town like that," the man said. "The mayor — well, people might think she's up to no good."

"Yes, sir," Daddy said and cleared his throat. "You hear the man, Sparrow? You can't go running off like that."

"Yes, sir." The man in front of me had splatters of blood all over his white apron and a big knife in the front pocket. What he been killing today? He scared me.

"Listen." The man leaned in toward Daddy. "Sinking Creek ain't a bad little town. We're a friendly community and loyal to each other. Most folks around here got no problems with you folks. But some do. I keep an eye out so's I can help, but I can't be everywhere."

He looked around and noticed the man

with the newspaper across the street was staring again. "That's Mr. Lawrence, he ain't nice. Stay away from him and don't go to his store. Don't go sittin' inside at the Soda Shoppe neither; sit outside. Coleman got pressured into the two produce sections a bit ago. But at my shop I'll serve anybody with money. Don't matter to me. Got it?"

"I appreciate your advice, Mr. — ?"

"Steve Tuttle. But everyone just calls me Butch."

"Thanks again, Butch. We appreciate your kindness." Daddy grabbed my arm and after he excused us, he walked me back to the grocery store.

"Girl, why are you doing this to your mama?" he asked as we approached the door. "What were you doing?"

"I was bored and wanted to look around."

Daddy gave me that expression that said he wasn't happy with me. But his face softened. He planted his hands on his hips.

"I told your mama you were probably just going to the bathroom."

Wasn't he gonna say anything else?

"I won't say more if you promise me to stop running off. I told you this a few days ago because of you wandering off into the woods." He released a long sigh. "Listen, Birdie, I know Mama's hard on you. Just be patient. Things will work out." He paused. "You praying for help?"

"Yes, sir," I lied. I stopped praying 'cause I was sure God didn't want to hear from me no more.

"Stop running off, hear me? No more having that Amish lady find you kids."

"Emma."

"What?"

"Her name is Emma. She's not just that lady." The surge of boldness made me proud. I had a white woman who seemed to care about me even though I'd told her that I'd killed my baby brother. "I like her."

Daddy looked at me like he was trying to figure out why this mattered to me and then shook his head like his thoughts were jumbled up. "You just do your best not to get up your mama's back. You hear?"

He stared at me until I gave him a small nod. We went inside the store and it was a whole lot fuller now, and everybody looked over at Daddy and me when we walked in. I just kept my head down. They weren't like Emma.

They weren't like Johnny.

Sunday.

Daybreak.

EMMA

The loud trotting of our buggy horse magni-
fied the quiet between John and me. We
were driving to a wedding, and since we
always held weddings on Tuesdays or Thurs-
days, John had to miss a day of work. That
never made him happy. This Thursday-
afternoon wedding was the only one this
season in our small community. We weren't
even near another Amish community, so
when we got visitors in for a wedding, the
entire district seemed lighter and more
cheerful. Otherwise, it was easy to feel
isolated, especially if one didn't have close
relatives in town, like me.

My parents had passed away several years
ago. They'd been old when I was born and
I was their last. My only sister, the oldest of
the five of us, moved to Ohio when she got
married, and two brothers moved to other
Pennsylvania communities. I had one
brother who lived here, though he and I had

never been close. The way I saw it, I was alone. I had no friends who knew of our loss or of John's secrets. None who knew mine. The secrets John and I kept from the church bound us together but were also destroying us from within. They would be our ruin, but we had no way out of them.

And it all began because of the little innocent one who was lost when we were at our happiest. We retreated from each other. He drank. I did other things. Things that, by the time I regretted them, I felt I had to continue because of the man my husband had become.

But today we could not be the people who lived like strangers inside our home. We would have to be the two people who all the community knew needed to remain faultless in the eyes of the church. My husband called on those who were at fault. And I was the wife who supported his good work.

What would they do if they knew the truth? They could never know the truth.

These quiet rides made me miss the chattering of a child. Johnny had been that child as soon as he could speak. He didn't speak much now and would drive his own buggy today, as young men did. He would also attend the Singing after the wedding, which was tradition.

I did have some joy in our drive, however. I knew we would drive past Delilah and Sparrow's home to go to the wedding.

When we were close, my heart released a little tremor. Delilah was putting in a garden. She would've gotten a late start because of their move, and the ground had not been sown in several years. It was hard work, especially in the heat of the day, so I was grateful to see that she had gotten help from a local Negro man, Otis, who did day work around town. Though I'd never had any interactions with him, I knew of him and that he was a good worker. Sparrow was also helping, only at such a slow pace, I wasn't sure it was considered helpful. The younger children had small shovels. They dug playfully.

The house's siding was more chipped than I'd remembered. I wished more for a proud woman like Delilah. But the yard was expansive for being so close to town. I was glad for that and that Carl Coleman was a good, fair man. Not everyone in Sinking Creek would've allowed a Negro family to rent from them; even I understood that much.

Delilah wiped her brow with a hankie, then tucked it into her waistband again. Just like I would do. The younger ones started throwing clumps of dirt at each other, and as we drew closer I could hear her voice mix with the clip of the horse's hooves against the dirt road.

Sparrow looked up and I offered a small wave. She started raising her hand until Delilah's voice cut through. I couldn't hear what she said but Sparrow's hand went down. But the gaze between Sparrow and me remained connected until Delilah turned my way. Her blank stare chilled me.

"Since when do you know them?" John asked.

"I met them when they moved in. They're a nice family."

"The bishop said to leave them all alone because there always seems to be trouble between them and the white *Englishers.* We aren't like either of them and need to keep to ourselves."

There was nothing more I could say to my husband in the moment. Though I had so much on my mind, I didn't want to arrive at church with the two of us arguing. We had never spoken about Negroes before. I had to admit that I hadn't given much thought to their difficulties until I found George in the woods. It wasn't something that had touched my life personally. But now that it had, I was stirred to understand.

The wedding was long in the new May heat. My sister, Judith, was visiting for the wedding since it was her husband's niece, Abigail, getting married. I had not seen her in several years. We quietly sat stiff-backed on our benches near each other. Her belly was swollen with her seventh child. Our lives were so different. Her life looked just like we used to talk about when we were both still home. Mine did not.

We had both been raised here, and when she left and joined a large Ohio community, I was jealous. Everything seemed easier for her. She had the life most Amish women longed for and, honestly, most got. A good husband and a large family.

"Emma, *sis so gut fa dich sehna,*" Judith said when we entered the house where we would eat after the ceremony. Then she hugged me. Delilah was the last person who had hugged me, and it was only because I was holding her son. Before that, I couldn't remember the last time I was hugged.

My heart overflowed in those few moments I was held by my sister. She alone had known of my pregnancy and the loss — besides John. I'd shared with her in my letters my intense grief and how I never wanted to go through that loss again. She knew that for a time I'd taken herbs to close my womb. And to have her here now brought up worries that she would not keep my secret. But even as I feared this, I had forgotten how much I missed her. Her smile had always won me over, regardless of our differences over the years.

The next few hours went quickly. Abigail Miller's family was large and our community was small. I had no responsibilities at the wedding. I appreciated finding a quiet corner, holding babies from time to time, and watching everyone catch up with one another.

Judith came up to me and asked me to take a walk. *"Kumm,* Emma, *vella geh lauffa."*

I didn't hesitate as I wanted to hear all the gossip from Ohio. A large community was always filled with news and it deflected any attention from my life.

Before we even reached the end of the long gravel drive of the home, I'd learned of a few youth who had left the church just before they were baptized. While this meant they would not be shunned, it also meant they were too young to be on their own. At sixteen it was dangerous and a recipe for a change of heart when they realized that living out in the real world was harder than they expected. The comforts of home would call to their sensibilities. They often did.

John had even left once for several months, saying he was going west to become a cowboy — though he'd already been baptized. But he returned, and after his confession and a brief time in the *ban,* we were married in short order.

"Alma-Ruth and Timothy will get married this fall, I am guessing. It hasn't been announced yet," Judith said of one of our cousins who lived near her. "I never thought anyone would ask her because everyone knows she can't have any children."

It was like the gravel we walked on had just coursed through my heart. She couldn't have children and wanted them, but I could and prevented it. Because it was unusual to have only one child, I had heard women talk behind their hands about how hidden sins had consequences. They didn't know about my buried baby or that there were good reasons I had not had more children. But they were right — hidden sins did have consequences.

"But Timothy is a nice widower and he has four children. I was relieved it worked out this way for Alma-Ruth. She's twenty-three and hasn't had many dates." Judith stopped walking. *"Vas veh dich?"*

I followed suit after a few extra steps and

turned to face her to answer her question. What about me?

"We're fine," I answered, hoping to avoid deeper questions. I kept my face angled away and started walking again. Then a little faster.

She took several moments before she was at my side. She grabbed my arm and made me look at her. "Then why aren't you as big as me? Why aren't you like this?"

"Judith, that's not your business." I shook my head at her. Old memories surfaced as my older sister yanked my arm, scolding me. She had often gotten her way as a child because I was so many years younger and did not speak for myself — she spoke for us both. But I would not let her parent me over something she knew so little about.

I had told her I'd taken herbs that first year so I would not get pregnant soon because I was afraid. My body was weak. I was weak. I wanted to have some control over my life. By the time I should've quit, John had begun drinking daily and wasn't the kind of man I wanted to raise another child with. I couldn't tell her that.

"Only God knows why I'm not like that." I gestured to her swollen abdomen.

"Are you still taking the herbs?"

"Of course, that's how I stay healthy.

Don't you take some?"

"But I don't take what you do. I don't take one that makes sure I don't —" She didn't finish her sentence. We were taught our whole lives that words like *pregnant* or suggestions of intimacy between even a husband and wife were inappropriate, even in a personal conversation like this one. But I knew that was what she meant and I didn't know how to respond.

Wisps of my sister's flaxen hair, which had escaped her covering, blew in the breeze. Her blue eyes looked as young and vibrant as they had in all our years at home. She didn't seem to tire even after so many children. Motherhood had been everything she had wanted it to be, and she would keep having children until the Lord Himself closed her womb. I loved her, but I resented how easy her path had been.

"You said you'd stop taking the wild turnip after that first year, but it's been over ten now — thirteen, maybe."

Thirteen years since I'd started taking the herbs, yes. And I'd learned later that because I'd been over halfway, it was called a still-birth, not a miscarriage. Why I'd not shared my good news with others was nothing out of the ordinary since many didn't and just let the size of their belly tell everyone without using embarrassing words. I wasn't so thin then. I had not lost all of my roundness from carrying Johnny. At around six months it was not very noticeable that I was expecting. She was so small. When she was gone, I had no one but my sister to share the sorrow with.

I looked beyond her and watched my community mill around the large farm. So much was in black-and-white except for the bright royal blue of the bride and the maroon of her attendants. Yellow-and-orange beams of sunlight cascaded onto the small crowd. The community of people glowed in the sun's rays and my throat was choked with resentment toward them — though they were not the ones to blame.

I'd allowed them to believe the lie that God had closed my womb like Hannah's was for a time in the Bible. It was an easier cloak to wear than the truth. Even if they assumed it was because of my own sin. Even Judith believed it was my grief that I held on to — but it was more than that. It was fear. It was John. It was raising a child with a drunk along with the fear of another loss. And what would John think if he ever found out? Things would be worse than they already were. How could I cast a stone at him about his drinking when I'd lied to him for so many years?

"I can't." I looked back at Judith. I shook my head and walked away from her. Soon she grabbed my arm and didn't let me pull away. She'd always been a force in my life and I should've expected that she would not take my walking away as the end of the conversation.

"This is wrong, Emma." Judith's words came to my ears and heart in equal parts accusation and concern.

I paused before I responded. "You don't know the whole story, Jude. I never had it easy like you did. *Dah mahn, dah kinnah.* You have what all Amish women want."

"This isn't about my husband or my children." She glanced around after she spoke, as she'd been louder than she should've been. No one seemed to be paying attention to us, thankfully.

"If you were married to him — if you knew —" I couldn't finish any of my thoughts.

"This isn't about John. It's about you. You said you'd stop taking the herbs. That you'd trust God. And this lie you are keeping from your husband —" She stopped speaking.

My arms were folded across my chest, putting layers of flesh and bone in front of my heart. But my palms slid down to my abdomen, like they had done so many times when I was expecting Johnny and after I knew I would have another. This safe place inside of me was not a refuge. It was my emptiness and my sorrow. It was the true grave of my daughter. Maybe there was someone somewhere in the world who understood why I couldn't relinquish this space, why being filled with possibility was too painful, but there was no one here who understood that. And no one understood how John's drinking had pushed me to it.

I let my arms fall to my sides, exposing my emptiness. I walked away and this time Judith let me.

DELILAH

As we drove in our rusty red truck down a long, dusty road, I kept thinking on how I felt like I was in some foreign land. The white farmhouse we drove up to didn't help none. I ain't never known nobody with a house so grand like that. It didn't have that sad way about it like our house. The driveway was a half circle and when Malachi drove in everybody started waving. So many smiling faces to take in. I used to enjoy parties, but anymore I couldn't find my joy in it.

When Malachi started to tell the kids to be mindful, they were already out the back of the truck and running off to play — Mallie had George by the hand. Sparrow didn't run off though. She just leaned against the truck. I made her wear her nice hat and had washed her church dress that she'd dirtied up in them woods. She'd been out of my hair for a few days. Even helped around the house a little. Didn't run off nowhere. But she always got this look in her eyes like she was hiding something. Not sure I cared as long as she behaved and didn't embarrass me.

Looked like the whole community had come out. Not just the scant crowd at church. Malachi would be making his rounds tonight to win everybody over. He was good at that and talked like them in that northern way — if they bothered to listen. Not like me and the young'uns who had a drawl from here to the last bend in the creek in town.

"Ready?" Malachi asked as he opened my door.

I scooted off the seat with a casserole in one hand and Grannie Winnie's gift in the other. We didn't have the money to buy something, but she was turning a hundred so I baked her some cookies and put them in a tin box I'd always loved and gotten as a gift when the twins was born.

I gestured Sparrow over when we left the truck and she came ambling along behind me. It wasn't that I wanted that girl to be distant from me and not make friends, but I just didn't know what to do with her or what she would do. She never seemed to grasp what she done that Saturday in

March. When a boy was stealing a kiss from her, what was really stolen was her baby brother's life.

After the food and gifts, I sat on a chair that was close enough to seem social but not so close that somebody would start up a conversation with me. I would need time before I was ready for that. Just a little more time.

While stories were retold and, I assumed, exaggerated for laughs, a small figure stepped toward me and was silhouetted in the brightness of the sunset. It wasn't hard to see that the shape was Grannie Winnie. How she had slipped away from the center of the circle, I wasn't sure.

"Deedee, it's so good to see you."

With my neck still craned up at her, I said, "Hey, Mrs. —"

"Ah-ah," she interrupted with a quick shake of her finger.

"Grannie Winnie," I corrected to please her and I couldn't help smiling. Old ladies always did know how to squeeze something out of nothing. "Why ain't you in the middle of your party?"

"Come on, let's go take a walk." Her eyes twinkled.

Laughter boomed from the group in the room, heightening the isolation I'd put myself in. I stood and followed the tiny woman out from the porch. I helped her old body down the stairs and it felt right nice to put my hands on someone in kindness.

"It's a nice house," I said after a minute's walk. "I ain't never seen a colored family with a house like this."

"The house, the farm, all this land" — she made a wide swipe with her hand — "was Brother Leon's granddaddy's place."

We took a few steps forward heading toward the path between two wheat fields. The land stretched out in front of us with those perfect rolling hills I'd grown accustomed to since our move. I wondered if there was something wrong with my land because it wasn't letting nothing grow yet. No little sprouts. Maybe what I'd sown and planted was grief so that was all I could harvest.

"Don't know any colored farmers in Montgomery — but one little old lady with a big garden outside of the city. My family was always stuck in the city." I felt a bit of a rhythm happening in our conversation, and even though I wanted to fight it, I didn't. The way she curled her shawl around her, reminding me so much of my own granny, wooed me some.

"Brother Leon's granddaddy was white." She threw those words out, then giggled.

"What? Why you laughing?"

"Because the way Brother Leon tells the story about meeting his grandparents for the first time is just about as funny as they come. His granny thought her son brought home a maid with a child — but he was their grandson."

"They weren't married, right?"

"Not yet. But in Pennsylvania here, it was legal — but most folks don't like it none — white or colored. But they eventually found a justice of the peace that agreed to marry them. And they lived out their years together in that little house right over there until Leon's grandparents passed and they moved into the farmhouse."

"The town accepted that?"

"You lost your mind?" She winked at me. "They made it hard for the family. The church. The local businesses. Everybody. But Leon's grandparents just had the one son and Leon was the only grandkid."

"Never would'a guessed it."

Then we just kept walking. The wind pushed against my back and whispered in my ears to be thankful. The crunch of old dried-up stalks of wheat crackled under our shoes and they told me to stay angry. In the

215

air, though, was all the peace. But it was thin and unreachable.

We walked like that for three or four minutes before Grannie said, "When you dream about your boy, you need to hold him and kiss him and just give him that mama love you got buried inside. It helps then, when you wake up."

I stopped walking and turned around to walk back to the house. I wasn't going to hear this talk. The crunching under my feet was loud — like a demon — and it egged on my anger.

"Don't you walk away. You gotta stop with all these walls. Ain't nobody trying to hurt you. Some of us think we might like you if you talked. Some of us might even be able to help if you'd give us a chance." Her voice had this proverb-floating-in-the-air feel to it. Couldn't take much of it in all at once, but you knew you got to listen — didn't want to though. This tone laced with age and wisdom was like sandpaper to my grief.

"Give you a chance?" I spun around. "What chance I got? Malachi do all the talking at church. My Sparrow act like she got straw for brains and you just wanna spout your wisdom like you think everybody just need to hear it."

"Except for the part about Sparrow, that

sounds about right." She walked a few steps closer to me. "But I ain't talking about her; I'm talking about you."

"Granny, just let me be. People always say they understand but they can't. All those people in that perfect farmhouse don't, people back home in Montgomery didn't, and you don't neither."

"You think nobody ever lost a child before? Probably feels that way. Like you're alone. But you ain't. None of that is true for real — and the more you believe it, the more you hurtin' yourself and everybody around you. I think you just mad because nobody is telling you that it's okay to shut out the rest of the world."

I couldn't find my voice because she was right and was the only one brave enough to say so — even Malachi was softer about it. But I wasn't wrong for shutting out the world. It was too hard to pretend to be okay.

"You already lost one child. You want to lose the rest?"

She didn't give me a chance to respond but just kept walking and left me standing there in the middle of that fresh-turned soil.

"How you know I dream about my boy?" My lips were shaking like all the feeling in my body living in them.

She turned and looked at me and a tired

217

smile crossed over her face.

" 'Cause I still dream about my baby sister and it's been about eighty-five years."

"That's not the same thing as losing a child."

The old lady pursed her lips and stared off into the distance. I didn't press her. It was clear her memories were just on the other side of the thin veil of time, like looking through water. After a long minute she turned back to me.

"I was the only mama that girl ever know'd." She paused. "Mama died when she was just a babe and gave me Rosie as my own. I failed them both."

"But how old were you? Just a girl?"

"Fifteen." She smiled.

I stiffened. But there was a big difference. I hadn't asked Sparrow to raise Carver but just watch him. Just keep an eye on him and George. I hadn't asked too much of her. My jaw clenched. "Do you think your mama ever forgave you?"

"It would've been hard, but I think she would've if she'd been alive. But really it was about me forgiving myself. I just wanted to die."

Die.

The word was so small but so big.

SPARROW

I could feel the water in the air as soon as I stepped out of my house. The sun wasn't up yet. The moon sat low in the navy-blue sky and gave me some light as I walked toward the woods. Toward daybreak. Toward Johnny.

Barely slept. Just thinking on Johnny. What would we talk about? Why did he want to meet me? I was just me.

I couldn't help but wonder what it would be like to kiss a white boy. Maybe it wasn't no different. But why was I thinking about kissing? Last time I kissed a boy my brother died. And for all I knew I could meet up with Johnny and he could have a whole bunch of white boys there to hurt me. I heard of stuff like that all the time. I didn't think he would do that though. I hoped not.

I looked back at my house and because the moon was dim, it looked like a ghost house. Then there was the fog that hung in the air around me. Because of that I trusted myself to click on Daddy's flashlight.

It was easy to follow the trail I'd now taken a few times. The last time I was with Emma. My friend. My white friend. The night sounds were louder than before. Crickets and toads for certain, but I didn't know what else was singing. I was used to hearing the sound of engines and police sirens in Montgomery.

Once I crossed over the creek on them smooth stones, the way got even easier. I just had to follow the flow of water. The creek ain't slept all night neither. It called to me as I walked alongside it so I started humming with it. Like the water and me were making music. But my voice didn't blend well, so I quit. The water knew too much about me and knew my sins.

Daddy always told me that all the water in the world was connected. So if something happened in one river, did it also happen to the ocean or a pond? He said it was because water traveled underground and in the air.

I thought about how this made me happy and sad. When water brought life, all the water was happy, but when it wasn't life — it was the other thing — did all the water know it? Did all the water rejoice and grieve together? Could it do both? If it could, then could people too? Did what happened to one person happen to everybody everywhere? People were everywhere like water — even underground and in the air.

Halfway there a sliver of light slipped through the trees — but I still needed the flashlight. I rushed my steps because I didn't want to miss him and make him think I hadn't showed up. I just kept looking for the clearing by the creek.

Then a burst of panic rushed through me. My breathing got heavy. My thoughts fought with each other. What if he never came or he did but we couldn't find each other? Would he think I had lied about coming? But what was I thinking meeting a white boy in the woods? What if he strangled me dead? What if he did worse than that and raped me?

I stopped walking. The trees around me looked so big and I felt so small. They hovered over me like I was just a little piece of nothing — which was true. The breeze through the leaves made a hissing sound. *Hiss. Hiss.*

I didn't turn around but I took a step backward. I couldn't do this.

A rustling brushed up against my ears and I wondered if I was too late to turn back. I imagined Johnny's tall, slim body walking

221

toward me. I couldn't see well enough in the distance, so maybe the noise was somebody else and I'd be dead in a minute.

Like a baby would suck on her thumb to calm down, I needed something too. But I didn't know what. Daddy's metal flashlight in my hand was damp with sweat.

I should run back to the house and let Johnny think I'd never come at all.

A thud on the ground near my feet made me realize that I'd dropped the flashlight. It was shining on all the weeds off the trail. It almost seemed like they were looking at me. I wanted to touch them. They wanted to touch me.

In my hysteria I squatted down and touched those plants I saw. They were the stinging plants Emma had told me not to touch. My hands felt the burn — a good burn — and like they changed my color to red. But I looked and they were still brown.

The stinging turned into tingling that was almost a tickle. My skin felt like it was sparkling and a bright coolness washed over me. I let out a deep breath that could've been Montgomery air I never did let go of 'til now 'cause it was so deep in me. I just kept staring at my hands as I held those ripped-up plants and rolled them in my palms.

I eased the corners of my mouth into a smile. The earth wasn't trying to hurt me, but it was giving me something new.

"Drop those." Johnny's voice was urgent. I hadn't even seen him coming. "You're going to hurt yourself."

"It don't hurt." I lifted the plant from my hand to show him that my hands was just fine.

The last few steps toward me were big, and when he yanked the green weeds out my hands, he winced. He tossed them away from us and took my hands.

"See, it ain't nothing. It just tickled a little." My cheerful voice felt foreign to my ears. My heart skipped a beat. I felt like a bird. Light and ready to fly. I felt like the water running over them rocks in the creek. I felt like the easy breeze that made my hair puff up. I felt free. I felt alive. I felt.

"You're blistering already." He had a tight grip around my wrists. I giggled when he pulled me toward the creek. My hands continued to feel cool and warm, like bird feathers were fluttering over the top of my skin. But I didn't like him yanking me none. I didn't want the feeling to end.

My hands was in the coolness of the stream in a moment and Johnny used his hands to cup water and pour it over the growing blisters. He scooped up some of the heavy clay at the edges and layered it on my skin. The feather-like tingle went away because of the cold mud. I wanted to go back to how it felt before.

"This don't feel good." I tried to pull my hands away.

"The nettles have little needles." He layered more mud on my hands. "The clay can help relieve the sting once it dries."

"But now it hurts." My voice sounded whiny and I tried to pull away again.

"I'll wash it off." He was panicking. He washed the clay off over and over. The blisters were hurting now and even though the clay was gone, he kept washing.

"Stop. You washing me now."

He looked at me and then at my hand.

"The clay gone. That's me you washing now. That's me, not the clay."

Maybe he didn't know the clay was all washed off because it was the same color as me.

His blue eyes took in my brown ones in big gulps. For about half a blink I thought he was leaning in toward me, like he gonna kiss me, but I was wrong. I was glad to be wrong. But I wasn't glad about how he squeezed my hand like a tug-a-war rope. I already missed that good tingle and loosened my hand from his hold and dabbed my hands dry against my dress.

My hands were covered in blisters. They didn't feel good no more. How was I gonna explain this to Mama?

We didn't talk for a few moments. The sunrise had come and the dampness in the air was lifting up and sitting on the tree limbs above us. I imagined the little droplets in the air sitting next to the birds in the trees and looking down at us, sparkling like diamonds. The toads from earlier were quieter now, or maybe not. Maybe I just couldn't hear them because Johnny was so close. Well, that's how I felt anyhow. I didn't know if that's how he felt.

After another few moments he rocked back from kneeling to sit on the ground. He rested his arms on his knees. I sat back also and made sure to keep my dress tucked under me and kept my knees together and down. If Mama ever found out I was out here, she would have my hide. But if she knew I wasn't sitting like a lady, it would make everything worse.

I was getting a little nervous that he wasn't saying nothing. And I peeked over at him out of the sides of my eyes. The sun wound its way through the leaves and landed right on us. I saw how the sun didn't shine off his skin the same way it did mine. I noticed how the sun would shine up hard against the chests and shoulders of colored boys when they took their shirts off to swim. I liked it.

But Johnny was handsome in a different way. He made me think a little about them cowboys from books. Like he was one of the good ones, but because he got that devil-look in his eye, that made me think that he ain't all good cowboy. There was a little something extra in there too.

"Why were you holding the nettles?"

I shrugged. "I just wanted to."

"Didn't it hurt?"

I shook my head. But right away I worried about what he thought of me. I remembered his mama telling me not to touch them because they would sting. But the sting felt nice. And the more the blisters were left alone, a little of that good tingle came back. I looked at my hands and the raised blisters now pulsed against my skin.

"Where did you move from?"

"Montgomery, Alabama. You ever been?"

He shook his head and smiled. "I've never been anywhere." He chuckled. "Well, I visited family in Ohio a few times, but that's all. What's Alabama like?"

What was it like? It was my heart and a

nightmare at the same time. I'd known of no other home my whole life until now. I dreamed of still living there with my friends and my old neighborhood where everyone lived so close together. I dreamed of Carver and him being alive there and him dying there.

I shrugged again. "It's all right. Real hot."

He nodded. "Why'd you move here?"

"Are you your mama's only kid?" I didn't want him to know I was a murderer.

Johnny sat up a little and pulled up a single wide blade of grass. "I think she lost a baby once. But I don't know anything more. So it's just me." He put the grass between the lengths of his thumbs and I thought about Emma losing a baby. I felt sad for her. I lost a baby too — just not the same way.

"What happened there?" Johnny pointed at the big scar I had on my calf.

I pulled my legs under the skirt of my dress. I didn't want to talk about how I got that. It was an ugly scar too. Puffy and off-colored. And it marked something I didn't like to think about but always did.

I gave him a weak shrug and he left it alone. And a few moments later a shrill, thin wheeze came from Johnny blowing through that blade of grass between his thumbs.

I jumped a little. "What you doing?"

"You've never made grass whistle?"

I shook my head.

Then he sat next to me. He pulled another blade of grass and without hesitation waved for me to raise my hands. He positioned the grass and even though he took care to avoid my blisters, he wasn't afraid to touch me.

He didn't touch my hands just to help me. He touched me because we was making friends. Or something like that.

"Now blow." He showed me with his own hands again.

I tried and it worked. I laughed so hard I fell back into the morning grass and so did he. We watched the trees dance in a breeze as the sun kept getting higher. Johnny rested his hand next to mine, and it was warm.

EMMA

There was a hum in the air I had never heard before. I stood still and tried to find the source. My view landed on the white-steepled church with its cross emblazoned in the citrus sunset. I listened. It was singing. But had a different sound from my church with slow-moving tones and long-held words. I always loved the portion of the service where we sang, though I never sang loudly. Just above a whisper. I loved the sound of togetherness and the unity.

But this was different. It wasn't just sound. It was music.

It was a perfect Sunday evening. Tomorrow morning would be a week since Johnny had found Sparrow in the woods. All week I knew I should return Delilah's pan but I hadn't. I was afraid that once the pan was returned, we would have no reason to see each other. Like the pan was that small connection we had.

I walked toward the church, crossing through Delilah's yard and the road and onto the short gravel drive of the church. Other vehicles were parked at the side in the grass. Maybe eight. Of course this was no place for me to be returning her pan. I could've just put it on the porch and walked home — but for my strong curiosity.

The church door was cracked open. The music now was louder and glorious. I could hear a rhythmic clapping I'd never heard before with singing. Their bold voices sang of freedom and of the River Jordan and of heaven. I envied the freedom that trilled in the evening air. I'd never heard that word used in church. Not in the preaching or in our songs.

The small congregation went into a fit of clapping and hollering all mixed together when the song was over. Then a singular voice broke through. It was an old woman. The quiver in her tone and pitch reminded me of Matilda Yoder who, when she spoke, sounded like a sweet, wrinkled-up song.

I held my breath to hear every word. The song was slow.

"Shine on me. In the morning, shine on me."

As the woman sang out, a humming of deep voices began. What was the woman pleading for? As I was trying to understand the words of this song, a man's voice broke in and the song picked up with more clapping. We didn't speak or sing with these words. Asking for a lighthouse to shine on us. We used the *Ausbund,* the oldest songbook that was still used and filled with four-hundred-year-old hymns. Some having come from my ancestors, the Swiss Mennonite, while imprisoned in Switzerland and written to encourage endurance.

"O may thy servant be endowed, with wisdom from on high."

These good words I had known as long as I could remember — it was a line from the second song we sang every church Sunday. But in this moment I realized that I didn't think on them anymore. Least of all did I pray them. But hearing these new words felt like the hastiness of a stream; I felt the force of them. There was a story in their words too — a different story from mine.

When the door flew open a pack of small children poured out, running. As they saw me, they slowed. As if I were a rock in a stream, the children flowed around me. They walked with their eyes going from excitement to concern. When they were past me, they ran to the other side of the church where a patient ball had been waiting.

Then there stood Sparrow. She was silhouetted by the yellow glow of the lights inside. She walked with her head down and held her Bible close to her chest. She wore the same dress Johnny had found her in.

I should've followed my instincts and not my curiosities. I should have put the pan on their front porch and gone home. I was intruding on them — but their songs had washed away my good sense and I had lingered.

Sparrow looked up and saw me. She rushed down the stairs but remained on the bottom one, so she was taller than me now.

"What you doing here, Ms. Emma?" Her voice was so small, it sounded as light as the chirp of a bird.

I stumbled over my words. I couldn't find them.

"Your mother's pan," I stammered and showed her.

"But why you here?" She pointed at the place where I stood. "You white."

My knowledge of white and colored was so incomplete. But for the bare bones about the Civil War, I didn't know much of my own country's history. And as for any town issues I'd heard of, our bishop always told us those things were for the world in all its sinfulness to wade through. They were not for us. But why?

"I don't know." I said it plainly enough that I felt like a child. I pushed the pan into her middle and her Bible flopped inside it as she grabbed it. I turned around and started walking away.

I made it to the other side of the road when I heard my name. I didn't stop. It wasn't Sparrow's voice and I was afraid to turn around and see Delilah's disappointment. I'd done something wrong. I'd overstepped a boundary. I'd been naive and stupid. John had been right. I should've minded my own business. What purpose was there in making friends with anyone who didn't follow the same patterned life I led? I didn't know who I was if I was just the white woman standing at the foot of a church I wasn't supposed to notice or look at or befriend. Was I just a white person and Deedee just a colored person? Was that all we were? Could we ever be just two people — friends — even though we came from different worlds in our one earth?

"Ms. Emma. Wait." The voice was more urgent this time and I could hear fast steps behind me.

I stopped in the grass next to her garden. My breathing was labored and when I turned around Delilah's breathing matched mine. Both of us tried to talk but for a few

233

moments we couldn't. My running and fears had made my heart beat too fast to speak. Maybe Delilah felt the same way. We stared at each other as we caught our breaths.

Were we not more same than different in this moment? Maybe in many moments?

"I'm sorry," I said between breaths. "I was just returning your pan when I heard the singing." I shook my head. "I didn't mean to intrude and I keep doing it." I looked beyond Delilah over to the church and several stared our direction from the small crowd that congregated.

Delilah, who had not taken her eyes off of me, didn't speak. She didn't want to speak with me, I knew that much. Did she despise me? I'd always been known by what I wore and how I lived, but not by my skin. I didn't know what it was like to be known by my own skin.

"Why you crying?"

I began wiping my eyes with the palms of my hands like a child would do. I shook my head because my throat was too full with tears. I could not remember the last time I'd shed any real tears. They'd been numbed or frozen or absent for so long. Sometimes I believed I cried invisible tears. I could feel them, but they couldn't be seen.

"Why does Sparrow always remind me that I'm white?" I blurted out, ragged and confused.

Delilah tucked her chin and raised her eyebrows.

"You know better than that. You know our colors don't mix. You live your life. I live mine."

"My bishop says the same thing. To keep to ourselves — separate from *Englishers.*"

"Are *Englishers* your color or mine?" Delilah spat out.

"It doesn't matter."

"It always matters. You white, you know that."

But I didn't know that it mattered, until now.

"Is it what you want — to be separate?" I couldn't think of anything more honest to ask.

Delilah's sharpened eyes softened. Her brow furrowed and with the tilt of her head I knew she was surprised at what I'd asked. I didn't know what to expect next.

"We were fixin' to have cake and tea. How does that sound?" She raised an eyebrow, making me believe she was doing what was right more than what she wanted to do.

"Why would you invite me over? I —" I couldn't find the right words to say that I'd been an intruder and didn't deserve it.

She bobbed her head toward the house. "Come on. Besides, Malachi would be upset with me if I just let you walk off without being neighborly and . . ."

I followed her and moved into step. "And?"

"*And* I don't know," she said plainly, and I knew she was being honest.

"I don't know either."

"Then I guess we can agree on that. Come on with you."

DELILAH

When I saw that white woman running away like that, I just knew I needed to see what was going on. When I asked Sparrow why she came, she just showed me the pan. But no one run away like that without something the matter. But if someone would've told me that I would be inviting her to my home, to have cake, to fellowship — that would've brought back the laughter I'd lost so many months ago.

On the porch I told her that I'd get the tea and cake, thinking she'd rather not come right into my house, but then she followed me inside. Though she'd also done that when she brought Sparrow back. I don't think she knows the way the rest of the world is about stuff like this. For the first time since I'd met her, I liked her a little bit. That brick wall I been building around myself got a few bricks taken down — not a whole row, mind you.

"Mama, we having cake?" Mallie asked as soon as I walked in. When he saw Emma, he zipped up his lips like they were sewed shut. He just stood there and then put a hand on Harriet's shoulder and she stopped her hopping around and looked at me and then at Emma. The whites of their eyes kept bouncing back and forth between us.

So distant and far from our world was it to have a white woman in our home or one of us in their homes. It wasn't the way things went in Montgomery, unless it was for a job interview. But then you weren't a guest. I'd worked in various homes since I was a child, all white, all nicer homes than mine. None of them had been mean to me, but they never invited me into their lives in any way but as a housekeeper.

"Children, this is Mrs. Mullet," I said to them.

"Please, I'm just Emma." Her voice was soft and lilting. "Everyone calls me Emma."

I saw her checking out my home and I was glad it was cleaned up.

"Hello, Ms. Emma," Sparrow said, bounding down the stairs. She wore a smile she only wear for Ms. Emma. She'd combed her hair back and her skin had a glow to it. I was glad at least that she'd added a *Mizz* ahead of her name.

"Y'all can call her Ms. Emma, if that's all right."

She smiled. "That would be fine."

Sparrow stood so close to Emma I couldn't think straight. I introduced the children and I about fell into a fit when Mallie bowed and Harriet curtsied. Like they never met a white woman before. I supposed it was because she was Amish. They knew a little about them but not much, and none of them ever met any of them.

"Sparrow, get the tea. Harriet, get the glasses out. Mallie, get the plates."

I took off my hat and put it on the hook — I excused myself to put my Carver purse on my bedside table. That's where I always kept it. I pulled off my earrings while I was in there too. My ears felt all pinched up. When I got back into the kitchen she was still just sitting there. Part of my head wanted to be annoyed that the woman was in my home. She had barged into where she didn't belong, but I had such guilt over my feelings toward her when she ain't done nothing wrong.

I turned toward her. "Why don't you have a seat right there." I motioned to the seat that usually sat empty.

George walked up to her. He had that usual George-look in his eyes, innocence

239

and something akin to a comfortable blanket. He'd been the soft one between him and Carver. Carver was like a pogo stick covered in butter. You couldn't slow him down or hold him in one place.

I shook my head to get the image out of my mind.

"Hi, George," Emma said.

He waved hi, even though he was close up. "Hi." His guttural voice didn't seem to shock Emma. He must have spoken his few words in the woods that day, outside of all that crying. He didn't say much and his voice didn't sound like no other child.

He pulled out his own chair, which was next to her, then he grabbed out a small ball from his pocket. Emma watched him intently. He rolled the ball down the table to her. She wasn't fast enough and the ball fell to the floor and bounced. She giggled as she picked it up and rolled it back. I watched for a few moments while I was cutting the cake.

"Birdie, your hands," Harriet's loud voice said. "Them blisters?"

Sparrow shoved her hands under the table so fast I knew I had to deal with her.

"Blisters?" I said and my eyes threw darts at her while I served the cake. Sparrow made no move to show me and kept staring

240

down. "What blisters?"

"I just got myself caught in some stinging weeds. Don't know what they're called."

"Nettles?" Emma gestured for Sparrow to show her. She reached out and took Sparrow's hands like it was nothing to touch her.

Sparrow shrugged.

"How that happen by accident?" I asked.

"Just walking to church. I thought they was flowers."

She had come after the rest of us and I didn't know what nettles were or looked like.

Emma's brow was all knitted up and when she bit her lower lip, I knew she was thinking on something that she wasn't sharing. But if Sparrow confused a stinging weed for a flower, I wasn't surprised. That girl just didn't have her head on straight no more. For a while there I thought she was going to be somebody. I wanted more for her than I had.

Saying that in my head sounded so bad. It wasn't that I didn't want what I got. I wanted to marry Malachi from the first day I met him in that lighthouse. I wanted to be a preacher's wife. I wanted to be a mother to a whole brood of children. But I never had a chance to go to college and learn more. I wanted that for all my children. It was hard enough for a colored man to go to college, but a colored woman — it just about made my heart jump into my mouth.

But now that was all gone for her. She couldn't do nothing without something bad happening. She couldn't even walk to church without getting blistered hands. What was wrong with that girl?

My thinking felt big and heavy. Did Emma think on this sort of stuff about her son? And I didn't know if she had any other children. I never asked.

"What is this?" She sipped the tea and then drank another longer drink.

"Sweet tea?"

"I've never tasted anything like this." She drank more.

I nudged Harriet to make her cup full again. I just shook my head for these poor northerners who didn't know about sweet tea. "You got other children? Besides the boy?"

"No," she said, still drinking the tea. "Just Johnny."

"All right. Just Johnny."

Malachi said that Amish folks had big families. She got me surprised saying she just got the one boy. And he's older than Sparrow. Couldn't help but think what was wrong with a woman with only one child. I knew a woman back home who was that way, but she had a whole line of little angel figures on her sink windowsill. Each one of them count as another baby in heaven. Did Emma have little angels all lined up some-place?

My mind got all curious about her. She didn't seem like other white women I met before. She didn't look down her nose at us.

"I'd love the recipe for this cake and the macaroni from last week," she said.

"Well, this is my grandma's recipe and I don't think it's written down nowhere. Same with the macaroni. We just make it."

She nodded and smiled. "Us too."

I thought maybe I could ask something about her husband, maybe what his job was when Malachi came roaring in like he on fire. That man got his eyes all ablaze and he was holding his suit coat in his hand and his tie pulled loose. He got some sweat under his arms and a big smile on his face.

"Woo-wee," he hooted. "It's been a good day, praise the Lord. Our biggest service yet. Did you know that Brother and Sister Morton drove forty-five minutes to fellowship with us tonight? I should've invited them over, but we got to talking and I just —"

He'd noticed.

"Hello there," he said.

"You remember Mrs. Emma Mullet, don't you, Malachi? Our neighbor."

"Sure I do — sure I do — yes, from the woods," he said and continued smiling as he walked closer. He held a hand out to her. "How nice to have you in our home, Mrs. Mullet."

"Thank you." She shook his hand. "Call me Emma."

"All right then, Ms. Emma." He looked at me then like he was searching for some explanation he knew I couldn't give him just now. I gave him my big eyes that said *later.*

"You want some cake?" I asked.

"Oh, no." He rubbed his belly. "Sister Marlene forced a cinnamon roll on me. I couldn't help myself and ate it while I stood there talking to everybody. A few of the ladies were looking for you. I told them you needed to get the children to bed."

He and I both knew that wasn't the whole truth.

Emma tensed a bit in hearing that. I thought to tell her that she'd saved me from talking to everyone, but I wasn't sure which I most wanted saving from. The ladies at church or her. Neither fit into my life. I

244

didn't want a friend right now. But I didn't like to see Emma running off like that. It didn't seem right.

"I'm going to retire early myself," Malachi said. "I have to be at the grocery store by five."

Mallie stuffed the last bite into his mouth and Harriet stole the rest of George's piece of cake. She smiled at me when I gave her my face. They both knew that if Daddy was ready for bed, then they got to be ready for family prayers.

"Come on, my family," Malachi said with his arms stretched wide and still holding his suit coat in his left hand. Our children folded up their hands — even George and Sparrow — and bowed their heads with their eyes all squinted shut.

I looked over at Emma and I thought about how Malachi could've waited until she went home. Or he could've said something to make her feel included or welcomed. Or something. I didn't know. But I got a bad feeling about this.

"I should go." Emma looked like she going to shake right out of her skin.

Malachi had just shut his eyes and was ready to say some real holy prayer that would've impressed the angel Gabriel, but his eyes flew open and he looked at her. My eyes were already on her. Everybody else looked at her.

"I am intruding again." She pushed back her chair so fast and hard that the scrape hurt my ears. She stood and gave me a nervous smile. "It's late and — my husband."

I stood also and gave Malachi the stink eye for making her feel uncomfortable. And then I thought about how white she was and how we made her feel in our home. Would this bring us trouble? I didn't know.

"You didn't do nothing wrong, Ms. Emma," I said. "I'm glad we sat down together."

"Thank you." She tucked the chair all neat like and turned toward Malachi. "Your family." Her voice broke. "You have a beautiful family."

And then I thought I saw something happening in her face that made me pay more attention to her. She got this softness about her but she kept it from coming out, so she also got a hardness.

"It's dark out, Miss Emma." Sparrow stood. "You got a flashlight? You allowed to use flashlights?"

"Girl, don't you ask foolish questions." What was she thinking? Her face grayed and she stared down at her hands.

"I didn't think I'd be out this late," Emma stammered. "It will be okay. I know my way home."

I held my finger up for her to give me a minute. I went to the cabinet and didn't know why I couldn't find our good flashlight — the nice big one — so our small one would have to do. She would need something. There was no way I'd go in them woods when the sun was setting down. That would mean it was darker in the woods than it was in my backyard. Ain't no way.

When I turned around I see that Malachi was ushering the kids, except for Sparrow, over to the stairs and whispering something to them. Maybe for them to say their prayers up in their rooms alone or something. Then George got away and gave Emma a hug around the tops of her legs. Was that his thank-you to her for finding him that day?

"I'm sorry," I said, getting over to her fast. I unwrapped his arms from around her. "He loves hugs."

"I don't mind," she said in a near whisper and kept her eyes fixed on him.

"Mama?" George said. By the sound of his voice, I knew what was coming next but there wasn't nothing I could do to stop it. "Carver? Where's Carver?"

"Come on, son." Malachi picked him up

and went up the stairs. Mallie followed him. And don't you know but my baby George cried Carver's name all the way up them stairs. It would've broke my heart in a million pieces if it weren't already all smashed up.

"Carver was my baby brother," Harriet said to Emma at the bottom of the stairs. "But he's dead."

"Harriet," I snapped and Malachi did too from the top of the stairs. She ran up like my hand was swatting her behind.

Emma and I caught eyes.

"I'm so sorry," Emma said with glistening eyes.

I nodded my thank-you and I had to force myself not to turn toward Sparrow just then. I wanted to give her that look I do when I wanted to remind somebody of something. But I didn't. And I knew Emma got a bunch of other questions in her mouth, but she didn't ask. I was glad because I didn't want to say nothing more.

She went to the door without warning and opened it and left. She didn't say good-bye or nothing. After I told Sparrow to go to bed, I followed her.

"Ms. Emma," I called after her. I clicked the flashlight on and handed it to her. "Here, take this."

In the light of the coming moon and the dim glow from my flashlight I could see that she was crying.

"Here," I offered again with a mouthful of tears.

She took it with shaky hands and turned around in a hurry.

I couldn't help but watch the glow of light as she ran through the yard. I had a feeling she'd keep running until she got home. Something was wrong. Something was real wrong.

EMMA

The many night sounds nagged and badgered me, reminding me of my burdens. I ran as fast as I could. Everything I saw tonight brought back Judith's words. The way Delilah was with her children like a mother hen. The way Malachi came in like a king. The way George hugged me. Sparrow's blisters. All of it needled me.

It was as if everything Judith had chastised me over had played out in front of me tonight. A house full of children. A husband who loved his family. A picture of everything that a woman was supposed to want and have. What I had wanted out of life. But I'd been making sure that my body was the last place a child could grow. What was worse was that my husband didn't know. I was a liar and a cheat. I had cheated my husband out of a family.

How disgusted would Delilah be if she knew? I wouldn't want her to know but I still wanted to know her. To understand her. And Sparrow. The girl had not left my side. She had hung on my few words. She had a beautiful smile.

But the blisters.

Nettles could not be mistaken for flowers. This and what she said about killing her brother. I didn't understand her.

It wasn't long before I was wet up to my calves from running through the small creek. The small flashlight didn't stay lit long and I had to walk in the dark. John would wonder why I was out after dark, or maybe he'd drunk enough to be in such a stupor that he wouldn't notice, even though he didn't usually drink on Sunday. But I prayed that his sin would make it so he would not see the guilt pouring from my eyes. That I would not have to face him shrouded in lies.

What kind of wife was I to wish sin upon my husband? The most burdened deacon in our district. No one would ever suspect that he was also the most sinful. That their honored deacon was a drunk — a *ztiffah*.

That was all I could think of when I saw the beauty of Delilah's family — that my husband was a drunk. My womb was not safe. And how it was all my fault.

I continued to follow the stream and then

I rolled my ankle on something and fell. My ankle burned. I felt around for what had tripped me. It was a big flashlight. It looked new. I clicked it on and it was as bright as day in the circle around me. I suspected Sparrow had dropped the flashlight and I was glad for the extra light.

The moon shone on the surface of the pond, and the yellow light of a kerosene lamp glowed through my windows. I was sure John was sitting and waiting for me.

I would have to look at him and know what I'd kept him from. I would have to look at him and know what he had put me through daily.

I kept walking.

I didn't want to go home.

When I got to the porch I clicked off the flashlight and stepped in quietly. If he had fallen asleep or had passed out, I didn't want to wake him. I shut the door and leaned against it. It didn't make a sound.

I put both flashlights in a drawer. The less John noticed and saw, the less he would question.

"Sis schpoht." His monotone voice said it was late and my heart skipped a beat.

"I lost track of time." I tried not to sound nervous. I looked over at him and pasted a smile on my face.

He closed his Bible and zeroed in on my eyes. "With those people?"

"What do you mean?"

"The Negroes — with the pan."

"Oh — *ja.*" My hands gripped the back of the wooden chair.

"Why were you there so long?"

"Just being neighborly."

He didn't say anything so I continued. "Did you know that Malachi Evans is a preacher? I bet you two would have a lot in common."

"I doubt it." He set his Bible on the end table next to him. "It just worries me — what kind of people they might be."

"They're nice people." I turned my back on him and busied myself. I folded and refolded the hand towel. I washed the sink and scrubbed in places that already showed my reflection. After a few minutes I hoped he'd return his attention to his Bible. But he was right behind me.

"Don't draw attention to us." He reminded me of this anytime attention could be gained. He twitched.

I looked past the ticks and saw his height and the way he tilted his head. For a moment I saw my husband, not just the drunk.

"Wouldn't you — we — be happier if I had given you more children?" I said it breathless and fast to get it out before I could pin it back inside the pocket of my heart. "Don't you think things would be — ?"

What word could I use? *Different? Better?* What did I mean by that? That he would be different or better?

"Why are you talking about this now?" He scowled. Not upset, but I could see frustration. "Was this because of Judith? Did she make you feel bad? She knows it's not our choice."

He turned away and ran his hand through his dark waves. He cleared his throat. He fidgeted. He kept his eyes from me.

He was saved from further talking when we heard a buggy driving in against the dry gravel. It was early for Johnny to come home from the Singing. The grandfather clock said it was before nine. He wasn't usually home until after ten.

John and I held a brief gaze and then a knock came.

Johnny wouldn't knock.

I stopped my pretend chores and looked over at John. He didn't move toward the door.

"I'll get it." I walked around the table and to the front door. I was surprised to find the new young preacher standing there.

"Mervin? Come on in."

I stepped aside and he took off his hat as he entered. He had a tall frame and was a handsome man. I guessed he was little more than thirty. Even as I looked out into the darkness and saw no one else, I still asked if Lena and the children were with him. With his wife it would be a friendly social call, but alone it was church business. The sort that no one wanted. It was late for either, however.

"Neh." She hadn't come. His tenor voice had a pleasantness to it, which was nice in a preacher. He put his hand out and I shook it hard and strong as we were taught.

"Mervin." John approached the younger man and they shook hands. He carried with his height a few added inches, with a boasted seven or eight years of life and the weight of a secret. The deep lines he wore on his face were a small reflection of the promise of deeper sins. "What brings you by?"

"Vella anah hookah." Mervin gestured to sit at the kitchen table.

"Coffee?" I asked. My concerns deepened when he shook his head.

John's agitation heightened when he sat. The nerves that came with an unannounced visit from a preacher were enough to push anyone, but for him it was worse. He chewed the inside of his mouth, tapped his fingers, rubbed his face, cleared his throat, moved his chair out and then back again. When his eyes met mine I saw the familiar pleading for help. No matter how much I hated his sin and what it did to me, he was like a magnet to me. He was my husband. I didn't know what else to do but help him — help us.

"I'd still like coffee." I feigned cheerfulness. "John?"

He nodded and cleared his throat again.

I readied the coffee and sliced a few pieces of lemon cream pie. My mind couldn't concentrate on the men's small talk for the twisting in my soul, like a swing in the wind.

Whatever it was that the preacher wanted to discuss tonight, there was no returning to life before losing my marriage to the amber-colored bottle. There was no growing young for my son so he could be brought up properly. There was no going back to not taking my herbs to prevent a soul, or many souls, from growing beneath my heart.

I was ashamed of myself.

I was also ashamed when I tipped a few swallows of John's wine into his coffee mug. It would quench any suspicions at his strange behavior. How often had I done this? How many years?

The first time I'd done it I meant it as an insult to him. A brazen declaration of his dependency. I stood across the room when he too̲ ̲ ̲ ̲ ̲sip and our gazes met instantly. His jaw clenched. His back straightened. He was horrified. He was pleased. He hated me for it, I was sure. But he never told me to stop and we never spoke of it. We never spoke of his drinking at all. My veiled remarks or actions were enough.

Of course, we never spoke of my herbs either. How many children had I said good-bye to before the possibility of a hello? The church said that God provided our children and that nothing should come in the way of His providence. Couldn't He, if desiring, make my herbs fail? He had made the herb. He had made me, and He allowed my failings.

But I would not allow myself to fail in the eyes of the church. We had too much to lose. I would appear the proper Amish woman wearing my prayer covering that, in truth, poured grace over nothing. It was just a covering over my flaxen hair. The grace that was enough for my sins couldn't come from a piece of fabric. Would grace arrive in allowing me to continue hiding my sin? Or would accepting my consequence be grace

257

— as it would free me from the bondage of my secret?

John and I were both lost in our secrets. We created them, ate them, and drank them. But we had been on this path together for so long, we were partners in it and yet enemies. My secrets were like a rubble of words that sat on the other side of my tongue, waiting to be spoken. What if I confessed everything to this young man who was my church leader? What if I spoke everything out of my mind? I pinned my mouth shut.

I placed the coffee on the table — making sure to give John the correct one. I also put several plates and forks along with the half-eaten lemon pie on the table.

"I wanted to come by and talk to you about some things." He paused and looked at John. "As our *aumah deanah,* I know you carry a great burden."

He stopped and looked at me. I stopped breathing. "Maybe I'll take some coffee after all."

By the time I'd given him coffee, he had plated a piece of a pie for himself. John and I watched him eat. No one said a word. The sounds of the fork against the plate, the deep swallow of the thick lemon cream, and the slurp of the coffee frayed my nerves.

"I'm here because of Johnny." He spoke midswallow of his last bite.

In that moment I realized what a terrible mother I was. I was relieved that this preacher had come to my house to speak of the ill behavior of my son. I was relieved that he saw my son's sin so my sin could remain unbidden from deep within my heart. I was thankful. Was this grace?

"What's the boy done now?" John rolled his eyes.

"It's not just him, John. That's why I'm out here later than usual for these types of calls. Johnny seems to be a ringleader of a handful of boys, a few girls, and a few *Englisher* kids too. They've taken to drinking together. I know your neighbor boy is one of them." He bobbed his head in the direction of our neighbors. "He has ways of getting beer. When we think our sons are driving our daughters home from a Singing, they go to your neighbor's barn and drink. Some of the drink is coming from your cellar too."

When John didn't respond, I nudged him with my foot under the table.

He looked at me. His face was blank. Then he took a too-long drink from his coffee and turned back to Mervin.

"He has become too familiar with the

English," John said. "I think that makes it easy to fall to these worldly sins."

"Do you think that his working at the lumber mill with all the English is causing this? You're an adult and can turn away from the world's pull." Mervin's brow furrowed and his head tilted in sincerity. "But Johnny's only a boy."

"No, I don't think so. I think there are other things."

"The other families' hearts are broken. They did not know that their children had fallen like this. Drunkenness is a mockery, and we don't want to lose these young ones to the world."

Tears shone in his eyes but did not fall. He blinked them away. Preachers and deacons were known for their tears, though I questioned the sincerity. Was it just a way to heighten our guilt? Or was it from the great burden they carried in these difficult conversations?

He went on about the wiles of the world and how strong drink ruined lives. I was living this ruination and did not need this sermon. I imagined that the other mothers he'd spoken to earlier had lost many tears, but I had none to shed. I'd already shed everything else in my life for the sake of secrets and had nothing left to give outside of confession. And now we had a scandal that we didn't have to hide. I felt a sick gratefulness in that.

"Emma is too comfortable with the English neighbors. I don't think that helps Johnny." John didn't look at me.

"I'm neighborly is all." I tried to stay calm.

"So neighborly that even though you didn't want to go to the Singing tonight, you instead spent time with that Negro family?" He tipped his head to the direction of the woods.

My gaze went from Mervin to my hands around my full coffee mug. I couldn't hold his gaze, not because I was guilty of what John was accusing me, but if I let Mervin's steadiness dwell on me any longer, I feared I would spill all the sin inside of me. There was so much I would drown. We would all drown. It would be a solace — a relief.

It would be my grace.

Sparrow

Miss Emma had water all down her front when I walked through her yard. I saw her through the open basement door. Mama thought I was reading out back but I had to find Daddy's flashlight. He convinced Mama to let everyone wait for school until the fall — just a month left anyhow. Then he winked at me. I smiled.

When I got as far as the stream where Johnny and I had met, I didn't see the flashlight nowhere. Maybe Ms. Emma found it or Johnny. So I kept walking. I didn't know what gave me the right to walk right up to that white house. But I did.

Emma was pushing clothes through one of them old washers like my grandma had for a while before she sold it. Some folks in Montgomery used them and even outhouses. But this was the first time I seen one used. Her skirt was pinned up a bit and it looked funny. I didn't like the smell neither. It was coming from the motor on the side of the wringer washer.

She was just inside her basement and didn't see me where I stood watching. And the motor was loud. Her forehead was all scrunched up. I'm not sure it was 'cause of the washing because she's not doing the hard part of the labor, or maybe she's got a load of something on her mind. I watched for a few moments, unsure of how to get her attention.

"My mama is also doing the washing today." I hated my squeaky voice.

"You don't help her?" I think Emma was just about as surprised that she said it as I was to hear it. She never said that stuff to me but just always made me feel good about being around her. But now I seem like a lazy girl who ain't any help.

"She don't want my help." Mama didn't want to be around me. Before Carver I used to iron all the clothes, but now she wants me out of her hair.

"Does she know you're here?" She glanced over from her work long enough to wipe across her face with the side of her arm.

I didn't answer right away but listened to the sloshing of the water. "Sorta. She don't really care — as long as I don't make no trouble."

Emma was quiet for a bit — maybe thinking. What's she got on her mind to be thinking on? She only had one child. Probably her husband was working at a good job. She was home alone. It seemed like it was easy to be Ms. Emma. But right now she got these burden lines going across her forehead and water trickling down the sides of her face.

"I'll take your help then," Emma said. "I've always wondered what it would be like to have a dau— to have help."

I swallowed hard when she almost says *daughter.* I almost wanted to walk — no — run away because it just ain't right to talk like that. Could put ideas in my head. But it does give me a thrill. I was so used to being the daughter who let Mama's boy die and got no good inside. What would it be like to be a different kind of daughter?

"Why you pin your dress like that?" I took off my light sweater; it was steamy in the basement.

"Keeps it away from the motor." Then Emma showed me how to hang up the clothes that were already washed. I already knew how to hang clothes. Mama taught me when I was real young and could reach with a stool, but I wanted to learn Ms. Emma's way. Like I was her daughter. Like she almost said.

She seemed to shake off a bit of that burden she was wearing and laughed at me when I didn't want to touch her husband's drawers. She even let me push some laundry through the wringer and pulled my hand away just before it got wrung up with her dresses. My hands were soaked and wrinkled and weren't so different from hers by the time all the laundry was hung. It felt good to work. It felt good that somebody wanted me around.

When she handed me a lemonade on her front porch, I took it and sipped from it quickly. It was a hot day and I had sweat through my clothes. Then she handed me the flashlights. The big one felt heavy and so did Miss Emma's expression.

"It was next to the stream about halfway between us," she said. "When did you leave it out there?"

"When I — Sometimes I walk out there when it's still dark." It was a half-truth. "I like the woods."

She watched me, but I just looked off ahead. They had this big barn on the other side of their drive and the road ahead of that was quiet. Then I watched the laundry flapping in the breeze and the rushes around that big pond blowing. Everything being

265

pushed by the wind. I wish it would just blow me away.

"I like the woods too," she said and set her hand on my shoulder.

I turned toward her and she had an expression on her face I wished Mama would still give me. She used to. She used to look at me like I was all she ever wanted. Not like she liked me better than the others, but just that she was happy with me. But it was buried deep down with Carver and it won't never come back.

"Does your mother know you're going in the woods — when it's dark?"

I shook my head. "No, ma'am."

"You shouldn't keep things from your mother." She took a sip from her lemonade. "Will you promise to tell her?"

I lied and said I would. Mama didn't want to hear nothing from me. I would smooth things over with her and tell her just enough so that if Ms. Emma asked about it again, I could tell her that I had. Or something like that.

"Your blisters look better than last night. Why did you lie about the nettles and the blisters? Nettles can't be confused with flowers."

I was surprised that quiet, soft Ms. Emma would just come out and say stuff like that.

I shrugged. "Just got confused."

She didn't say no more.

Ms. Emma hugged me when I left late that morning. I didn't deserve that hug. She shouldn't have given me nothing like that.

When I walked home, I got this itch to do something I knew Emma wouldn't like. Johnny wouldn't neither. Something that would make Daddy sad and that Mama wouldn't care about.

I sat down by the water and I used my sweater to pull up more of them stinging weeds — *nettles.* I unbuttoned the top of my dress and pressed the wild plant against my chest — by my heart. I let the tingling spread through me. My blood stirred up all over my body. I heard a deep moan and it took a moment before I realized it was coming from me.

I kept on until the tingling wasn't coming from the plant anymore, but it was my chest tingling. The blood in my veins did it on their own. With my hand still covered by my sweater, I threw the used-up weed into the stream. I couldn't let Mama or Emma see nothing. Or Johnny. Being confused about a plant once might be okay, but if they saw blisters on my hands again, they would know I was lying. They'd make me stop.

I didn't want to. Especially now after this second time was even better than the first. I was afraid maybe the first time wasn't real — that the relief I got from them wouldn't happen again. But it did. The numbness of grief and guilt just fled when the nettles were against my skin. They were all I felt then. I pulled some more out and wrapped them in my sweater. I needed them for later.

I went to Miss Emma's once more that week. Just like she was ready for me, she gave me a slice of pie. It was delicious and tasted like kindness and love and knowing someone. She also taught me to darn socks. When I had Johnny's socks in my hand, I rubbed the nubby fabric between my fingers. It made me feel funny inside. It made me feel.

Then the next Sunday at sunrise, Johnny was at the water's edge before me. He was waiting for me this time. He was making two marks on a small tree nearby. Later he told me that it was a birch tree and the marks were to count our meetings. He had this big smile on his face that made me forget for a minute that I killed my baby brother. It didn't happen long but just for half a blink I got to feel that something that came with his smile. Why did he smile at me anyway? What made me special enough?

I doubt I'll ever get the answer to that but don't care. He was my only friend now — besides his mama.

"How long you been here?" I asked.

He shrugged. "Ten minutes."

Before I sat next to him I looked at his socks. Were those the ones I darned? My thumb rubbed on my pointer finger where I stuck myself with the needle.

"What are you thinking about?"

"Your socks." I smiled. It was the same one I used to give the neighbor boy I was kissing when I should've been watching Carver. The thought rattled me for a moment.

"My socks?" He looked at them.

"Your mama teached me how to darn them." Now I couldn't take my mind away from the last time I was with a boy and what happened. And how my flirting killed my baby brother. Just talking to Johnny would get me into trouble again. Who would die this time when I sinned?

"How are your hands?"

"They fine." I showed him. "It was nothing."

I said it like I meant it but I didn't. It wasn't nothing. It gave me something else to feel for a bit instead of the guilt. Didn't know how it did that, but it did. Thinking on this stuff made me run my hand over the cotton fabric of my dress. If Johnny wasn't with me, I would do it now when I felt a little nervous or bothered or needed to feel that good hurt. Because I wanted it so bad, I had to take some deep breaths so I wouldn't start acting crazy. I needed to calm down.

Could I sneak some in with me to church? Maybe I could sit on it with the weeds under my dress or just put it right in my underclothes.

Water splashed on my face. "What you do that for?"

"Just wanted to see you laugh," he said.

I forced myself to smile. He didn't know why that bugged me. He didn't know about Carver.

"What you do at church?" I changed the subject and church was all I could think of.

"We sing a little and then there's preaching. Sometimes it goes longer than it should."

"That's about like our church." I waited for a second. "Ours goes a little long sometimes too. Usually 'cause of all the singing. Not 'cause of the preaching. Daddy's our preacher, you know."

"Mine's a deacon."

Our eyes met and we smiled, like we saw

how similar our lives are.

"Why you meet me here?"

He shrugged. "You're not like other girls around here."

"Because I'm colored?" I wanted to raise my eyebrow like what Mama did, but I didn't.

"Well, you're different from the other girls in my church." He nudged me with his elbow. "But you're from somewhere else and I wanted to get to know you."

He paused.

"And you're pretty."

My face felt warm. "I gotta go." I got up.

I wished we met more often. Last Sunday he touched my hand when he washed it and when we lay back in the grass. I wanted to feel that again almost as bad as I wanted the stinging weed against my skin. They were so familiar to me I could find them fast now. But his touch had to be given to me. I couldn't just find it lying around the woods somewhere.

He got up and faced me and, like he'd read my thoughts, his finger grazed my jawline before I had time to flinch. "I *like* the color of your skin."

I leaned my head away out of embarrassment — far enough that I lost the touch of his finger. My skin color was never given

271

good attention, unless it was from Daddy's sister Edna. She was possessed like a she-devil with her light skin and said I wasn't quite as light as her, but pretty light. So when Johnny said something I ain't never heard before, I just about wanted to be a turtle and crawl into a shell.

"What's this?" Johnny turned over my collar where a patch of fresh blister had peeked through.

"Nothing." I buttoned up the top button.

"That was a blister — like your hands." He grabbed my arms.

"It ain't nothing." My voice squealed, but I didn't try to get out of his grip because he didn't make me afraid.

He looked at me so hard I thought my face would crack. "Are you doing it on purpose?"

How had he figured it out? Now he would never want to meet out here in the woods. He wouldn't want nothing to do with me.

"I'm not doing nothing." My voice was even higher. "I gotta get back. Mama's gonna notice if I don't hurry."

But he just held me, and even though his hands were tight, he wasn't rough.

I thought he was gonna kiss me. Did I want him to? Would I even let him? But I realized I was crazy because he let go of me.

"Why are you hurting yourself?" His brow got all wrinkled like.

"It don't hurt." I was honest this time.

"But the blisters. That can't feel . . ." He shook his head. "But why?"

I shrugged.

"I don't want you to hurt yourself."

"But it helps." I put my hand on my heart. All my sadness bubbled up and my voice didn't work well when I talked again. It warbled like it was running over the creek bed. "I hurt real bad because I killed my brother." I swallowed. "The nettles cover that hurt a little."

"What happened?"

I paused for maybe a whole minute.

"I wasn't watching him and a real bad thing happened." I told him what that *real bad thing* was — I whispered it because I couldn't say it out loud. But I didn't tell him I's kissing on a boy when it happened — I didn't want him knowing that. I told him how Mama hated me because of it. How the stinging nettles made my blood turn alive again.

Then he held me real close with his arms around me. At first I didn't know what to do. But then I put my arms around him too and tucked my head in close to his chest. I smelled his soap — probably Ivory — and a hint of cigarettes. I heard his heart.

I didn't know a boy could be like that. Hold me without trying to touch me in places he shouldn't. Mama and Daddy didn't know that a few boys had tried to touch my bosoms and tried for somewhere else. I always slapped their hands away, but the boys just laughed.

The neighbor boy tried to but I didn't slap him away. Ever since, though, I couldn't say his name. But I said it in my mind today. *J. D.* — that was what everybody called him. But his real name was John David.

As Johnny stood in front of me in them woods, I wondered if it was a second chance at being good. Maybe God was testing me to see if I would sin again and again.

DELILAH

Of course the little white church couldn't heal my heart. Nothing could do that. Even if it could, it wouldn't happen in a month. A month with weekly visits to the grocer where a white man does his best not to act like he's better'n me. I don't hate him for trying. Each week we go to church and today the pews were full.

A pile of new families coming who, by the end of service, were clapping and having themselves a good ole time. Malachi made a point of talking to every adult, every child — everybody. He was made for this. I had been too — before.

We all ate together for Sundays and, like a good preacher's wife, I got it all laid out. Chicken, greens, black-eyed peas with salt pork, and a couple of pound cakes and plenty of sweet tea. We got a whole mess of biscuits too. They usually got eaten up first.

All this work made it look like I was meant

for this life of a reverend's wife, with all its thinking of others first and putting self last. To take care of the needs your husband couldn't.

But I knew the truth.

I knew I wasn't that kind of wife no more, not in my heart, anyhow. There'd been a time when I relished it. My husband filling hungry hearts and I'd fill the hungry bellies — not that I made all the food, but serving it out and making sure everyone got enough — that was what I'd loved most. But I was so darned empty now — I couldn't do no filling.

Sparrow stayed in her room now during these lunches. Harriet always took a lunch up to her, even though nobody asked her to. She just did it because that's the kind of girl she was. Maybe I taught her to be that girl once, but I know it's not because I've been teaching her how lately.

Later, when I was sitting up in bed, I knew I should've been happy with the day. Malachi was.

All I could do was think of how empty I was sitting there looking at my purse full of Carver dirt. I had planned on putting the dirt in a canning jar so I could see it better, but I hadn't done it yet. It just came with me everywhere as if it were Carver. Once I grabbed it forgetting what was inside, but the weight of it was a quick reminder.

I was angry that I'd forgotten. My baby boy deserved better than that. My baby boy deserved better than most of what happened in his little life. What was God thinking giving him to me? About giving Sparrow to me? What was I thinking giving Carver to Sparrow that day?

Oh, the weight of grief.

It was so heavy and I couldn't put it down. That would be like walking away from Carver and letting him die all over again. I put the handbag on my lap and opened it. The dirt inside was dry and still. It's the same dirt it was before but it looked different. It was lighter. There wasn't no life in it because I took it out of the ground. There weren't no seeds inside ready to grow. No moisture from the earth or the sky. No nothing. It would need water if something was going to grow out of it. Water for life — the idea of that choked me.

It was the dirt of the dead.

Malachi walked in and paid no mind to my sitting there with Carver's dirt on my lap. Sometimes I think he should sit with me and get angry all over again that we lost our child, and then other times I think that if he came near me, I would slap him. At

277

first we had both grieved and it was the glue that held us together. But then he started acting like himself again and I had to carry his grief along with mine. Didn't take long for it all to become mine.

I closed the handbag and set it back on the nightstand again. Malachi was sitting up in bed reading when I slipped under the covers with my back to him. It was too hard to be soft for him or anyone anymore. There had been a day when all I could think about was how much I loved being a mother and a wife. I never told nobody but I also loved what happened in the darkness of our bedroom. Knowing another life might form but if not, at least he and I enjoyed each other. Wasn't that what Solomon wrote about? Wasn't that what made all the ladies in Sunday school blush if Solomon's songs from the Bible was ever referred to, even if not in mixed company? I just didn't feel nothing like that now.

"Can you believe how many new folks we had today?" Malachi spooned up next to me.

I closed my eyes and arched my back away from him. "Mm-hmm," was all I could say.

"Did you hear the singing?" His voice smiled so hard it broke my heart. No, I hadn't noticed because I hadn't cared. "I'm thinking of asking Brother Daryl to lead our songs. What do you think?"

He nuzzled my neck and I knew what he wanted. He was my husband, of course I knew his ways. We hadn't done nothing like that since Carver. He'd been as patient as a man could be.

"Maybe it's a little soon." Too soon for Brother Daryl, he'd only come twice, or too soon for what he wanted — I left the interpretation up to him.

"Nah." He took a long pull of my scent. "Sister Liberty was just as excited to be at church as Daryl."

"Gracious sakes, that name," I said before I caught my tongue.

"Oh yes, *that name.* Now those were wise parents to give her that name."

I knew a Bible verse was coming. He had the voice and the inspiration.

" 'Stand fast therefore in the liberty wherewith Christ has made us free, and be not entangled again with the yoke of bondage.' " His arms wrapped around me in the moment after his quote from somewhere in the New Testament. His arms got tighter. He got closer.

I wanted to run away. The weight I'd gained in my grief and the heaviness of the grief itself was stuck to my hips, butt, thighs, and heart. Because of that his hands felt like a million spiders crawling on me. I wanted to claw out of my skin. It wasn't his fault. I just didn't want to be touched no more. Didn't want no pleasure — didn't seem right.

"I think asking Brother Daryl would be fine," I said, trying to keep my mind on the conversation, thinking maybe it would distract him into church business instead of other things. But it didn't. Now he was stroking me from my waist down the curve to my hip and down to my knee.

"Marlene and Titus's boy, Kenny, is having some troubles. He got eyes for Mr. Coleman's daughter."

"What? What is he thinking?"

I felt Malachi shrug.

"He's a stupid young man." Malachi was serious but also added a little chuckle. Kenny wasn't the first and wouldn't be the last to set sights on the wrong girl. "I'm going to try to talk some sense into him."

Then a weighty pause filled the room.

"But I don't want to talk about Brother Daryl or Kenny or anybody at church right now." His words were whispered now and his mouth was just behind my ear.

I just looked at my purse full of dirt and I couldn't catch my breath with all the grief packed around my heart. My lungs were full of the burden and it all lived stuffed up in my throat. The handbag with his dirt just sat there almost like it was staring at me. I thought it was like having him with me or at least a part of him, but it wasn't. What I brought with me was a load of dead dirt.

Malachi thought he was comforting me, as if I was comforted his way. He didn't say a word and my body became like bread dough in his touch and I got no strength. He turned me over to face him, but I couldn't really see him. I just looked through him. It was like the muscles in my body didn't want to work no more.

I knew what was going to happen next and I knew it was right and it was healing for him and it was oneness. It was good. He was my husband. But I wanted to run away.

EMMA

The voice came to my ears from the other side of the pond. It was Sparrow's "hello" like the chirp of a songbird. She walked out to the dock and waved at me. I looked up from my basket of wet clothes and waved back. I looked forward to seeing her several times a week. She had become a fixture to me already and it was only June. She seemed more familiar than someone I'd met not many weeks ago.

In that same amount of time, John had yet to speak to Johnny about the drinking that Mervin had tasked each parent to handle privately in hopes of quelling it. Johnny and the other young people were not baptized so a confession would not be required. Several nights each week he would be out late. It made me nervous, but John didn't speak a word. Not to me or to our son.

His comments to Mervin about my visit

to the Evanses' had caused a greater chasm between us than ever before. He began to understand when he sipped the plain coffee I served him when we had company. Well into his too-sober, agitated state, his expression declared panic. Our stare lingered and I wanted him to know that I wouldn't help him anymore.

While our life together had divided more than ever before, we had a rhythm to our days. Upon waking, he would take a quick swig from a bottle he thought was a secret — I was always already awake. He'd dress first, then through our open windows I'd hear the outhouse door creak and slap. Then I would ready myself. We did our chores in silence with little acknowledgment of each other.

We ate our breakfast quietly and then while Johnny hitched up the buggy, John disappeared into the basement. He always took his *Bivell* with him. However, his behavior blasphemed the holy Scriptures rather than blessed them. Johnny would get the lunches I'd packed for them the night before and wait in the buggy for his *dat,* and then they would leave. For most of the day I was alone.

If it was Monday, I did laundry. Then in order of the weekdays I ironed, mended clothes, cleaned, and baked. When someone was in need, I'd take in ironing, mending, or washing. It had been the same for as long as I could remember and the same for my mother who had been raised far away from this valley. This routine was the same at most Amish homes everywhere.

After work John and Johnny would clean up. We would have a quiet dinner, prayers, evening chores, and some time to sew or crochet. John would feign Bible reading or write a letter. Johnny retreated to his room or would slip out without a word. I would hear him return later when I lay awake in my dark bedroom. This was my life. It was set out before me like blocks and bricks.

But Sparrow.

She'd become the brightness in my gray.

These thoughts passed through my mind like fog as Sparrow tried to skip rocks across the calm pond. Her efforts were in vain. She gave up and ran down the dock and then toward me. In that moment I saw my daughter. Our skin colors didn't match, I wasn't blind to that, but she was so much of what I'd always hoped for in a daughter. She was eager to learn. She had bright eyes and an eternal smile. She wanted to be around me. I think she loved me.

But instead of her hello I heard the words

she had spoken weeks earlier.

"I killed him."

It plagued me. But still the words had pulled me closer to her. Hadn't I killed a handful of children — the ones I'd refused to conceive? Maybe if we'd had a house full of children John would've changed his ways. Maybe if I'd been the right kind of wife he wouldn't despise me.

"Does your mother know you're here?" I asked every week, though it was more to clear my conscience. She answered me the same each week. That her mother just wanted her out of her hair.

We didn't talk much while we partnered to do laundry. Today I had extra loads for a family who had taken ill.

Sparrow and I worked for several hours and she was a good helper. When she used the wringer, her clothes were getting about as dried as my own. Then we hung everything out. I had never had such full lines. Walking through the rows of little-girl dresses in blues, browns, and greens pulled me away into a world that was not my own. In a moment would my little girls run through the yard with their giggles floating around them and beg for lemonade? I would always say yes. My imaginings always lived in sunshine.

"Ms. Emma?" Sparrow's voice reminded me of my reality. None of these hung dresses belonged to me. Any daughter I might have had would never be. Would their souls just linger in some in-between world? How would God's plan reconcile with my sin?

"Yes?" I replied to Sparrow.

"Why don't you got more children?"

I had considered that Sparrow was able to read my thoughts before now. Or that she at least sensed my feelings. Her sensitivity somehow understood how my mind worked. What I didn't know was if she would know when I lied.

"We need to trust God's will." I waved for her to follow me into the house.

"Does God decide who lives and dies then?"

I didn't know. "Are you thinking about your brother?"

Our eyes locked.

"Does God decide who lives and dies?"

I couldn't stop hearing the question in my head. It went from her songbird voice and changed into mine. From her asking me to me asking God. I wished I knew the answer to her question. The answer to my question. Abel died. Cain lived. Job's children died. Job lived. All of creation died. Noah and his family lived.

My baby died. I lived.

I wanted to ask her how her brother died, but I didn't. Wouldn't she tell me if she wanted me to know? But was she really to blame? Was that why Deedee wanted her out of her hair — because she blamed her for his death? If I knew how Carver had died, would I lay the blame on her also?

The house inside was as humid as the outdoors. I went to the mudroom and retrieved the lemonade from the refrigerator. My heart was in conflict. I wanted to be with Sparrow, but I didn't want to be near her questions. I didn't like what they aroused. These questions I'd pushed away, thrown out, and buried years ago. Who did I blame for the death of my daughter? John? Myself? God? I supposed I blamed all of us. My willful barrenness proved that.

"Why did God choose Carver to die instead of me? Was it to punish me because I was with — ?" She stopped talking.

I turned toward her. She stood in the doorway between the mudroom and the kitchen with her brown eyes so wide and questioning. Maybe her coming so much wasn't the best idea. My stomach was swirling now.

We walked back into the kitchen — Sparrow at my heels — and she stood close to me when I put the lemonade pitcher down and opened the cabinet for two cups. The short moments felt so long and my mind thrummed with her questions.

Yes, I believed God was punishing me. I'd done so much to be punished for.

"I don't know. But I know that God loves you." I'd never said that before. Not to my son or any person. Not to myself. Did I believe it? Of course I believed that God loved Sparrow. I wasn't as sure if He loved me, however. Didn't think He could — and I added John to that as well.

"Daddy says the same thing." She smiled at me and took the lemonade I handed her. She took a sip and when she was done swallowing, she started talking again. "Mama don't say nothing to me no more."

Still air mutes the voice of nature.
Wind without a song.
Water without breath.

"John doesn't speak to me anymore either," I wanted to say, but I didn't.

DELILAH

I was in Coleman's Grocery inspecting how our bananas had turned brown. Mr. Coleman wasn't asking much for them and banana bread did sound good — but so did a yellow banana. The white section had a good selection of bananas. I thought that Mr. Coleman's daughter and the Carter boy may be what made him care less about what was put in our section. His produce had been so good since our move.

"Banana bread?" Granny Winnie said with a wink and a giggle. She'd asked me on Sunday to help her grocery shop. Her vision was getting worse. Of course I said I'd help.

She said that Marlene couldn't come into the grocery right now because of Kenny.

"You want some tomatoes, Granny?" I pointed.

"Gimme three nice ripe ones," her little voice said.

I picked the three best ones and put them in my grocery buggy when the butcher barreled in. He was a huge man and after one visit, I was done with him. Malachi did the meat buying after that. He was tough-speaking to everyone in his store. He was not unkind, but he scared me something awful. Malachi said his name was Butch, which suited him, of course.

"Carl," Butch yelled. "Carl."

Malachi came out from the back and looked around a little. His gaze told me to be cautious and keep an eye out. Butch yelled a few more times.

Granny grabbed my hand. "That Butch? Sounds mad."

"Yeah, that's Butch."

The half a dozen women in the produce section all stopped and looked toward the booming voice.

"Butch?" Carl came from the back of the store where he had an office and seemed as confused as the rest of us.

"You better get down to the station," Butch said between deep breaths, loud enough for everyone in the market to hear.

"Did he say station?" Granny asked. "Oh no."

"Yes."

Butch started toward the door and pulled

Carl's sleeve, urging him to follow.

"They found your Shirley with that colored boy again," Butch said as he and Carl turned to leave. "They want to go find him. He ran off."

"I don't want him hurt. I just want him to leave Shirley alone," Carl said as he left.

"If they catch him, they'll hurt him," Butch said.

I kept myself from speaking or even sighing so as not to draw any attention to us. "Stuff happen like this a lot around here?"

"Now and again something starts stirring up stuff between everybody. Not often." Granny kept her hand on my arm and gripped tightly. "Last time it was something about a job at the mill, and the time before that it was because the clinic saw a black child ahead of a white woman." She shook her head. "It's always something."

She paused for a moment. "This ain't good though. And it's my great-grandson."

All the white ladies were watching me and Granny. We didn't have anything to do with this, but that didn't matter. Malachi rolled the cart over and whispered to us, "You should go."

"What? We ain't done."

"Go straight home." Malachi didn't give me a chance to say nothing and rolled his

cart off. He didn't look at the white ladies around us or even me but just did the job he was paid for.

At that moment I understood and did as I was told. Granny had her arm linked through mine, and after I put the produce back, I led her through the canned good aisle and out. As we walked to my truck, anyone who was on the sidewalks looked at us.

"Get out of town," a man snarled at us outside the diner. He used another word a moment later and my ears stung.

"Just keep walking," Granny said. "Lord loves them just like He loves us."

I got Granny in the truck and ran around the other side and locked the door as soon as I was inside. I leaned my head against the steering wheel.

"I heard that Kenny got a shine on this girl, but this all sounds a little more serious than that."

"I told Kenny many times to leave Shirley be. But he does love her and she loves him back."

"So this Shirley girl wants him back?"

Granny Winnie nodded and got a sadness in her eyes.

I wanted to judge Marlene Carter over this because she was always so high and

mighty. Now her boy would make things harder for the whole colored community in town. It wasn't right that they were after him for nothing illegal, but that wasn't no surprise. It wasn't right that her boy was bringing so much trouble to us.

When we got to the house, Granny grabbed my phone and without even asking me she told Marlene to come on over. I didn't want Marlene to come on over.

"Marlene's gonna need us now."

"Us?"

"I'm her granny and raised that girl. You her reverend's wife — yes, us."

The back door started rattling like it was going to be pounded through. Granny and I both jumped and before I got over to the door Kenny came tearing in.

"What you doing here?" I spilled out.

"Reverend said I could hide out in the basement." His eyes were wild. "Just for the night."

"Get your butt down there, boy." He listened to his granny and moved like the devil was chasing him.

"What's going on, Mama?" Mallie asked.

"Nothing," I lied. "You take the other two outside and play."

He knew I was serious and they left. I didn't know where Sparrow was, and if she wasn't upstairs in her room she was in the woods. Didn't know what she spent all her time with in there.

"Oh, Granny," Marlene said and I turn around to find her walking through my front door. Then five other ladies came in with her — none of them knocked. Whose house was this? She didn't even know that her boy was in the basement and Granny gave me a little head shake. Better Marlene didn't know. If she was asked, she wouldn't have to lie. All the ladies were sitting around her in the living room like hens. Consoling her and praising the Lord that the white men hadn't found Kenny.

"Deedee," Granny said. "What you thinking about all this?"

All the ladies stopped tittering and turned to me. A heavy silence filled up all the leftover spaces of our little house. The kind nobody liked or could lift away. I wanted to be a little mad at that old lady for putting me on the spot like that, but she was a hundred — she was allowed to say just about whatever she wanted.

"Y'all should send him away to kin someplace else — far from here. Get that girl out of his head."

A collective hum and raised eyebrows told me that many of the ladies agreed with me.

Maybe they were good ladies, even though I hadn't gotten to know them.

"I can't send my boy away for doing nothing wrong — nothing against the law." Marlene cried harder.

I lowered my chin to my chest. "Well, you gonna have to give him up one way or another as I see it. Problems like this makes it real hard for the rest of us. Or you can send him away — to an aunt or something — and he can find a nice, good colored girl to love and let him move on with his life." I said this like I got wisdom to share, but I knew better. I wasn't wise. Look at the mess with Sparrow. Maybe I could just be wise about somebody else's kids.

"But I wouldn't see him. I don't want him to move away."

"It's better'n jail — or worse," I reminded.

We all knew what *worse* meant and down south we just saw it more than maybe they did up here. Marlene didn't acknowledge anything more from me, and Granny left with her and the other ladies within an hour. But here I was left with Kenny in the basement and waiting for Malachi to come home from work. I knew how this sort of stuff went. One colored person do something white folks don't like, but all of us could pay for it at any time. Even if we got nothing to do with it.

After a few more hours went by my gaze didn't leave the window, watching for Malachi. He usually took the truck in, but because I needed it today he would have to walk home. I didn't like the idea of that. I thought about how I could go get him myself, but I got dinner cooking on the stove and in the oven. I couldn't leave.

I didn't want the children to know I was worried so I tried to act normal. Which for me, lately, was to keep my distance — even from my own kids. I realized this more as I made an effort not to let them see how agitated I was.

Of course, stuff was different down south. Nat King Cole had been attacked on his own stage in April. He was just minding his own business playing a concert. And in Montgomery if a colored boy walked in the wrong nice neighborhood, there might be police escorting him away fast. At the very least there would be strong language telling him where he could go. I got real roughed up once by some white girls when I accidentally bumped their shoulders passing them by. I never made that mistake again.

Sinking Creek was a lot smaller than Montgomery though. Maybe it wasn't as dangerous as a large city. It was in the North too. Things were safer up here and I was glad for that. But it didn't mean I wasn't worried for my husband.

The kids were watching TV — even Sparrow. Should I stop dinner cooking on the stove and go find Malachi? He should've been home by now. Then he came inside real fast like. I left the kitchen and ran over to him and threw myself into his arms. When he held me, it almost felt like old times.

"What's wrong, Dee?" He didn't try to get fresh with me like he would've in the past when we was alone but sets down a grocery bag and then just holds me tightly.

"I was so worried." I sniffed a little and realized I had a few tears rolling down my face.

"You don't need to worry, Dee. I'm careful and this ain't Montgomery."

We let go of each other but stood close.

"What about Mr. Coleman's daughter and the Carter boy? You saw how mad Mr. Coleman and Butch were. What's going to happen? And Kenny." I made my voice real quiet. "He's in the basement. Why did you tell him he could come here?"

He pressed his finger to his lips, then kissed me before he went down to the basement. He came back up a few minutes later and promised me Kenny'd be gone by morning.

"He'll have to figure this out with his parents. It'll give the local authorities some time to cool down." Then he showed me the groceries he had picked up for us and Granny, since we had to leave in a hurry. He'd gathered up what we might need.

He done good. I told him so with a smile, and then I started to cry.

"Hey, hey, hey, Dee?" He came to stand next to me and put his hand on my shoulder. "I'm all right, see?"

"It ain't that, Mal. It's this. It's us. It's like old times."

He tried to tell me that it was okay and it was good. And I knew he was right. It was the best evening we'd had since Carver, and while it felt good, I also felt like vomiting all at once. What would happen if anyone found out that Kenny was in our basement? I thought of his mother when I made him a plate of food and Malachi took it down to him. He needed to be fed. I wouldn't be able to look Marlene in the face if I didn't feed her son.

I was relieved when I woke and he was gone. The whole night before I'd dreamt of him but then he turned into Carver. I tried so hard to see his little face, but it was like I was looking through water. I tried to wipe it all away but it didn't change. I could just hear a giggle that sounded so close, but I couldn't get to him.

SPARROW

I didn't tell nobody that I dreamed of Carver — but he was dead in every one of them. I didn't tell Emma, even though I saw her a few times every week. I didn't know why she liked me. I didn't tell Johnny neither, even though we were still meeting at daybreak on Sundays. I didn't know why he showed up every time. There were six tally marks on the birch tree. Every time I went out there I expected to sit there alone. But he came every time.

"I brought some salve," he said this week after he put his hat on my head. Something he'd started doing a few weeks ago. He handed me a small circular tin.

"What is that?"

"It'll help with the blisters." He sat down close to me.

I was ashamed of myself. Every Sunday morning he would ask and I couldn't lie to him. But I couldn't stop with the nettles

300

neither. Then he'd want to see the blisters. His eyes would be sad and he'd ask me again to stop hurting myself. But I couldn't stop.

I put some of the salve on the outside of my left thigh without lifting up my skirt too high. It was from late the night before because George had started crying at bedtime, calling out for Carver. Then he ran to Mama's room and wanted to see her bag. We all knew it had Carver's dirt in it. George took handfuls of the dirt and threw it everywhere. Mama closed the purse before he got too far.

While Mama and Daddy dealt with George, I ran outside. Didn't take much to find nettles. I'd already made sure that everything around the house was pulled because I didn't want the little kids getting stung. So I went toward the woods and started pulling up patches.

"Did you hear about what happened in town?" Johnny's voice was soft and brought me back.

"You mean Kenny Carter?" It was July now and the whole Kenny situation wasn't much better.

"I don't know his name. Just know that a couple of fellas found him and beat him up."

He was beat up, all right. After a few days

they stopped looking for him and then things cooled off after a few weeks. But somebody saw him sneaking around town one night and he got jumped.

"The Carters come to our church."

"He's not in jail, at least."

"Well, he didn't do nothing against the law. But Mama said he probably should've left town. Might make it better for the rest of us."

"What's he going to do now? I heard they'll arrest him if they find him around town."

"For what?"

He shrugged.

"I think he's going south to family."

He nodded and we were both quiet.

"I wouldn't have beat him up."

I looked Johnny right in the eyes, trying to untangle his words.

"I just wanted you to know I wouldn't have hurt him."

We sat in an uncomfortable silence for a few hefty moments as his words hung there in the air between us like ornaments on a Christmas tree. If we was found together I figured I'd be the one in trouble, not him.

He finally said something. "Have you ever gone dancing?"

"Dancing?" I was confused.

"We're not allowed to dance but I've always wanted to."

I took his hat off and put it on the ground, then stood. "Come on."

When I put my arms out, he stood and took my waist and my hand and didn't hesitate none neither.

"I never went to a real dance, but Daddy used to dance with me now and then before —" I swallowed back the rest of my words and I started moving how Daddy used to, even though I didn't know what I was doing. I didn't care, and by the smile on his face, Johnny seemed to enjoy our dancing.

His hand was so warm on my hip, and our swaying back and forth was nothing special except that we was together. I didn't know when it happened, but our swaying got slower and we were much closer than Daddy and I danced. He'd dropped my hand so both of his hands were around my waist now.

"I can't stay long. Church is at our house today so I have to help set up." We were so close I could feel his breath on me.

"What do that mean? Your daddy preaching?"

He released a guttural laugh at the same time he said, "No. My dad doesn't preach. It just means that church is held at our house. Our whole district will come for church and lunch and then the Singing tonight."

"Singing?"

He looked away with a shy smile and I didn't know why — but he was still holding me close and we were still swaying just a little.

"It's for the young people. Like us. The girls and boys my age get together. We sing. Play some games. Eat pie."

I understood — it was dating for the Amish.

"Oh." I didn't know what to say. I didn't want him to sing, play, and eat pie with some white Amish girl. I cleared my throat. "Kind of like a date at church?"

He had that shy smile again and laughed it off. "I better go," he said but didn't take his hands off of me. "I wish you could come."

"Me too." I had what felt like a dopey smile on my face.

"See ya later, alligator." He still held me.

My smile grew. He knew the song too and it made me giggle.

"After 'while, crocodile," I said back in the tune of the song and it made us bounce to the beat a little.

He smiled and looked at me for a long

moment. "You're the prettiest girl I know, Sparrow." His words were raspy and my heart flopped around like a fish. He squeezed my waist and it made me wiggle and I missed his warmth when he stepped away. He bent down to pick up his hat and put it on his head, then turned to go home.

"Johnny?"

He turned and walked backward, waiting for my words.

"I'm gonna try to stop for you." I held up the salve, but I was sure he knew what I meant without that gesture.

He smiled and tipped his hat at me, then turned and jogged off. I didn't walk away until I couldn't see him anymore.

Hours later I went back in the woods. I had done my best to be as invisible as possible during church. All everybody talked about was Kenny Carter having to leave town. Lots of people was crying over it. Daddy preached how David had to flee Saul's kingdom but how he was still protected and chosen by God. Kenny's mama and sister cried the whole service. I almost felt bad for Belinda, even though she'd been so mean that first Sunday and never talked to me after that. I thought about smiling at her, but when our eyes met she clenched her jaw and looked away. I didn't try again.

During lunch I had stayed out of Mama's hair and washed the dishes without sticking my head in the water. I just didn't want to get any attention today because I wanted to slip away later. I wanted to see what an Amish Singing looked like from the woods.

Right now I was on the other side of Johnny's pond. The windows of their house were open and I could hear them singing. Similar to our singing, one person led into the song with a few words before everyone joined in. But the speed of the song was different. Their singing was slow and sounded a little sad. They held their notes for a long time and their voices were loud and strong. There were a whole bunch of voices, but it all sounded like one big voice.

I listened to a few songs and then I heard the sound of scraping and footsteps. They came out to the porch. A line of boys, then a line of girls. They were all about my age. I couldn't hear everything that was being said, and even if I could, I didn't think they'd be talking in English. Everyone was paired up and in a long line. They had their arms around one another. Some were closer than others. The long column of people came my way so I hid a little deeper. It wasn't very dark yet, being just after eight, so I had to be careful. Before the group was very close they made a turn and passed in front of the pond.

In the fading light I saw him. Johnny. He was near the front of the line. As they snaked around the yard, he tapped the shoulder of the boy in front of him and all the boys advanced forward by one girl. The boy at the front of the line went to the back. Johnny did this again until he was the one forced to the very back of the line.

When he paired with the girl in the back, he held her closer than he had the other girls. He walked slower. He didn't keep up with the rest of the long row of couples. He didn't tap the shoulder ahead of him, and when someone else did, he and the girl he was with were so far behind, they didn't change partners.

When they came around again in a wide circle, he moved closer to the pond. The sun was setting and everything was blue and purple. They were whispering. I heard her giggle. She had bright-orangey hair. I imagined she had freckles. What was her name? Probably something nice and normal instead of a dang bird.

Johnny had lied to me. I wasn't the prettiest girl he knew. This girl was.

I didn't want to burn my skin with the nettles though. I wanted — needed — more.

307

I knew where I could go and I wouldn't even have to leave the woods. As soon as I could move from my spot without being noticed, I did.

There was just enough light that when I came to Johnny's clearing where he and his friends would smoke, drink, and look at naughty pictures, I saw the glint of a tawny-brown broken glass. My relief. My salvation.

EMMA

The cicadas' song mixed with the voices of my community at the Singing. It had been a long day — which was typical when hosting church. The excitement of that first time was, however, significant for an Amish couple, suggestive of their maturity and sensibilities. Our first turn came even before we had Johnny.

And now I watched the young couples walk about the yard, pulling one another close. Johnny was well liked and favored among the young people. I fought pride in knowing that many girls found him handsome. He was so like his *dat* at sixteen when I'd fallen in love with him. I was fourteen and had to watch him from a distance, however. How I wanted to play Walk-a-Mile with the young folks and have him tap enough shoulders to get to me.

Johnny did just that as he made efforts to get to Dinah. The bright, shining daughter of the new Lancaster preacher with a name those native to the valley considered fancy. She still wore her Lancaster heart-shaped *kapp* and attracted many young boys, but she preferred Johnny. She was pretty. Her eyes were almost lost in her smiles and she was covered in freckles. No one looked like her.

I watched as Johnny and Dinah's walking slowed and soon they were far behind the rest of the group. Johnny had done this on purpose. I knew this because it was an old trick — one and the same John used when I started to attend Singings.

Then I saw movement from the woods. From my porch view, as the sun was starting to set, it looked like a girl running through the woods. Sparrow. I knew I shouldn't go. But I knew I would.

I returned to the kitchen. A few older couples sat in the living room with John. They were talking about what had happened to the young Negro man and the grocer's daughter. A situation we'd kept our ears open to for several weeks. We didn't get involved in town matters, but it seemed everyone had an opinion about it anyway. I listened for a minute. It worried the bishop to have this type of conflict in town.

"Makes everyone suspicious of everyone

else." His old voice threaded the air. "We just need to leave it be and keep to ourselves. Tell your families. This is not our fight."

Everyone agreed with him and not without fear in their eyes. He encouraged us to work among ourselves and patronize *Englisher* businesses, Negro or otherwise, as a last option. No one knew of my friendship with Sparrow and the desire I had to know Deedee. We were kind to everyone, but a real closeness should be with our own community members.

I was distracted from the conversation when I saw my husband's agitation. More than normal. The stress of the day having caught up with him, he tapped his empty coffee cup. He looked across the room at me and his jaw clenched and unclenched.

I looked away. I didn't care. But I did care. His enslavement to the drink was as strong as mine was to control my womb. If his unusual behavior made someone recognize his sin, then he deserved it.

Mervin and Lena had stayed along with several others. Lena smiled at me and started to get up, but I whisked the flashlight from the drawer and tried not to make eye contact. In a moment she sat back down.

One of the older ladies whispered something to her.

As I reached for the doorknob, I saw John stand. He said something about not feeling well. His face was pale and moist and his hair glistened even from this distance. He looked at me again and pain filled his eyes. I didn't let it affect me and lifted my chin and went out the front door.

I didn't want to draw attention to myself, so I didn't turn on the flashlight until I was in the woods. There was still a little light left, but once I entered the woods, everything was dark.

I rushed headlong through the path. I knew it well. After a minute I stopped to listen. I could hear movement and night sounds and my breathing. I shut my mouth.

"Sparrow?" I called out in a loud whisper. "Sparrow?"

I didn't hear any real words but was sure I'd heard a muffled gasp or a whisper or a cry. I didn't know. It might have been an animal.

I walked farther in. My beam of light didn't show anything out of the ordinary. I clicked off the light and stood and waited for several long minutes. Nothing but the usual rustling of nighttime in the woods.

Maybe it had just been my imagination. I

turned back and walked past the youth who were moving on to another game, but Johnny's eyes found mine. His brow furrowed and he turned in the direction of the woods where I'd come from and his stare lingered. He didn't pay mind to the older boy who was explaining the next game. He didn't notice that Dinah was smiling at him, awaiting his attentions. He just watched the woods.

By the time I went to bed, the youth had all left. Johnny wasn't home yet from driving Dinah home. Of course, this was more than a drive. She would have pie or cinnamon rolls waiting for him when he arrived at her home. Because I knew the Masts' house, I knew she would invite him to sit in a dating room.

For most families it was just the main living room. They would eat, talk, giggle, and likely kiss too much for the next few hours. I silently prayed he wouldn't expect more from her and that there would be no detour to Arnold's barn.

The bedroom was dark when I opened the door and I shielded my small kerosene lamp, not wanting to disturb John. I was careful to set it down and undress without a sound. Before I got my nightgown on I heard a rustling from the bed.

"Emma."

His raspy, weak voice jolted me, and I shimmied the nightgown over my body and rushed over to him. He was covered in sweat.

"John? *Bish du krank?*" I asked without thought, but the moment the words left my mouth, of course I knew he was not ill. He was sober.

"I tried — to go to bed — without." His breathing was rapid and he shook.

We had gone through this before, and no matter how often I despised his ways and distance from me throughout my waking hours, when he was like this, my heart filled with desperation to be that helpmeet I had married him to be.

"Vas kan ich du?" I asked what I could do. Though I knew.

"The cellar," he said a few times. "I can't. You can."

In these moments I wanted to tell him no. I wanted to tell him that we could go back and start again with our marriage, before the alcohol and before my herbs. Before all our sin and begin again.

"I'll help you." I started to cry. "We can do this together. No one needs to know."

"Emma." He called out like he was not just in pain but in agony. "I tried — almost

314

three days. You didn't even know it."

"What?"

"I tried for you." His breathing was loud and he gripped my arms. My skin squeezed between his fingers. It hurt. "I know you hate me — Johnny does too."

I shook my head and hot tears fell from my face fast. My conflicting love for him was like a weight so heavy I couldn't even see clearly. "Let's just leave this place."

"No. Go to the cellar. I can't do this. Get a bottle. Get two," he growled.

"We can — together." My throat was too filled with emotion and the yell that had scraped against it.

Even in the darkness I could almost see his eyes come to life. He pushed me away and leaned over the side of the bed and sat up with his legs hanging over the side. He lowered his head and groaned. I touched his back and it was as slick as if he'd just showered. The bed beneath him was soaked.

"Go get me a bottle, Emma." He spat his words as he grabbed the small tin trash can and retched.

There had been a time several years ago that we'd gone through something similar. Our bishop came unannounced when John was drunk. I somehow distracted the bishop from noticing and pretended to check for a fever and took John to our bedroom. The bishop seemed concerned but never questioned it. We went through the withdrawal from the alcohol for a week because of our guilt, but then John returned to his sin as a dog returned to its vomit.

My heart still grieved over that time over ten years ago. I'd told him if he took another drink, I'd know he loved the drink more than Johnny or me. I'd promised myself I'd never have another child with him. Though I'd wavered in my herbal practices before that and promised my sister I'd quit. Sometimes I did for months at a time. But it was never long enough to regain the trust I needed in my husband or God. I always returned to my deceitfulness.

Considering this as he pleaded with me to get him a bottle made me angry. Wherever that overflowing of love had come from, it was gone minutes earlier. And now I felt angry and hurt and back to those early years when I'd wished so much for him to stop drinking.

"I won't." I moved away from him.

In the dim moonlight his face was ragged and looked older than I'd ever seen. It was jarring. I couldn't even see the handsome man he used to be. Not behind his raging eyes, not tucked in somewhere between his anguish and pain.

"Please, Emma, I can't do it. Will you do this for me?"

"I won't."

I barely got my words out when he lunged for me. He pinned me to the mattress with his forearm tightly on my shoulders, the pressure almost at my throat, and was on all fours on top of me. His sweat dripped on me and I struggled to get free. He wasn't hurting me but maybe showing me that he could if he so desired.

"Stop it, John," I yelled and with no great effort pushed him away because he was weakened.

"I'll send Johnny away if you don't get a bottle."

I stopped and turned. "What?"

"I wrote to *Mem* and *Dat.*" His breathing was labored, but he still found the strength to stand to his full height. "I told them what's been going on with Johnny. *Dat* said he could fix him up fast."

"Because you can't." I spat my venom at him. "Because you're a drunk and you can't fix anything."

He still shook and was wet with sweat but had gained some leverage with me with this. "I'll do what I please." He stumbled toward the stairs. I hoped he'd stay there in the cellar to drink.

I looked over at my drawer that held my herbs and the precious words that came from the nature around me. Neither held what they used to anymore. The herbs not only had kept me from the possibility of losing another child but also had kept me from an honest marriage. And my book full of poetry lines and thoughts — I had nothing left to put in there.

How had we gotten to this place in our marriage? Our sin and destruction needled so deeply into my soul, I couldn't breathe.

John didn't acknowledge my panicked breathing when he staggered back into the room. All that mattered was the one open bottle and the two more he brought with him and how little I cared about what happened to me anymore. I wanted — needed — the pain to go away.

hat?" I stopped and huffe...
...ittle. When Sparrow didn't an...
...away, I raised my eyebrow at...
...t?"
...y bit her lip before answering m...
...elled like Uncle Thomas — but...
...he aftershave."
...ill catching my breath when I re-
...at she meant.
...ther Thomas was old and broken
...ouldn't see him for months but
...ould come around, pass out drunk
...ouch for a few days, and then be
...e children would watch him at a
...He always tried to cover up his
...ell by wearing too much after-
...didn't help like he thought it did.
...ght." Now I knew what we were
...ith and started running again.
...e close to the pond when I saw
...nning down Sparrow's leg. "You
...monthly?"
...a'am." She cleared her throat —
...ys meant she was hiding some-
...e looked back a little but then
...orward and kept running. "I fell
...and cut myself. It must have come
...t yourself falling? Where?"
..., don't worry 'bout that right now.

DELILAH

I could just about see the whites of Sparrow's round eyes from a distance when she came tearing through the haze of the woods. She was screaming. I was at the sink finishing breakfast dishes. The last time I had heard her scream like that was — well, I didn't have to say when it was. Why was she in the woods? What was she doing? Who died?

"Mama, Mama." A tug comes to my skirt and when I turned around, all I could see was Carver. I gasped. "Water?" he said.

Carver's asking for water? That don't make sense. Sparrow's screams were coming closer.

"Mama." She was yelling it by the time she flew through the screen door. "Mama, come, you gotta come."

"But Carver," I said out loud, and when I did I got hot in my face. Of course this ain't Carver. It's George. Her scream took me back. I wished she'd just leave me alone. But when I wished it was Carver, did that mean I'd rather have Carver than George? I hated myself for the mistake.

"Mama," George kept saying and yanking at my skirt. "Water."

"Mama," Sparrow interrupted. Her eyes were round, white, and wild. "It's Ms. Emma. You gotta come."

It took me a few moments to get my bearings.

"What you talking about, girl? Ms. Emma?"

Sparrow was breathing so heavy she couldn't get her words out. She came at me and yanked my arm and tried to pull me toward the door. Her fingers pinched my skin and I pulled out of her grasp and swatted at her. I missed.

"You got to come now." She broke up her words like I did when I really meant them. I looked in her eyes. She was afraid and serious. It was different from Carver though. I didn't see the guilt like before.

"Mallie," I yelled but my eyes stayed right on my daughter. The boy came running down the stairs like the devil after him. Probably used my mean voice without trying to.

"Yes, ma'am." He st[...] soldier.

I gave him strict instr[...] or in the backyard awa[...] Harriet and George. G[...] my skirt the whole tim[...] Mallie to do that first[...] seriously and I'd thr[...] braided-up switch, so I[...]

"Mama." Sparrow's [...] yelled and waved at m[...]

As I ran toward the [...] already getting a cup [...] was using a calm voice[...] even looked at Sparro[...]

When I ran my legs [...] bunch of matchsticks [...] hot and getting hotter.[...] woods, the sun wasn't[...] no more and it did c[...] wasn't until we was h[...] slowing down. My sid[...] needed to walk for a [...] was far ahead of me an[...]

"What's the matter[...] Emma need me?" I[...] breathing.

"She won't wake u[...] and she was —" Sp[...] and I tried again to ke[...]

"Sh[...] puffed[...] me rig[...] "She [...] Spar[...] "She [...] withou[...]

I wa[...] alized [...]

My [...] up. We[...] then h[...] on our[...] gone. [...] distan[...] booze [...] shave. [...]

"All [...] dealing[...]

We w[...] blood [...] got you[...]

"No, [...] that al[...] thing. [...] turned [...] yesterd[...] open." [...]

"You [...] "Man[...]

We got to get there." She waved at me to hurry up. There was only one other time I ran so fast and I took it hard to recall those memories.

When Emma's house came into view and we ran across the warm grass, I got nervous. I wasn't invited. Marlene's boy Kenny was all busted up for loving the wrong color of woman. What if I got arrested for running headlong into a white person's house? I stopped at the bottom of the porch steps.

"Sparrow, I can't," I said between deep breaths.

"Mama, you gotta." She wasn't crying but she might as well've been.

"She a white woman. This a white man's house. I can't just barge in there." I turned in a circle, thinking it over. Then I turned back to Sparrow who was still standing on the porch just looking at me. "Why you act like you know this place anyhow?"

She breathed in a few times. Looked away over top my head. Her forehead furrowed and then she looked back at me. "I been coming here every Monday and some other times ever since that day she had cake with us." She started to cry. "Ms. Emma and I do laundry and she taught me to sew. She wants to teach me how to bake and garden."

I don't know if I should laugh or cry. What

did my daughter and this woman think they was doing? Playing house with each other? I was on the other side of the woods tending to my little ones and they was over here pretending to belong to each other. So when I was getting hot and sweaty doing laundry at my house and Harriet was helping me like a good girl, Sparrow was helping another woman that weren't even her mother.

Then I thought about all them Mondays when Sparrow's meek voice had asked if I needed her help. I always told her to just go and do something. So what did I expect? I didn't want nothing to do with Sparrow ever since Carver. I hadn't given her none of myself ever since he gone. Ever since she let him die.

"Please, just come. She needs you. I don't know what to do."

My sensibilities flew somewhere out of my head and I bounded up them stairs after Sparrow and through the front door. The house was so still inside a chill went through me. Breakfast dishes were lying around. A greasy pan rested on the woodstove. Broken eggshells lay around on the countertop, their insides pooling. I just knew this couldn't be normal.

"This way." Sparrow waved for me to follow her up the wooden staircase.

They were just about the tallest open stairs I'd gone up in a long time, but the wood didn't creak none. Sparrow was up at the top in no time, springing on her toes. I took longer than she wanted, but I was tired from the run and felt spooked being in a house I wasn't invited to. What would Malachi say?

"She's in here." Sparrow waved me over to a room when I got to the top. I could see the corner of a white metal bedpost. Then she pushed open the door.

I stood in the doorway. If the room wasn't so disheveled it would've been pretty — elegant even. It was so simple and so white. The quilt on the bed had some other colors on it, but there was more white than anything. The curtains were a light blue and made the walls seem whiter. The chest of drawers and nightstands were a darker wood but they looked nice and clean. The windows were open and the curtains moved in time with the breeze. But that's where the nice stopped.

I stepped in farther. I smelled the sick inside. It did smell like my brother Thomas.

But what wasn't nice was the way Emma lay there. The sheet was only covering her from the waist down. But she was all over naked. Her breasts was bare and she had gotten sick on herself. It was in her hair and on the sheets around her.

I took the sheet and covered her. My heart was hurting because I got a bad feeling about all this. Nobody like me should be seeing a nice white lady like her lying naked in her own filth.

I looked around and all that prettiness I first saw was gone. There were empty bottles rolling around on the wood floor. The top drawer of the chest of drawers was cracked open and her undergarments were hanging out. Some type of gray-green powder was all over the place. A small glass jar open on the floor. It wasn't empty but looked like it was what the powder had been in.

I don't touch nothing though. I know better than to touch white folks' stuff.

What was going on in this house? I didn't know. And here my daughter been spending time with this woman and I think right now that she must be a drunk and have a hangover. Who did she think she was, caring for and coddling my girl when she got this kind of filth in her heart?

"Mama," Sparrow said and I was reminded that she was with me. She was standing next to Emma's bed like she wanted to touch the woman but didn't know what to do.

I walked over to where Sparrow stood and happened to kick one of the empty bottles. It clinked against the metal bed frame.

"Move over," I said and stood in front of Emma. "Ms. Emma."

I repeated her name a few times, but she didn't do nothing. Sparrow elbowed me — it said *do more.*

I let out a little groan when I exhaled. This was not a good idea. *I shouldn't be here,* I kept thinking.

I took the woman by the shoulders and shook her a little. At first she felt like a limp rag. But the second time I did I could feel her muscles under my hands coming awake. I shook her a little more and said her name again. I ain't seen a hangover like this in a long time. She got herself good and drunk.

My brother Thomas did this often enough to yell profanities at my children when they were too loud. Sparrow had asked me once if drinking would kill him. I remembered telling her, *"Maybe, if he drink enough for his fat rear end."*

I got a bad feeling about Ms. Emma. How much drink would it take to poison her good? She was so skinny. When I touched her shoulders I could feel how bony she was.

"Ms. Emma," I yelled and she made a low groan. I looked at Sparrow. I shook her harder and yelled louder.

Her eyes fluttered a little and a low, sad sound came out of her mouth again.

"Ms. Emma," Sparrow said and pushed me away. She'd started crying and I hated that that bothered me. I ain't seen Sparrow cry since Carver died and her first tears were over a white woman? That just don't sit well with me. She barely even knew this woman. "You gotta wake up. Come on, Ms. Emma."

She put her face on Emma's chest and cried. Then a few moments later Ms. Emma's hand rose and she weakly rested it on Sparrow's nappy head. Her fingers tapped a little.

Sparrow jumped up and was about two inches from Emma's face. "I knew you was in there. I knew you would hear me." She sniffed from all her crying. "I knew you ain't dead — you just couldn't be dead."

I wanted to leave the room because it just about turned my stomach to see my daughter act that way about another woman. But I knew that Emma was in trouble — with these empty bottles, the powder all over the place, and a whole houseful of secrets or lies or both. She was going to fess up today whether she liked it or not.

I pulled Sparrow up by her shoulders,

which felt meaty and strong compared to Emma's, and I took charge.

EMMA

I was walking through the woods and the sun beamed through the trees so brightly I squinted. It was a beautiful day. But then the trees went against me. They started bending down and hitting me. They whipped me around and pulled me one way and then the other. Then one tree, a big beautiful willow, grabbed my shoulders and shielded me from all the others. And it told me to wake up.

Wake up?

I didn't want to. I wanted to just walk in the forest for the rest of my life.

The willow tree kept shaking my shoulders and told me again to wake up. To open my eyes.

It was so hard though. I didn't want to.

But then I heard a sparrow singing. The bird flitted around and I wanted so much for it to stay with me. But it didn't. So I tried to reach for it and tell it not to fly away. It told me to open my eyes too. And for this little helpless bird, I would do anything.

The first thing I saw was the chocolate-colored skin of Delilah. It seemed very strange to see her and I thought I was dreaming. My eyes didn't want to stay open. I opened and shut them over and over again. Every time I opened them they stayed open a little longer. I never knew how heavy eyelids were. And my head had never hurt so bad before.

When they opened a little longer I saw Sparrow too. I inhaled deeply and looked about me. John? Was John hovering over me? And the events of the previous night came back. He'd drunk his fill before falling asleep. But I didn't want to be with myself anymore. I had lost my dignity with each swallow. I folded myself back into the bed somehow and hoped I would never wake up.

I was no longer Emma Mullet.

I was just pieces of her. Hollow. If I looked in a mirror, I wouldn't have a face anymore because I wasn't me. I was gone.

"John?" I asked and it was so hard to speak.

"Your husband ain't here, Ms. Emma," Delilah said. "Do you want me to find a way to get him? Where do he work?"

I shook my head and groaned the word *no.* I let it linger in my mouth as long as I could and it tasted like a small bite of freedom to declare outside of my own mind that I did not want my husband with me in this dark moment. There was a small bit of strength caressing my skin. My head ached though. And I was afraid if I sat up I would throw up the nothing that was left in my stomach, or maybe I'd vomit up my heart, stomach, and all the lies that I'd eaten for so many years. I wasn't alive anymore on the inside anyway.

"Sparrow came and fetched me." Delilah was talking so loudly.

I squinted, but when my eyes closed she shook me as hard as that willow tree so I opened them again. And the trees hadn't been beating me, they had been keeping me alive so I wouldn't walk too far away from myself.

"I'm going to sit you up now. You need to get up and get some air and some energy."

I groaned when she pulled me up and she said something about how I felt like an overgrown doll. I felt as empty as one.

Sparrow straightened my pillow and Delilah helped me lie back. The room started spinning. My stomach reacted and I began dry heaving. Nothing came up. I had nothing inside. Nothing left.

The trash can was put in front of me anyhow and a warm hand rubbed my back. It made me feel nice. When was the last time I'd been touched so nicely?

I began crying and pushed the trash can away, finding Delilah's chest to lean on. She shushed me like a mother and held me with the kind of care I didn't know what to do with. Was she my friend now? Because she'd seen me like this? This was when I realized that I was naked and why Delilah had made such careful tucks around my body.

I didn't know how long I cried. I had so many tears to get out. I was full of tears and sadness and guilt.

"You need something to eat." Delilah lifted me up when I seemed to be done. "Some water and something to comfort that soul of yours."

Her words were a comfort. But I had to brace myself against her tone. I knew she knew about pain. We had different pain, but sometimes pain spoke the same language. I was glad ours seemed to.

She cleaned me up and made me comfortable. And the idea that I needed help to clean up my own vomit disgusted me. It was humiliating. She helped me into my nightgown that was rolled and crumpled on the floor.

"Thank you for helping me."

Even in Delilah's careful helping, she couldn't let her gaze land on mine. She didn't want to see my shame. Her kindness moved me. But I stiffened when she released a deep exhale with a smile that looked forced. I knew all about forced smiles.

"I ain't done yet, Ms. Emma, so hold on to your thank-you. You might not like me so much in a few hours."

She made me get up and she and Sparrow helped me downstairs. They helped me into the outhouse, but I couldn't go. Then she wanted to make me some food. I watched her work in my kitchen and while she did, Sparrow cleaned it up. John and Johnny had left a mess and I wondered what my husband had told my son about my absence from our morning routine.

Sparrow and Delilah worked together in the kitchen like a real mother and daughter. Without many words they knew what the other needed or wanted done.

I just sat at the table wondering how this had become my life. And how with all the community of people I was surrounded by, none of them knew me the way these two did. In part because I had hidden my truth

334

but also because I knew that the ugly parts of my life were unacceptable to talk about unless I was ready to be put in the *ban.* This would fall on both John and me. I knew that. I had my own hand in everything.

Delilah put a plate in front of me. Just one scrambled egg, sliced tomatoes, and some coffee. "Eat." She didn't give me any room to refuse. So I ate. The coffee tasted good and hot and filled another hollow space in myself. The egg made my stomach turn in circles after a few bites. I didn't eat the tomato.

Delilah was sweeping the floor when she took a step closer to me and focused right on my eyes. "Don't you retch on me, Emma. Take yourself a few breaths and tell yourself you ain't going to do that."

I listened to her and it worked. I kept my food down.

Next, with a little direction she made Sparrow get a bath ready for me. She asked me if she could help me with my nightgown. I said I could handle it. That simple act gave me back a small slice of dignity. Delilah took down my hair and washed it and let me wash my body. Sparrow was told to go out and start the laundry. She knew how.

"You fixin' to tell me what happened now, Ms. Emma?" Her hands worked over the soap in my hair.

I wasn't sure I'd felt anything so good before, but I was conflicted over whether it was her strong fingers massaging my scalp or the tenderness it took to wash another person's hair.

"Emma. Please, call me Emma."

"All right, you gonna tell me what happened, *Emma*?"

"Why is Sparrow the way she is?" My hands fisted, holding on to the truth about the lies I lived.

I heard a heavy sigh behind me.

"It's a long story," she said, but it was a sad voice and I understood.

No one liked to talk about why we wanted to walk away from our lives. No one wanted to talk about why we drew invisible lines around our hearts and expected everyone to stay far away.

She rinsed my hair and in a few minutes I was out of the bath and she helped me pin myself into a clean dress. My hands were weak and shaky.

"This is some kind of dress," she said with a lifted eyebrow. "Don't know how you don't draw blood every time."

"But you just did it — and there's no blood." And I offered a smile.

She poured us both some coffee and put

the mugs on the table. Then she checked on Sparrow and returned to the table.

"Don't know what you done to that girl, but she's washing like she know what she doing."

"She's a good girl," I said without realizing how it must sound. "I mean, she wanted to learn, so I taught her."

We sat in silence for a few minutes.

"I caught something from a church friend and it made me sick." I took a sip of my coffee.

"Is that right? You got the influenza?"

I nodded in agreement.

"That must've been a bad one because I ain't known nobody who can't even wake up without being about shook to death. Huh?" Delilah pursed her lips at me. I looked away.

Another minute passed. I thought I heard footsteps on the porch and was thinking how wonderful it would be to have Sparrow here. She would relieve this tension.

"So your husband's a drunk, ain't he? And you drank yourself silly 'cause you think it'll take some of the hurt away." Delilah didn't say the words sweetly or whisper them but just spoke them out.

I never said anything louder than a whisper; I was afraid of true words. But she didn't live by my ways.

I shook my head. She had gotten some of it correct, but not all of it. She didn't know about my herbs that kept me from getting pregnant all these years. Last night he hadn't forced me to drink. I drank because I couldn't stand being around myself anymore. I wanted the stupor that my husband had to forget the pain and the guilt.

"Emma, you ain't gonna lie to me." Delilah wagged her finger at me. "Don't your church preach against lying to your friends?"

"Are you my friend, Delilah?" I asked it so fast after she spoke that I knew the shock in her face was real.

She paused for a moment. I knew what I wanted her to say.

"Yes, Emma, I 'spect I am." Her jaw quivered and I didn't know why. "So you better call me Deedee. All my friends do."

"Okay, *Deedee.*" I paused for a moment, adjusting how I sat, the snake of burden wrapping tighter around me. And it hissed at me as I tried to loosen the burden by talking to Deedee.

"I lost a baby girl over thirteen years ago," I started and Deedee cleared her throat and blinked quickly. I told her how no one knew I was expecting because no one talked about such things. You just waited until it was obvious. "Then one day, my body just let her go."

I looked out the window and bit my lip when a warm tear trailed down my face. I didn't want to talk about this. Deedee wiped her face and sniffed. She was crying too.

"Besides John and my sister, no one knew." My voice faltered but I continued. "And even though I never knew my daughter, I couldn't forget her and I couldn't move past the pain. So I started taking herbs to close my womb — I never wanted to feel this pain again." I paused and swallowed hard. "And the worst part about all of this is that I've been lying to John for all these years. He has no idea why we have no other children."

I told her about the alcohol too.

I also told her how I aided John when we had company because I didn't want the church to learn of our sins. She wasn't shocked. I had just laid out for her all the reasons she shouldn't be my friend and why I was a terrible person. But she stayed quiet and just sipped her coffee and looked at me like I was her equal. I hadn't felt that for a long time. I may have never felt that way.

I told her about the night before. How he'd tried to stop drinking for a few days but couldn't. How he brought three bottles to our bedroom. How he hadn't drunk much but I had because I hated myself so much. I drank more than I ever had before. So much that I thought I would die. So much that I prayed I would.

SPARROW

I was soaked with water when I went to the house for a towel. But when I heard Mama asking about Ms. Emma's husband, I decided to just listen instead. Mama's voice was so loud it carried well. But when Ms. Emma spoke I had to get real close to the closest window so I could hear. It was open and a breeze made the curtain inside press toward the screen.

I wouldn't be able to catch it all. But I heard things like deacon, drunk, and that she lost a baby. Johnny had been right, then. She didn't cry, but sometimes she was quiet and I wasn't sure what was going on. But then I heard Mama again.

"What does your mama say?" Mama questioned.

"My mother?" Emma's voice was a little louder, like she was shocked. "She died several years ago, but I never would have told her anyway."

"Why?"

I could almost hear Emma laugh in that way people do when something wasn't funny. I could hear her say something about how they didn't talk about that sort of stuff in their church.

"That ain't your church, it's your mama," Mama corrected.

"Same thing to us."

"Then I'm going to tell you what I think, Emma. And you might not like it."

There was silence for a few moments.

"You got to either tell him it's enough or you're going to tell the church on him and they can do whatever you was talking about. The business with the shunning." I imagined Mama's eyes getting big and round and serious. "Will he beat you if you tell the church?"

"I can't do that, and no, he won't hurt me."

I heard a chair scrape. I suspected it was Mama getting up because I knew better. If she dished out some advice and the other person ain't interested — she wouldn't waste her time. I ran for it and got back over to the laundry. Then I heard wheels rolling over gravel into the drive. I peeked around the side of the house and saw one of them Amish buggies — that was what

Emma called them.

Would it seem like Emma got hired help? In Montgomery a whole bunch of white folks hired coloreds as domestics. But that's not what we were here. We were friends and we came to help. I didn't know if I should wave or just keep doing the laundry or run away. Should I call Mama to come real fast?

But instead I just stood there and said nothing. I held on to the wet white sheets that had been on Ms. Emma's bed just an hour ago all filthy with sick. And I knew I got to wash it clean for her. I wanted to help her because she helped me.

The wet sheet dripped everywhere and added to the puddle on the ground. It dripped between my bare toes 'cause I knew better than to wear my shoes. My toes wiggled on the wet concrete slab and the water splashed the top of my foot.

The water. The water always found me when things went wrong, like now. It wasn't just because of Ms. Emma being sick — or something like that — but the feeling I got about visitors coming made my stomach hurt.

Two women got out of the buggy. The one woman was large and reminded me of Mama's mama. But this woman's face was softer. The other woman's face looked like she could henpeck you. They both wore the same kind of dresses that Ms. Emma wore. And even in the warmth they had on their large dark bonnets.

They looked over at me and I looked back at the sheet in my hands. They didn't move from where they stood. They just stared at me. I moved my hands and pushed the white sheet through the wringer and held my hand out the back to hold it carefully. Still they watched. When the sheet was all the way through their eyes were still on me.

I didn't like the way it felt, and when my gaze found theirs they jumped a little, like I'd said *boo.* If I wasn't so nervous I would've laughed. I didn't know what else to do so I said, "Hi." They smiled and said it back. Okay, now what?

They made the next move and they left me and walked up the porch steps. They was gonna walk into the door and see Mama and Ms. Emma sitting there talking stuff about her husband and what she done to herself. That's when I decided to do what I done.

When I started screaming it wasn't because it hurt as bad as what Ms. Emma had said it would. It was because I needed to make it sound like it do so everything that was happening stopped and something else would happen. Besides, there wasn't much that hurt me no more. Not the stinging nettles or the blisters that came after. Not the broken glass that cut up the back of my leg that had opened up when I started running. And not sticking my fingers in a wringer washer.

My yelling brought them Amish biddies running and then the door flew open and Mama came running. Ms. Emma wasn't running but she was coming too. Everybody looked at everybody else with this surprised expression on their faces. 'Course, nobody knew what was going on. All at once they was asking what happened and was I all right. Imagine that, white people — strangers — worried about a colored girl like me. But I saw in their eyes that they were.

That's when I pulled my fingers out real hard and fast. Don't know how I done that either because they were so tight in there. It hurt a little more than I thought it would then and I see that my left hand was all eaten up from my fingertips to the middle of my hand.

"Sparrow." Mama yelled it like she used to. I ain't heard my name in Mama's mouth much. "What you done, Sparrow? What you done?"

She took my wrist and we was both shaking so bad blood was dripping everywhere. I was afraid she'd shake my hand right off my wrist. She just kept repeating, "What you done?" over and over. She did that when she got nervous — repeated herself.

I remembered what she said that day with Carver. *"I know you got a breath. I know you got a breath in there, baby."* He didn't. There wasn't no blood that time though.

Ms. Emma was just now at the bottom of the stairs and then it was like them old ladies knew it was up to them. The big fat one came running at me. On the way she grabbed a white towel I hadn't washed yet.

I couldn't understand what they said but the two ladies pushed Mama back and started wrapping my hand. Tight. It was so tight I just about thought I would lose my breath. They kept saying words in their language and were gentle even though they worked fast. The fat one did most of the wrapping and the pointy one held my hand still at the wrist and put her other hand on my shoulder. She even patted me a few times. The washing machine motor turned off and I think it was Emma who done that. Everything seemed so quiet after that.

"Emma," the big one said and added a bunch of other words I didn't know.

Emma looked at me. She looked a little

stronger than before but reminded me of a branch of a willow tree. She might just fly away if the wind picked up and bent and turned like she just a little bit more than nothing.

"Bring her inside," Emma said in English. "I have a Sam's salve that will help."

Then everyone spoke English after that.

We all walked inside and the Amish ladies walked on either side of me. One held my hand up and the other had her hand on my arm on the other side. I wasn't hurting all that bad but they were so nice and meant well — I didn't want to turn down their friendliness. Mama was somewhere behind me. I imagined her face in my mind — pursed lips and raised eyebrows like she got a mouthful to tell me.

When we got inside I saw that Mama hadn't poured out the water from the tub yet. A wet towel hung near a window to dry but otherwise the kitchen looked nice and tidy. Maybe those old ladies wouldn't think so much about it. Either way I'd given Ms. Emma and Mama some warning. I knew it wasn't every day Emma got two colored folks at her house when she was supposed to be doing laundry.

Emma went to a cabinet and pulled out the salve. It was close to empty and I knew why. It was the same salve that Johnny had given me for my blisters.

"I thought I had more," she said and came over to me, "but I think there's enough."

While they unwrapped the cloth and put salve on my wounds, Mama just stood there. When I winced for real she even touched my arm. I wondered if I lopped my whole hand off next if Mama might hug me. Maybe she had a little left for me inside of herself. What would she think about the cut I gave myself on my leg? It wasn't bleeding just now but I could feel it as I sat on that wooden chair. I didn't want her care over me to go away, so I winced again even when it wasn't so real.

Her hand squeezed my shoulder, like she was giving me her courage.

Did I have my mama back?

Delilah

Those Amish ladies with their big black bonnets were something else. I watched them care for Sparrow and just let it happen. I didn't know why. I should have cut in and taken care of my girl myself. It wasn't like I didn't know how. But I just trying to get used to the idea that I cared about what happened. When she screamed like that it didn't make me think about Carver or nothing like that. It just made me think about what was happening to my daughter. But it had been a long time since I cared for her like that and watching them ladies bandage her up was enough for me just then.

I've seen worse wounds, but I think the way it happened scared the girl more than anything. She'd never been a real tough girl even when she was young. When I touched her shoulder I thought about how it was the first time I touched her in a nice way in a real long time. I done a lot of slapping in the weeks after Carver. I squeezed her shoulder when his name come to my mind again. Like my hand winced.

Made me think about the pain that my baby was in when he died. How afraid he would've been. It was a whole lot worse than scraped fingers. I gave her a pat on her shoulder one last time, kind of like saying *you okay now,* and took my hand off her shoulder and crossed my arms in front of my chest. I gave what I could.

"Now, how does that feel?" the fat lady asked Sparrow as she and the other lady untied their black bonnets and set them down. Shame on me for calling her fat. I knew I might be bigger than that someday if I don't stop eating like I was a month into grieving.

"It feel all right now," Sparrow's little bit voice said. "Thank you."

The other lady, she looked kind of like a woodpecker if I was being honest, patted her arm again but didn't say nothing. She did give up a nice smile though. They looked at Emma who was sitting down at the end of the table with her hand hugged around her coffee. More like she was gripping it. She don't look good and it wasn't just because she was still pale and tired.

"*Nah,* Emma," the big one said and

slipped into their language.

Emma's eyes flashed to me and then back to the woman who was speaking. She interrupted the long stream of words.

"Betty, this is my neighbor Delilah." She gestured toward me.

"Delilah?" The thin, quiet one spoke for the first time. She spoke to Emma and even though I didn't understand a lick of their language, I knew she said something about what manner of person has the name of the biggest hussy in all the Bible. When Emma didn't respond she turned back to me. "I'm Joyce Yoder." She extended her hand out to me and I was surprised by her grip.

"We're sisters," Joyce said. "This is Betty."

Betty reached her hand out also. Her grip was also quick and firm.

"Neighbors?" Betty asked Emma.

Emma gestured with her head. "On the other side of the woods."

The sisters looked at each other. Their eyes were wide and it was like they was reading each other's minds. I could see Emma trying to find the right words, the right story, the right excuse about why we were here. I got this feeling, though, that it wasn't because I was a colored woman but it was because I wasn't Amish. Maybe both.

"We should finish that laundry for you,

Ms. Emma," I said and poked Sparrow. I added that *Mizz* back to try to show that I was respectful. "You just have a nice visit with your friends."

"*Ms.* Emma?" Betty said and laughed. "Now that does sound fancy."

"My girl here heard that *Emma* was under the weather and we had a mind to help her out." I tried to find the right words to help Emma.

"She heard?" Joyce looked confused. "How?"

There was a short pause before anyone answered. I didn't know how she'd heard. Why had I said it like that?

"Sparrow helps me with laundry sometimes on Mondays." Emma spoke but she didn't meet anyone's eyes. "Deedee is kind enough to lend her daughter to me. When she came, she saw I was sick and asked her mother to come help."

"Now, that is a good neighbor," Joyce said. "But why don't you ask one of Martin's girls? There are so many of them."

Emma cleared her throat.

" 'Cause Ms. Emma know'd I like to do laundry," Sparrow said with her small voice and peeked at me from the tops of her eyes.

The two old Amish ladies giggled again and repeated the *Mizz* part. I don't know why they found that so funny.

"Our way of life must seem so strange to you *Englishers,*" Betty said.

"Would you like some coffee?" Emma changed the subject.

As they agreed and Emma's feeble body went for mugs and coffee, I pulled Sparrow's sleeve and we slipped out the door. I let out the breath I was holding when we get outside. My lungs empty of all that nervousness and by the time I get down the porch steps I caught the giggles.

"What you laughing about, Mama?" Sparrow looked at me funny.

"Those ladies." I yanked her sleeve again toward the basement. I try to stifle my laughter.

"I thought they was nice."

" 'Course they are, but did you see how their eyeballs just about fell out of their heads when they heard our names and that you was helping *Mizz* Emma with the laundry?" My laughter started to slow down and I don't remember the last time I laughed so hard. It was a long time ago.

"Mama, you laughing."

It was sad that as soon as she said that I felt like a balloon that had just got popped and all the air was out of it. All my giggles just flew out of me somewhere and it was like they had never even been there.

We finished the laundry and when we left just before lunch the two ladies was still inside with Emma. I didn't want to make nothing of it, but my heart hurt a little for the woman I'd called friend. I figured only time would tell if we were friends like she want. But she was in a bad way with her husband and with her life of secrets.

EMMA

I watched Sparrow and Deedee's slow walk part the grass behind the house and wished they were the ones who remained with me.

"Now, how did you meet *sellah frau*?" I supposed *that lady* meant Deedee. I turned to face Joyce, and by the looks of her eyes, she wanted the whole story.

"We met in our woods when I was out walking." I decided to keep it as simple as possible.

"They were in your woods?" Joyce scrunched her lips together and made her whole face appear beak-like.

"You know John and I don't care about that, unless it's hunting season."

They let that part go. I was glad they didn't realize that there was no way for Deedee to know that we were so lenient about our property being walked by our neighbors.

"And you just started talking to them?"

Betty asked. "Weren't you scared to meet up with strangers in your woods?"

"Scared?" I questioned. "Why? She has children and a husband — who's a preacher. They are not so different from us as you might think."

Betty and Joyce looked at each other with raised eyebrows.

"I don't know as I really care so much that they are Negro," Betty said. "I just think they do things different than us. Just better to abide by the bishop's words to keep more separate from them and from all *Englishers.*"

"With all the problems that Negro boy was causing in town, I agree," Joyce piped up. "I heard he was following that girl around everywhere. The family couldn't get a moment's peace. That would unnerve me if I was the girl's *mem.*"

All the words. The emotions. The fear. I wanted to run up to my room and hide. I didn't know how to respond and I knew little about the current situation but had a feeling we weren't getting the whole story. We'd never much concerned ourselves over the way the rest of the country was bothered by the color of people. We just kept to ourselves. Did I think that people should be judged that way? No. But with that, I'd always been taught that it wasn't my concern. I suppose I'd believed my whole life that I was just to mind my own business — until George. I realized that no matter the color, I would've helped him. Just as Joyce and Betty had helped Sparrow, I supposed. They hadn't hesitated to help, but their understanding of the Negro community was questionable, as was mine. The fear everyone had about one another was what struck me the most.

When they left I fell on the couch and didn't wake up until I heard a knock at the door. It wasn't a loud knock, but everything else was so still it woke me. My head felt better by measures and my body was less achy.

I walked to the door and could hear Deedee's voice calling my name like she was still worried about me. I opened the door and saw her standing there with all my clean clothes from the line in my basket.

"Well, I can see you're feeling a mite better." Her voice was in that same rich, loud manner, but there was a little bit of a smile behind it. "I'm glad to see it."

"Yes. Me too," I said and looked over her shoulder.

"Sparrow's at home with the kids. I think we plum tuckered her out this morning anyway." She raised her eyebrows. "Can I come in?"

I opened the door wider and watched as she walked in and headed for the couch. She put the laundry basket down and grabbed the top piece. A pillowcase. She snapped it about as good as any Amish lady I'd ever seen.

"You gonna help or just stand there?"

I'd never met a woman like Deedee before. She was named after a villain in the Bible. One of the worst kinds of women. A liar. A loose woman. Someone you couldn't trust. But she wasn't a villain to me. She was my friend and seemed like my only friend.

I made sure Deedee was gone at least an hour before I expected John to return. In that time I put the smallest details in the house to rights. I didn't want there to be any question as to how I'd spent my day.

Johnny came in first and put his hat on the hook before he looked at me. He looked at the counters and then at me. His gaze lingered and it was almost as if I could see the words travel from his mind to his mouth.

"Bish bessah?" I wasn't sure how to take him asking me if I was better. Of course John probably told him this morning that I was sick. But I also had a notion that Johnny knew more than I had been realizing. His

father and I were not the only ones with secrets in this house.

I gave him a short nod.

He said he was glad, but the room was filled with the anticipation of the words that were inside the pouch of his cheek and remained unspoken.

"I hope you don't get sick like that again." He stuttered his words a bit but he looked at me the whole time.

"*Ja.*" I agreed but couldn't hold his gaze. I knew what I'd done. What would my son think of me if he knew I'd prayed for death the night before? Death would leave him motherless. Maybe he was already motherless since I was little more than a shell anyway.

When footsteps came up the porch, Johnny's eyes and mine made quick contact before he went to wash up. My insides turned and flopped. What I saw in Johnny brought something all the way up from my toes that I could feel at the top of my scalp. Was it the courage to be more? I never again wanted to wish to be dead.

John came in and looked around in the same way Johnny had. I knew by his expression that he'd expected to see something else. What else though? Did he think I'd be dead when he came home and the house would be in the same state of chaos as it was when he left that morning? Or did he expect me to pretend nothing was wrong and to give him a clean house? I didn't know.

"Surprised?"

"Vas meansch?"

"You know what I mean, John," I spat at him. "Last night."

"Don't blame it on me. I saw this morning that you drank more than I did. I didn't make you do that." He put his hands up in defense of himself. "Looks like you're the one with the problem, not me."

"I wanted to die. Our lives are a lie. And now you're threatening to send Johnny away." I walked closer to him. "I'm telling you now and you'd better hear me — I'm never going to help you cover up your drunkenness again. If you don't —"

"If I don't what?" He challenged me but his eyes darted erratically. He was afraid.

"If you don't stop, I'll tell the bishop everything."

He laughed at me.

"This is all just because you're ashamed of yourself. You're the one who was drunk far into the morning. You drank yourself sick. You're embarrassed and you want to take me down with you." He spoke everything in a loud whisper. He got closer to me and I was surprised at the anger in his face. "You couldn't have killed yourself with what you drank but you're not smart enough to know that. You just gave yourself a bad morning. Do you really want to get shunned? You want to embarrass Johnny? You want to ruin his life?"

"The church can punish me all they want, John." I matched his whisper but with more passion in my words than he was accustomed to. "It's better than living with guilt."

His face winced. My threat worried him. He didn't even know all the guilt I lived with.

"Things will get better, I promise." His chastising had changed to pleading.

I wanted to believe him, but I didn't. But I didn't know if I could be brave enough to follow through with my threats. What would happen if anyone found out that John wasn't the deacon he claimed to be? I didn't know. Once you were voted in as a deacon, only death separated you from the position. Being exposed would crush our marriage and our son. His parents would be in despair. And wouldn't it be contradictory to the church? For their own deacon to be a man of sin instead of a man to follow after?

"I won't help you again — no matter how

bad it gets for you." The gravel in my throat came out in the rasp of my words. *"Hausch mich?"*

My asking him if he'd heard me was maybe going too far. He grabbed my fore-arms, and even though I knew he didn't want to hurt me, it did hurt.

"You can't tell anyone." His words smelled like drink and sweat coming through his teeth. *"Hausch mich?"*

I didn't see it coming but we were almost knocked off our feet when Johnny pulled his *dat*'s hands off of me. Johnny pushed John's chest, making him fall hard against the door, busting open the screen. Johnny stood between us and faced his dad with clenched hands.

"Don't you ever put a hand on her again," he yelled.

SPARROW

When Mama asked me to go to Coleman's Grocery for Granny Winnie, I wished it would start pouring down rain so I wouldn't have to go. She never sent me out on errands, well, not since Carver. There hadn't been any errands that day, but she sent me off as the responsible one. I looked at Mama like she was growing a third eye when she asked me today.

She even said, "Why you looking at me like that?"

"What if there's trouble?" My panic swelled and I wasn't sure I could do what she wanted.

"You going to make trouble?" She raised an eyebrow.

"No, ma'am."

That had been the problem before. I had made trouble.

"If you don't make trouble, then there won't be trouble."

I knew she said it in hopes of believing it herself. There were all sorts of colored folks who didn't make trouble but had a whole lot of it anyhow. That boy Kenny hadn't done no wrong, but now he was still hiding away ready to move south.

But that girl he loved, she didn't hide nowhere but was gonna go east to beauty school in the fall. New York or something. Imagine that. Beauty school. Was that where you learned how to be beautiful? Wasn't she beautiful enough?

"Daddy's there. He'll keep an eye out."

Granny hadn't been feeling good and she always made chicken cabbage soup when she felt bad. I had to go get the stuff she needed and then walk it to her. Then I had to walk all the way home.

I knew the way all right, but I ain't never had to walk that far away from home alone since we moved up north. Even in Montgomery I didn't have to go far. Everything I walked to was close by enough and I was never alone. We neighborhood kids always did everything together when we wasn't in school. Just like that Saturday when Mama had sent George and Carver with me and my friends to get them out of her hair. I didn't want to have them with me because it would be harder for me to flirt and carry on with J. D. And then I lost Carver and he died.

I grabbed the list and the small zipped pocket Mama gave me with the money in it. She said that Granny would pay me back when I got to her house. I was to put the money pouch deep in my pocket and not mess with it. I did just like she said and as I walked the heaviness of the coins would bump the side of my leg. It was close to the cut I'd made but not right on it.

I hadn't hurt myself since I stuck my hand in the wringer and that was over a week ago. Maybe I was all better now because Mama had touched me nice. Or because Mama and Ms. Emma was talking like they was friends. We got to see her a couple of times this week even.

Maybe I didn't need to hurt myself no more. Maybe there was other things that would help me. Just thinking about it though made the scab on my thigh itch something awful. But my fingers were mostly healed up now. All my nerves about going into town started making me feel like I was fighting a battle. If I gave myself just a little cut, it would help me not feel so nervous. And what if Johnny found out I hurt myself after I told him I wouldn't no more? What would Mama and Ms. Emma think if they ever found out? They couldn't — so I couldn't.

I passed by the white neighborhoods and just walked like I knew where I was going and I wasn't gonna make no trouble. I didn't walk too fast, might seem like I was running away from something bad I done. I didn't walk too slow because it might look like I was snooping. I just paced my walking by singing a song in my head.

If I walked to the rhythm of "Swing Low, Sweet Chariot" it was just about right. Felt a little awkward to measure my steps, but I did it anyway and made sure I didn't step on no sidewalk cracks. Didn't want nothing bad to happen.

On Main Street the bright-pink sign that said Soda Shoppe was just about waving at me to come on over but I don't. A few people sat at their outside tables licking up the dripping cones. They was bouncing their shoulders and heads to the music. It was a song that was new just before Carver died and I found myself saying it in my mind. *"See you later, alligator . . . after 'while, crocodile."* But when I moved my body just a little I thought about Johnny and got warm all over. I stopped and started back on my "Swing Low" song in my head.

Mr. Coleman was standing outside the

grocery, like other shop owners. Sometimes they would come out to have a cigarette or to yell a conversation across the street or just to stand in the sun for a few minutes. Mr. Coleman didn't pay me no mind at first until he threw down his cigarette to extinguish it and it hit my shoe.

"Sorry about that . . ." He lengthened his last word as if seeking my name.

"Sparrow."

"Sparrow, yes." He had this half smile. He looked around me. "You're here alone?"

I just nodded.

He nodded in return but he didn't look too happy about it. But he opened the door for me anyhow. "Let me know if you need anything, Sparrow."

I waited for a tiny little second before I dashed through the door. When I got inside I was glad that almost nobody was there. My coin pouch hit against me again because of my fast, big steps. The money was still there, so was my scab near it. That cut was never so far away from my mind. Knowing I could do it again if I needed to. To help me.

I grabbed a buggy and put all four things on Granny's list inside and, like a lady, walked up and paid for them. The cashier never even looked at me. I was hoping he would so's I could show what a nice girl I was.

"Sparrow girl." Daddy's voice came up from behind me. I'd been so wrapped up with acting grown that I'd forgotten to look for him. "Well, lookie here, my girl is just like her mama."

He smiled and I tried to smile back but felt embarrassed for acting like Mama when he was watching and I didn't know it.

He reminded me where Granny lived and how to hold the paper bag so it wouldn't rip open. He watched me all the way down the sidewalk 'til I had to turn the corner toward Granny's neighborhood. Then we waved at each other.

The houses got smaller and a little run-down the closer I got to Granny's. Long and narrow type of houses — a lot like Montgomery. Like all us folks had to live the same way. But still, they was nothing like the run-down houses in Montgomery but sure wasn't as nice as the white ones. There was the railroad tracks that cut between the neighborhoods, and that seemed to be the way towns and white folks liked things. But it all don't mean much to me. Saw worse in Montgomery.

Granny's house was a chipped-up yellow. She called for me to come inside before I even knocked.

She was sitting on the couch and looked smaller than ever. Her skin was saggy and reminded me of a rubber band that had stretched too far for too long. The house was clean and smelled nice and the furniture was nice — even though it was old.

Granny told me to put the food away and pointed to the fridge. I found another four heads of cabbage and four bunches of carrots and celery inside. She had all the stuff in there. Why did she need more? I opened the bread box and there wasn't no room for the bread I bought.

"Granny, you got lots of —"

"Money's on the counter, Miss Sparrow." I saw right away that it was the exact amount I'd spent. Down to the penny. I put the money in my little pouch, then back into my pocket.

"What do you think about being called Sparrow?" The old woman's voice was almost breathless.

"Don't know." Of course I hated it.

"You know the Bible talks about sparrows."

"Sure."

"It's like the most measly little scrimpy offering someone can bring to the Lord."

I just looked at the old lady, and when she

patted the spot next to her for me to sit, I did.

"Only the poor people offered sparrows. You understand."

I nodded.

"But you know what's so nice about that?" She smiled.

I shrugged.

"It just showed how God cares big for even the littlest, tiniest, scant thing like a sparrow." She patted my hand and leaned her head back and closed her eyes. "I'm going to take a nap now. Would you wait here with me for a few minutes and then you can go on home?"

"All right."

"Straight home, mind you." She opened an eye to look at me.

I smiled. "Straight home, yes, ma'am."

"Home," she whispered and fell asleep.

By the next Sunday Granny Winnie was just 'bout dead. While she was lying in her bed with family around her, I was waiting for Johnny to meet me in the woods. Just like every week I didn't know if he would come, but he always did. Anytime he might realize *who* he was meeting. A colored girl. A liar. A killer. Wasn't that who I was? But he knew all of it and still came.

But I couldn't stop thinking about him

with that red-haired girl. She got that kind of look to her that would make just about any boy's head turn. Maybe even colored boys. I was sure that Johnny would kiss a girl like that too. I was jealous.

"Didn't think you'd come today," I said.

He furrowed his brow at me and sat down real close. He put his hat on my head.

"Why? I always come." He hung his arms over his knees, and when he turned to me his face was close to mine. So close that I could smell his soap.

I looked over at him and then looked back at the stream and threw another little rock. It made me nervous to have him so close even though I liked it.

"What's the matter?" he asked while he made another tally mark on the tree.

This sort of stuff was too hard to figure out. I didn't have my friend Mira with me to ask her what you was supposed to say to a boy. But even Mira wouldn't know because Johnny was white and none of us talked to white boys in Montgomery.

When he was done making the mark on the tree, he sat even closer than usual — and pushed me a little with his shoulder, teasing.

"What happened with your hand?"

"Didn't your mama tell you?"

"Why would she?"

"I hurt it on your washer. You know, she wasn't feeling so good on Monday. She was retching and —" I shouldn't have said nothing to him. Ms. Emma wouldn't want her husband and son to know that we were the ones who found her. And I didn't have to be told that it was because she had been drunk and was sleeping off her stupor.

"You were doing our laundry?"

"I was just helping your mama." I couldn't think of how not to answer him now. "She wasn't well."

"Did she say that?" His voice got a little louder.

"What do you mean?"

"Did she tell you she was sick, or how did you know?"

"What does it matter?"

"It does." He was so insistent.

"I came over like I do on Mondays to help with the laundry and saw she had got sick all over her bed." Why had I opened my big mouth?

"Why did you come into my house?" He stood and was almost yelling.

"I got worried when she wasn't doing the laundry." My voice was getting high and squeaky and I couldn't control it. Hot tears felt ready to burst out of my eyes. I stood and faced him. "I was just fixin' to help her but she weren't there."

"You shouldn't just walk into someone's house." The leaves just about rustled from his yell.

"And you shouldn't lie to people," I yelled back, then took his hat off and tossed it on the ground.

"Lie?" His brow furrowed up.

"I saw you with that girl." I started crying. "I came back. I wanted to see what a Singing was. Looks like all it means is that you get to go tell another girl about how pretty she is."

I tried to control my tears but couldn't. When I cried everything hurt. I didn't have any fresh wounds because I'd had a good week with Mama. But the cut hadn't healed on my leg and it just burned like a cigarette sizzling on it. It was like I could feel the skin on my fingers being pulled off little by little. Why do tears hurt so bad?

"Dinah?"

I didn't want to know her name because hating someone you didn't know was easier. Now that I knew her name it made her real. Dinah. That was prettier than Sparrow. She was prettier. She was white like him.

"What do you expect? I can't date anyone outside my church." He spat the words at me. "Can you?"

I hadn't thought about it that way. I shook my head.

There was a heavy silence for what seemed like half the morning, but it was probably for just half a minute. Then he came closer to me by one step.

"You gonna see her today?" My voice sounded like one of them gnats that would wheeze in your ear. I hated my voice.

He shook his head. "We don't have church today — just every other week." He paused for a moment. "I didn't mean to yell about coming to the house." He looked at me and then looked up over the trees. "It's because of my dad though. Not because of you."

"Your dad? Ain't he nice?" My regular little voice had returned.

He shook his head. "Just don't come around if he's home, okay?"

He touched my face and it surprised me. I looked up at him. "I promise."

His eyes told me that he got pieces of words in his mouth he was trying to sew together.

"You got something more to say?"

He looked at me and it was clear he was wading through something in his mind.

"Sometimes I just think how nice it would be to have a fresh start like you got when

374

you moved here."

"It ain't all you think it is though." Because it came at a price. It was a consequence and not a reward. "But you're my only friend. You got to stay."

He looked over at me and didn't take his eyes off of me for a long while.

Then he kissed me.

I didn't think a whole lot more about anything but that kiss. Would he kiss me again if I stopped hurting myself? But every time I walked past some nettles or I tapped the healing scab on my leg or my hand ached from the wringer washer, I thought of that relief and was tempted. But the kiss was so nice. And I wanted him to do it again. Over and over I replayed how his hands held me close and how strong his chest was against my soft one. And how I could tell he had kissed a lot already because he wasn't sloppy.

Was it just a kiss to keep me from talking about Dinah, or was it because he wanted to kiss me? I didn't care though. Not now anyway. Maybe it was because he wanted to see if colored girls kissed differently than white girls?

Was it a dare from his friends?

What would Ms. Emma think?

That last thought halted me right where I

was. Would Ms. Emma hate me for it? Would she send the police on me? If she didn't, would his daddy? He told me not to go near him. Didn't know why. But after I had snuck to hear a little of what Ms. Emma told Mama about why she was sick that day, I figured that Johnny's dad wasn't so nice a man.

When there was a lot I didn't know, I would go back to the one thing I knew for certain.

I liked the kiss.

It was soft and sweet, like he wanted to give the kiss to me and not just take one from me. That was different from any other kiss I ever got. Was that how white boys kissed, or was that just how Johnny kissed? Why did it matter what color he was anyhow? My eyes was shut when he put his lips on mine and I reckoned his were too. Maybe everybody else's eyes should be shut also. It weren't their kiss. It was mine. Nobody could take it away from me and besides, kisses ain't got color — they were just kisses.

DELILAH

Marlene was too broke up to sew Granny's white burial dress so I did it — it was the right thing to do. Sparrow was one of the last to see her before she put herself to bed and said it was time. In a week she went from all her sass to shallow breathing. I couldn't think of nothing but the funeral. It was tomorrow. I was afraid Malachi would make me go. We had a day still to argue over it. I didn't like to argue on the Lord's day, but I would if I had to.

It was July and the church was hot, sweaty. Even in everybody's grief the songs got more energy than ever. Every so often someone called out Granny's name, like they telling her to celebrate in heaven. I didn't feel the same way about things.

"When I got over to Granny's house to pray with her, Sister Marlene told me that in Granny's kitchen there was six cabbages, six bunches of carrots and celery, and more than six loaves of bread." Malachi winked and everyone chuckled. It also set a few to tears. "Brothers and sisters, there was more than enough to feed everybody as we stood around the clock with Granny for all those days. Granny was always taking care of everybody."

The laughing and the crying came together like a choir. Marlene said that they knew she was hoarding food, but they couldn't make sense of it so they let it go.

Malachi went on to say some of the old wise words that Granny used to say and how nothing got past her. He said how even when he was a little slippery boy of six he knew that Granny always gave hugs, hard candy, and, now and again, some swats. How sometimes that love came in the form of some harsh words. There were quite a few "mm-hmms" that joined together, creating a bit of a hum in the small crowd.

Hearing these words made me sure I wouldn't be going to no grave site. It was too soon to go to a place like that where I'd buried my heart. I looked over at Sparrow. She looked just about as dead as I felt inside.

In the last few weeks spending some time with Emma and knowing that when Sparrow wandered off she was with Emma also, it brought back something I knew I'd lost. I had a whole herd of friends in Montgomery I all but shunned after Carver. But in this new place there was one woman who saw me as a friend and I felt it deep. Like I didn't want to let her down. I'd let Granny Winnie down though. She'd tried to be my friend and I didn't want to hear nothing she had to say.

Sparrow had let me down. She done more than that.

I 'spect she could feel my eyes and mind on her and she looked up at me from her seat in the pew; the rest of us was standing. I turned away. I just couldn't linger in her eyes. Maybe she was thinking on that last conversation she had with Granny or maybe she was thinking about the funeral tomorrow. I don't know. But whatever it was, I couldn't try to figure it out. I didn't want to see her. I wanted to get away.

I pushed out of the crowd and passed Brother Titus and his kids, passed all them folks who wanted me to be a good preacher's wife, and passed Marlene who cried pretty and made me want to run faster.

When I got outside it didn't help. The humidity was thick, even though I could still feel the breeze that almost always came through the valley. But it was still too thick for my lungs. I stepped down from the church steps and kept trying to breathe in thinner air and came up with nothing. To my right I saw the makings of a town that don't feel like my own yet.

Past the house were the woods and without willing it, my feet started moving. Maybe it was that I desired the coolness of the woods or maybe it was because the woods were becoming like a passage to another place. Or maybe they just took me somewhere else inside myself.

Maybe it was nothing like that and I just wanted to be where nobody could see me.

Even though I didn't plan it, I knew where I was walking. I was walking to Emma's house. It was Sunday. I knew she wouldn't be there. She would be at church herself. But I walked that way anyhow.

I'd walked in the woods a bunch now so it didn't just seem like the place where I nearly lost two of my kids. I liked the sound of the stream. The valley breeze swirled around me and brought me a measure of relief. The hum of the trees blowing around took away thoughts about Granny's funeral. These woods was good to me today.

I kept walking and when I got to Emma's pond, I saw what I didn't expect. A whole bunch of people was there. Them black buggies were all lined up at the side of the barn and through the whole yard. A voice wafted through the distance, like a whisper. I didn't dare move closer to hear what the voice was saying. A few minutes passed before singing rang out. Loud voices that almost made the pond ripple. It wasn't that it wasn't pretty, but it was just different from other singing I'd heard. I kept listening.

And when everybody came out of the house in nice, neat rows, they all looked like they belonged to the same family. Their dresses were like uniforms made up of about five or six colors. Some wore black bonnets and some wore the white ones. The young men gathered in a huddle and I recognized Johnny.

I imagined myself in the middle of a swarm of Amish ladies getting a meal together. Not so unlike my church, but we didn't all wear the same clothes. But wasn't it similar? Weren't we alike in many ways?

Malachi was probably done preaching and I was missing the lunch at my own house. They would all be wondering where I was and I didn't have a good excuse. But here I was running through the woods again. By the time I got back to the house, I was huffing and puffing. Our yard ain't filled with buggies, but we got a bunch of cars lined up in the churchyard.

Like at Emma's, my house was full with my church family. Malachi saw me walking up and he didn't look happy.

"Where you been?"

"I just took a walk."

"In the middle of my sermon?"

"All that talk about heaven and death." I kept walking because I wasn't about to have this argument with him. "I just needed to get outta there. I don't need to explain that to you, do I?"

He grabbed my arm and stopped me in my tracks. What was he doing? I looked at his hand around my arm and then up at him. I hadn't seen those sharp eyes in a long time.

"Let go of me." I pulled my arm away.

"You got to stop this, Dee." He planted himself between the house and me.

"You want everybody see this?" I said this since my husband didn't like scenes any more than I did and as the preacher he had to be a good example.

"Stop it, Dee. It's not just about leaving church — but that does upset me — it's about all of this. You agreed to come here. We agreed that this move would be good for our family, but I don't see you trying. All I see is your anger and bitterness about our boy."

"Somebody's got to grieve him, Mal. You ain't, so I got to for the both of us. You already moved on and forgot all about him." I used my mean whisper when I spoke because I didn't want nobody to hear me.

He laughed. It was that laugh that made me want to smack his face.

"You losing your mind, woman. What you mean I forgot my son?" His diction was slipping so I knew he was passing frustration and had gotten to angry fast. "Then you go off and start making friends with that Amish woman and don't pay no mind to our flock here."

"You have a problem with the Amish now?"

He rolled his eyes and took a step back and let out a quiet groan of annoyance. Then he inhaled and turned back to me. "Of course I don't have a problem with the Amish. They seem like nice people. But why you making friends with this woman but none of the women from our church?"

Nothing I could've said to him would've made sense. Maybe it was 'cause Emma was like me. All broken and busted up inside because her life didn't go like she thought it would. I thought she was pretty brave and stupid to try to lie to me — but it made me see her like she a real person and not some perfect Christian who never sinned. I was pretty sure she knew I'd lied to her too. But she didn't push me to tell her the truth — not about Sparrow or Carver — and I was glad for that.

Malachi was waiting for my answer.

"I like her. Don't know why you got a problem with her."

"What I have a problem with is that you ain't making friends with nobody from our own church. Sister Marlene be hurting right now because Granny just about raised her, and there's the stuff with her boy that you don't even care about. She said you told her to send the boy away or he'd get killed."

"She said that, did she? And when was that? Was Brother Titus — her husband — with y'all when she told you what I said to her?"

"Dee, stop it. I know what you tryin' to do. Marlene don't mean nothing to me like that, and of course Titus was there. But I just wish you'd try to make friends with her — or somebody from our church."

"You know this ain't about me spending time with Emma. She got nothing to do with this. This is about you wanting me to be more like Sister Marlene. Maybe she can take my place and act like she's the preacher's wife then. Maybe that would make you happier."

"It don't matter what I say right now, Dee, you are going to fight with me. You could say you're thirsty, but if I gave you a cup of water, you'd still refuse to drink it. You can't see nothing that's standing right in front of your eyes, woman."

"You've abandoned me, Mal. You just left me alone to grieve for our boy and deal with that girl in there." I pointed to the house.

"That girl in there?" He also pointed toward the house and leaned toward me at the same time. "That girl in there you're making out to be a murderer is just a girl — our *daughter*. You made her into what she is right now. And you so angry at God but you won't admit it — like out of all these feelings *that one* is the one you should be ashamed of."

"You saying some pretty nasty stuff to me, Malachi Evans," I spat at him. I tried to walk away but he kept me by grabbing my arm.

"Ain't nobody out there in the world who could've saved our baby but Jesus, Dee."

"Then why?" I yelled without caring who heard me. I yanked my arm from his grasp.

" 'Cause it was his time," he said with tears rolling down his face. "It could've happened walking down the street or asleep in his bed. I don't like saying that, but I can't see it any other way."

I wanted to tell him not to preach at me. That he got no right. But he was right and I didn't have enough inside me to do nothing about it.

I walked away from him. I could tell that even though we'd been a mite away from the house and crowd, enough people could see that we wasn't happy with each other. I had half a mind to put myself to bed and forget that I had a house full of people — my own people. Did Emma ever feel that way?

I turned myself around and walked back into the woods.

EMMA

A little boy down the bench from me at church pulled a frog from his pocket and I smiled at him. He was still young enough to sit with his *mem* instead of his *dat* for church but old enough to be scolded for bringing the frog. His bottom lip pushed out and he put it back in his pocket. His *mem* administered a quick pinch to his arm.

The ache for my own son washed over me.

A pinch or a scolding wouldn't mend or fix anything anymore. I had failed Johnny. The guilt was no longer heavy only in my chest but had moved to every joint of my weak body. It was palpable on the surface of my skin. It was everywhere. I had become my sin.

This was all thought of during our second week holding church. Each family took two church weeks in a row, which had a week of no services in between. Sparrow had helped me make pies a few days ago and had asked questions about our services and the Sing-ings. I asked if she'd been the one in the woods the other Sunday, but she didn't answer.

She had been quieter than normal and moved slowly. I didn't ask why though.

I could see John from where I sat. He chewed on a peppermint leaf and kept his gaze on Bishop Atlee Hostetler. When John's gaze wandered and found me, it was short and pained. I knew he felt what I did. Guilt that was greater than our graces.

Johnny held it within himself as well. As much as he had defended me to John, he avoided me as well. Was it shame? His shame of me and knowing I was not without sin.

Even while I washed the first set of the dishes where I could see Johnny's group of friends through the kitchen window, I thought on these things. They looked like young boys when they were all together like that. Laughing and joking. But now in the grass and trees I saw my guilt. Even our still-as-glass pond was like an enemy as it fed and nourished all of nature — the very nature I'd used to betray my family.

Behind me many of the men were out on the porch or in the living room talking, and the women were either tending to children or with me, cleaning the kitchen.

"I just wanted you to know that I could spare Linda on Mondays for laundry," my brother's wife, Dorothy Byler, said as she grabbed a towel to dry dishes. Dorothy and I had gone through our *rumspringa* together, but we had never been close. "Betty and Joyce told me you were looking for help. You're not well?"

The way she said it made me cringe. That sounded as if either I was sick or she suspected I was *so* — that a baby was on the way. Of course, neither was true and I didn't need help with the laundry. I needed Sparrow. Saying it in my mind brought a charge through my body like when a light-bulb blew in a flashlight.

"Oh, *ich muss net helve.* But that is kind of you to offer." I would have to come up with a reason why I didn't need help now but had just told the Mast sisters that Sparrow helped me.

"Dahn du bish net so?" She gestured to her own belly.

No. I wasn't *so.* I was not expecting anything but the boon of guilt.

I shook my head.

"Du bish krank?"

"I'm not sick," I told her but didn't meet her eyes.

389

"Then why do you need help? There are only three of you."

"I don't need help." I was not one to debate or contradict others. I kept to myself. I spoke quietly or not at all.

Dorothy tilted her head at me and then looked past me.

"Betty, didn't you say that Emma needed help with laundry and had been getting that Negro girl to help?" This was why Dorothy and I were not close. She meddled and was persistent about it.

Betty stuffed half a cinnamon roll in her mouth with her head bobbing up and down. With her mouth still full she said, "Sure enough."

"She had a funny name. It was a bird," Joyce yelled over to us.

I wanted to squeeze my eyes shut and get away, but if I did I would draw even more attention to myself.

"It was Dove," Betty said. "No, it wasn't. What was it?"

"It wasn't Robin," Joyce offered.

"Was it Blue Jay?" someone else said, chuckling. "Or Starling?"

Several of the women added their laughter.

"Emma?" Dorothy said.

"Sparrow," I said no louder than a whisper.

Several women said how unusual that was and how they would never give their girls such a strange name. And all I could think was if I had gotten the chance, I would name my daughters ones they would laugh about over the dime-a-dozen Sarahs, Ruths, or Barbaras.

"Her *mem* had an even worse name. Didn't she, Emma?" Joyce called over to me.

I found myself wishing that some sickness would overtake me so I could leave the room.

"Vas was deh mem sah nameh?" Another woman asked what the mom's name was. All the women looked at me with such anticipation.

"Delilah." The whites of Betty's eyes shone, suggesting shamefulness.

Several ladies gasped and giggled and talked it over and questioned who would do that because of the biblical reference to the woman of the same name.

I pulled over a stack of dirty plates to be washed, trying to refocus myself. They weren't mean people and I'd thought Delilah was an unusual name just like they did, so I understood the surprise. I hadn't laughed over it though. I didn't laugh at much. Why did *different* cause such a reaction? If not laughter then judgment, and if not judgment then fear. Shouldn't it cause us to seek something more valuable, like understanding? But fear and judgment were easier.

"So, this Sparrow." Dorothy got close. "She's the one who helps you on Mondays?"

"Just recently, yes." I poured myself a cup of coffee and leaned against the kitchen countertop. Dorothy did the same.

"But you don't need the help?" Dorothy shook her head.

"She likes to help." I thought it was the best answer.

"Oh," she said with a sour expression. "Is she simple? She doesn't know you don't want her to come?"

"No, she's not simple. She's a nice girl and likes to help me. She's good company."

"And her *mem* comes over too? I don't know any Negro people. I thought they kept to their own — like we do."

Dorothy was simply being honest. Our district was small and we helped one another and didn't do much with the English community of Sinking Creek or the surrounding towns. We didn't leave town much.

"They live like we do but they have electricity," I said.

"You've been to this girl's house?"

"I wanted to welcome them. They have four children and her husband is a preacher. They garden and eat meals together and work hard. They aren't so different from us."

"Really?" Dorothy raised her brows. "But you don't want Linda to come help? Then you could tell the Negro girl she didn't need to come. Shouldn't she go help someone in her own church?"

"I won't need Linda's help," I said, then left saying I had something to check on. Though I didn't.

Because there was no place to go, not even my bedroom where several babies slept on my bed, I walked toward the woods. I walked to where my baby lay asleep, beneath the blanket of grass, but found Delilah sitting near the creek before I got there.

"Kinda nice being out in the middle of all this." She gestured around her.

I walked a few more paces in the quiet. "I know."

She nodded and sniffed. "The trees. The birds. This creek even."

"It's peaceful, isn't it?" I walked closer. "Why are you here?" I knew there was a reason.

"Just needed to get away."

"Me too."

I sat down and we were quiet together for several minutes.

"An old lady from our church died yesterday. It just brings up stuff I don't want to think on. Funeral's tomorrow but I won't go to it."

"I understand."

She looked up at me and the glassiness in our eyes was the same.

"I know you do, and I think you might be the only one."

DELILAH

The late-July weather was warm but nothing like the red-hot days back home. I still got to fan myself as I sat listening to Malachi preach. His face was glistening with sweat — that would happen on the coldest day, though, when he was preaching Jesus. George wiggled next to me and I patted his knee and then gave him the little plastic farm animals from my bag. Harriet was sitting where Granny used to sit. All the little girls her age were. They used to sit with her every week because Granny Winnie just loved them and she always had a hard candy for them. Mallie had his eyes glued on his daddy.

"We've talked about prayer this morning. We've talked about the endurance it takes to move forward in our lives. We know that the apostle Paul encouraged the early church to turn away from what was behind and move toward what was ahead."

He paused and made a show of looking up in the sunlight shining through the old, cracked-up stained glass window above the door.

"What does that look like?" He held his Bible up over his head. "This right here, brothers and sisters." He took his time to trace his gaze over all of us sitting there, like he making sure we're listening. "Brother Titus and Sister Marlene know about the power of prayer, don't you?"

Brother Titus called out an "amen." Sister Marlene raised her hand up while she cried a little. And I started thinking that she better be crying. Because of her boy's mess, some other of our boys went into Mr. Coleman's grocery and knocked over a bunch of his canned goods, denting them all up. And pulled the plugs on his refrigerators and a bunch of food was spoiled by morning. There was a big ole mess in that place. Those two young men were arrested fast and now in the county jail. They weren't so big now, were they?

If they'd taken to Reverend King's message about the bus boycott that hate for hate doesn't work, then they wouldn't be in jail and my husband would still have a job. That's right, Malachi got fired by Mr. Coleman. Malachi didn't fight none about it but just took it. But now we got to figure out how to keep our stomachs fed and be afraid that he'll kick us out of our house next.

Malachi went on to recite scripture in that poetic way he was always so good at. I tried to listen. I tried to hear what he was saying. When he said that we were to accept what we're given and face our challenges in order to move forward — and to do so with the fruits of the Spirit, nothing lacking — I wanted to roll my eyes and scoff. I felt like he was always harping at me to move forward. I ain't planning to disrespect my son by moving away from my grief. My mind wandered after that. Wandered back to Montgomery and that great big river and that tiny little grave.

Before I realized it Brother Daryl's deep baritone sang off to my left and everyone was standing and clapping. Malachi had come down from pulpit and was standing at the front of the aisle. He was clapping and his tenor voice was a perfect blend with Brother Daryl. I tried to sway in rhythm with George and Mallie at my side. Sparrow just stood at the end of the pew doing nothing.

In the next moment Mallie left the pew.

"Mallie," I whispered loudly, "where you going?"

That dear boy turned to me and his face just about glowed. His eyes was big and wise looking, with a face so much like my daddy he should've been named after him. But Malachi was the kind of man who deserved a junior.

"I'm going to tell Daddy that I want to be baptized." Mallie's smile just about stretched off his face.

I didn't have nothing to say so he turned away and walked up to his daddy. When he got up there the song was just finishing up, but there was still a collective hum of voices and Marlene was yelling out for the Lord Jesus to help her boy Kenny and Brother Daryl's loud praying kept up the energy for the next song to come.

And there was my Mallie. Here he was just so proud and I just about want to faint. Then Harriet's little voice filled the whole sanctuary with her vibrato. Like a bird she trilled in song and I didn't even know she could sing — well, not like that anyhow. Everybody followed the child.

"Precious Lord, take my hand . . ." were the words she sang when Malachi took Mallie's hands. My husband leaned forward to hear what our son wanted to tell him. His eyes

opened wider in surprise and he pulled
Mallie into his arms. My husband's gaze
found mine right away. Like he knew. He
might be happy. But I wasn't. He knew why.

I didn't think of much else in the next few
days than Mallie wanting to be baptized.
And then my sister sent me a letter and my
nerves just about couldn't take it. The bus
boycott was still happening down south, and
my nephews and the young people in our
church thought they were so big because
they following right along with the Reverend
King. It wasn't that I didn't want change,
but I didn't want those young people to be
hurt or worse. And along with that I got the
picture of my sweet baby's grave site. I
looked at it for a small moment. Couldn't
take it in more than that just then.

My thoughts were all jumbled up when I
found Emma in the woods bent over a patch
of grass like she was tending to it. I still
didn't know how we were friends when we
got a whole church full of ladies who looked
like us and believed like us that we could be
friends with. Of course right now I was
thinking she might be harvesting that herb
that kept her from getting pregnant all these
years.

I wasn't very quiet in the woods with my
walking so she soon saw me. She smiled but

it wasn't that nice, soft one I knew well. It was like she got something to be nervous about. She was holding something behind her back like I don't know it. Did she think I was stupid?

"You tending to something?" I gestured with my head to the patch of oval grass.

She was quiet for a few long seconds. I didn't interrupt her thinking. Her shoulders settled and she looked back at me.

"This is where I buried my daughter." She brought out from behind her a handful of them pretty white flowers and bent over the spot. She laid them flowers down with some kind of reverence by the big old rock that sat at the top of the little space.

"I see." I understood, but I couldn't help but judge a little. She ain't never knew her baby and was still grieving after her. I knew mine for four years. Wasn't my grief worse? I felt like a bad person for even thinking that since grief ain't measured like that. Was this her grieving over all the babies she didn't have because of what she done for so long?

I looked around and found a few of them pretty purple lupines and pulled a few. I squatted next to her and put them down too. She looked up at me when I did and I smiled at her.

"It something we can still do for our babies," I said. "Give them a nice resting place."

In a minute we was both sitting on our backsides on the forest ground. Just being there together.

"But you're so far away. Doesn't that hurt?"

She just came out with these questions that I don't want to answer. But ain't nobody else bothering to ask me, so I supposed it was all right that Emma did.

"My sister Deborah said she's making sure Carver's grave looks nice." I cleared my throat. I don't feel like crying today. But, of course, I got my own grave I carried around with me almost everywhere I went. "You know what I got though?"

She shook her head.

"I got his dirt."

She looked confused.

"I put a bunch of handfuls of dirt in my purse." When I said it I shook my head and let out a little embarrassed laugh. But you couldn't admit that you put dirt in a purse without thinking how that might sound. "I just wanted his dirt to come with me. Something from him."

"Does it help?"

401

I don't know how to answer her, so I don't.

"I got a letter from my sister today," I said without thinking and wished I'd just answered her dang question instead. I pulled out the picture that was inside. "This was with it."

I handed it to her. She looked at it long and hard and I appreciated that.

"The flowers are beautiful." She handed it back to me.

I slid it into my pocket without a glance. I'd already cried over every detail of the picture earlier.

"Is that picture what's on your mind today?" Emma asked innocently.

I looked at her with my lips all buttoned up.

"You said we're friends." Her voice, again, was so opposite of mine. Her words come out like vapor in the air and mine were like a whole waterfall coming out all at once with some force I didn't often control.

She was right and if I wanted to be friends I'd have to make an effort. But it was about stuff that folks like me got to think on, and I don't know any white folks who wanted to talk about how we was fighting against their laws and ways. But Emma did have a different way about her.

"Deborah wrote about the bus boycott. Many from my church are getting involved and following the good Reverend King."

She looked more confused now than before.

I told her about Rosa Parks and about how we were fighting against the segregation of the public bus system. How we were driving around on our own and how hard it was to figure out how to get from here to there. I told her that Reverend King was a good man and he was strong and fighting for colored rights and he got a peaceful way about it too. When I told her how this wasn't just about buses and how every place we went was designated for whites or coloreds, she shook her head.

"It's like another world to me." I believed her. "We are so far away from all of that here."

I raised an eyebrow at her. She thought we was so far away but we got our own problems in this backward town. "You think so?"

"I've never seen signs on the doors like that."

"They do it without signs here, Emma." I tried to keep my voice even. "I can't buy or even touch the produce from your section. They told me to use the grocery buggies that the whites don't use. The dentist don't see none of us. Did you know that? And there are a whole heap of lies going around about the Carter boy."

There was more, but I wasn't sure how much more she could handle. She was a naive one, this woman.

Emma looked down at her hands and after a time I thought I should get up and leave her to think on things. Then she spoke.

"I don't know how to change any of that or about boycotts. All of these things are . . ." She paused like she was searching for a word. Then she looked up at me. "I know it's not right. But I don't know what to do."

We both released a sigh.

"But I will promise to stand by you."

EMMA

It was a muggy late Monday afternoon when a knock came to my door. Maybe it was Sparrow coming after all. It had rained all day, and when Sparrow hadn't come this morning, I didn't want to do anything. I decided not to even do laundry. I didn't care anymore. I missed her and she hadn't been coming as often, though Deedee and I had begun to build the sort of friendship I had never had before.

I set down my sewing and rubbed out some of the day's aches from my hands as I walked to the door. When I reached for the knob, the knock came again. It wasn't Sparrow. She always knocked twice. Short and light. These three bold knocks came steady against our solid wood door.

"Hello, Mrs. Mullet," said the deep and smooth voice of Malachi Evans when I opened the door. He was wearing dress slacks and a collared shirt with the sleeves rolled up. The forward-tilted hat looked more formal than his clothing, but I liked it. He smiled and his face was so pleasant I smiled back. His skin was darker than Deedee's and Sparrow's and his eyes shone even brighter. I liked him.

I looked over his shoulder and saw an old truck in the drive. "I didn't hear you drive up." I opened the door farther. "Come on in."

"I'm wet, ma'am." He chuckled as he pointed to his shoes. "Out here is just fine."

Relief settled over me. I didn't know how to be alone with a man who wasn't my husband. And John would not approve.

"I just put water on for coffee. I'll bring some out."

"That's mighty kind of you. Thank you." He gave me a smile so genuine and so like young Harriet.

As I made the coffee, I left the door open as he stood on the porch.

He yelled through the door things that I never heard from my Amish friends. What a nice house we had and how nice the wood-work was. Of course, to me Amish homes often looked much the same. Some were bigger than others, but communities often had similar cabinetry, tables, flooring, furniture, and curtains. Even the dishes we used were similar.

I wasn't used to hearing words like that about my home so I wasn't sure what to say. As a little girl I once said how much I liked my cousin's new bed my uncle had made for her. My mother scolded me, telling me that compliments like that caused pride. That we needed to see where God was in the beautiful things of the world, not man-made beauty.

Maybe not at age ten, but over the following years I thought about how God had made my uncle and he was a fine carpenter. Wasn't that praising God by admiring my uncle's work? But that was not the way we lived as a church. Being uniform and consistent was our way, with solemnity and not showiness.

"Did your husband build this house?" Malachi asked through the open door, breaking my thoughts. "I'm so used to smaller city houses, living in Montgomery. These big, beautiful farmhouses are like a whole different world. Just beautiful."

I cleared my throat when I heard that word. *Beautiful.* I'd never described any part of my life that way.

"Thank you," I said, trying not to sound proud. I poured two mugs of coffee. "John, my husband, didn't build the house; he bought it. He did put up the barn though."

I walked onto the porch and he took one of the mugs from me. The whir of the rain was our backdrop and made the several long moments of silence okay. My hands clutched my mug as I sat across from him on the porch swing. My toe started moving my weight on the swing forward and back. I sipped the hot dark liquid and so did Malachi. Why had he come to my home?

"My oldest son, Malachi Jr. — Mallie — you've met him?" He raised his eyebrows.

"Yes."

"He wants to be baptized."

All of this was so unusual. First, a Negro preacher was at my doorstep, and second, while I knew his family, I did not know him. He seemed to be here with something to say. I was sure he would say that he had learned of all the time Sparrow was spending at the house and that he didn't approve, but instead he brought up his son. And baptism?

I must have shown confusion.

"I'm sorry, Mrs. Mullet." He moved up to the edge of his chair, sitting erect and looking right into my eyes.

"Emma, please."

"Emma. I'm confusing you, I realize. Here's why I came. I wanted to see if we could use your pond for the baptism. There are several others in my church, besides my son, who want to be baptized. None of my members have a pond or a deep enough river on their properties, and because of everything that's going on right now, we would rather not use public property."

"You need that much water?" I asked before I thought. We used less than a cup for each person, not a whole pond full. And Mallie was so young. Our members had to be at least sixteen to join, but it was more common to be older than that.

"We baptize the way Jesus was baptized." His eyes were so bright, I'd never seen the likeness.

The baptism of Jesus was never referenced when our youth were baptized, but I had heard the story. There had been a voice from heaven. There had been a dove. The man had buried Jesus under the water and brought Him back up. It didn't resemble the baptism I'd had or that our church practiced.

"When?" I took a sip of my coffee and considered this.

"In a few weeks, maybe a month?"

Of course I would say yes. There was no reason not to. However, the church and John were nervous about any ties to their community because of the current issues. Our preachers did not understand everything that had occurred between the white and Negro *Englishers,* but they wanted us to stay far away from all of it.

If they came while we were attending church, it could work without John even knowing — or the church. It was best left to the bishop or my husband to answer, but I chose to give him my own instead.

"Sure. In four weeks would work."

We would not be home that morning.

"Sister Emma, I really appreciate this." He leaned forward and the eagerness on his face couldn't be hidden.

Sister Emma brought an unusual feeling to me. Like he accepted me.

The *clip-clop* of a horse's hooves could be heard coming down the road. John and Johnny. The rain started to fall slower, but my heart did the opposite and began to race.

"Everything all right, Ms. Emma?"

"My husband. You need to go."

He didn't say anything but handed me his mug and ran to his truck. He pulled out fast and I wondered how he understood without me saying much. John would've seen him pull out since his buggy was in the driveway a moment later.

I washed Malachi's mug, dried it quickly,

and put it away. I put the potatoes I'd peeled on the stove to boil, then pulled out the ground beef to make gravy. It was ten minutes before they both came inside.

"Who was here?" John asked before he even had his coat off.

I heard Johnny move off to his room quickly.

"What?" I kept my back to him and stirred the gravy more than needed.

"There was a truck that pulled out. An old one." He was closer now but still at arm's length.

"Oh, that. Just someone new to the area — just stopped to ask a few questions." I closed my eyes for a brief moment and hoped my lie of protection would work and could be forgiven. It was partially true. I held my breath. I took the gravy off the hot part of the stove and then drained the potato water. My hands were busy enough that he wouldn't notice I was shaking.

"Was it one of those Negroes?"

I nodded. I did my best to pretend there was nothing to be concerned over by grabbing the potato masher and turning to the counter. "The bishop just said not to get involved with the town's issues. He didn't say we couldn't be kind and neighborly."

He turned me around to face him,

411

grabbed my arms, and backed me up against the stove. I dropped the masher and tried to stay on my feet. My palms sizzled on the stove top and I screamed. Even though I lifted them the pain consumed me.

"This isn't about them — or the bishop. I can't, you can't —" He couldn't finish any of his thoughts through my scream.

"My hands," I cried. "My hands."

Something in his eyes changed and he let go. Instinct brought my hands forward. The burns were bad. John's eyes grew larger. He looked at his own palms at the same time and backed away from me.

"Vas hap ich geduh?" He questioned himself about what he'd done as he stared at his hands. Then he peered up at me and he couldn't catch his breath. "Emma?"

I couldn't do anything but hold my hands out in front of me. He turned to the sink, but the water from the spigot only trickled. It would take several long minutes for the generator to force more water through our pipes. He grabbed me by the wrists and pulled me to follow him. He took me to the pump, but the bucket that hung there was hungry for water. He groaned.

"What are you doing?"

He gathered me in his arms like I was a small child and ran with me to the pond.

He was out of breath when we reached the small shore, and he sat me down and scooped the cool water and splashed it over my hands. Over and over. We were both soaked. His breathing was heavy and he didn't say a word.

The pond water soothed the burns, but my skin was already white and red and raising into blisters. Then he looked around and in a moment he was gone. With the lack of constant cool water over my burns, they heightened in temperature. Where had John gone?

He returned with a broadleaf plantain. I had no idea he'd ever paid any mind to what I had used to help with bites and burns over the years. He broke off strips of the wide green leaf and folded and bit them, releasing the juices, and with careful hands laid the paste on my shaking, upturned hands. The act was so intimate my heart thudded.

Then we sat together, my palms still turned up and burning, though there was some improvement. We were both soaked and dirty, sitting on the shore of our pond. The rain was a drizzle now and the sky hung low and gray. The insects and frogs started to chirp.

"Forgive me," he said and his breaking voice filled the space around us.

My jaw clenched. I could not forgive him.

He repeated his words with weeping and continued his pleading for forgiveness.

I still could say nothing. How could I forgive him?

"I don't want to be this man," he sobbed. "It was just one time I had too much because I was angry about something at work. It wasn't even anything important."

I turned toward him. I'd never heard any of this.

"That was the night you went into labor," he cried. "I couldn't help you because I was so drunk and see what happened? I couldn't look at you anymore. I was so guilty — then I couldn't stop."

He wiped his face with his shirt and sniffed. He looked at me for a good long while and then walked away. I stared straight ahead. I could hear him walk through the yard and then I heard the basement door open. Did he want forgiveness for all that he'd done? Or for what he would continue to do? Did he want forgiveness for his temper or for his drunkenness? Was he going to come back into our bedroom drunk and blame me for pushing him into hurting me?

"Mem?" Johnny walked up behind me.

I turned. He looked like a grown man to

me now. Not a sixteen-year-old boy. He helped me up. He didn't ask me what happened but just helped me walk to the house.

As we got closer we heard John. We stopped. The sounds of crashing and yelling were deafening over the din of the evening noises that continued to grow louder.

I didn't say anything to Johnny but urged us to continue walking.

"Are you going to do something?" my son asked.

"No."

SPARROW

I was way over a hundred taps under the water in the bathtub. I opened my eyes and saw the ripples on top of me. Almost like I was buried in water instead of under the dirt. It was peaceful under here. Granny was buried now but Mama and I didn't go. I had heard Mama and Daddy arguing over it. Mama won. I didn't even have to ask. I just told them I wasn't going. Nobody cared about me anyway. I didn't cut myself because I kept thinking about seeing Johnny on Sunday and how I told him I'd stop hurting myself.

The next Sunday morning I sat on the side of Johnny's pond in the warm and heavy air. The house was dim, unlit from the inside. I imagined him moving about to come meet me. Hoping. My stomach swirled. I had beat the sunrise. But even when the sunrise eventually came, Johnny didn't. This was the second time he hadn't come. Not since the Sunday he kissed me.

I looked around for something to cut with, but I didn't have nothing. I banged my head with the heel of my hand as hard as I could. It didn't cover up the hurt for Johnny missing two Sundays. It didn't give me no relief. It didn't leave a scar. I needed to see what I done. Like a notebook on my skin of all the sad I got inside. So I ran home. I would find something there.

But Daddy woke up before I could do anything and hugged me good morning. I pinched the soft part of my underarm all through church though. That hurt got to count for something, don't it?

But it kept coming to mind about how I would mark myself for Carver. How that mark couldn't just be some cut on my leg or slapping and pinching myself or the stinging nettles. Because of the hurt I done, that mark would be deeper.

Later in the week I was supposed to be watching the little children in the backyard. Mama was with Emma. The kids were playing like they just got nothing to think about. I don't want to hate them but I kinda do — a little anyway. They don't know hurt. They will keep forgetting Carver too. But they won't ever forget what I done.

Ain't nobody watching me so I started

walking away from home going toward town. The same way I walked when I got drenched in mud-puddle water and when I got them groceries for Granny. I got through the white neighborhood. The door was open to Pretty'd Up Salon, and when I walked by I heard them laughing like they was having the best time.

I passed Coleman's Grocery. Mr. Coleman didn't wave or smile — but I knew he saw me. At the butcher that big man was barking at his worker about the meat being cut too thick. I whispered the word *cut.* A lady walked by me and scowled and pulled her daughter closer. I didn't even care.

I kept walking until I found myself standing in front of the lumberyard where Johnny worked. A loud bell rang out and little by little men started milling around. Some of them were Amish like Johnny but most weren't. Ain't none of them like me though. None that I saw anyhow. They had their lunches and laughs and conversations. Didn't even notice me.

Then I saw Johnny. He was walking with a few others who weren't Amish. His eyes glanced over to where I stood. I could see his confusion even at a distance.

I waved at him, then realized what I'd

done and knew right away that I shouldn't have.

His expression went from confusion to something else. His eyes darted back and forth from the group around him. Then I saw Arnold. He grabbed Johnny's shoulder and pointed at me and let out a loud holler. I tucked myself out of sight. What had I done?

"Hey, Johnny." That redheaded devil boy said the word that I hated and called me dirty and laughed at me. "She's following you."

I heard some shuffling around but didn't dare look around the corner. I heard footsteps coming near me. I turned toward the sound to be met by Arnold's red face instead of Johnny's.

He grabbed me by the hair and pulled me out from the alley and into sight. The lumberyard was now full of men eating lunch. I had hold of Arnold's wrist but couldn't free myself. Johnny arrived a step after.

Arnold was yelling nasty stuff at me when we both ended up on the ground. Johnny had punched him and brought us both down in the process.

Then he pulled me up fast and back into the alley. "You shouldn't be here." Of course

419

that was the first thing he would say. He was right. I was stupid.

"I — I —" I didn't know what to say. My throat felt as little as a spaghetti noodle and I didn't know if I could breathe. I gasped for a few breaths, but when he took my forearm and gave me a good shake, I caught myself and started breathing normal again.

"Stop it, Sparrow." He looked behind him, then turned back toward me. "You're going to get us both into trouble."

"I'm sorry, Johnny." I pulled my arm from his grip.

His hands trembled when he set them on my shoulders. In my own nerves I tried to smooth down my hair where Arnold had grabbed it.

"Go," he said with a breathless voice. "I don't want you to get more hurt."

I did. I ran and I didn't turn around. What kind of fool was I to walk into town like that and go see the white boy who said I was pretty? Who had kissed me? Who probably liked Dinah better than me anyway?

Nobody at home even noticed I had been gone. Nobody noticed that I'd just come back. Mama returned a few minutes later. Then we ate lunch. My hands moved to my bologna-and-cheese sandwich and I knew I ate it, but I couldn't feel my teeth bite it or chew it or swallow it. I couldn't hear the conversation around the table, but I saw the mouths of my brothers and sister moving. Mama didn't talk much; she never did no more. Maybe she used up all her words with Emma.

I helped clean up. I washed George's face. I even smiled at him. He smiled back. Then I went to my room and pulled out a sewing needle I'd stolen from Mama. My heart sped up real fast knowing what was coming.

I needed two things — the sting, the tingle, the shiver, and the mark to remind myself of the many things I hurt over.

For the kiss.

For Johnny saying I was pretty.

For Arnold's meanness.

For me being stupid.

For George's smile that was too much like Carver's.

I only bled a little when I pricked myself a dozen times — it wasn't enough. So I started to scratch the needle against my skin 'til it bled, like tally marks. I pulled out that old river shell from my nightstand and let it cut against my skin. It didn't break my skin much, but it was a good idea to use the shell anyhow. Like Carver was getting revenge on me — he deserved to. I was happy that I'd thought of it for his sake.

My bed was already marked up with blood from the first cut I made when I saw Johnny with Dinah. That one broke open too many times, so a little more didn't matter. Mama would think it was just my monthly blood. She couldn't know of this. But if she did, she wouldn't care. Why would she care?

The relief reminded me of the way a little baby rested in its mama's arms. It got nothing to do but rest there and be warm and be heavy. That's how it felt. It was part of me now like my finger or foot or nose. I needed it. I imagined that the relief took up the spot where my soul used to be. I figured I lost my soul when I had killed Carver. Ain't no God who wanted somebody like me in heaven. But now I got these magic cuts that made the pieces of me come together.

But it didn't take everything away. It just made me feel something else for a little bit. I still knew what I done would never go away. I was like Cain and I would be forever marked. Daddy had said that we'd see Carver someday when we died. But that weren't true for me. When I died I would crumble like dirt into the ground that Mama wouldn't take up in her bag. When I died I got no reason to make it to heaven. When I died —

■ ■ ■ ■

A few nights later, when everyone was asleep, I left the house, awaiting the Sunday dawn and Johnny. I didn't even take a flashlight. The moon was bright and I knew the woods so well. I sat on the dock watching for Johnny, even though I knew it would be hours before daybreak. And he probably wasn't going to come anyhow because of what I done. But I was still going to wait.

It wasn't but an hour before a truck turned into Johnny's driveway. The driver of the clunker turned off his headlights when it rolled in. Then I saw Johnny step through the front door of his house with a bag over his shoulder.

I didn't know when I decided to run, but I did. But not away. I ran toward him. He didn't see me or hear my feet brush against the lawn.

"Johnny." My voice was raspy. "Don't you leave."

He turned toward me.

"Sparrow?" The same disappointment and surprise filled his eyes like at the lumberyard.

"Psst," the driver said, and it was that awful redhead, Arnold. "Johnny, come on."

Hadn't he just punched him a few days ago? And he was gonna climb into a truck with him? I took a few steps back and scowled something awful. Did I know Johnny at all?

"Come with us," Johnny said and ran up to me. He held me so close and I knew Arnold saw us. His mouth was by my ear. "Come with me. Let's go out west and start over together."

I pulled back and looked at his face. "What you talking about? With him?" I looked past him and saw another Amish boy was inside also. Arnold gestured to me with his fist. Johnny didn't see him.

"I won't let him hurt you."

I peeled his hands off me. "He'll kill me. I can't go anywhere with that boy."

"He'll never get close enough. And as soon as we get somewhere, we'll go off on our own." He put his hands on my arms. He was so warm. His eyes didn't move from my face. He was serious about his invitation. But I wouldn't go nowhere with Arnold.

"Stay, Johnny. *Please* don't run away."

"Johnny, come on," Arnold whispered, leaning out the open window in the door.

"I have to leave — I can't stay here anymore." He touched my hair and my face and traveled down my neck. "My parents — my dad — I don't want anything to do with him."

"What about your mama?"

His gaze went to the woods behind me. He shook his head. "I can't stay." He looked back at me. "Things are too hard here. Just come with me."

I think I loved him because he understood, but my fear of Arnold was stronger.

I stepped back and closed my eyes. When I opened them again I saw Johnny step backward, still facing me, with a pained expression.

"I'll come back for you someday."

And then he was gone.

DELILAH

I heard a banging on the front door when the sky was still navy blue. I blinked a few times and then turned to see that Malachi was still asleep. Why would someone be here now? What day was it? Even on a Sunday morning I don't have to be up earlier than the sun.

I sat up and rubbed my face to wake myself up before I swung my legs over to get my slippers on. "Malachi," I said in a loud whisper. "Somebody at the door."

He groaned a little at me. I waved a hand at him and grabbed my housecoat and headed for the door.

The knock came again.

"I'm coming," I said, and not real nice neither.

I tied up my housecoat and cleared my throat and reached for the door when another knock sounded. They sure was impatient. I pulled the door open and found a big figure standing on the other side. I didn't open the screen door though. I wanted to know who it was first.

A light was shined in my face. It hurt my eyes and I squinted and put my hand up. "Gracious — what you do that for?" I asked before I caught myself.

"We're here to talk to Reverend Evans?" The loud voice didn't sound familiar. He repositioned the flashlight so's it's not right in my eyes. I saw a uniform. "This is Police Chief Crabtree here to see the reverend."

"Give me a few minutes. He's still in —"

Then he pushed the door a little. "Can we come in?" Police Chief Crabtree interrupted.

"Let me go get my husband." I stepped back as the door opened without my invitation. He got some nerve. He was a large man. Not just tall but had a big, round belly. But it was the way he thought about himself that took up the whole kitchen. Behind him came another man in uniform. A small man in comparison.

"I'll wait here," he said with his gruff voice.

I didn't act like I was nervous until I was all the way inside my bedroom. I didn't want that man to see my hands shaking. But when I got the bedroom door closed, I ran

427

around the bed and started shaking Malachi awake. He was bleary eyed and didn't know what I was talking about.

"The police chief is here," I said in a loud whisper and shook him back and forth again. "Police Chief Crabtree. And I don't know why."

"What, Dee?" He sat up. "You having a wild dream or something?"

"Mal-a-chi. Listen to me. The sheriff is in our kitchen and he got something to say. I'm scared."

"Crabtree? Is here? Now?"

"I said that twice. Now get your butt out of bed. Don't you make me cuss and you know I might 'cause you know how I get when I'm scared. We ain't never had a police chief in our house. Not even when —" When we lost our Carver we had to deal with the police, but they didn't come into my home.

Malachi came to himself and stretched when he got out of the bed. He was in an undershirt and pajama bottoms. He would never want to be seen in them, but he ain't got a choice right now. I grabbed his robe and handed it to him and rushed him to tie it. My hands and my breath was shaky.

Malachi rubbed his face again and he clicked on the light on the nightstand. He grabbed his watch and looked and groaned. "It's barely five."

"You got to get out there, Mal." I yanked at his arm.

"I'm going, Dee." He put his watch on, like it dressed him up or something.

I walked behind him and had his robe fisted in my hand. My toes hit his heels a few times and I apologized under my breath, but I wanted to know what was going on and was all nerved up. He pulled the robe out of my hand but I stayed close behind him. When he stopped in front of the police chief, half my front was against his back.

He put his hand out. "Good morning," he said and didn't hide that he was vexed. "What's this all about, Chief?"

"Reverend Evans, I'm Police Chief —"

"Yes, I know who you are. We've met before, a few times, actually. This must be important since it's pretty early and my family and I were still asleep, you see."

He got just about too much confidence, this husband of mine. He got to be nice and instead he was dishing out his annoyance with a fork and spoon. What was he thinking? Police — or any white person — sure didn't like that kind of attitude from a colored man.

429

"Do you know anything about Kenny Carter?"

"Kenny Carter?" Malachi didn't act surprised or nothing.

"What do you know about his whereabouts?"

"I was told he was sent down south. That's what his folks said and that's all we know."

Malachi was telling the truth, though I had not been in all of those conversations.

"I know there was some trouble with the Coleman girl, but he's really a good kid. He doesn't want any trouble. I don't think he means to come back," Malachi said in the tone he used when he was counseling folks. Real trustworthy and gracious.

"I'm not so sure about that." Police Chief Crabtree looked over at the other police officer and they raised their eyebrows at each other. He turned back toward us and took a deep breath. "We believe he may be responsible for the vandalism during the night at the Sinking Creek Community Church."

"The what?" I said before Malachi could respond.

"Vandalism?" Malachi said all high-pitched like. "That doesn't sound like Kenny."

"A vehicle was driven into the side of the

community church." His gaze shifted back and forth between Malachi and me.

"A vehicle?" Malachi and I both said.

"Yes, that's correct."

"Why do you think it was Kenny? Was it Kenny's car?"

"It was against the *white* church and as far as the vehicle, well —" The chief looked over at the other officer who shrugged, then whispered something behind his hand. "It's the Johnson boy's car — Arnold. He told us it was stolen and he was pretty beat up when we talked to him. We need to know where Kenny is, Reverend, and we expect you to help." He leaned forward then. "I know you don't want no trouble to come to you and your church. Maybe you could go with us while we talk to his parents?"

"You're talking to me before the boy's folks?" His voice was higher than my raised eyebrow.

"We believed you'd be more" — he stumbled over his words — "forthcoming with information and help us with the boy's parents."

I supposed I was glad they thought he was honest, but it was a sad state that they thought the Carters weren't. Malachi told them he would drive himself to the Carters and would be there after he changed his clothes.

Chief Crabtree and the other officer nodded with reluctance and let themselves out while Malachi and I just stood there.

"What we gonna do, Malachi?"

"There isn't anything we can do right now but for me to go with them." He walked toward the bedroom. "I'll talk to the church this morning that we really need to be praying for our town over all this. And make sure that Kenny isn't in town anymore."

"You don't think he did it, do you?"

He didn't answer.

"Malachi, you can't believe he'd do something like that."

"Why not, Dee?" He moved past me to grab his clothes from the wardrobe. "He was mighty upset and he made lots of threats."

"But they are the ones who run him out. He didn't do nothing against the law."

"Yes, they ran him out. Why are we surprised about that? But that doesn't excuse bad behavior from anyone. I need to go talk with the Carters and see if Kenny really did go south like they said."

That was what Malachi harped on over and over in all the years I heard him speak. He didn't excuse all the prejudices against our community, but he also didn't excuse any response that was against the law. He always went back on that old phrase that two wrongs don't make a right. I wasn't sure I always agreed with him. If someone did harm to any of my children, they would have to deal with me. It wouldn't be nice neither.

"Daddy." Harriet stood in the bedroom doorway. "What was that police car doing in the driveway?"

"It ain't nothing you got to worry over." I kissed her forehead. "You go back to sleep. It's real early."

"Why do I have to stay in bed if Sparrow ain't?"

"What do you mean, Sparrow ain't in bed?" I asked.

Malachi pushed past us both while he tied his tie and went into the bathroom. It was like he didn't even hear what Harriet was saying. As usual, his mind was caught up with something else — church — instead of his family.

"She ain't in her bed. I thought she was down here." Harriet's eyes rounded large with question.

I went into the kitchen half expecting to see her standing there. But she wasn't. I looked out the front window and saw the police car pull out of the drive, red taillights glowing. The church was silhouetted in a calm sunrise. I went to the kitchen window and looked out back. She wasn't there.

I went up to her room next. Of course Harriet couldn't have imagined Sparrow's empty bed, but I had to see for myself. I pulled the covers off her bed and all I found were blooms of red blood on her white sheets. I sucked in a breath. Even though I knew it could be her monthly, I got a bad feeling about seeing that blood.

"That blood?" Harriet made a stink face looking at it.

"Harriet, you gonna need to be a big, grown-up girl and stay home with your brothers." I know I sounded breathless so I cleared my throat to put some oomph in my words. "If George wakes up you just give him a bowl of cereal and some orange juice. You tell him Mama will be home soon."

"Where you going?"

"I got to get your sister." I ran down the stairs almost missing half of them and changed into an old dress as fast as I could. I didn't even put on any stockings but slipped my feet into my shoes.

"You going somewhere?" Malachi asked when I got to the kitchen where he was grabbing an apple.

"Sparrow's run off again. I think I know where she went."

He stopped me with his hands squeezing my forearms and didn't speak until I looked at his face. "Dee, you okay to deal with her?"

"What choice do I got? You go to the Carters and I look for the girl — you don't know where to look anyhow." I didn't know why I was so panicked at her having run off again, because I knew she'd be in the woods or at Emma's house. What trouble could she get in? But there was something like a boulder in my stomach and I knew something wasn't right.

"Delilah." It meant something when he said my whole name. "She's your girl. Don't forget that."

"I know that. Now let me go." I reminded Harriet of my instructions and then ran out into the yellow, dewy morning.

My feet were wet by the time I got to the stream. I didn't worry about using the stones and splashed through the few inches of water. I ran as long as I could and then I did that fast walk-run, all the while looking around for some sign that maybe Sparrow was near.

I was a little over halfway when I saw her fuzzy black hair sitting near the clearing by the stream. The sun wasn't all the way up

435

yet but the light shined through the trees, and I looked up and breathed a thank-you to God. She was humming something I didn't know and rocking front to back in rhythm. She didn't hear me come closer even though I was breathing heavy.

"What you doing, girl?"

I thought I'd see my girl turn toward me but she didn't. She looked up at me with what looked like two round, hollow circles in her head and then looked back toward the water. I didn't even recognize what I was seeing.

"Sparrow." Was more breath in her name than sound.

She didn't look at all this time.

I took a few steps closer and her whole body came into view. The skirt of her green dress was pulled up to the middle of her thighs. Her legs were sticking straight out, her feet bare. She was holding something in her hand and still rocking a little, but the humming was only in spurts, and snatches of it seemed a mite familiar. I walked closer and stood almost in front of her.

My scream didn't echo so much as it just shot right up through that sunlight beam. My whole body was shaking and I didn't know what I was looking at. Her legs were a mixture of brown and red. She got blood all over herself.

Blood.

I kneeled down and starting rubbing her legs with my skirt. "How did this happen?" I said between panicked breaths.

She didn't look at me but handed me a piece of amber glass. Sharp enough to cut but too thick to go deep. I grabbed it from her hand and threw it in the water. I scooted toward the stream and cupped water in my hands and washed it over her legs.

She still don't do nothing. She don't talk. She don't wince. She don't move. She don't even act like the cuts hurt. It's like she wasn't there no more.

I kept cleaning her legs and found cuts all over the tops of her thighs. None of them were awful deep, but there were a whole bunch of them and they didn't stop bleeding. I didn't know if I felt disgust or fear. Why would she do such a thing? Was she possessed by a demon, because no one in their right mind does stuff like this, right?

"Sparrow." I slapped her face. Not hard but hard enough to get her attention. She didn't move. My stomach moved up and down like it wanted to come right on out of me but I wouldn't let it. Maybe it was my own demon.

I grabbed her by the hair knot on the back

of her head and yanked with a strength I didn't know I got. I flipped her forward toward the stream and stuck her face in it hard. The water rushed past her face and rushed over her hair and my hand. It was cold. After a few seconds I pulled her up.

She was breathing hard and her eyes were alive and her nose was bleeding now. I pushed her down too hard. But I got her knowing and hearing me now. But for how long?

I pulled her up. She seemed weak and hung on to my arms. She was dripping and breathing in gasps and her nostrils were flaring.

"What you done to yourself, Sparrow?"

She wasn't answering me. But she wasn't blank no more. I got this feeling that she been doing this for a while and I hadn't paid no attention. The blood on the bedsheets — yes.

I unbuttoned her dress and she didn't even try to stop me. I looked her body over. She was wearing a bra, but I saw on her shoulders and chest some slips of lightness, like scars that were still healing. I touched them. There was a ripple of skin. "You done that?"

She nodded. Her breathing was more normal now but her nose was bleeding still, and it was dripping down her mouth and onto both of us.

"With what?"

She pointed to some weeds on the other side of the stream.

"Weeds?"

"Nettles." Her high-pitched voice was raspy and hurt my ears to hear.

I remembered Emma talking about nettles and that you couldn't touch them without burning your skin.

Around her waist were more blister scars from the nettles. I lifted her skirt and her underwear was blood red and not from her monthly. She got a whole lineup of cuts still bleeding down the side of her legs and some rows of little marks. Just like the tally marks on the tree — counts of five. They were scabbed over and puffy.

"What you done to yourself?" I let go of her dress and stood.

She didn't bother closing her dress but just stared at me. Both our chests rose and fell hard and we didn't sound like ourselves. I didn't even feel like myself. Just like when Carver died and I saw his little body lying there all wet. I just thought I got to be somebody else because Delilah Evans did not have a dead child.

Delilah Evans did not have a child who

cut herself like this.

But she did. I did. I fell onto my knees. I couldn't hold myself up no more. I got no bones inside me — I was just filled up with grief. It took up all my spaces.

Then Sparrow ran.

EMMA

The morning sunlight hadn't even crept through my windows when I heard the banging on my door. I sat up with a quick exhale. John was asleep and wasn't roused in the least by the sound. My senses were at the very surface of my body and I took in everything fast, like how the room was filled with the scent of sweat and humidity. My husband's breath was even and calm. It had been so erratic lately because he decided to stop drinking. He needed my help but I didn't want to give it. The taste of guilt never left my mouth now.

The knock was louder the second time I heard it and I got out of bed — being careful of my burned hands. The knock came a third time before I made it to the front door. Anyone showing up at my house so early made my nerves tense.

I opened the door to find Sparrow on my porch. Something was wrong. She looked as

441

if she'd been attacked — her legs and face were bloody and her dress hung open. Deedee came a moment later, shaking and breathless. Her dress was bloody also.

I glanced up the stairs. No John. I closed the door without a click and joined them on the porch. I didn't want John or Johnny to wake. Whatever was happening, I had to deal with it on my own. Even though it was warm I wrapped my arms around myself, holding my nightgown closer to my body.

I looked between mother and daughter, startled at what I saw. Deedee was on the ground in front of the porch steps staring up at me. Her chest rising and falling deeply. Her face grimaced in pain but not because she had been running. I knew the expression too well and it ran deeper than anything physical. Sparrow was on the porch several paces away and breathing so loudly that each exhale made a sound.

I looked back at Deedee. "What happened?"

"She ran here, Emma. I tried to catch her before she woke you," Deedee said. "I don't know what come over her. What happened to your hands?"

I looked down at the strips of cloth I had wrapped around my burned hands but didn't answer Deedee. "Sparrow?"

"He drowned, Ms. Emma," Sparrow yelled, ragged.

"What? Who?" I looked past Sparrow and saw Deedee crumble and hold on to the porch rail to keep from falling.

"Carver! Carver drowned in the river. While I was kissing a boy my baby brother was drowning down the Alabama River. It was my fault. Mama blames me and she hates me for it."

I didn't know what to say. Deedee couldn't meet my gaze. She just looked down at the ground, shuddering with sobs. Carver had drowned. I couldn't think of a more terrible way to know how your child died.

"Why are you telling me this?" I didn't know why I asked this, but I knew Deedee didn't want me to know or she would've told me. I didn't know why telling me made a difference.

"Because I can't live at home no more," Sparrow yelled. "Please, Ms. Emma. I know I'm not white and can't be your daughter. But maybe I could work for you. Maybe I could live in the barn or the basement. I don't care. I won't make no fuss. I can do your laundry and your ironing and your darning."

"Sparrow." I wanted to fold her into my arms. I wanted to fold Deedee into the same hold. There was nothing I could say that would make this right.

"Mama and Daddy moved here to start over but I didn't get no fresh start. I need to move someplace else now. Emma, can I?" She begged like she believed and meant every word she said. "Mama wishes I drowned instead of Carver."

Then Deedee fell onto her knees. I squeezed Sparrow's shoulder but had to move past her on my way to Deedee. I would help her up. Bring her inside and give her hot honeyed peppermint tea. It wasn't that I was choosing to comfort Deedee over Sparrow, but I knew she would never ask for my help as Sparrow would. And maybe not accept it either.

When I got to the bottom of the porch, I knelt by Deedee and put an arm around her shoulders and helped her up. She let me.

That's when I heard a buggy pass by the house. When a second went by, I paused. Then the third came, but instead of moving on, it turned into the gravel driveway.

I pulled Deedee up the porch steps and waved at Sparrow to go inside. I didn't know who had driven in and I didn't want to have to explain something I didn't under-stand myself — why had Sparrow brought her confession now?

I sat Deedee on the kitchen chair and she looked at me with a sorrow I didn't know was possible. I wanted to stay inside. But I couldn't. In a few moments I stood outside on the porch again wishing I'd grabbed my robe. Whoever was here was not someone I'd want to see me in my nightgown.

After a few moments I saw that it was Mervin Mast driving the buggy. Why was he here? Deedee and Sparrow were sitting in my kitchen and at any moment John and Johnny could wake up and wonder the same. I turned around but couldn't think of a fast solution, so I turned back to face the preacher as he climbed out of the buggy. It looked like his daughter Dinah sat in the passenger side.

Mervin walked around to the back of the buggy and opened the door. Dinah came out the other side and went to the back of the buggy with her *dat*. I just stood there. Then Mervin shuffled around the side of the buggy with Johnny's arm hanging loosely around him.

"Johnny." I ran to him. Even though I touched him — his arm that hung at his side, his chest, his face — I knew right away what was the matter. There was no wound for me to mend. There was drunkenness. I

445

knew it well. "Bring him over here."

I took the other side of Johnny and helped him up the stairs and onto the porch swing. He moaned now and again but didn't say anything. Dinah followed soundlessly. She was dressed, but her eyes were red rimmed and her face blotchy, as if she'd been crying.

The veil between the church and our sin was as thin as the nightgown I wore. My breath was caught in my lungs and I just stared at my son until Mervin spoke.

"Do you want to get John?"

"He's not well," I said too fast.

His expression slipped — like he knew something. He looked at his daughter, then back at me when he spoke. "Dinah, *sis nah zeit.*" He told her that it was time.

I jerked my gaze toward her and imagined that my eyes were too big to stay in my face. I could hear my breathing. Johnny's moaning. And I had two Negro neighbors in the house. And upstairs my sleeping husband was ill from being too sober. My knees weakened.

Mervin grabbed me and helped me to the rocking chair. I sat at the edge and tried to catch my breath.

"Johnny, Danny, and your neighbor boy," Dinah started, then looked at her *dat.* He gestured for her to continue. She did with tears in her eyes. "They've been making plans to run away."

My hand stifled my gasp and she paused. Her *dat* nudged her to continue.

"Arnold crashed his truck and Johnny got awful mad. He beat up Arnold pretty good, and then they both started drinking again. Danny didn't know what to do so he dropped off Arnold at his house but brought Johnny to my barn. I was the only one who knew what they were planning."

A commotion erupted in the house.

"Vas ist en auh geh?" John came outside asking what was going on. It was easy to see he was filled with confusion as Sparrow and Deedee followed him. Sparrow's gaze was on her feet. Deedee looked like she might faint and her face shook with weeping and fear. My heart was beating so fast it felt like it was in my throat and my ears felt drowned with the sound of it.

"John," I said, then looked at Mervin. I couldn't think of anything I could say that would distract from how unusual this was. "These are my neighbors — they were in need this morning."

"Now, listen," Mervin began saying in English for Sparrow and Deedee's benefit. "I'm not sure about everything that's going

447

on here, but Dinah didn't know what to do with Johnny so she came and got me. I brought him home so we could figure this all out together."

There was a pause so heavy and great that I didn't have the strength to lift it with a response.

"John, you have to get ahold of your family." Mervin meant well when he said this, but I winced. "You have a son who is out of control and you could've lost him overnight. He and Danny were in the truck when Arnold crashed it into the church in town."

Deedee gasped, but when I looked at her she pursed her lips like she had a lot to say but didn't.

Mervin opened his mouth to talk again when Johnny spoke. "I kissed her." He had sat up without anyone realizing. He looked angry.

I looked at Dinah, who had stopped crying but looked as shocked as all of us.

"What?" I said, not understanding.

"I kissed her," he said, pointing at Sparrow. Then he looked at Mervin. "My *dat*'s a drunk. That's why I wanted to run away."

I knew my tongue was in my mouth, but it was dry and dusty and I couldn't speak. He'd kissed Sparrow and confessed John's drunkenness to our preacher. I couldn't

448

breathe, I couldn't speak. No one was speaking, but it wasn't silent.

John stuttered something about Johnny not being in his right mind.

Deedee looked at Sparrow, but Sparrow's and Johnny's eyes were locked on each other.

Dinah started crying again and ran to the buggy.

"Is this true?" Deedee gripped one of Sparrow's arms and shook it hard. "And don't you lie to me, girl."

Sparrow looked away from Johnny to me and then down at her feet.

Deedee pulled Sparrow by the arm toward the porch stairs. She got to the bottom and turned toward me. "Emma, you best get your son in control and keep him away from my daughter. And don't you lie to your preacher and tell him that Johnny ain't telling the truth about your drunkard husband." She turned her eyes on John. "A young man in my church is being blamed for your son's foolishness. You better go to the police and make sure they know the truth. You're getting one of our young men in a whole heap o' trouble over that wreck. You hear me?"

Johnny started groaning and mumbling repeated words, but I was distracted by

John's agitation. I was sure he'd never been spoken to like that. Deedee half dragged Sparrow across my yard and toward the woods. I hadn't had a moment to take in the things Sparrow confessed this morning and the burden that weighed heavy on Deedee, and now they were gone. But I had another set of problems in front of me.

"Mervin, the boy is drunk. *Glaup ein neht.*" Of course John was telling Mervin not to believe Johnny. My husband would rather have anyone believe that our son was the drunk and liar in the family. "And that Negro *frau* doesn't know me or anything about my family. You can't believe a word she says."

Johnny suddenly rushed to the side of the porch and vomited over the railing. After several heaves he lay down on the floorboards and groaned.

"I'm so sorry, Mervin," was all I could say. I was sorry that my son was rebellious and drunk and had destroyed the church in town and hurt his daughter.

"Who was that lady and the girl?" Mervin asked, still confused.

"Neighbors." My head gestured toward the woods. I knew he wanted more information than that, but that was all I would say. "The preacher's family on the other side of our woods."

"What do you know about them? What about this girl and Johnny?" His voice was calm but firm. He wasn't looking for a conversation but for answers.

I knew enough about them and they knew everything about me, but I could find nothing I was willing to say to him.

"I don't know why they were here this morning." I looked up at Mervin and then at John. I knew that didn't answer Mervin's question. "I know they needed help. They know I will help them."

"And what Johnny said about the girl?" Mervin asked.

I shook my head and my eyes burned. "I don't know." I exhaled. "Johnny?"

He didn't move.

"Johnny," I yelled, and the rasp in my voice scratched my throat. "Answer me."

"You don't want the truth. None of you do." Johnny's words weren't so slurred anymore. He was coming back to himself. He wouldn't be able to take back the words he'd thrown out into our morning.

"And what about the other things he said?" Mervin looked at me for a response, not John.

But I could not speak. It was like some unseen demon was holding down my

451

tongue. Was it because I couldn't be honest anymore? Was it because I loved my husband so much that I didn't want to see his ruination? Sadly, that was not true. It would be *our* undoing. I was protecting myself along with him. But hadn't he asked for my forgiveness and I withheld it from him?

I could not forgive him.

I wanted him to suffer. I should tell Mervin everything.

"Tell him, Emma." John looked at me and my skin prickled. Then he added, "Since it looks like Mervin here wants to hear it from you and not me."

Was he angry or scared? Both?

I looked down at my hands and what he'd done to me. I looked at my husband. Somewhere far deep into what was left of my heart I loved John. He'd hurt me and destroyed our marriage, but what I'd vowed to him was wound around us tighter than the bandages around my burned hands.

"Johnny's drunk." I didn't lie. But I wasn't honest. "I don't know what he means by everything else. He's —"

"Mem." A storm brewed in his voice. *"Esch sahk ein."*

Just tell him.

"*Nah schtopes,* Johnny." John pointed a thick, calloused finger at our son and told him to stop, then turned it on me.

I looked at his hardworking hand with his finger close to me, pointing at my heart. It shook. I looked at his face. His eyes pleaded with me. I could hear his words asking for me to forgive him and to help him start over.

"Emma, *geh ins haus.*" While his order was only whispered, I knew I needed to obey and go into the house.

"Mem." Johnny's exasperated tone made me hesitate, but not long.

John's gaze left me. The weight of it was somewhere else entirely, but it wasn't on me. I should have been glad, but I felt loss instead.

I went inside and left the three of them outside.

When someone was voted in as a deacon or preacher in our church, they left that position only through death. But what about sin? What about the death of their righteousness and soul? Was there such a thing?

SPARROW

My feet splashed in puddles and through wet grass and hit against the rocks. Mama was rough with me walking through Emma's yard, but when we was out of view it got real hard. She pulled me through them woods like I was some kind of dog. She had me by the collar of my dress and if her hand fumbled she'd grab my sleeve. I'd closed the front of my dress when we was inside Emma's house, waiting. But not all the buttons was there no more. Mama had popped some of them off like dandelion heads.

We was both breathing heavy, but sometimes she would say something like, "I just can't believe you," or "A white boy," or "Here we go again." She even stopped once and let go of my dress. She tried to talk but that irritated laugh of hers came out more often. Like she just couldn't believe how stupid I was. 'Course she right.

"Didn't I tell you boys was off limits?"

Her finger jabbed at my face.

I nodded.

"But you didn't listen and you go and kiss that boy?"

I nodded.

"What was you thinking?" She turned in a circle, shaking her head. Then returned to me. "What. Was. You. Thinking? And stop nodding your head at me. Answer me."

I didn't say nothing.

She smacked my cheek. Hard.

I looked over her shoulder and then she grabbed my dress again. This time the front was rolled up in her fist. Another button popped off. "Oh no, you don't try to run away from me." She whipped out her mean smile. "I saw you looking past me like you was ready to run. I have had enough of that."

We walked, her pulling me, a few more steps. Then she turned toward me again. "You hear me, girl, loud and clear." Her voice was shaky and with lots of breathing. "You gonna stand by me, walk by me, sit by me, and lay by me. You ain't gonna have any time without me."

My eyes filled.

"And do you know why?"

My vision was so blurry, but I wouldn't blink out them tears.

"Because you can't be trusted with nothing." That word *nothing* came out with a spray of spit. "And every time you so close to me you know it's because you are like nothing. Because girls who are something can be trusted and don't act like they's nothing."

The tears were hotter than I thought they'd be when they finally trailed down my sweaty face. Mama had them too.

"You crying now?" she asked. "Where was all this crying when you let your brother drown under that river? When you should've been watching him instead of kissing J. D.? You let that happen. You. And it was all because of a boy."

I was full on crying now. I didn't know how to stop the crying when it started. That's why I hadn't cried before.

"Stop crying." Her words lashed me hard.

My tears wet my neck and slid down between my bosoms. My knees hit the hard earth. I kept crying.

"Get up." She pulled at the shoulders of my dress. "Get up."

"I can't, Mama," I said between heaving. "You don't want me to anyhow. Just leave me here."

"Get up." Her voice got a shudder to it now. She pulled at the back of my collar but it didn't even move me an inch.

"I killed him, Mama," I yelled into the ground, but I know the words make it to her ears and might've reached all the way down to the water in the earth and gone all the way to Carver.

"Don't you talk about him. Don't you talk about him." Mama's voice was wild and full of poison.

"Then we can talk about me, Mama. You like to do that, don't you? You talk about how bad I am all the time. Especially that day when J. D. was kissing on me and I let him and I liked it." I spit out my words like they was pure water.

"You a little tramp, that's what you are. A tramp that don't care 'bout nothing but herself."

She'd never called me that before. I couldn't even say it. I'd said it before about the girl down the street — everybody did. She was doing it with just about every boy who wanted her. I never done that. I never showed my body to nobody and I never let the boys touch me down there.

"No, I ain't. I was just kissing. I didn't let him touch me there or there." I sat up and pointed to my chest and between my legs. For a split second I watched the tops of the trees swaying and I felt bad that they got to hear all our ugly yelling. Then I kept at it. "He tried, you know. He was trying when Carver was calling for me. He was calling my name, Mama. He was calling for me. 'Birdie, Birdie,' he kept saying. But he called it three times before I looked because I couldn't get J. D.'s hands off of me."

"But you was still off with him — kissing — when you should've been watching. Don't you blame it on that neighbor boy and make it sound like it was his fault because he was trying to feel you up. You shouldn'ta been kissing on him nohow."

She was right. I never should have walked away from the river. Mama and Daddy and every other adult told us that a hundred times. I didn't listen. It was still my fault. I had picked J. D.'s kissing over keeping my baby brother alive. He got four years on this earth and died. I got ten more than him and I wasn't deserving. Nobody had to tell me that. I just knew it.

"I know." I yelled so loud I heard birds fly away.

She ain't never spoke to me about that day but for what I was doing. Even the little that Daddy tried to tell her of what I told him, she wouldn't listen. I didn't even know if she knew that the whole reason it happened was because George and Carver was

458

just trying to be like Daddy. Now Mama hated me and sometimes I wondered if she hated Daddy too.

"They was playing preacher, baptizing each other in the river." My voice was like a crow's caw. Ugly and raspy. I wanted her to know this stuff in case she didn't, because I wanted her to hurt as bad as I did.

"Stop it." Her words were captured inside her wailing cry. "Don't you talk about it. Don't you talk about him." She wagged her finger at me before she turned and started walking away from me.

She'd walked away from me every day since Carver died. Her steps were heavy and like her joints was hurting every time she stepped. Like she was carrying a load on her back. She was wearing her old blue dress. The same one she was wearing that day, and I wondered if she even realized it. I remembered it because everything that day was stuck in my head like a picture that don't move or change except that Carver went from smiling to dead every time that picture came up.

"He pushed George to the big log that stuck out. But he couldn't catch it himself." I'm quieter now but I know'd she heard me. "That's when he started yelling for you."

Mama stopped walking and just stood

there facing the other way, away from me. I could see her shoulders shake and her whole body shudder.

DELILAH

My eyes were open but all I saw was flashes between white and black in front of me. Like my vision was going and I didn't want to see nothing no more.

I hadn't let her tell me nothing about that day. Not Malachi neither — but he tried and he would say things I didn't want to know. Like how Carver was playing preacher and trying to baptize George. But I didn't want to hear about how my baby died. I just knew he died, drowned under that Alabama River. Didn't nobody need to know more than that.

I didn't think nothing could make it worse than it already was — losing a child. But baptism. Wasn't baptism supposed to bring you a new life? It brought my baby death. I didn't want to hear nothing more about that. Nothing. But that girl kept talking and my legs couldn't move. I just fell on the dusty old trail under my feet.

"Carver saved George, Mama, but couldn't save himself. I jumped in but I couldn't get to him. He was yelling for me and you one second and then he wasn't. I couldn't find him. He was under there somewhere and I couldn't find him, Mama. But I looked. I looked until the police pulled me out."

The girl had been wet all over when I saw her. Shivering and acting crazy like. The swimsuit dress my aunt made for her was torn and it just about showed too much of her. Her legs was scraped all over and she got a big gash on her calf where you could see too much of the stuff inside. But she won't let nobody help her. They had to hold her down so she didn't jump back in that dang river. My sister Deborah had to fight with her to get her stitched up, but I never bothered myself with it. Later that night Deborah also gave the girl something, don't even know what, to make her sleep.

Gave it to George too. He was just having fits all over the place. Wetting the bed and slapping, biting, and scratching everybody that came close. Lost most of the handful of words he said. Only kept a few.

That mark on her leg, though, always stared at me. It got infected once and Deborah had to deal with it. But now it was just ugly and puffy. But it go along with all them other cuts she got. Like she didn't want that to be her only mark. I never did see the old Sparrow again from that day on — the one I'd raised. I reckoned she was dead somewhere in that old Alabama River too.

But I didn't grieve for her. I just grieved for my baby boy.

SPARROW

I was glad Mama kept her face turned away from me because I wouldn't have been able to look at her. I heard her heaving great big sobs now and she stepped backward, like she couldn't hold herself up, and collapsed. She don't get up neither. Not for a good long time. She moaned for Carver over and over. I don't know when she left but she did.

She left me in them woods alone. But the trees was still moaning *Carver, Carver.* The birds didn't sing those nice pretty songs, but instead it sounded like *Carver, Carver.* Slow and sad and like it came from deep in the ground, his name growing inside the dirt like a seed. The warble of the stream was low and deep, and when the rain came, I felt like God was saying *Carver, Carver* in the thunder.

I went back to that day. I could feel the crispy grass between my toes while we walked to the river. I could feel the hold on my hand and the pull of my heart. As I hid behind the bushes with J. D., I could feel his few kisses on my lips. They made me warm all over. There was laughing and giggling and running back toward the river.

But I knew I wasn't there. The birds were singing and the sun was up high now. I been out here for a couple of hours just lying in the trail.

An arm came around me, but my eyes just saw the ground in front of me. I let that somebody lead me away. They sat me down in a chair somewhere. I obeyed and didn't care who was with me or what would happen. A towel was pressed against my head and hair and I felt the wetness lift off of me some. My mess of a dress was taken off me. I don't know if I lifted my arms on my own or not. I didn't have a lot of control of my body no more. My wounds were dressed with nice hands. But I couldn't see nothing much. My eyes were about swollen shut 'cause of all the crying and they just didn't want to see nothing. Then the hands put another dress on me. It didn't fit just right and it didn't feel right but I didn't much care.

I knew I walked somewhere and then I heard Daddy's voice and another voice. I knew them both, but I couldn't think about who the other one was. I just stood there until Daddy took my arm and he walked me up to my room. I thought he asked me about eating something, but I couldn't say nothing. I knew enough that I was on my bed so I turned to face the wall away from Harriet's bed and from Daddy who stood there. I kept my eyes from his face because I think seeing him would kill me dead.

But then I think, *Ain't I already dead?*

EMMA

It was late afternoon when John found the strength to drive me and Johnny into town. He knew that we needed to see the church that he and Danny had driven into with Arnold. I didn't know how John was managing after he'd been shaky and weak the whole day. Maybe it was because he knew it was something we had to do. Something we'd never had to do before — contend with our local police to see what must be done and not just our Amish church.

No one talked the whole way into town. I wasn't sure if Johnny was even breathing, he was so quiet. It was later in the day, but we knew we needed to go make things right. We didn't want another boy getting blamed for something Johnny had done. Perhaps John realized our son needed a father.

When we got there I was surprised to see so many people there. The damage was bad. Worse than I'd imagined. The yard had deep tire grooves through it and the hole exposed the inside of the church.

A police car was there and several Negro families, but I only recognized Malachi. No one seemed to notice us as we parked a short distance away. John tied the horse on one of the hitching posts placed sporadically throughout the town. He walked stronger than I thought was possible and had Johnny's shoulder under his grip. He told Johnny to tell the police what he'd done. I walked behind them.

The Negro families moved over a little when we arrived, and as I stepped on the other side of Johnny I looked around and listened. The same large police chief was there and a tall Negro man was talking to him. Deedee's husband stood next to him and patted his shoulder, as if trying to keep him calm.

"We've been talking about this for hours in our homes and now here," Malachi said. "We know Kenny didn't do this."

"Unless you can prove he didn't, we will put a warrant out for his arrest for the destruction of public property." The police chief leaned back and folded his arms. He seemed to think a lot of himself as I'd seen this same stance on several men in our church I tried to avoid.

"My son has something to say." John's loud voice brought everyone's attention.

No one said anything. Everyone just looked at us.

"What was that, Mr. — ?" The police chief made one step toward us and squinted.

"John Mullet," my husband said plainly.

"Mr. Mullet, then. I'm Police Chief Crabtree." He cleared his throat and looked around at all the eyes watching the exchange. "I'm sure you don't have anything to offer in this situation." He fixed his belt around his big belly. "This isn't anything you need to worry about. We are keeping the town safe for peacekeeping folks like you."

John held my gaze as he patted Johnny's shoulder.

"It was me," Johnny said just loud enough to be heard. "My friends and I were drinking and we ran into the church — it was an accident. We didn't mean to do it."

The murmur that resulted among the dozen people who stood by was louder than expected. I heard everything from how it was typical that a colored boy was blamed for what a white boy did to how it was a good boy who would step up and confess his wrongs.

"Surely you're not saying that you — ?"

The chief's eyebrows knit together and he gestured toward the gaping hole in the church. "But you don't drive cars."

"My friend, who's not Amish, was driving, but we were both drinking." Johnny looked at his *dat,* who gestured for him to continue. "I want to help pay for the repairs and do as much of the work as I can myself. I know carpentry."

"Now, son," Chief Crabtree said with a great big smile on his face. "Aren't you just a stand-up fella?"

He continued to give Johnny accolades for his uprightness and I watched as the spirit of the Negro community declined. Their young man had just been threatened with arrest for the damages and my son had been given a pat on the shoulder and a smile.

I felt myself shrinking and wished I'd stayed home. The police chief, John, and Johnny walked toward the church and continued to talk about what the repairs would look like and how much it might cost. I was standing there alone. I'd never felt so exposed.

"Next time tell your son to fess up before my boy gets accused and we have to defend him for hours," a tall woman yelled over at me. I could see she'd been crying and she still held a handkerchief.

Several others agreed with her and I didn't know what to say. I just stood there. I thought of all the things Deedee had told me about all the rules they had to follow in order for them to survive in a society that wouldn't give them equal rights because of the color of their skin. How could I defend myself or my son? He had done wrong.

Then after a few quiet moments Deedee came from behind the crowd and padded through the churchyard to stand by me. "She done her job. She brought her boy here to make things right. The boy done what he was supposed to do."

"But why did they wait so long?" the same woman as before yelled. "You know what we've been through today, Deedee."

Deedee looked up at me and pursed her lips a little. Her whole face was ashen and tired looking. My face probably looked the same in her eyes. I knew she was still upset at how the morning had gone. Who wouldn't be? I still didn't understand all that had happened. And I knew she knew that it had been Johnny all the while but hadn't turned him in to the police. Maybe she knew we would do the right thing. Did she have more faith in my family than I had?

She stood with me as proof of that.

DELILAH

I walked through them woods holding on to that dang green Amish dress that Sparrow came home wearing. I made sure to gather up every pin and weave them through the fabric, and I put it in one of Emma's baskets she had brought one day. It was full of herbs and friendship that time though. If I hadn't used up them herbs already, I would've thrown them out or given them back too.

Just because I stood by Emma at that white church didn't mean I wasn't upset. And it didn't mean that any of us missed how Police Chief Crabtree treated the Mullets differently than the Carters. Was that the Mullets' fault though? And if the tables were turned, I was sure that Emma would've stood with me. I hoped anyhow.

Couple of days had passed by now and Sparrow was still little more than a rag doll. She wouldn't eat or talk or do nothing. Nothing I did worked. But all I did was try to get her to listen to me, thinking she might snap out of it. But I knew she wouldn't. She was done hearing me. I don't know but to just leave her be for a time. Malachi said I was wrong.

Right now, though, I want to take back the dress and the basket and tell Emma that she got no right putting an Amish dress on my daughter. She got no right to bring her by and walk away without no explanation, leaving Sparrow for Malachi to find standing on the front porch. She got no right making my girl prefer her over her own family. Sparrow ain't Emma's daughter. She ain't her kin. She ain't her color. She ain't her religion.

It don't matter that I don't know what to do with Sparrow or what I think about her. She was still mine and Emma got no right to coddle her. I couldn't get out of my head how that girl was begging to be Emma's servant.

I put on a church dress and my hat and my nice shoes, even though it was Thursday. It did make it harder to walk through the woods and creek. With all the rain we got on Sunday it been dry ever since. Like bone-desert dry. Like we-ain't-never-gonna-get-more-rain sort of dry. It was like all the water in the air got harvested up and stored up someplace else.

When I left the woods and entered Emma's yard, I took a deep breath. The problem with this business was that I liked Emma and it pained me to lose her as a friend. It wasn't that I never liked no white woman before. In Montgomery there was a church, a white church, with a group of ladies who came around sometimes — to be nice. At first I didn't like them because I didn't want no handouts from white people — I didn't want them to act like they were *missionaries* to us — but when I gave them a chance, I saw they weren't doing that. They were all either old schoolteachers or nice white folks and wanted to stop drawing lines between the races and instead learn from each other.

Still not always sure what they wanted out of us, but they were real nice folks. Otherwise, I had only worked for white ladies. And I don't think that a lot of white ladies got colored lady friends. We all just keep to ourselves and what we know and what's easier. Wrong or right, that was how I saw things.

When I saw Emma on her porch I stopped my step. I stood there for a second and watched. She wasn't wearing her normal bonnet but just a knotted handkerchief. I done that so many times, just like that.

When I started walking again my feet brushed the dry grass and she noticed me. It was almost like the air around me was pulled into her inhale. She stood. My steps felt like when you walked through water. You got to push your legs harder and watch for a sure step.

"Can I get you some lemonade?" Emma said when I stood at the bottom of the porch steps.

"No, ma'am. I just came by to deliver back your things."

"Deedee." Emma's voice dropped at the end, like her tone said, *Why you acting this way?*

Why wouldn't I though? *Come on, Emma. Your boy kissed my girl. You dressed my daughter in your clothes like she was your daughter.* I wanted to say that but I didn't.

"Will you at least come and sit for a minute?" she asked.

I done my own big inhale and exhale and took those steps up and sat opposite of Emma. She had beans she was snapping in a bowl. Her hands still got a few bandages on them and I wonder why.

When neither of us spoke for a few minutes, she started. "I'm sorry about Sunday." Her voice was so thin. Like a starved piece of voice that was just about ready to break.

"It don't matter now." I didn't meet her eyes. Not like all of Sunday was her fault, but I didn't say that. "I brought back your basket and the dress."

"Dress?"

"You didn't think she should keep it, did you? You shouldn't have put it on her to begin with. She ain't your daughter, Emma." My anger rose and I'd slipped and called her by her first name instead of using *Mrs. Mullet* or *ma'am*. I wanted to show her that we wasn't friends no more. I got up and put her things next to the big stainless steel bowl of green beans.

"I don't know what you mean. This is my dress but I never put it on her."

"On Sunday?" I wrinkled up my face. "You brought her back and she was wearing this dress. She had that salve all over her cuts too."

"Deedee, I don't know what you mean. I didn't leave my home except to go into town — with Johnny." Her voice faded at the end.

"What you talking about?" I pulled back my chin and looked at her like she must be losing time or just crazy or something. "Then who — ?"

Then I knew. Emma knew also.

"Johnny," we both said.

But we both knew it wasn't the kind of right answer that was right. It just made more problems. Now I got to worry about her being naked in front of a boy. I got to worry about if that boy done something to my daughter. And if she ever got a baby in her belly, Lord help me, I would send her away.

"He wouldn't do anything to her," Emma said like she reading my thoughts.

"What you mean, he wouldn't do nothing to her? He already done something to her." I shook my head with a laugh that I hoped told Emma she was stupid. "Your boy kissed my girl. You want your white son kissing on a colored girl?"

She inhaled but didn't answer.

"He undressed her and put that dress on her." I pointed to the ugly green dress sitting there.

"You don't know if he undressed her. She could've put that dress on by herself."

"You don't know what Sparrow's been like, Emma." I started yelling and stood. "She don't eat, don't talk, don't make no noise even. When I wave my hand in front of her face, she don't blink. She don't do nothing but lie there in her bed. She peed the bed and didn't mind to lie in it."

"What?" When Emma stood she upset the

bowl of beans and it made a loud hollow sound against the wood porch floor. "I need to see her."

"No, you don't." I wagged my finger at her. "You got to stay away. Don't you see this is your fault?"

"*My* fault?"

"And your son's. He done caused her to get all messed up in her head. She don't know what's up or down no more. They been meeting in them woods of yours. And then your son kissing on her and probably kissing on that redheaded Amish girl also. And who knows who else. And maybe it was more than kissing."

"But, Dee —"

"He getting drunk and driving cars into places and then colored boys getting blamed for it." I spat out the words. Why was I the only one who saw the problem here? "Don't you see? You white folks just do what you want but we get the blame."

"But, Deedee, I thought — well, when you stood by me —" She stepped toward me.

"Don't you get it? What are you, stupid? Your son is as dumb as you and as drunk as your husband." It didn't matter that I regretted it as soon as I said it. She wasn't dumb. But I couldn't stop my tongue now. "You best get ahold of that son of yours."

478

"And what about Sparrow?" Emma's voice was as thick as tree sap and she got some courage coming into her all at once. "She came to *me* like a little girl looking for a mother."

"Don't you talk about Sparrow."

"Why? Because you can't face how much you've hurt her?"

"You need to stop talking." I wagged my finger again, then stepped down the porch. Then I turned around to throw a few more words at her. "She ain't your daughter. You don't got no daughter and you don't know nothing about mine."

Her husband came out just then. He looked like a ragged piece of man. His hair was too long and stuck to his forehead. His shirt was hanging out partway and it was a good thing he was wearing them suspenders because his pants looked so big on him, I think they would've gone right down to his ankles.

His gaze landed on me and then Emma and then back on me. "What's this?" He was breathless with just those mite words.

"You aiming to dry up, Mr. Mullet?" I threw my words out to him so fast he twitched a little. "I know all about you and what you done that the church too naive to see."

479

"Deedee, don't," Emma said with the force of an invisible wind.

"Y'all think you better than everybody else, don't y'all? Like y'all above everybody?" I almost got to laugh now, seeing the two of them standing on that porch acting like they don't know all they done.

"My wife hasn't done nothing to be ashamed of." His tone was so honest it surprised me. He believed what he said — like he got some saint for a wife who been putting up with his drunk ways for years.

"You a fool for not knowing that for years — *years* — your wife been taking birth control herbs."

Emma hung her head, weeping. John looked over at her and back at me when I couldn't keep my mouth shut. And my own tears burned my eyes.

"Now you know, like you should have all this time." I was ashamed of my words. Emma looked at me for a moment with all that water in her eyes. She stepped around her overturned bowl and left. John followed her inside.

Then I stood alone. I knew I'd done wrong but I couldn't take it back. My fear had taken over my mouth. What was worse was I didn't want to be honest about what I was afraid of but I cried the whole walk home. When I got there and found Malachi sitting at the kitchen table looking at the checkbook, I was so angry with myself I got nasty with him.

"You counting all our money?" I said real mean like.

Malachi didn't pay me no mind so I kept biting.

"When you found Sparrow on the porch, she wasn't alone, was she?"

"Dee," he said in that voice that always meant *leave it be*.

"You tell me the truth, Malachi Evans."

He tapped the pen on the table a few times.

"It was the boy." He looked at me.

"And you didn't think you should tell me?"

"It wasn't important right then. Sparrow was." He stood and the scrape of the chair against the floor plucked my nerves. "But you don't seem to be worried about her, do you?"

"Don't you talk like that to me." I glanced over toward my bedroom where my purse sat filled with Carver dirt. I had this vision of two purses sitting there, side by side. What if I lost her? I shook my head. No. That wasn't going to happen.

"I can't fix her, Mal." My voice broke so

481

hard my throat hurt.

"You don't need to fix anyone — you just need to forgive her for what was an accident. Carver's death was an accident."

"I can't!" The little ones at the television turned at my hollering but I didn't care. "I can't do that. It just hurt too much."

"Dee," he started with his nice, soft voice, but I interrupted.

"I think maybe I should call my sister." I looked away from my husband. "The little ones and I will go back to Montgomery — at least for a while. Maybe you can get through to Sparrow. But I can't."

EMMA

I remember my *mammie* telling me once that sins didn't go away with the setting and rising of the sun. Sin remained in its state of needing forgiveness and would still have consequences even after the sun rose and set on it — and then there was the guilt.

"I'm sorry," I told John when he closed the door behind him.

"It's true?" He choked on his words. "All these years?"

I couldn't speak so I just nodded. My tears heated my whole face.

"But you said —" he started but didn't finish.

I knew what he was thinking though. I'd told him those first few years that it was up to God, not us. My first lie. Then, after several years of no pregnancy and after so many bottles my husband had consumed and after so many powdered herbs I'd swallowed, I told him it was because of his

483

drunkenness. I told him we couldn't conceive a child as long as we had a hidden sin. My second lie. But I believed it. I believed that God didn't want us to have more children because John was a drunk and I was a liar. He didn't know my hidden sin though. He didn't know that I was too afraid to have another child. Because of the pain of loss. Because of him. I had made the decision for us without him.

I couldn't go back. It was the truth. And now he was trying to change and my lies had surfaced. If we weren't a drunk and a liar anymore, then who were we?

"You didn't even care that she died," I cried. I'd never said that to him and how it broke my heart. His ignoring me had hurt as much as losing her. "You never even looked at her or helped me bury her. I had to do it alone." I pointed toward the woods.

"I wasn't in my right mind. I hadn't thought things through about — the baby. You wouldn't talk to me. You were so angry, I didn't know what to do." He threw his hands in the air. We'd never spoken like this to each other. "You were so sad and I couldn't fix it."

I considered what he said. There was some truth to it. He was right that I wouldn't talk to him. I retreated into a new hiding place

— the woods, my words, into my quiet — anywhere but near him.

"How could I talk with you? You were drunk all the time." I threw my accusations back at him.

He sighed. "I know and I'm sorry. I can't take it back though." His attention didn't waver from my eyes. "I did wrong. I admit it."

I couldn't respond. I was still so angry and the feelings I had when I placed that tiny box into the damp earth were sown into my soul. He wasn't there. He cared more about his wine than he did me.

"I did see her though." His voice filled the heavy quiet. "The morning you buried her." Tears fell down his cheeks and his face contorted. "I'll never forget the way she looked. And I still visit her grave some-times."

"The black-eyed Susans," I whispered.

It was not long after I'd buried her that I found black-eyed Susans scattered every-where around the tiny grave. Because no one knew where I'd put her grave, I had convinced myself it couldn't have been John. I'd stuffed it away and anytime those flowers lay over her grave again, I always refused to believe they were from him.

"I always thought of her as a Susan —

since that day."

I took in a sharp breath. He had named her too.

"I'm sorry — about the herbs." I meant my words, but my voice sounded hollow and empty. I looked up at him and saw the eyes of the young man I'd married. A ragged face and body encased those eyes, but he was in there and, oh, how I'd loved him. I began to weep and lowered my gaze to my lap. "Forgive me, John."

He watched me for a long time, but I couldn't return his gaze. How could I plead for his forgiveness when I had not extended it myself?

"I forgive you, Emma," he offered too early and too filled with grace. I was undeserving.

In these moments realization settled into me. I had not harvested any wild turnip to dry. There was still some time, but maybe somewhere deep inside of me I knew it was time to stop. The secrets and lies had made my soul more barren than my womb.

John and I didn't talk about the herbs again. As far as it appeared, he had moved beyond that with the unspoken expectation that I would not continue lying to him. And I wouldn't.

The sun set and rose even while the

consequences of our closely held sins lingered and wrapped around us like vises. If sin was a river, I would've drowned long ago. I was drowning even now.

I saw my years of lying to my husband in the growing of the grass. When the trees blew I heard the secrets between Johnny and Sparrow. When the sun roasted the gravel on the drive, making it hot to walk across, I thought of John's drunkenness and desperation to start anew — but not knowing how. The dips in the driveway from old puddles, the dry eaves, the thin air that didn't wave in the distance was John pleading for my forgiveness that I wouldn't give. I'd based my lies and secrets on my husband's sin and I could not get out of the web I'd created.

I had not cooked a hot meal since that Sunday morning when our lives crashed before us. John was in bed most of each day. He hadn't gone to work at all this week and I didn't know how to help him. I was afraid for him. Could *not* drinking kill him?

Since he learned about my lies I thought he wouldn't want my help, but he accepted it every time. When I held his shoulders when he couldn't keep down a bite of food, he would always turn toward me with sorrow-filled eyes and thank me. When I climbed into bed finally, as late as possible, he would move ever so slightly toward me. Just enough to where his back grazed my own rounded back. Like he needed to be near me, to know I was there.

Dealing with Johnny did not have the same softness to it. He had returned to work but kept to himself when he was home. He wasn't leaving the house in the evenings anymore though. For that I was grateful.

"Did you do anything more to Sparrow than kiss her?" I blurted out over a cold dinner of egg salad and tomatoes.

Johnny shook his head.

"What about the dress you gave her? My dress."

"She was lying in the woods — alone." He banged his fist on the table.

"Johnny," I reprimanded.

"Sorry," he said quietly.

I waited for a few moments.

"Did you undress her?" I swallowed hard.

"I promise I didn't *look* at her." He looked into my eyes and I knew he wanted my understanding. "Have you seen her cuts?"

"What do you mean?"

"She hurts herself because she's so sad. They're all over her legs and she has scars in — other places. I tended to the fresh ones."

I swallowed a bite too early and it stuck in

my throat. I drank some water and tried to think about what Johnny was saying. She'd been cutting — hurting — herself and I didn't have to be told why. Hadn't I been hurting myself with herbs, forcing barrenness out of bitterness and fear? Hadn't I attempted to hurt myself when I drank alcohol that night? The pain of sadness had been too great and I did what I despised most. Had I not seen myself in Sparrow from the first moment I saw her in the woods? Only I'd lied to myself, saying I saw my long-deceased daughter instead.

"Why her?" I asked.

The silence seemed to last for an hour.

"From the moment I saw her I knew I needed to know her." He smiled a little. "Don't you think she's beautiful?"

I couldn't trust my voice and nodded my response.

"She was so different from the girls I knew." He paused a moment. "And I think I was supposed to know her so I could help her. She helped me too."

"How?"

He shrugged. "She taught me things I didn't know before. Maybe because she's different from me. Maybe because she needed me. I don't know."

What I heard between his words, in pauses

and stutters, was love. And I found I was proud of my son even in my nervousness and fear of our family's circumstances.

"Someone's here." Johnny pushed his chair back and his hands shook as they ran through his hair.

I hadn't checked on John in hours. The morning hours up until lunch had been a back-and-forth of peace and chaos with him. Once he'd been asleep for longer than an hour, I took to the woods, going the opposite direction of the Evanses' home. I'd followed the creek all the way to the Detweiler farm and its perfect order of things and then walked back.

"Should I go get *Dat*?" Panic laced Johnny's expression. "Can he even get dressed?"

"Try."

He took long strides toward the stairs as he glanced through the living room windows to his left. Then I stood and went to the door, hoping it would slow down the progression of them entering the house before John was ready. If he could even get out of bed.

When the front door clicked behind me, a wash of nerves spread throughout my body. I stood there with my hands still on the knob behind me as Mervin Mast and Simon Detweiler stepped out of the first buggy.

Mervin looked at me for a brief moment before turning back to Simon. They spoke to each other, but I could not hear. Simon's gaze darted around and his jaw clenched and unclenched.

"Hello there." I moved toward the porch steps only to stop in confusion at the appearance of another buggy. I looked at it and then at the barn door, which had been opened though I had not realized it. Our buggy was missing.

"*Dat*'s not in bed," Johnny said as he opened the door and then noticed our buggy in the driveway instead of the barn.

Our ancient bishop, Atlee Hostetler, exited our buggy on the driver's side, then walked around to the other side and helped John out as if he were a woman in labor. He had an arm around John's hunched shoulders as he walked toward us.

John looked up at me. His pale, sick complexion made his eyes stand out, and though weary, they didn't waver from me. He was barely dressed. He wore pants and a shirt, half untucked, his suspenders were down around his knees, and he wore no shoes or hat.

"You didn't notice the buggy or the horse missing when you came home from work?" I asked Johnny, breathless, as John continued to stumble with Atlee up to the porch. Mervin and Simon walked behind them.

"I was too distracted," he whispered back. "What do you think he told them?"

"Ich vehs neht." This was true. I didn't know what John had said to these men or why he chose to do this. I considered that he came up with a plan to find a way to cover what Johnny had confessed. I shouldn't have been surprised that he'd gone on this mission without so much as telling me. Had he told them about the herbs?

"John? *Voh hosh due gah?*" I asked what he'd done and tried to keep my voice steady.

I explained that he'd been sick for days and I was worried that he'd left the house at all. He needed to get back to bed. He was too weak to be out.

John looked at me but didn't say a word. Atlee had John up on the porch now and all I could do was stare at my husband's feet. They were bare and dirty.

"Er hoht mich allies saht," Atlee said in his plain, monotone voice.

John had told him everything. Johnny and I exchanged a pained expression.

Everything? My ears rang and I couldn't hear what Atlee said to Mervin and Simon. But they moved from the side of the house to the basement. My heart pounded like the rhythm of a hammer striking a nail. Everything was trapped inside. I was trapped inside.

"*Hoch annah,* Emma." Atlee's tone telling me to sit was nicer than I deserved.

When I didn't move, Johnny guided me to the rocking chair and helped me sit. John sat on the porch swing with sweat dripping from him. He rested his elbows on his knees and looked up at me through strips of hair. Our eyes were fixed on each other and for the first time in years I found comfort in them. The edge and stubbornness in his forehead had been replaced with regret and age and the wisdom that tortured you when in sin. I knew it well.

"I'm sorry, Em," John said and began to weep.

He hadn't called me Em since we'd first been married, but no tears came. I dropped his gaze and looked to Atlee.

"John came to me today. He has told me everything," Atlee's thin, old voice said.

He paused when Mervin and Simon walked up to the side of the porch.

"He told us the truth, that he smashed the bottles," Mervin said.

Atlee looked back at me. "John will be *schtill schtella.*"

John would be silenced in church — as a member and as a deacon.

"After some time John will need to make a confession," Atlee continued.

"And me?" I straightened my back — awaiting my sentence. "What about me?"

Had my life not been a forest filled with weaknesses and secret hurts and judgment? Had I not worked against God Himself with my efforts to remain barren, with hiding sin, with my hate? My secrets were well folded inside John's sin.

Atlee looked at me with confusion.

"Emma has done nothing to harm the church." John's weak voice broke and caught achingly. "This is my sin."

He was wrong and he was right. I had done nothing to harm the church in the way he had, but I had done much to be ashamed of before God and my husband.

I had hurt my marriage and couldn't see it until now. Suddenly I saw the years I'd kept a babe from my womb. How many children had I said no to? Children I had desired but was afraid to bear — for the possibility of loss. How many women had I blamed for my own loneliness? What joys had I missed over the years because spiting my husband was more important?

It was like lamenting over thirst while the

solace of water was close at hand. But I'd remained empty, and instead of taking a long drink of healing and offering forgiveness, I'd poured the water onto the earth to satisfy the bitter roots I harvested daily. Could water even satisfy my thirst anymore?

SPARROW

Mama washed me up. I don't know which day she done it, but I could feel the wet washcloth against my back. She lifted my arms and washed under my arms and even washed my feet. That tough expression in her face wasn't there though. She cried a lot but I couldn't talk even when she begged me. She just got mad at me when I didn't.

How long would it be until one day I woke up dead? Would Mama wash me before she buried me?

After a bit I did start getting out of bed. I even went to church. Nobody there knew the difference in me though. I never talked anyhow. I didn't sing the songs with them. I just sat there and waited until Daddy was through preaching and then I'd go home.

But today was different.

The Carters told everybody they were moving, now that Granny was gone and they'd sent Kenny away. They was gonna go far away to Mississippi where they got kin and nobody knew what happened up here in Sinking Creek with Kenny. Belinda cried all the way through the service. They were gonna leave after the baptism service. And when I think about that, I think about too many things. None of them were the good things that Daddy always said about baptism neither.

Daddy said we were baptizing everybody at Emma's pond. Mama ain't let me see her since that one Sunday. By then it'll be a few weeks — I think. I missed her but I knew she didn't want nothing to do with me because of what she knew now about me and Johnny.

I think about Johnny, who I ain't seen since that day neither. He was the one who helped me that day, and when he undressed me he stood behind me and kept saying out loud how he wasn't looking at me. I didn't care if he did because I was just skin over top of nothing. But I couldn't tell him that because I couldn't talk no more. He was so careful when he put the salve on my cuts.

The baptism was what I kept thinking on though. Would I see Carver there somewhere floating around in the water? Wasn't that how the police found him? George was holding on to branches at the side of the

Alabama River's current, but Carver wasn't there. The snaky fingers of the river took him away all because of my sin.

All Carver wanted to do was baptize George like he seen Daddy do with the church folks. That's all. But the current didn't know the boys was playing. It just did what currents do and washed them away. Water just did what it did and got in all the cracks and went in all the emptiness it could find. It didn't even have to try hard. It was just how water worked. Sometimes it was giving and sometimes it was taking. Because water can do both.

I heard Mama and Daddy fighting about the baptism late at night when they thought I was asleep. Mama said she ain't going. Daddy said she was and that she can't miss Mallie's big day. When they stopped fighting and I figured they were asleep, I got up and walked around the woods.

The next morning when Mama came up and got me out of bed, like she got to do now, she saw the dirt my feet tracked in. My white sheets ain't white down by my feet. But at least it ain't blood. At least I'm not marking myself no more. It doesn't work no more anyhow. It doesn't give me the relief I need because it doesn't go deep enough.

"You walking around in them dark woods?" she asked, but she knew the answer. She just sat there and cried but I couldn't do nothing.

Then Daddy started sleeping in the kitchen so he would hear me if I got up. But I still got out because I stepped over the squeaky step and could open the door real quiet. Before I left, though, I grabbed Mama's purse — the one with Carver's dirt in it — and took it with me. It was Sunday and Johnny would meet me at daybreak. I was sure of it this time.

But when I got there I was alone. He wasn't there. He was in a whole heap of trouble with his folks, his church, and even with the town. But I was still hoping he'd come.

I traced my fingers against the marks on the tree that told me we'd met eight times. Then I sat and listened to the water moving over the rocks. Then I walked to Emma's pond. Nobody saw me. I dumped Carver's dirt out of the purse and into the pond. It would make Mama hate me even more.

Then I walked home. Daddy was still asleep in the chair and I put Mama's handbag back on her nightstand. But when I went up the stairs the creaky step whined and Mama woke up. She yelled at him and then got me to sit down in a chair and washed my feet again.

DELILAH

I don't know what to do when on Sunday morning my washrag gets brown and red from Sparrow's dirty, bloody feet. She don't seem to feel nothing. Her feet were getting cut and scraped and she didn't even care. I didn't know how to keep her in her bed besides tie her down and I couldn't do that. She made me think about that hospital for crazy folks I saw once and I started to wonder if there's one around here because I don't know what to do.

I'd lost the battle with Sparrow when I decided I wouldn't forgive her for losing my baby boy and I lost the argument with Malachi about Mallie's baptism also. And after I got myself dressed and ready, I got Sparrow ready. Poor Harriet was acting like she was Sparrow's age and she fed the boys their breakfast and straightened George's little tie for him and told him how handsome he looked. She asked Mallie if he had his clothes ready to change into after he was done getting baptized. He said yes, but she still had to bring him the towel he'd forgotten.

Before we left I grabbed my handbag — had to take Carver along. But it weren't heavy.

I opened my bag up in a real hurry and found only a few tiny grains of dirt around the cracks and corners. The dirt was gone. I didn't even question who took Carver's dirt from me, and when I looked over at Sparrow I didn't see my daughter no more. I didn't know this girl who I gave birth to. I set the open purse down on my bedroom floor and left it there — I was emptier than the purse now.

I touched Carver's grave photo that was on my nightstand too. It sat next to a picture of the twins when they were about two. He was smiling at the camera but George was looking down and away — he didn't like looking in people's faces. I clenched my jaw so hard my teeth 'bout broke.

My grief scared me now. It scared me so bad I just about don't know what to do with myself. It don't taunt me like somebody laughing, but it felt like something just crawled on my back and, besides how heavy it was, squeezed me so darn tight I couldn't breathe no more.

And it was more than just a feeling. It was a thing with flesh on it. It lived and walked with me. It slept with me in my bed and shared my pillow. It ate with me and fed me more than I needed. It was a living, breathing, heart-beating kind of grief. It was more alive than me.

When we came into Emma's yard their driveway was filled with the cars from our church folk. They were standing at the pond near the shore, swatting flies. The children stood reverently with their parents, but when that dumb young mother ain't watching her little boy near the water's edge, I just about want to push her in myself.

"The water is still, Dee," Malachi had said earlier. He said how there wasn't no current to drag nobody away. It would not take Mallie to his death. This wasn't the great Alabama River that got a mind of its own. But then I'd reminded him that it was still water — and water was alive. It just did what it did and ain't nobody could tame it.

Malachi asked me to get Mallie ready for the baptism. I put Sparrow in the back of the crowd. The sun shined on her and gave her such a pretty complexion, but I looked away.

"Birdie pretty, ain't she?" Harriet said.

"Harriet, you hold her hand." She tightened her grip on the limp hand of her big sister.

I pulled Mallie back toward the house. I slipped a robe over his head and with a shaky hand patted his head and shoulders.

"It'll be all right, Mama. Besides, I know how to swim." He gave me his best smile before he ran off to the pond. I had taught the kids to swim because of the river, but the twins were so little and the river was so big.

I stood there for a long minute. The sun had come out, but the dryness made my skin feel funny. It hadn't rained since that awful Sunday morning two weeks ago and my heart was like a brown paper bag that was used too many times. All dried up. Even the grass was turning yellow. Malachi started talking about the meaning of baptism and about Jesus' baptism in the Bible. When he started talking about how it was a symbol of the resurrection, I just couldn't listen no more. It weren't no rebirth or resurrection for my boy. It was his death.

"How's Sparrow?" Emma's feathery voice, as light as it was, broke into my thoughts.

I turned to find her standing in the shade of her porch. She looked tired and thinner than usual. Her hair didn't just turn gray in two weeks but it was almost colorless.

I pursed my lips and shook my head and took in the sight of my daughter's back and Harriet holding on to her hand. I thought about my handbag sitting on my floor at home. And how I was waiting to find out when my sister's husband could come up and get the little ones and me to take us back home to Montgomery. Then I could kneel in Carver's dirt and that damp earth as long as I wanted.

"She bad." It was a relief to tell her. Like some weight had just lifted and with that came the well of grief to the surface and I started swallowing hard to keep it down. Her voice sounded like forgiveness and kindness. I didn't deserve it. But it wasn't grief over Carver, I knew. It was grief over Sparrow. My dead, living daughter.

"I found footsteps." Emma's voice was so quiet and sad sounding, it just about broke my heart if it wasn't already so crushed up. "I think she's been coming onto my porch and on our dock."

I didn't know what to say. At least I knew where she was going when she slipped out at night. I took a breath and kept my gaze fixed on the pond. "How's your husband?"

She said nothing for a long pause. "He's been silenced."

I turned to look at her and by the expression on my face she knew to explain.

"He's not allowed to speak in church or to other members during this time while they decide what to do." She sighed. "John will be put in the *ban* for at least six months, maybe a year, but eventually he'll be restored to the church."

"He still dry?"

"It's the longest he's ever gone."

"What about your boy?" I asked it but it wasn't easy.

"He and the other boys have to pay for the damages — and help with the repairs." Her mouth quivered and she swallowed real hard. It's a hard thing to have grief from our children, I knew.

We both paused for a few moments and listened to Malachi, who stood at the edge of the pond.

"Water can do many things, can't it? There are no doubts as to what water gives to us. It's indisputable. To some of you it brings enjoyment but to others it brings fear. To some in our history it brought freedom when they crossed over rivers into free land and even further back *through* the sea away from enemies. To some it brings restriction because it can't be crossed easily or at all. When it's still it is peaceful. When there's a storm it can be downright destructive."

He found my eyes then.

"To some it quenches a deep thirst and gives life. And to others the water is too much and brings death." He choked a little on that last word, then cleared his throat. "But God gave us water and the water gives and gives to us — in so many ways. And Jesus promises living water to all who are thirsty."

His voice switched gears now and he gestured to those getting baptized. "This pond isn't filled with special water. And those of you who are getting baptized today, you need to know that baptism is about dying. About dying to your old self and coming out of the water new in Jesus. It shows everybody here on the outside what God has done on the inside."

Then he waved in the first person.

"I know your boy did what he could with Sparrow to help her — that day, I mean." I angled my voice up to Emma on the porch and I bit the inside of my cheek to keep from letting all my emotions come out at once. My whole body full of tears now.

She nodded but didn't say nothing.

"They go all the way under," she said after the first person was finished.

"Mm-hmm," I said, and my heart fell

down into my stomach. "All the way under."

The small crowd cheered when Brother Darren came out of the water with his son Moses. The boy's mama and the rest of his family moved off to the side and threw a towel around him. Mallie was standing on the shore ready to walk in and my heart was beating so hard my eyes felt like they was pulsing. I don't want him to go in that water.

Malachi already stood in the pond about waist deep and I couldn't see how he could do this after what happened with Carver. I looked at Harriet and how she patted George's head. That boy was just picking at the grass at her feet. He got no idea what's about to happen.

Malachi waved Mallie toward him and he walked into the water. He put his arms out to steady himself like what he's stepping on was slick and he don't want to lose his balance. But he got to his daddy and the water came up to his chest. Made it hard for me to breathe.

"What a special joy and privilege it is to baptize my son, Malachi Jr." Malachi smiled at the boy, who smiled up at him. That boy loved his daddy. Just like with the other people he talked about Mallie making a decision to follow Jesus, and just like everybody else Mallie fairly glowed.

Malachi raised his hand to face the sun and in his loudest voice began. "In obedience to the Lord's command, I baptize you, my son — and brother — Malachi Jr., in the name of the Father, the Son, and the Holy Spirit. Buried in baptism." The boy went under the water and I held my breath until he was pulled out a second later with a toothy smile on his face. "Raised up to walk in the light of Jesus Christ."

The small group cheered and Brother Titus raised up the song "Wade in the Water" and the clapping and singing was in full groove. The baptism had gone off and no one had drowned.

Sparrow stood there next to Harriet. George on the other side.

Sparrow turned around. Her empty stare fixed into a real gaze into my eyes, but the next moment it flew away.

EMMA

The little bird with its nest in my eaves tapped on the window. I hadn't seen her in weeks and thought she'd left for good. The tapping continued, longer than usual. My eyes blinked open to watch her. Ever since I'd sighted her, I'd wanted the bird to be a sparrow, to take it as a sign from or about Sparrow. But it wasn't. It was just another martin making a mud nest in my eaves. Without warning it flew away into the dawn that pushed against what looked like storm clouds in the dry spell we'd had for weeks.

Another week had passed and this was an in-between Sunday. But even if it was a church Sunday, we wouldn't have gone. John wasn't ready for church or to go back to work. When we did return to church, he would have to make his confession and officially be silenced.

John was sleeping peacefully now, but he'd been thrashing around much of the night and would still shake uncontrollably but for shorter spells. I felt a strange mixture of pride and frustration over him. He'd chosen to take this path, but I was the one who had to walk with him — again on a trail of a decision I'd not made for myself and had no control over. He'd not said another word about my lies or whether I would continue taking my herbal birth control. Or if I would ever forgive him.

Then I heard singing. It sounded so distant I couldn't be sure I wasn't imagining it. I got out of bed to go outside and investigate. I ran on tiptoes through the house and when I stepped off the porch, I heard my name being sung. Over and over. It was just loud enough for me to follow the sound. When I saw Sparrow standing on the edge of the pond dock, I wondered if I was awake. I looked up to my bedroom window and I could see the mother bird flying back to her nest. Was I upstairs sleeping and this was a dream? Mist hung in the air for the first time in weeks.

"Sparrow?" I yelled across the yard.

She looked at me.

Her hair was out of the usual knot she wore and it was splayed around her head like a lion's mane. She was wearing a white nightgown, not so different from what I was wearing. The breeze picked it up and it swelled around her body. This was when I saw for the first time how dangerous the pond could be. It was larger than most backyard ponds, and John had always wished it was a baseball diamond instead.

"I got to get Carver," she said and pointed into the water.

"Sparrow?" Had I heard her right? That she had to get Carver? She then lay down on her belly and grazed her hand over the water. She started singing again. *"God's gonna trouble the water."*

"Come inside." I tried to keep my voice light as I walked toward her.

"I need to get Carver." She pointed into the water again. "And Daddy said that the water brings new life."

I stepped closer.

"New life," I whispered to myself. I walked toward her, but she was still far away on the opposite side of the pond. "Carver's not in there, Sparrow. Let's go have some hot cocoa and we can talk."

"Baptism is about dying. About dying to your old self and coming out of the water new in Jesus," Sparrow said. "You heard Daddy, right?"

"Mem?" Johnny's voice was behind me. *"Vas ist letz?"*

He knew what was wrong when his eyes found Sparrow. When he swore I didn't reprimand him. Sparrow seemed not to notice Johnny or care — I didn't know. She stood. She was so close to the end of the dock I was certain her toes hung over the edge.

"I can get to her."

But as soon as he said that, we watched as she got into John's small fishing skiff, and with the oars pushed it away from the dock. She tried to row a few times, then pushed the oars into the water with a flat-sounding splash.

"Go get Deedee — go as fast as you can."

And my son ran.

DELILAH

When I see that white boy come tearing through my yard I just about stop breathing. The children were asleep upstairs. I was still in my nightclothes. I hugged my arms around myself and felt the thinness of the fabric.

Sparrow.

Of course she was the first thing I thought about when I saw that boy. But Malachi said she was in her bed. Only a little bit ago, less than an hour, Malachi woke me up to tell me he was leaving to help the Carters pack up their stuff. They were moving today — on the Lord's day — packing up before church and leaving right after. I scoffed just thinking about it. Malachi had slept in the kitchen all night to keep her indoors. Right in front of the door, he said. Sparrow had stayed home all night. So he couldn't be coming because of her.

But why would that boy be running at my

house right now? It had to be about Emma. Something happened. I rushed to the door, but he got to pounding on it before I opened it. I thought he was going to break right on through.

"Sparrow," he was yelling when I opened the door. His nostrils flared out and his face was sweaty.

"What you mean *Sparrow*? You can't see her," I said, a little irritated. "You think it's okay —"

"No, I'm not here to see her. She's in my *dat*'s boat — on the pond." His words was all broken up. "Something about baptism and Carver."

"She what?" I started to think I was losing my mind.

"Just come, you have to come."

None of this made a lick of sense — but it also made a whole bunch of sense at the same time.

"I'll be right back." I left him standing on the porch in front of my open door.

I ran up the stairs. Maybe Sparrow was still in her bed where I'd left her the night before and that boy just gone plain mad. Of course Sparrow wasn't there. Of course she'd slipped out in such a short amount of time. It was like she planned it.

I shook Mallie awake. I explained just

515

enough, gave him instructions, and reminded him to behave. His bleary-eyed gaze
offered up a smile. He promised, then
turned over and tucked himself close to
George who had his thumb hanging out of
his mouth. Maybe I'd be back before they'd
all wake up.

A deep rumble sounded. Even though I
knew it was thunder it felt like it came from
under my feet. Like something under the
ground was stirring stuff up. We ain't had
rain for weeks but sometimes the lightning
and thunder came anyhow.

I hear the boy calling for me to be quicker
and I just about turned my ankle on my way
back down the stairs. Johnny was bouncing
up and down out of his skin. I told him I
wanted to get dressed. The wind had picked
up and I felt it whirl around me with the
door still open. I felt almost naked.

"There's no time," he said and waved me
out.

Over his shoulder I saw a storm rolling in
hard and fast. It looked big and dark and
all the light we got at dawn had fallen away.
Johnny don't take me needing a minute for
an answer and he put an arm around the
back of my shoulder and urged me out. He
kept his hand on my shoulder as we ran
through the yard. I was wearing slippers, at

least, and that made the running a little better. But I didn't know what I was running toward.

Johnny took my hand to help me over the creek and helped me over anything that had fallen in the wind. The woods were so dark even with the daylight coming. But I couldn't see no quiet yellow sun. The leaves were flipped over and rustling loud. The creek rushing faster than I ever saw. The thunder quaked and trees cracked. The storm was going to be bad.

Emma was in the yard waiting for us.

"Sparrow was at the dock when I woke, then she got into the boat — she's saying something about being baptized and finding Carver," Emma yelled over the bustling world around us.

"She talking?" I asked.

They both nodded.

I looked past Emma's shoulder and saw her. There was my daughter. I didn't know what to do.

"I can swim out there and pull the boat in," Johnny said. He unbuttoned his shirt and pulled it off. He was a handsome young man and when I saw his urgency I 'spected that he did care for her — maybe he loved her even. Maybe it wasn't just about stealing kisses — or more than a kiss.

"It's so deep. Can you even swim well enough to get to her?" The wind threw Emma's voice around.

The sky was so dark now and I couldn't rip my gaze away from Sparrow. Her mouth was moving but we couldn't hear what she was saying.

"She was singing," Emma said. "I could hear her before the storm came in. Like a lullaby."

She loved to sing. Before. Last year her teacher said she thought I should put her in music lessons because she could sing. We had often sung together while we worked in the kitchen or on walks, using the rhythm of the song to pace ourselves.

But then with Carver. We all lost so much. I didn't even know if she would ever go to school again. The burden I got over this just about bowled me over.

Then she started yelling "Mama" over and over again. Fast and wild sounding.

"Is she saying Emma or Mama?" I whispered.

Emma and I looked at each other and at first I wasn't sure myself. At this distance it could have been either. But then I knew she was saying "Mama" because that's what Carver had yelled, she said, besides calling for her too. I tried to call back but she

518

couldn't hear me. She flapped her arms and I almost thought she might start flying — because my life ain't going nothing like I thought it would, ever since Carver gone.

Johnny was on the dock now so he could go get my girl. Emma grabbed my hand and we ran toward the dock. It was awkward, almost like a three-legged race as a child, but she didn't let go of me. Her grip tightened — so did mine.

We stopped together at the start of the dock. It was long and went far out into the water but still nowhere close to Sparrow, who was bobbing up and down inside the boat. Beyond Sparrow the usual clear water I'd always seen here was black and had this endless, hollow look to it. The pond had never looked so big and mean as it did now.

When Johnny jumped in I saw that he wasn't a strong swimmer but good enough, I hoped. Emma and I just stood there and watched, hand in hand at the end of the dock. We watched as Sparrow backed farther toward the side of the boat like she was in her own world.

The rain started slowly at first with big, heavy drops. We were soaked through in a few minutes. I looked at Johnny struggling and then over at my girl.

I didn't know how she did it, but she

looked into my eyes and Emma's at the same time. We both felt it — don't know how. We both gasped. Then she closed her eyes, put her arms out to her sides, and fell backward toward the water. We both screamed when we heard her smack against the surface and then she was gone underwater.

Then we jumped together.

But as soon as we hit the water our hands were ripped from each other and Emma went under. She couldn't swim.

SPARROW

The water filled me up like a bucket. I got heavier and heavier and I couldn't keep myself from sinking. It was darker than I thought it would be under the water and I kept my eyes open.

I had to do it. For Carver. For Mama.

But I don't see nothing. It was too dark. I felt around, but it was real deep and I couldn't touch the bottom and maybe not even get close. I just started swimming down underneath it all. I could hold my breath for a long time because I been practicing. This was nothing like the time I got baptized. I went in the water and back out and I felt like my skin glowed. But now I jumped in myself and there ain't nothing glowing about it. It was just dark.

Mama and Emma looked so scared on the dock, I couldn't keep looking at them. I had to get into the water and do what I needed to do.

Something grabbed my dress and I start hitting and kicking. I couldn't see what it was, but when we got to the top of the water I saw it was Johnny. I pulled my dress out of his grip. Then he came for me again. I used my heels to kick and I knew I hit him. The rain was coming so fast it's a wonder the pond don't fill up and dump us out. Johnny came up and he's got blood running down his face.

In the distance I could see Mama in the water too. But she didn't notice me. She looked like she was yelling herself and tried to swim, but even though I'm a good swimmer, it was hard. The rain was coming down like darts. I didn't see Emma though. Not on the dock or in the water. Mama was having a hard time and she was yelling and thrashing around and coughing like she swallowed half the pond. Then she turned and saw me. Her mouth was big and round and I could tell she was yelling for me.

But I couldn't worry on that right now. I just needed to get down, all the way to the bottom, and get Carver back for Mama. So I go under.

EMMA

When I jumped in I didn't think the pond could swallow me. The turbulent storm transformed the calm and even surface into an entirely different pond. I didn't know how to use my legs or my arms. I was sinking. I could feel the bottom of the pond. The muck and clay sucked me down farther.

I opened my eyes and looked up. I was feet away from the surface and I saw a crack of lightning skitter across the sky. Was this the last beautiful thing I would ever see? The last thing I would ever see?

But I kicked and fought and wrestled with the water and found my way back to the surface.

Then I saw a hand extended toward me. Deedee. I took her hand.

DELILAH

When she went back under that black water, I don't know what to do no more. I put my hand on the dock and held myself there and looked around for Sparrow to surface. But I kicked my feet like a maniac because I hadn't been in water so deep since I was young — and a much better swimmer. The water was swirling around and the rain was coming down so hard now, I couldn't see nothing.

Finally, I saw Emma splashing and carrying on. But just when she came up she went back under. I moved toward her and put my hand out. "Emma," I yelled a few times.

I felt her hand in mine and I squeezed and pulled her to me and toward the dock. "Can't you swim?"

Emma shook her head and looked like a rag doll.

"Why you jump in?"

"Because I stand with you," she yelled all

ragged like.

I knew she was telling the truth.

"I don't think we can save her," I hollered.

Our gazes darted around, looking around the pond, but we didn't see Sparrow coming up nowhere.

"Johnny won't stop until he finds her."

Lightning flashed across the sky.

"Sparrow!" I yelled for my daughter over and over.

The rain came down harder. I couldn't hear myself — how would she hear me?

Johnny swam back to the boat to rest for a few moments. He found Emma with his gaze and I could see the fear in his eyes. He hadn't seen Sparrow in a good long while.

"Come on." I waved Emma to follow me.

We used our hands to work our way down the dock until we could stand up. Then we pulled ourselves onto the dock. We didn't talk and I was thinking how it was because we both know we failed.

I failed Sparrow and now I might lose my daughter for the last time.

SPARROW

Daddy told me once that all the water was connected in some way. But I been in this water for a good long while and I don't see nothing that made me feel like Carver was close. Of course, all his dirt was mixed together with the other pond dirt, but I thought that maybe God would keep it safe for me somehow.

When I knew I couldn't find the dirt and that Carver wasn't down here, I didn't think I could face Mama again. We all came here to get a new start. When I drown here in this water, will they move again to get another fresh start?

My lungs started to burn but I don't want to get another breath. I don't deserve air. Carver deserved air. I was all the way at the end of the pond with a fistful of pond weeds to keep me far under the water. I looked up. The sun was starting to peek out and the glow made the water shine like glass and diamonds. The world looked pretty through the veil of water, but I knew the truth. I knew the world was ugly and hateful. And I was no good in it.

My lungs burned so bad now. I was really hurting for a breath. I looked up one more time and could see somebody up there. There were footprints on the water. Somebody was walking up there right on top of me and there was so much light shining now. It was so bright.

Then everything went black.

DELILAH

The reflection of the sun's yellow light was bright on the surface of the pond. My throat was hoarse by the time the pond went still again. I looked off into the distance and around the edges. But I don't see nothing but Johnny's head. How long had it been since I seen her come up? Ten minutes? An hour? A year?

Where was my girl?

That was who she was. She was my girl.

But now she might be dead somewhere under all that water that now looked still and settled.

Across the pond Johnny came out from the shore and was bent over. Was he giving up or just catching his breath?

I pushed up to my knees to watch.

Emma had her eyes on Johnny too. She stood. Her nightgown stuck to her skinny, bony legs. Then she looked at me and helped me up. We started running.

Johnny got Sparrow in his arms. But she ain't moving.

EMMA

I believed that a mother's grief could make ripples on the surface of the still water or cause the sun to move. Deedee's wailing pierced through me with that force.

The grass around the side of the pond where Johnny was coming from was tall and carried the weight of all the water that had just fallen. The grasses had been pushed aside because of the wind and rain. Deedee fell twice as I pulled her. The temperature hadn't cooled with the rain and a heavy mist settled around us. We ran through the vapor, were wrapped in it and ate it.

"Johnny." I heard my voice, but it didn't sound like me. It sounded ragged and aged and desperate.

"Birdie." Deedee's voice was rough like mine, but she used a name I'd never heard from her before. It felt like a gift to my ears.

Johnny tried to run but he couldn't. I heard him groaning as he carried her. His body was too spent. His arms shook. I didn't know if he was crying. Was the exertion too much, or was his heart as pained as mine? A little blood ran from his nose.

"Lie her down, lie her down," Deedee said when we got close. "I got to see her."

He placed her in the grass. Her eyes were closed. He wept. Her head lolled to one side. He buried his head against her body. Her lips were pale and motionless. I think he was praying.

"Oh, Birdie, don't you be dead." Deedee's hands moved over Sparrow's body. Everything was so limp. "Help me roll her on her side. She probably swallowed some water. We just got to get the water out."

We listened to her say this over and over — "We just got to get the water out." Maybe twenty times. Maybe a hundred.

Johnny pulled her body toward him and I pushed against her back. She was on her side. Deedee started to bang on her back and yell for her Birdie to breathe.

DELILAH

I put my hand on my Birdie's cheek and I was reminded that we were just the same shade. She was mine.

I couldn't say that I knew all the things that made up a mother and daughter, but when I looked at her it was like I saw that little baby when she was first born. Like I was holding a new little brown bird with big eyes, just staring up at me like she knew I was her mama and knew what that meant.

She finally coughed and sputtered and spit up a whole lot of water, but she came 'round. Just like all those years ago, her big brown eyes looked up and found mine. And I knew we was going to be all right.

We all coddled her and cried and praised the Lord for a few long minutes. Then she talked. I didn't know how much I'd missed her voice until now.

"I saw him, Mama," she mumbled between choking. "When I was under the water, I looked up and saw him."

"Who, baby? Carver?" I said, still crying.

"No, I saw *Him. Jesus.* He was walking on top of the water above me and He put His hand out to me and I took it."

It didn't matter if it was a dream or an illusion or Johnny's hand — she was safe. She didn't even understand that she'd been unconscious when she was found. But maybe that was exactly what happened and she'd seen Jesus. Maybe she'd been right and I'd been wrong all along.

SPARROW

Mama was different after she thought I was dead in the water. I was too. A whole lot of stuff was different.

Everybody from church came and brought food. From our church and from Emma's church — them sisters Joyce and Betty sat for tea with Mama even. We got more food than we know what to do with. This time the food don't got that bitter-dead taste. They got something else that tasted real good. Daddy spent more time with me than the church folks.

Emma helped at the house and it was nice to have her close. Mama said she ain't worried about me running away no more, but she still sat with me a lot. She said she left me for too long already and we both just about died because of it. She made me stay in bed for two weeks straight — except to use the bathroom. Even the white doctor came out to the house. He was nice and said I would be just fine.

Lois and Cassie, some girls from church who never talked to me, came to see me and said when I was feeling better that we should go for ice cream. Mama said I could so I told them yes.

I had changed too. Before I just took all the bad things in my head and let them sit and spoil rotten, but now everything came up and out of me. Maybe it was 'cause I was afraid I'd go back to before when talking was too hard and I just needed to stare and walk in the woods. Or maybe it was 'cause I just needed to hear Mama's voice and mine together in the same room that we was both alive in.

"You mad at me for dumping Carver's dirt into the pond?" I asked her one of the quiet days in my room.

She lifted her eyebrow and gave me that look that only she could but then softened. She might just have been surprised at what I asked.

"I'm not mad about it no more. Maybe a little sad." Mama was always honest.

"I'm sorry, Mama. I was just real mad."

"I know."

"I thought it would make you see that I needed you. I was sad as soon as I done it because it was all we got left of him."

"It ain't though." Mama put one hand on her chest and the other on mine for a few beats of my heart and then put them back on her lap.

I was quiet for a minute and both of us were looking far away from each other.

"I wanted to get the dirt back. I wanted to die and be reborn like what Daddy said baptism was." Our eyes found each other's real fast and we held on. "I know now that he didn't mean it like I took it — my mind wasn't working right. But I did see Jesus walking on top of that water — He saved me."

She took my hand in both of hers. It was warm and I felt safe. "He saved me too, baby."

"But what about Carver?" I leaned over and pulled that old river shell out of my nightstand. I touched it and thought about the Alabama River, the last place I saw Carver alive, and the reason I wanted it on his gravestone and why Mama didn't. My skin tingled thinking on what I'd done with it once.

"He's in heaven, baby." Mama's voice was that soft kind she used to use — like the soft fuzz on caterpillars. She smiled at me and patted my arm. Her eyes were sparkling, and even though she got tears in them, I didn't see the hate no more.

"Are you and the little kids still going back to Montgomery with Aunty?"

"No, Birdie." She shook her head. "We're staying right here."

"It's still my fault about Carver though, isn't it?"

She looked away and through the window toward the church. I got worried at what she was thinking and what she was gonna say.

"Not like what you're thinkin'. This stuff is so hard, Birdie, and I done a lot of wrong. I think that I just got stuck in a bad place because I missed Carver so bad — but I'm not blaming you no more. Or myself. Or nobody."

"I was stuck too." I paused for a long moment. "Are we unstuck now?"

Mama put on her pretty smile. "I think we're getting out of it together."

"Why did Carver die instead of me?" I said the words so fast because it was something I been thinking on for so long, and if I didn't say it fast, I wasn't sure I'd ever say it.

"Don't know that. We don't get to choose. It was his time — we don't know why. But it wasn't your time." Mama's mouth trembled.

"Carver ain't never coming back though." I said it and I had always known that it was impossible. I knew when someone was dead they was dead. But Mama had been bringing Carver back to life every day — every hour — since he died.

"He ain't but we will go to him — someday."

DELILAH

The next two weeks were like a gray shadow of the months before. Like when you put your hand through water . . . Some of it goes between your fingers but your hand still gets wet. We passed through the water together — Malachi and I both was hanging on to our girl and each other.

I let my broken heart start beating again, which hurt almost worse than when it broke. But it was time to start living on in this world. Sparrow was talking now. A lot. So much that sometimes I wanted to clip her mouth shut with a clothespin, but she made me hear my own voice answer questions I'd been asking myself but was too afraid to answer.

"Do you think Carver was scared?" Sparrow asked me one morning when we sat on the porch and together watched the world rouse. I even let her have some coffee. She held that hot mug in her hand just like me and sat with her legs crossed just like me.

I swallowed hard — like I got a bunch of pond scum stuck in my throat with this question.

"I hate it, but he probably was." I paused and felt that ache from the roots of the hair on my head to my tippy toes. I thought about his path to dying and how it might have been for Carver — but my mind didn't stay on that bad stuff but settled on how his path of dying took him home. He was happy where he was and, even in my mourning, I was finally glad he was happy. "But he wasn't alone."

"Do you think Jesus was with Carver?"

"I do."

"Then why didn't He put His hand out for him to grab — like He done me?"

"I think He did, Birdie. But neither of them let go. He just took our boy the rest of the way with Him. All the way to heaven."

"So Jesus let go of me?"

The tremble in her voice broke through my hurt and reminded me that she was just a child and had never asked for none of this. She was just that daughter of mine with the bushy hair that I couldn't tame much, with a voice like a bird, with scars up and down her legs, and a broken heart trying to mend. To Sparrow, thinking that Jesus let go of her

540

would mean that He didn't want her.

"He knew you weren't done down here." I squeezed her hand.

She was quiet for a good long time, but she kept rubbing her hand over mine like she needed to feel me being there with her.

EMMA

After Sparrow and Deedee had rested inside for a little while, Johnny, John, and I walked with them through the woods back to their house. It didn't seem right that we'd gone through so much that morning and then it all ended so simply. John had woken up and didn't question anything but just became a part of our story together.

All day I thought about how I witnessed Deedee unclench her fist filled with anger and offer an open hand to Sparrow. It worked over me like water smoothed a rock.

The oil lamp was lit low in the living room where John sat. His Bible was open on his lap, but his head had fallen back in sleep. He looked peaceful for the first time in weeks. I watched him fight so hard for what he wanted in staying away from the drink his body loved so much. Maybe he loved me more than the drink now.

I walked over to my husband. I had

touched him often in the last weeks. More often than in the many months before. I'd held him when he shook so much I didn't know if he would die. I had often put a hand on his shoulder when he vomited the only swallow of water in his stomach because I didn't know what else to do. I'd washed his face from his drenching sweats. Each time he tried to catch my gaze, I looked away. I washed his hair for him and I bathed him. But in all those times I had touched him out of duty, not love.

But tonight I wanted to touch him. I wanted to touch the face of the man who had confessed his sins to his spiritual and earthly authority and would endure a humiliating confession in front of the church in order to right things. But within that, folded neatly, I realized that regardless of his standing with the church, the state of our marriage was separate from that. It required an answer from me and not just an approval from a group of preachers or an *Ordnung* that we lived our life by.

I moved his dark hair away from his chiseled forehead. The lines were deep, but his strong brow was rested and not furrowed as it had been for many weeks. His face twitched a little at my touch. It felt foreign to be gentle with him and to admit that I wanted to regain our love and all we'd lost.

"Em?" he questioned when he opened his eyes.

I knelt next to the chair and took his hands. He looked at me and at our hands laced together and tilted his head toward me.

"I want us to move away." I hadn't known this until I said it.

John sat up a little and let go of my hands. He closed the Bible and set it on the table next to the chair. Then he looked at me with confusion. *"Vas?"* He needed an explanation.

"Remember Atlee talking about the new community starting in Kentucky?" I began to draw energy from my own words and the promise of a new beginning. "I think we should move and start fresh."

"It's going to be a Mennonite community."

He looked at me for a long time. My hands were resting on his knees. Our gazes were locked together. This was the most intimate we had been in more than a decade. I didn't want a repeat of the past but wanted something new with John and a chance.

I thought about Deedee and what the move was for her and how it had been filled with such heartache as long as she held tightly to her hurts and her grief. How even in grief one could have an open eye toward what was to come and what could be and be okay with the slow and steady process of grief that made it easier to live life. To let go of fears and to give forgiveness. But it was so hard to say the words.

"Will you forgive me?" I wasn't sure I'd meant any other words more in my life.

He cupped my chin and seemed too overcome to speak. He nodded. Of course he'd already told me he had that day Deedee had spilled my secret, but I needed to hear it again.

"But," he choked out, "I don't deserve to ask you to forgive me."

"I already have." My eyes burned with tears. "I want a new start for you, me, and Johnny."

He didn't have to say much but smiled when he said yes. Then we held each other. And for the first time since the loss of our child, he comforted me in my tears and I let him.

SPARROW

I didn't want to break Mama and Daddy's rules by sneaking out of the house, but I just got this feeling inside me that Johnny would be waiting for me at daybreak. It was August now and it seemed like a whole lifetime ago that I'd met him the last time. I pushed that out of my head because there had been so much confusion since then. But a lot of good stuff too.

I'd been in bed for two weeks and my body was itching to walk outside in the woods where I found Emma and Johnny and a new life.

I wore my new lilac dress and made sure my hair was smooth — Mama had braided it nice the night before. Would Johnny still think I was pretty? Then I wondered if he ever had or if it was just something he said to make me feel good.

My heart started pounding and carrying on when I stepped around the creaky step and made sure the door didn't click too loud. My little house was still dark and I would make sure to be back before they woke. I didn't need to give heart attacks to nobody. When I got into the woods I did my best not to run like a wild girl. I walked like a nice, smart girl.

When I saw him sitting there by our tree, my heart got all soft and gooey and I felt a smile grow on my lips. When he saw me he smiled too. He started to mark the tree like we used to do, then stood waiting for me.

"I was hoping you'd come." His voice got this soft, brushy feel to it. "I came last Sunday, just in case."

"Mama wouldn't let me out of bed."

"But you're up now." He winked at me.

We both looked down at our feet.

"You want to sit down?" He pointed.

I sat real nice like so I wouldn't get my new dress dirty. He sat real close to me. His shoulder was touching mine and it made me feel warm all over.

"So you're doing — better?" His face was close to mine when he spoke.

I shrugged. "I'm feeling a lot better."

"Good." He nodded.

"Mama said you're moving away."

"Kentucky. A new Mennonite community is starting there." His blue eyes brightened.

I didn't know what to say because I didn't want him to move away, but I could see that he wanted to go. Maybe, like my family, they needed a fresh start. I was glad it wasn't because he was running away.

"What happened?" I asked him. I knew he knew what I meant.

He shifted how he was sitting. "After I said good-bye to you, we drank and then we argued and got in a wreck."

" 'Bout what?"

He looked over at me. "You."

"Ruined your plans, I guess."

He shook his head. "No, it saved me. You saved me."

I smiled and just watched the creek. Looking at him made me wonder if I wouldn't just melt into a puddle of water in a second.

"Whatever happened to —" I stopped.

"Arnold?" He shrugged. "He left town. Don't know where he went."

He quickly talked again.

"You look really pretty today."

"You mean it?"

"I've always meant everything I've said to you." He pushed his shoulder against mine. I giggled.

The warmth from my face traveled through my body and settled in my stomach. It swirled a little and I didn't remember ever

feeling quite like that before. I finally knew
I don't got to question everything he said
no more. I trusted him and I figured that
was even better than love. But with that feeling came sadness. He was leaving. Probably
would never see him again. I wondered what
girl he would kiss next. I stared down at my
hands that were twisted together.

Then my dark hand was in his light hand
and it looked so nice like that. Our fingers
all braided up together. He brought my
hand up to his lips and kissed it.

"Do you think we'll ever see each other
again?"

His gaze went all over my face. I didn't
know if that was a good thing or a bad
thing. He let go of my hand and brushed
the back of his finger against my jawline.
He took off his hat and put it on my head.

And then he kissed me.

DELILAH

From a distance I could see that little spot of green grass I was sure Emma would be at. She was picking weeds and tossing them to the side. She put a handful of some bright-yellow black-eyed Susans in the center and brushed dust and dirt from the large rock marker. I watched this because it reminded me of myself not so many months ago. It was different but it was the same.

"We thought we'd find you here," I said with a smile. She smiled back and I saw that old mixture of joy and sadness in her eyes.

"Hi, Ms. Emma." Sparrow gave her a warm, breezy kind of smile. She bent down and hugged Emma and my friend's hold on my daughter was tight.

"In a few minutes I get to go for ice cream with my friends," Sparrow said when she pulled away but stayed kneeling next to her. "And I get to start school on Monday. Right, Mama?" She turned toward me.

"Sure you can."

Sparrow turned back around to face Emma. "I'm sad you're moving though." She stuck her bottom lip out like a young child, and it reminded me that she'd grown young in the last month and was almost all back to that silly, wild girl I'd raised on buttermilk and whippings.

Emma nodded but didn't speak — like she couldn't trust her voice. Sparrow gave her another hug, like she knew Emma needed it.

"I don't want you to go," she said into Emma's shoulder. She pulled away and two big tears streamed down her face. Emma's trailed too.

"I know." Emma cupped my girl's cheek in her palm. It was just about all the beauty I could handle for the moment and I turned away to blink the tears gone.

"I love you, Ms. Emma. Mama said I could write to you."

Emma smiled at me. *"Ich liebe dich,"* she said and Sparrow giggled.

I knew what she'd said — they were the only Amish words I'd learned. Sparrow had taught me.

"Now run off and be back before dinner," I said and Emma and I both watched Sparrow run off.

"You're not afraid anymore?" Emma asked. "That she'll hurt herself or — ?"

I shook my head and my sigh filled the woods. "No. I can't explain it. It was like when all that happened at the pond, everything changed. Like something lifted out of me and I got to see who she was again."

I'd told her all of this before but I repeated it often — like it was a testimony of what a miracle was done.

"I thought she was dead." Emma said this every time I saw her too.

I raised my eyebrow and looked at Emma with that expression that said *me too*. I'd admitted to Emma another time that if my girl had died, it would've been my fault.

"We ain't over it all," I said. "I ain't over my grief or that it just seems like it shouldn't have happened. But Sparrow and I — we're working through it."

I paused for a moment and considered what to say. I had so many words like water flowing around in my head. "But I can't lose a second child because I'm so sad over losing the first."

We both looked down at Emma's little oval plot. There wouldn't be a time now that I'd walk these woods — if the next owners allowed it — that I wouldn't notice this little one sleeping below the ground. "You know you can't run away from all this. Wherever you go, you pack it with you."

Emma snorted. "Is that your way of keeping me from moving?"

I shook my head. "No." I sat on the ground next to her and patted her hand. "I think y'all need a fresh start. But you got to know that all the good and the bad go with you. You still going to remember this little tiny soul you lost but also all the good you gained here. You taking with you everything. You ain't losing nothing."

"I'm losing you" — Emma snuffled her tears — "and Sparrow."

I shook my head again. "Don't you say that." I smiled to keep my mouth from shaking in my own tears. "And just think. There's an *Emma* waiting for you somewhere in Kentucky. She gonna find you out and take care of you like you done took care of me and my girl. And I'll write to you. I promise."

She was quiet for a moment and I knew it was time.

"I'm sorry, you know," I said.

"For what?"

"For what I said to you and John — that day with the dress and —"

Emma shook her head and interrupted me. "You don't need to say sorry. It was

553

time he knew."

"But it wasn't my place."

She released a little chuckle that got sadness mixed through it. "I don't know. I think friends are supposed to keep each other honest."

We both got up from the ground and walked toward Emma's house, mostly in that nice, quiet way that friends could do with each other. When we got to the pond we both looked over it. The soft, sandy shore was at our feet. The pond seemed new again. Like I never seen it before.

"Let me teach you to swim?" I giggled. I started taking off my shoes.

"What?" Emma laughed. "Like this?" She gestured to our dresses. "Right now?"

"Right now's all we got," I said and I saw something spark in her eyes. She took off her shoes and stockings and covering and her gaze skimmed over the pond once more.

I reached out my hand to her and she took it. Together we stepped into the water.

The water was the same color as my hand and the same color as Emma's hand — but the difference in color didn't change what it was. It was still water. And in that, I found solace.

EMMA

Water pulls at us
Believe
Drawing us together
Trust
Wraps coolness around
Us
Plunge into the deep
Breathe
We are reborn
Together
Solace

BY EMMA MULLET

DISCUSSION QUESTIONS

1. When Deedee and her family arrive in Sinking Creek, Pennsylvania, they encounter a new type of racial segregation. How is what they discover different from what they knew in Montgomery?
2. Emma's entire life is clouded over by shameful secrets. What is the effect of burying a secret for many years?
3. Deedee and Emma have experienced unique losses, yet their pain binds them together. How can grief or painful experiences help us better connect with others?
4. Describe Sparrow and Emma's relationship. Why do they take to one another, and how does Deedee understand their friendship?
5. Why do you believe Emma is afraid to have another child? Why does she take the herbs?
6. Deedee's grief over Carver manifests itself in various ways. Can you relate to

any of them? How have you experienced grief, and if anything, what has helped you cope with it?

7. Both Deedee and Emma feel that they are outsiders in the communities to which they should belong. How does that play out in the story? Have you ever felt like an outlier?

8. Though the novel is set in the past, does it echo within the present? Have times changed? How do we see racial and religious differences playing out in our modern world?

9. Why do you think Deedee helps Emma after her bout with drunkenness? What role does vulnerability and transparency play in their relationship?

10. What does Sparrow's young perspective add to the story? How is her experience with loss unique from her mother's?

11. Can you imagine a time or place in which Sparrow and Johnny could be together?

12. How do the characters in this novel perceive God? For them, what role does God play amid their anguish and loss?

13. Both Emma and Deedee have strained relationships with their husbands. How does grief burden a relationship, and how do you see the women's marriages evolv-

ing throughout the book?

14. Do you believe the novel has a hopeful ending? Why or why not? And if so, what is the source of that hope?

ACKNOWLEDGMENTS

— To my mighty heavenly Father. Without You I would have no words to write. Receive my thanksgiving as I cling to Your Word that tells me that if You have set me on a task, You will see me through.

— To my one true love, my dream husband, Davis. You deserve numerous accolades and awards for dealing with this author-wife. What a wild ride we have been on lately. Your love and devotion mean everything to me. I love you for all of time.

— To my dear daughters, Felicity and Mercy. I love you both more than SkinnyMe chocolates and "I Ain't Doin' It" videos — true story. You are the most supportive children an author could ask for. You are my dream daughters.

— To Natasha Kern, literary agent extraordinaire! What a journey. Your industry wisdom is unmatched, but truly our long talks about all the other parts of our lives are so special to me. So much gratitude and love to you.

— To my publishing team at Harper-Collins Christian Publishing. Daisy Hutton (I will never forget our first phone conversation), Jocelyn Bailey, Becky Monds, Amanda Bostic, Allison Carter, Paul Fisher, and the amazing sales team. I'm so honored to work with each of you. Your enthusiasm, support, and expertise are unmatched, and I am extremely grateful.

— A huge shout-out to Kristen Ingebretson for designing the breathtaking cover. You are pure magic!

— To Julee Schwarzburg for editing and editing and editing — and for befriending me, Delilah, Emma, and Sparrow. Their story is better because of you. I couldn't have done this without you — but I did just add a boatload of words in these acknowledgments. Forgive me?☺

— To my amazing family. Big thanks to my mom and my sister, Emmalene (one of the inspirations for my name choice for Emma), for hosting my family while I was on deadlines. You have no idea how much I appreciate the understanding and for feeding my girls while I worked. An extra thanks to you, Mom, for answering my random Amish questions. And Dad, Brandalyn, Joseph, and Johannes for your cheers and prayers and for the laughter that reminds me to chill out. And a wink-wink to Emma Mullet, my great-aunt, for inspiring my name choice as well. I love you all!

— To Pam and Alicia, to whom this book is dedicated. Without your constant friendship, prayers, and unwavering faith in God and in His work in our friendship, I could not remain sane. This story is about friendship and how God makes matches. As far as whose name came first in the dedication . . . I drew names because you are equally important in my life. I thank God for you both and for unlimited data plans. I dearly love you both!

— To Kelly Long . . . for *everything.* You gave me a gift once that said our souls are old friends. Yes, they are. You're so important to me, and I love you.

— To Kim Cash Tate, Markus and Amber Hayes, and Erma Pointdexter for being willing to answer questions and read pages. Thank you for hearing my heart and looking past my awkwardness and nerves. I can say without reservation that your input and honesty have made this book what it is. You each have blessed me in the hugest of ways, and I pray the Lord's blessing over your lives. I will always hold your openness and kindness close to my heart.

— To friends and allies in life. Carla Laureano, who gives me courage. Carolyn Baddorf, because Orvieto and all our talks. Angela Crisp, for taking the girls for a whole day when I was on deadline. Amanda Dykes and Joanne Bischof, because pizza, new friendships, and encouragement. Jennifer Naylor, who gives amazing Christmas hugs. And so many more . . .

— To my amazing Influencer team (you know who you are). To have each of you in my corner blesses me more than I can express. I truly couldn't do this without you. I am humbled and grateful. I cannot say thank you enough.

— To you, the reader! I thank you because a book isn't finished until you've read it. Thank you for being on this journey with me. May we go on many more together.

ABOUT THE AUTHOR

Elizabeth Byler Younts gained a worldwide audience through her first book, *Seasons: A Real Story of an Amish Girl,* and is a RITA nominated writer. Elizabeth lives in Central Pennsylvania with her husband, two daughters, and a cockapoo named Fable.

Visit her online at
ElizabethBylerYounts.com
Twitter: @ElizabethYounts
Facebook: AuthorElizabethBylerYounts
Instagram: @ElizabethBylerYounts

The employees of Thorndike Press hope you have enjoyed this Large Print book. All our Thorndike, Wheeler, and Kennebec Large Print titles are designed for easy reading, and all our books are made to last. Other Thorndike Press Large Print books are available at your library, through selected bookstores, or directly from us.

For information about titles, please call:
  (800) 223-1244

or visit our website at:
  gale.com/thorndike

To share your comments, please write:
  Publisher
  Thorndike Press
  10 Water St., Suite 310
  Waterville, ME 04901